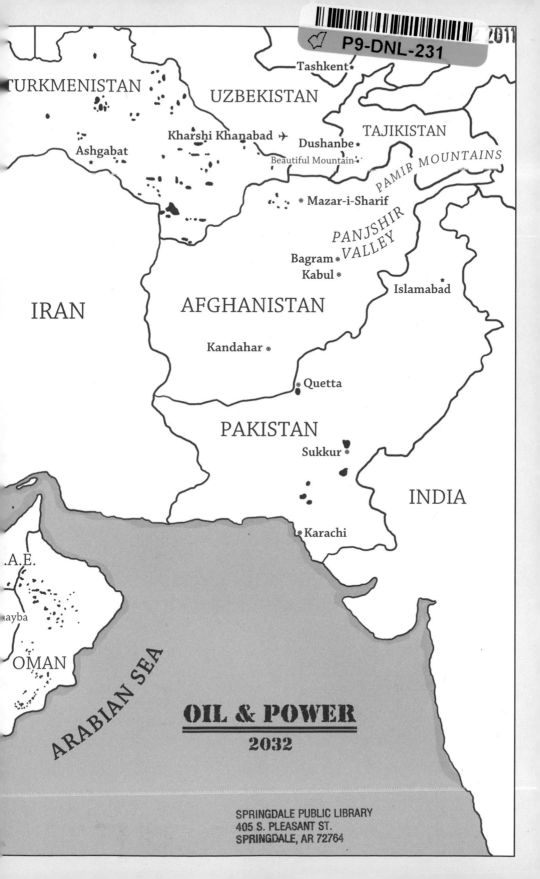

THE
PROFESSION

THE PROFESSION

A THRILLER

STEVEN PRESSFIELD

CROWN PUBLISHERS
NEW YORK

This is a work of fiction. Names, characters, places, and incidents either are the product of the author's imagination or are used fictitiously. Any resemblance to actual persons, living or dead, events, or locales is entirely coincidental.

Published in the United States by Crown Publishers,
an imprint of the Crown Publishing Group,
a division of Random House, Inc., New York.
www.crownpublishing.com

CROWN and the Crown colophon are registered trademarks of Random House, Inc.

Library of Congress Cataloging-in-Publication Data
Pressfield, Steven.
    The profession : a thriller / Steven Pressfield. — 1st ed.
        p.   cm.
        1. Americans—Middle East—Fiction.   2. Mercenary troops—Middle East—Fiction.   I. Title.
PS3566.R3944P76 2011
813'.54—dc22   2010047384

ISBN   978-0-385-52873-3
eISBN 978-0-307-88858-7

Printed in the United States of America

Book design by Philip Mazzone
Jacket design by Jae Song
Jacket photograph by Benjamin Earwicker (flag)

10 9 8 7 6 5 4 3 2 1

First Edition

FOR OUR GUYS

THE
PROFESSION

1

A BROTHER

MY MOST ANCIENT MEMORY is of a battlefield. I don't know where. Asia maybe. North Africa. A plain between the hills and the sea.

The hour was dusk; the fight, which had gone on all day, was over. I was alive. I was looking for my brother. Already I knew he was dead. If he were among the living, he would have found me. I would not have had to look for him.

Across the field, which stretched for thousands of yards in every direction, you could see the elevations of ground where clashes had concentrated. Men stood and lay upon these. The dying and the dead sprawled across the lower ground, the depressions and the sunken traces. Carrion birds were coming down with the night — crows and ravens from the hills, gulls from the sea.

I found my brother's body, broken beneath the wheels of a battle wagon. Three stone columns stood above it on an eminence — a shrine or gate of some kind. The vehicle's frame had been hacked through by axes and beaten apart by the blows of clubs; the traces were still on fire. All that remained aboveground of my brother was his left arm and hand, which still clutched the battle-axe by which I recognized him. Two village women approached, seeking plunder. "Touch this man," I told them, "and I will cut your hearts out."

I stripped my cloak and wrapped my brother's body in it. The dames helped me settle him in the earth. As I scraped black dirt over my brother's bones, the eldest caught my arm. "Pray first," she said.

We did. I stood at the foot of my brother's open grave. I don't know what I expected to feel: grief maybe, despair. Instead what ascended from that aperture to hell were such waves of love as I have never known in this life or any other. Do not tell me death is real. It is not. I have sustained my heart for ages with the love my brother passed on to me, dead as he was.

While I prayed, a commander passed on horseback. "Soldier," he asked, "whom do you bury?" I told him. He reined in, he and his lieutenants, and bared his head. Who was he? Did I know him? When the last spadeful of earth had been mounded atop my brother's grave, the general's eyes met mine. He said nothing, yet I knew he had felt what I had, and it had moved him.

I am a warrior. What I narrate in these pages is between me and other warriors. I will say things that only they will credit and only they understand.

A warrior, once he reckons his calling and endures its initiation, seeks three things.

First, a field of conflict. This sphere must be worthy. It must own honor. It must merit the blood he will donate to it.

Second, a warrior seeks comrades. Brothers-in-arms, with whom he willingly undergoes the trial of death. Such men he recognizes at once and infallibly, by signs others cannot know.

Last, a warrior seeks a leader. A leader defines the cause for which the warrior offers sacrifice. Nor is this dumb obedience, as of a beast or a slave, but the knowing heart's pursuit of vision and significance. The greatest commanders never issue orders. Rather, they compel by their own acts and virtue the emulation of those they command.

The great champions throw leadership back on you. They make you answer: Who am I? What do I seek? What is the meaning of my existence in this life?

I fight for money. Why? Because gold purges vanity and self-importance from the fight. Shall we lay down our lives, you and I, for a flag, a tribe, a notion of the Almighty? I did, once. No more. My gods now are Ares and Eris. Strife. I fight for the fight itself. Pay me. Pay my brother.

I served once beneath a great commander who asked in council one night, of me and my comrades, if we believed our calling to be a species of penance — a hell or purgatory through which we must pass, again and again, in expurgation of some crime committed eons gone.

"I do," he said. He offered us as recompense for this passage "an unmarked grave on a hill with no name, for a cause we cannot understand, in the service of those who hate us."

Not one of us hesitated to embrace this.

BOOK ONE

EUPHRATES

2

ESPRESSO STREET

NINETY MILES SOUTH OF Nazirabad, we sight a convoy of six vehicles speeding west and flying the black-and-yellow death's-head pennant of CounterArmor. The date is 15 August 2032. In that country, when you run into other Americans, you don't ask who they're working for, where they're from, or what they're up to. You help them.

We brake beside the CounterArmor vehicles in the lee of a thirty-foot sand berm. The team is pipeline security. Their chief is a black dude, about forty, with a Chicago accent. "The whole goddam city's gone over!"

"Over to who?" I ask. A gale is shrieking, the last shreds of a sandstorm that has knocked out satellite and VHF comms for the past two and a half hours.

"Whoever the hell wants it!"

The CounterArmor commander's vehicle is a desert-tan Chevy Simoom with a reinforced-steel X-frame and a .50-caliber mounted topside. My own team is six men in three vehicles — two Lada Neva up-armors and one RT-7, an Iraq-era 7-ton truck configured for air defense. The outfit is part of Force Insertion, the largest private military force in the world and the one to whom all of western Iran has been contracted. I'm in command of the group, which is a standard MRT, Mobile Response Team. The overall contract is with ExxonMobil and BP.

The CounterArmor trucks are fleeing west for the Iraq border. The Turks have invaded, the chief is telling us. Or maybe it's the Russians. Tactical nukes have been used, near Qom and Kashan in the No-Go Zone; or maybe that's false too. "Get in behind us," he shouts. "We're gonna need every gun we can get."

I tell him our team has orders to enter the city. Five American engineers, civilian contractors, are trapped there, along with the TCN—Third Country Nationals—security detail assigned to protect them. Our instructions are to get them out, along with a technical brief they have prepared for the commanding general's eyes only.

"You can't go back there," the chief says.

"Watch us."

Nazirabad is a Shiite city of about three hundred thousand. They're all Shiite cities in Iran. You can tell a Shiite city by the billboards and the vehicles, which are plastered with pix of their saints, Ali and Hussein. A Shiite truck or bus is festooned with religious amulets and geegaws. Reflectorized pinwheels dangle from the rearview and outboard mirrors; framed portraits adorn the dash; every square inch is crazy quilted with talismans and mandalas, good luck charms and magic gimcracks.

Anyway, that's what we're seeing now—forty minutes after leaving the CounterArmor convoy—as Iranian civilian cars, trucks, and buses flood past on the highway, fleeing. Comms are still out, whether from the nukes, the storm, or man-made jamtech, we can't tell. Our orders are to rescue the engineers. Beyond that, we know nothing. We don't know what we're riding into or what our chances are of getting out. This is the bitch of modern warfare. Every technological breakthrough spawns its dedicated countermeasure, with each generation getting cheaper and more accessible. X knocks out Y; before you know it, you're back to deadfalls and punji stakes.

So we're relieved, forty miles south of the city, when two Little Bird choppers—the kind used by the Legion, one of Force Insertion's subcontractors—show up topside and communicate to us by line-of-sight that other friendlies are up ahead. Twenty minutes later we pick up radio traffic from Legion vehicles heading our way and, half an hour after that, two black bulletproofs—GMC Kodiaks with cork tires and gun-slit windows—roll up and brake, coated with gray dust. An operator springs down, wearing a tuxedo jacket and white linen shirt over cargo pants and boots. We can see, in the distance, the three-level overpass south of the city. The merc comes up, grinning in his black tie. My #2, Chutes Savarese, hails him.

"Where's the party?"

"We brought it, babies."

The merc introduces himself as Chris Candelaria and shakes my hand and the others'. His ring says SEAL Team Six. He wears another that I don't see, under the Nomex glove on his left hand: the Wharton School. The team he's leading is from DSF, Dienstleister Schwarze Flagge, the crack German–South African outfit that evolved in the twenties out of the Zimbabwean Selous Scouts. He just got out of Isfahan five hours ago, he says. Dried blood paints both his hands and arms; the shoulder of his jacket has been charred through; he's got a dust-caked battle dressing on his neck, above an ear whose bottom third is scorched black and slathered with green combat antiseptic. But he's grinning. Like me, he wears a beard. His hair is long and falls in a cascade of black ringlets.

"You guys going in there?" he asks. From our rise south of the highway, we can see Dragonfly drones in swarms over the city. Every punk-ass gang and militia is flying these little fuckers, some the size of kites, others no bigger than pie plates. The streaks of their rockets — high-explosive and flechette — blow away in the wind. "Want some help?"

The merc and I do a quick map orientation, marking the in-city locations and the routes, order, and sequence we'll use to approach them. What about supporting fires, I ask. Our team has zero; has he got Close Air Support, drones, anything?

The cupboard is bare, the merc says. "It's just you and me, partner. We are officially OOO" — On Our Own — "and SOL." Shit Outa Luck.

The contractor has a case of Jack Daniel's in the lead Kodiak. Standing at the rear doors, he passes us two bottles for each vehicle. He's got cups but no ice. He introduces the rest of his team, who are more comm guys than trigger pullers. I note two DSFers packing Heckler & Koch 416s, German superguns, with 40 mm grenade launchers underslung. On the truck's roof squats a donut satlink receiver in a fiberglass cover; inside the vehicle I note a bank of tech gear, including a Xenor encryption box.

"What kind of team are you leading?" I ask.

"We're a financial unit. I'm specking oil and gas contracts. Haven't had a rifle in my hands for seven years!"

I'm laughing now. So is Chutes. "Thanks for the help, bro."

"I'm coming from an embassy ball," says Chris, indicating his tux. He nods toward the trucks and guns. "We grabbed this shit and ran."

He tells us Isfahan is burning. Tehran too. Mobs are storming the U.S. embassy — and the embassies of the Russians and the Chinese. He doesn't know who's attacking whom. He has caught snatches on al-Alam, the Iranian satellite channel, about a rising in Saudi Arabia; the fear in the West, says the report, is of a Shiite sweep across southern Iraq and into the Eastern Province of Saudi Arabia. Or maybe it's all bullshit. The one thing the merc can tell us for sure is the nearest safety is across two hundred miles of hell. "Salter's at

Kirkuk with two armatures, moving toward the Iranian border. If we can get to him, we're home free."

He means our Force Insertion commander, Gen. James Salter. An armature is the equivalent of the old conventional-army airmobile division. The word comes from Latin, meaning equipment or armor. Force Insertion has, along the Iraq-Iran border, four armatures with all supporting arms including artillery (105- and 155 mm howitzers), drone and truckborne antiarmor, and air defense in the form of mobile Chinese I-SAM rocket trucks. Salter's air assault complement, we know, is at near full strength, meaning each armature has three battalions of extended-range Black Hawk and up-gunned War Hawk choppers, a battalion of heavy Chinooks, plus seventy-two owner-operated AH-64 Apache attack helicopters, all outfitted with the latest aftermarket Chinese, Czech, and Israeli missile technology, American and Indian avionics and satcomms, and flown by American, Russian, South African, Australian, Polish, and British mercs, most of whom have in the old days been majors, lieutenant colonels, and colonels in their respective conventional air forces. Our new friend eyes our ragged-ass gear, which looks like it came from Operation Iraqi Freedom, and the faces of our guys — Chutes Savarese, Junk Olsen, Adrian "Q" Quinones, Marcus Aurelius "Mac" Jones, and Tony Singh, our six-foot-four Hindu from Sri Lanka. He indicates the city.

"Gentlemen, as Sarpedon said to Glaucus, 'Let us go forth and win glory — or cede it to others.' "

Chutes is grinning. "What's your name again, man?"

"Chris Candelaria."

"Chris, you're my kinda dude."

They bump elbows. In we go.

Nazirabad is situated at the juncture of two highways — 8, which runs north-south, and 41, east-west. The three-level interchange and its security station, Checkpoint 290, is the funnel through which all motorized entry and egress is channeled. There's an industrial slum to the north called Ali City, from which most of the bad actors come — tribal militias, criminal gangs, Mahdi revivalists, cabals of displaced army officers, as well as Jaish al-Sha'b, "Army of the People," which has replaced AQP — al-Qaeda in Persia — plus every imaginable hue of nationalist, separatist, and irredentist forces, including foreign fighters — Turks, Chechens, Syrians, Saudis, Uzbeks, Tajiks, Uighurs, as well as Shiite Kurds, Afghan Hazaras, and Lebanese.

As recently as ten years ago, Nazirabad was a secure, attractive tourist destination. Brochures called it the "city of artists." The Old Town had four souks, one entirely for tiles, another for decorative ironwork — gates, lamps, chandeliers. Nazirabad had two synagogues, believe it or not, and a Christian bookstore. A woman could walk alone and bareheaded, even after dark. Eighteen months ago, when our team deployed, a foreigner could still get a private villa, with cook, driver, and laundress. No more. In the space of ten weeks, since the start of the third Iran-Iraq war, the place has degenerated to a level of violence equal to Baghdad or Ramadi twenty-five years earlier — and the last half year has been even worse.

We take side streets into the city, bypassing Checkpoint 290. The sun is dropping fast. Mac has made radio contact with our engineers; they have abandoned the company compound and made their way to a safe house (actually the home of their supervisor's father) on Espresso Street, a well-to-do boulevard so named because it has the only Starbucks within five hundred miles. The only problem is that Espresso Street has become the epicenter for whatever conflagration is currently consuming the city.

We approach from the west, so the sun is behind us. We can see Iranian-badged Hind gunships overhead, putting out rocket and machine-gun fire — probably at sniper teams on rooftops — and see the propellant trails of heat seekers and SFRs, shoulder-fired rockets, corkscrewing up in response. I'm navigating by the electrical power lines, which run along central thoroughfares and are the only objects taller than three stories in the city. In an urban firefight, you can't simply race to the action like a fire truck toward a burning building. You have to patrol up to it, employing "movement to contact," which basically means keep advancing until somebody starts shooting at you. Our engineers are talking us in over line-of-sight squad radios, which work for two seconds and then break up as buildings and vehicles intervene. "How close are you to the fight?" I speak into my mike.

"We *are* the fight!" comes the answer.

Espresso Street, when we enter it, is as broad as a boulevard and sizzling with spent shell casings, smoking bricks, rubble, and blocks of concrete-and-rebar and is pocked by craters from which ruptured water-main fluid floods, mingling with raw sewage, garbage, and gasoline to form an inch-deep burning lake across the welcome-to-hell cityscape. We pass one Russian-built Iranian T-79 tank coming out, protecting two gun trucks with wounded regulars inside and on top. Local civilians are running up to my window and Chutes's, shouting that there are snipers on such and such a rooftop or drone swarms above such and such a block. Unarmed boys race on foot toward the action, just for the excitement. We see a press pickup, with "TV" on the windshield in masking tape. Chutes is my driver. The boom box blares Bloodstone's "Death or Dismemberment":

Eat me, beat me
Wolf me down and excrete me
I'm here for your ass, motherfucker

Cars are burning in the middle of the street; we're jinking around downed phone poles. Adrenaline is flooding through me; I can tell because the pulse hemometer on my wrist reads out at 180/15. But my subjective experience is the opposite. I'm cool. The hotter it gets outside, the cooler I become. This is nothing I can take credit for or claim to have achieved by virtue of training or application of will. I was born this way. When I was nine years old and my old man would wallop the tar out of me for some infraction of his demented code of honor, I would stare up at him icy eyed and not feel a twinge of rage, even though I could have and would have killed him on the spot if I had taken a notion to. I was remote. I was detached. I felt like another person was inside me. This other person was me, only stronger and crueler, more cunning and more deadly.

I never told anyone about this secret me. I was afraid they might think I was crazy, or try to take this other me away, or convince me that I should be ashamed of him. I wasn't. I loved him. In sports or fistfights, in moments of crisis or decision, I cut loose my conventional self and let this inner me take over. He never hesitated. He never second-guessed. Later, in combat, when I began to experience fragments of recall that were clearly not from this lifetime, I knew at once that these memories were connected to my secret self. They were his memories. I was only the temporary vessel in which they were housed.

This secret self is whom I surrender to now, entering Nazirabad. I become him. I feel fear. At times it threatens to overwhelm me. But my secret self pays no attention. I hear the gunships overhead and see the vapor trails of their rockets. A man must be crazy, I think, to head of his own free will *toward* that. But at the same time, no force beneath heaven can keep me away. This is what I was born for. I'm geeked out of my skull — and I'm curious. I want to see what's up ahead. How bad is it? What kind of fucked-up shit will we run into this time?

In action there is no such thing as thought, only instinct. We blow past two sharp exchanges of fire and suddenly there's the house. Our engineers have spray-painted on the compound wall

THIS IS IT!!!

in block letters two feet high. I wave to the other trucks: Keep moving. We can't burst in on our own engineers or their bodyguards will shoot us, not to mention the wicked stream of fire that is pouring onto the compound from rooftops and circling drones and is now zeroing on us.

"I know the place!" Chutes is shouting across at me. We accelerate past the rusty front gates — seven feet tall and perforated like cheese graters by .50-cal fire — and swerve hard left into an alley. Chutes is bawling across the seat at me. I can't hear a word but I understand from his gestures: there's a way in, from the rear, which we can access from one of the myriad cross-channels if we can find it. I'm raising the engineers and telling them to hold their fire when they see the rear gate blow in. "I will throw a flash-bang," I enunciate with exaggerated clarity into the Motorola mike duct-taped to the right shoulder of my Kev-lite vest. "When you see the flash, run straight out to us."

Nothing works in combat the way you think it will. It takes us almost twenty minutes to cover the two hundred feet to the rear compound gate. By then our besieged engineers are too petrified to stick a toe out. Snipers are on every rooftop, with rocketmen racing up, more every minute. We break in the gate with our Lada Neva's tailboard and are just starting in reverse across the court to the rear entry of the house, when one of the security men — a Fijian, no taller than five-foot-two, probably making forty bucks a day — appears in the rear egress, shouting, "IED! IED!" and pointing to the dirt drive over which our truck is about to roll. Three 155 mm artillery shells sit unburied, big as life, with their wires exposed, lining the south side of the lane. "Brake!" I shout to Chutes. The Fijian dives back into the house, one nanosecond ahead of a fusillade of 7.62 fire that blows the jamb and the security door to powder. Chutes powers the Lada Neva back out through the gate, to safety behind the four-foot-thick main wall. "What the fuck do we do now?"

There's nothing for us but to go in on foot, blasting every hajji triggerman on every rooftop as we go.

Junk, Q, and I bolt back through the gate. The rear door of the compound is about sixty yards away. We dash past a line of parked Toyota trucks and Tata/LUK compgas cars; I can hear the sheet metal shredding as gunfire pursues us. We can hear Iranian voices everywhere, not just on the overlooming buildings, but on the flat roof of the compound building itself. They know exactly what's happening. They could trigger the IEDs right now and take us out, but they're greedy—they want our vehicles, too. We dive into an alley and take cover beneath two gigantic air-conditioning units supported by pipe stanchions. I can hear one gunner on an overhead taunting us in English. Another in a baseball cap pops up behind the roof wall and starts firing. I jack myself left-handed into the clear and blow his head off. "Man!" shouts Junk, whooping.

I'm shouting to the Fijian, telling him we're coming. "All!" I cry, pantomiming to the group. "Run for it!" Does he understand English? I can't see him. Where are the engineers? The Fijian pops out again, flashing five fingers and a thumbs-up. Again gunfire shreds his nest as he plunges back inside. Junk and I spring out. Hajjis are pouring gunfire from rooftops and upper-story windows. Out of the corner of my eye, I see Junk take a hit and drop. "Go!" he's shouting. "I'm okay!"

I reach the rear door. The engineers and two other Fijians crouch back in the dimness, which is dense with brick dust and smoke from the pulverized walls of the building. The engineers wear body armor and blue civilian Kevlars. The security men have on nothing thicker than khaki; one dude is in flip-flops. "There!" I point to the alley where Junk and Q have taken cover. "Now!"

The mob gets ten steps and the first 155 blows. It's the far one, the one closest to the rear gate. The dumb-bastard triggerman has pushed the wrong button. The blast still knocks every one of us flat and annihilates our hearing. I'm in the rear, driving the engineers forward. Everybody's still alive. My head is ringing like a Chinese gong, but I can still hear the Iranians on the roofline cursing their numb-nuts triggerman. Our gang plunges to cover under the air-conditioning units. Quinones is kneeling between the A/Cs, firing at the V of two tenement rooftops above us. The enemy keeps popping up between clotheslines and satellite dishes. Every time Q pings one and the pink spray blows out of their heads and they drop away out of sight, the engineers yelp with terror and relief. Q and Junk are cross-decking now, firing over each other's shoulders. We're halfway to the compound wall, halfway to safety. "Move now!" I shout.

The group bolts to the gate and wall, to Chris, Chutes, and the others. Q and I are dragging one engineer, who has lost sight and hearing from the concussion of the 155, with Junk hopping on one leg and hanging on to one of the security men. We plunge back to safety just as full darkness falls.

Chris's two Kodiaks, which we had held in reserve two blocks back, have come forward now, ready to take us out. They're revving in the alley, thirty feet north, in the safe zone shielded by an adjacent building. Enemy 5.56 and 7.62 fire is ripping into the wall above us. Now the rocket rounds start flying; our Lada Nevas and 7-ton truck have to pull back. Someone is helping Junk into the first vehicle. I hear one of Chris's DSF men shouting in a German accent, "Who? Who's missing?" For a moment I think they mean Junk. I look over. Junk is okay. Then I realize they're talking about someone else. I turn back toward the compound. On the ground beside the air-conditioning units crawls one of our Fijians.

Sonofabitch! The man is in the dirt, clawing his way toward cover. Furious fire rakes the ground around him. I see him scramble face-first into a cooking ditch, just as a full burst from an AK takes him square between the shoulder blades. Both elbows fly rearward, then flop; his neck snaps; he crashes face-first into the dirt. He stops moving. "Brake!" I'm shouting to Chutes. "Q! Chris!"

"Go! Get out!" Chris Candelaria is calling, waving the vehicles to pull back. He has packed Junk's wound and stripped his own tourniquet, worn lanyard-style around his neck; he's cinching it around Junk's thigh as he and the German DSF man help him toward the first Lada Neva.

"We're going back!" I shout.

"What?"

"The Fijian. We're not leaving him!"

A shoulder-fired rocket whistles overhead and blows the hell out of a house across Espresso Street. What little hearing I have left is now gone.

"We're not leaving without him."

It's my secret me who's talking. He has made the decision.

"What the fuck are you talking about?" This is Chutes, my tightest mate and most trusted brother. He sticks his jaw six inches from mine.

"We're going back," I tell him.

Junk curses. "He's not our guy, chief! We don't even know who the fuck he is!"

"He's dead!" says Chutes. "There's two more 155s in there, waiting to blow!"

Other faces stare at me.

"Leave the body," cries the Fijian team leader. "The man would say so himself if he could!"

I tell the Fijians he's not theirs, he's ours.

Chris Candelaria's two Kodiaks are hauling ass now; they know they're targets. Iranian rocket gunners are trying to blow down the building that protects our flank. As their rounds scream in, blocks of concrete the size of bowling balls sail a hundred feet into the air and fall back, crashing all around us. We scramble into the slit trench of sewage. Guys are trying to crawl up inside their helmets. I'm peering around the corner, back into the compound.

Chutes clutches my sleeve. "Bro, listen to me. We got the engineers, we got the report . . . that's what we came here for." He points past the gate to the compound, to the fresh enemy streaming in along the rooflines. "We go back in there, somebody's gonna die."

There's no fear in Chutes's voice. He's just stating the truth.

I meet his eyes.

"Fuck you," he says, jamming fresh magazines into his belly rig. "You hear me, bro? Fuck you!"

Back we go. Chris Candelaria comes with us. We can hear the enemy hooting with anticipation. In the interval they have brought up a Russian PKM, which fires Eastern Bloc 7.62 rounds with a nutsack-shriveling *rat-a-tat* sound, and these are tearing the hell out of the open space we have to cross. The foe has got his second wind now. He is going after our Lada Nevas and the 7-ton truck, which have stayed behind to cover us. Rockets are zinging across the compound like Roman candles.

We grab the dead Fijian and haul him facedown from the dirt behind the blown-down cookhouse. The IEDs never blow. Chutes curses me all the way back to the gate, curses me when I bag the security man's effects and lash them around my waist with 550 cord. And he curses me all the way out of town.

Two hours later, our team has reached safety in Husseinabad, in the fortified compound of an Iranian police chief whose real name is Gholamhossein Mattaki, but whom everyone calls Col. Achmed.

Col. Achmed has his own doctor, his cousin Rajeef. Rajeef has a pharmacy and a little surgical suite in a side building of Col. Achmed's compound. Rajeef is our team doctor. He supplies all our pills and powders. We call him "Medicare."

I have driven flat out to Col. Achmed's, to get Junk (and two engineers whom we discover have been wounded in the dash across the compound) under serious medical care. Our medic Tony is a superb under-fire practitioner, and the DSF tech is good too. But neither one is a surgeon — and neither one has Dr. R's goody-box of Vicodin and Percoset, Ultram, Fentanyl, OxyContin, and plain old central Asian smack. I also want to bury our Fijian in a site that won't be desecrated. While our guys rehydrate and wolf down a meal of lamb and lentils, I grab Chutes and Chris Candelaria and organize a pow-wow with Col. Achmed. We still don't know who's invading whom, how dangerous the situation is, or what the hell is happening east in Isfahan and Tehran.

Achmed is not just a police chief and commander in the paramilitary Masij. He is a hereditary tribal leader and a grandson and great-grandson of Harul and Arishi sheikhs; he is responsible for the safety and welfare of several thousand men, women, and children of allied families, clans, and subtribes. He's a serious man.

"Get out now," he tells us, in the tone that your favorite uncle would take if he were looking out for you. We are in the third of his four storage buildings. The place looks like Costco. On racks and pallets sit unopened packing boxes of air conditioners and computer printers; cartons of Pennzoil, Pampers, and paper towels. Achmed has cases of Evian water, V8, Gatorade; crates of Nike running shoes, T-shirts, and tracksuits. The IRGC, the Iranian Revolutionary Guards Corps, smuggles in half the goods sold in Iran; the stuff comes in, billions of dollars' worth, by launch and lighter from Kish and Qeshm, "free trade" islands across the gulf, via the port of Bandar Ganayeh — not to mention whatever the colonel's minions have looted from ExxonMobil and BP. Guns and ammo are everywhere, in and out of crates—M4-40s, mortars, boxes of 5.56 and 7.62 NATO cartridges. Col. Achmed's family, he tells us, is packing up. The women and children will flee to southern Iraq and then to Syria. Achmed's sons and goons fill the room, armed to the teeth. "Don't wait even for morning," the colonel tells me, Chutes, and Chris. "If you do, you and your men will be massacred."

I ask him who will come after us.

"Me," he says with a smile. "Everyone."

Col. Achmed explains.

"They will not be able to help themselves. First they will come for your weapons and everything of yours that they can steal, then for honor, to avenge the humiliation you and your countrymen have inflicted upon our national manhood simply by your presence and your blue eyes. Next they will come to get you before others do, for the greatest honor goes to him who strikes first, while those who hesitate will be accounted cowards."

I ask him what will happen in the next week or ten days. He gives it to me in Revolutionspeak, but the gist is this: Shiite Iran— meaning those Revolutionary Guardsmen, army colonels, patriots, tribesmen, and true believers who have been biding their time throughout this long, phony war will unite now with their Iraqi Shiite coreligionists and, casting off the yoke of the West and its hirelings, strike east along the arc of the Shiite Crescent that runs from the Dasht-i-Margo—the Afghan Desert of Death—across Iran to the Eastern Province of Saudi Arabia (not coincidentally the swath of real estate that contains the richest petroleum reserves on earth) and purge this land of those who do not belong or believe.

"Do my men and I have time," I ask, "to finish dinner?"

Achmed's tribal code mandates hospitality. He helps us bury our Fijian, though he insists, first, on declaring the man a convert to Islam (which Col. Achmed can do, being a mullah as well as a tribal chief, and to which none of our Fijian's mates objects under the circumstances), then tops off our fuel tanks and loads us up with Neda spring water and sixteen-ounce cans of Beefaroni. One of Achmed's sons brings a tray of delicious homemade *sohan* — pistachio candy.

Col. Achmed maps out the safest route to the frontier (the one he'll be chasing us on) and helps key into our GPSes the sequence of junctures — all unmarked desert and mountain tracks that we could never find without his help. Dr. Rajeef rigs mobile hospital beds for Junk and our two wounded engineers; he stocks us up with two dozen vials of morphine, plus sample packs of Demerol and Dilaudid with sterile syringes and a hundred ampules of methylephidrine, which we all need in our exhausted, postadrenalinized state.

We take our leave over cups of black Persian coffee. It's midnight. Our engines idle beyond the walls in the night. Achmed and his men leave us alone, for our final prep and words for each other.

"Chief." It's Chutes, stepping forward before the others. "I'm sorry for what I said back there in Nazirabad . . ."

"Forget it."

He apologizes for refusing, at first, to go back after the Fijian, whose name, we have learned, is Manasa Singh. Chris Candelaria seconds this. I thank them both. It takes guts to speak up in front of the others. The act is not without cost to proud men. I appreciate it and I tell them.

The men surround me in the headlight-lit court. Safety lies two hundred miles east, in the dark, across country none of us knows — back valleys and passes peopled by warriors who will know where we are, how many we are, and where we are heading. Every one of us knows this, and every one feels the fear in his bones.

"Because we went back when we didn't have to," I say, "we know something about ourselves that we didn't know before. You know now, Chris, that if you fall, I won't abandon you. I'll come back, if it costs me my life — and so will Q and so will Junk and so will Chutes. And we know the same about you."

A bottle makes the rounds.

"The contract we signed says nothing about honor. The company doesn't give a shit. But I do. I fight for money, yeah — but that's not why I'm here, and it's not why any of you are here either."

From inside the compound, Col. Achmed and his sons listen. Two hours from now they'll be hunting us as if we were animals. But for this moment they know us as men, and we know them.

"What we did today in Nazirabad," I tell my brothers, "would earn decorations for valor in any army in the world. You know what I'll give you for it?"

I grab my crotch.

Chris Candelaria laughs.

Chutes follows. The whole crew shakes their heads and rocks back and forth.

You have to lead men sometimes. As unit commander, you have to put words to the bonds of love they feel but may be too embarrassed to speak of — and to the secret aspirations of their hearts, which are invariably selfless and noble. More important, you have to take those actions yourself, first and alone, that they themselves know they should take, but they just haven't figured it out yet.

3

SALTER

MY NAME IS GENTILHOMME. Don't even try to pronounce it. My friends call me Gent. Even my wife does, or did while I still had her.

I'm from Algiers. Not the one in North Africa.

Algiers, Louisiana.

Algiers is technically part of New Orleans, but you'll never hear anyone from Algiers admit that. In Algiers, you're from Algiers. Remember the movie *No Mercy,* starring Richard Gere and Kim Basinger? That was shot in Algiers. Algiers is rows of white clapboard houses and parking lots paved with seashells. You get the best muffaletta sandwiches in Algiers and the strongest coffee in the South, straight out of the holds of the ships in the port. Algiers is gang country. Cops are crooked there, and so is everyone else. The town is full of Creoles and Cajuns and long-haired dope-smoking crackers; there's quite a few Greeks and Turks and lately lots of Russians. Gentrification has not hit Algiers.

Tehran is a lot like Algiers. So are Beirut, Mogadishu, Khartoum. Baghdad is too. Journalists usually compare Baghdad to Los Angeles — the sprawl, the palms, the hellish traffic. But Baghdad is more like New Orleans. Same heat and humidity, same bridges, same big river swinging through the center of town. When I got to Baghdad in 2016, I felt right at home. Both places are run by gangs. There's a boss in every neighborhood, and every man, woman, and child knows who he is. They say it's tribes and religion in Baghdad, and that's true. But in the end a militia is nothing but a well-armed gang. It may take to the streets in God's name, but it plays by the rules of gangland.

In Baghdad, the neighborhoods are segregated from one another physically and emotionally, just like in New Orleans. Each one is run by a different mob, and each mob is at war with every other mob. A man from Baghdad doesn't think of himself as a Baghdadi. He identifies with his *muhalla,* his "kitchen," his clan, and his tribe. Algiers is just like that. It gets down to specific city blocks. "Where you from, man?" When you hear that on some streets back home, the next thing you hear is a gunshot.

Baghdad is like Algiers too in the sense of time-in-place. In Iraq, tribes go back centuries on the same ground. No grievance is forgotten. The blood of wronged ancestors saturates the dirt; the law is revenge and payback. If you're born there, you're stuck in it.

Honest government doesn't exist in Baghdad or Algiers. You can't get a driver's license or a satellite dish without paying somebody off. There's no middle class in either place. In Algiers or Baghdad you rise or fall based on your connections to street power. Justice never comes from the state, only from the tribe and clan, the boss, the sheikh.

What Westerners call corruption is just life in 75 percent of the world. Americans still don't understand this. We think the rest of the planet is like us, or would be if it had the same advantages. We live in a bubble in the States. We make decisions and establish policy based on dream conceptions of the wider universe. We think everyone is the same as we are. We think they want the same things we want.

They don't.

They're not like us at all.

James Salter was the first general officer I ever heard articulate this. The press accused him of permitting a massacre once, in East Africa during the violence in 2022. He said, "I was obeying a more ancient law." And he was.

I first met Salter in Iraq, six years before that. I was a twenty-six-year-old platoon sergeant with 3/7—Third Battalion, Seventh Marines—in Mosul at the tail end of the second Iran-Iraq war. Mosul is a Kurdish city with powerful Shiite and Sunni minorities. It sits on top of two of the three biggest oil fields in northern Iraq. The Kurds claim it; the Turks want it; the Iranians went to war to take it.

Mosul's population was about three hundred thousand then, and every district was at war with every other. I was reading Hobbes's *Leviathan* at the time. It was my bible. We had a threat board on the wall of our company office, listing the various militias and self-defense fronts, religious armies, criminal gangs, kidnapping rings and tribal jaishes, jamiats, and arbakais that considered us the enemy. One time I counted the entries: thirty-seven. That didn't count the uniformed and mufti Iranians, Turks, Armenians, Russians, Georgians, Chechens, Syrians, and Saudis, none of whom recognized the legitimacy of any border and all of whom were certain that, wherever the border was, we Americans were on the wrong side of it. Mosul was then one of the two or three most dangerous places on earth. My company's AO, Area of Operation, included a dense urban district called the Sumer. The first day I saw it, I understood the place. It was just like home.

From the start it was clear there was no hope of "victory." My job from Day One was to keep my Marines alive. How did I do that? I protected my guys by making up personally to the boss of our neighborhood, a tribal sheikh named Abd el-Kadr.

When I was in high school, I was an all-city basketball player.

Because of this, I was known around town; I was friendly with a lot of the mob guys. I would sign balls for their kids or get them tickets to games, that sort of thing. Anyway, the day came when my future was going to be decided. The boss in our part of town was an old Cajun named Jean-Baptiste Robidoux—they called him Robbie—who had a fried chicken and oyster shack that was his "hooch" or his "spot." He was there every day, in the porch-fronted room off the alley. I forget how it was communicated to me, maybe by one of Robbie's sons, but it was made clear that I was to show up and pay my respects.

The scheme was exactly the same in Mosul, except when you went to Robbie's you had coffee and when you went to Abd el-Kadr's you had chai tea. But there was the same storefront shop, the same back room, same heat outside in the alley, same sons standing around with guns. At Robbie's, the weapons were out of sight; at Abd el-Kadr's, they were in the open. In both places the drinks were served sweet and in little tiny cups. In both places you smoked. In both places you talked about the weather or family for fifteen minutes before you brought up anything of substance. To rush things was bad manners.

I told Robbie I wasn't going to college; I would enlist in the Marine Corps instead. He asked if I had given this serious thought. I was a smart kid; he didn't want to see me screw up my life. I said I had thought about it a lot. Reluctantly, Robbie approved. A job would be waiting for me if I wanted it. I thanked him.

Robbie handed me three hundred-dollar bills. I was a man now. Actually he didn't hand me the money; he set it down on the corner of the table. I didn't pick it up; my daddy did it for me. I had Robbie's blessing now. It was understood that if the law ever pinched me, I would eat my own ass before I'd give up anything about Robbie or his business. At the same time, if my mother or sisters ever needed something that I or my old man couldn't provide, Robbie would make sure they were taken care of.

When I met Abd el-Kadr, I immediately understood the

drill. From the first minute, I was looking to present him with something—a gift of honor, to express my respect and to establish me and my platoon in the same relation to him as I had been to Robbie back home. I hinted around a bunch of times, but the sheikh would never say what was important to him. He was too sly, and the rules of the game said it was my job to figure it out. One day in another part of the city I chanced to come into contact with a young Iraqi hitter showing off his two-year-old Toyota Land Cruiser with a winch on the front.

How did I snug things up with Abd el-Kadr? I snatched that Cruiser. The move was more of a military operation than 90 percent of the raids, sweeps, and counter-IED ambushes 3/7 ran legitimately. I planned and rehearsed it with my guys for three weeks. The problem was that the buck who owned the Toyota was the son-in-law of the sheikh in his muhalla, who was way up in the Nawari, a powerful tribe in the city. These characters are like desert Bedouin; they still wear the traditional dishdashas, the Lawrence of Arabia robes. There would be a bloodbath if they knew who had hit them.

We set up a fake checkpoint and took the car in broad daylight, then made it disappear from the impound lot. We had fake names on our uniforms and everything. We took the Cruiser to a chop shop in el-Kadr's kitchen, where it was repainted, numbers swapped out, new seats, new upholstery; it was a better job than you could get in Detroit. This was totally off the books; if "higher" found out we'd done this, I'd be in the brig for twenty years. I presented the machine to el-Kadr, who of course already knew all about it. He loved it. The prior group in our AO had lost four killed and thirteen wounded during its seven-month tour; ours in the preceding two months had had three hurt, two badly. After the Cruiser, no one fucked with us. We were bulletproof on those streets.

The Toyota was how I first came into contact with Gen. Salter. This was long before his mercenary days. He was a passionate patriot then, a shooting star not only in the Marine Corps (he had already achieved two spectacular tactical successes—in Yemen and Nigeria) but in all the armed forces.

Salter came from a celebrated military family. His father had been a Special Forces major in Vietnam, who went on to wear three stars before he was killed in a chopper crash during Desert Storm; his mother's dad was Adm. Scott X. Vincent, who was chairman of the Joint Chiefs under Eisenhower and wrote, among a number of other books, *The Projection of Power,* which was one of the sacred texts of the neocons during the run-up to Operation Iraqi Freedom. Salter's degree is in history from Northwestern; he has a Ph.D. from Duke in political science and has studied at Oxford and the London School of Economics. Commandant of the Marine Corps was a sure thing for Salter, it was assumed, with chairman of the Joint Chiefs to follow. Salter is a widower; he has one son, Robert, a captain in the Marine Corps.

Salter's command at that time included all the Marines on both sides of the Iran-Iraq border. He himself was in the field all the time. That was his style. His Jump CP, his mobile headquarters, consisted of three unarmored OIF-era Humvees in charge of a six-foot-four, 240-pound gunnery sergeant named Dainty (his real name), with crews that Salter had trained himself, and an Iraqi "terp"—interpreter—named Sayeed who they called Sam and who Salter trusted with his life. Salter would show up anywhere at any hour and just flop down with his Marines and shoot the shit.

· I had to make a report to him once, during an operation about a month after snatching the Cruiser. This was at Bagofah, east of the Tigris, in the pancake country not far from ancient Gaugamela, where Alexander defeated Darius to complete his conquest of the Persian Empire. Gen. Salter kept a straight face through most of the report, then, when I was just about finished, he said, "I see your man Abe's rolling 'round the hood in a fine new piece of iron."

I said I'd seen the vehicle; it was definitely a primo ride.

"While a Land Cruiser just like it," Salter said, "went missing from Rashidiyah at just about the same time."

I said that Sheikh el-Kadr was an influential man; I was sure he had many connections in the auto sales world.

"Yeah," said Salter. "I hear he got a helluva deal at Gent's Motors."

Salter was one of us. He got it. It was Salter who plucked me out of the enlisted ranks, pushed me through four years of college in twenty-seven months, at Uncle Sam's expense, and got me to the head of the line for OCS and TBS, The Basis School at Quantico, when the waiting lists for both were eighteen months long. He changed my life. I wasn't the only one he helped either.

Salter's Marines loved him. Even after the debacle in East Africa in 2022, when Salter was stripped of his stars like MacArthur in Korea and forced to walk the plank in UltraHi-Def and 3-D, the mass of the ground-pounding grunts still stood with him. He was their kind of commander. Even now, a generation since he had worn the uniform of a conventional U.S. fighting force, he could still attract to his service the savviest military minds and the saltiest trigger pullers, not only from Uncle Sam's vets but also from seasoned professionals of every English-speaking (and Russian and German and Arabic/Pashto/Dari) outfit in the world.

We cross the Iraq border ninety-six hours after bolting from Col. Achmed's. Where are Salter and his armatures? It was under Salter's orders, relayed via his adjutant Pete Petrocelli, that our team made the run into Nazirabad to retrieve the engineers and the technical report that they were preparing.

We strike the UAV screen of the northernmost formation just after noon. A drone picks us up as we descend via smugglers' tracks from the Zagros Mountains. This is high desert country, cloudless, shadeless, waterless, with a sky so clear we can see the Firefly spy-bird, no bigger than a pizza box, soaring half a mile above us. With intense relief we transmit our security signature and report that we are carrying wounded who need urgent care. The fly's scanners give us the once-over; within ninety seconds, orders appear on the screen of the All Force Tracker on my dashboard. We are to proceed to a trig point twelve miles east-northeast, where we will be met by a CASEVAC chopper and two HSDs, high-speed picket cars of the perimeter security force. We will be VDBed — video debriefed — in place.

When the commanding officer of any outfit, battalion sized or larger, moves outside the wire — meaning into hostile or potentially hostile territory — he does so shielded by concentric rings of satellite, drone, air, and ground security. Like a flagship at sea, the number one cheese advances as the epicenter of a task force arrayed around him in defensive circles. That's the way it's supposed to be — the way, we assume, that Salter will be operating, as commander of the dominant Western combat force in a theater where tactical nukes have supposedly been deployed within the past 120 hours.

But when our team arrives at the debriefing point — a barren wash between two basalt ridges, which coincides with the eastern-most point of Force Insertion's advancing formation — we see not only the two light HSDs that are supposed to meet us, but a cloaking truck, two satcomm dish cruisers, a three-vehicle CAAT anti-armor team, and a pair of eight-wheeled MI-1 fuel tankers. That's a Jump CP if I've ever seen one.

We pull in and brake. The CAAT teams' missile tubes track us all the way. The comm screens on our dash depixelate, jammed by the cloaking truck. A surveillance satellite looking down would see nothing but fuzz.

"Peace, babies!" Chris dismounts, still in his tux jacket. "It's only us chickens."

He and I step forward, readying our scan-tabs to verify our identities. A bearded officer intercepts us. "Drop your drawers, girls. The only ID I trust is a full cavity search."

"Hayward," I say. "You asshole!"

The officer clamps me in a bear hug.

I ask him what scam he's running in this hellhole.

"Watching out for the boss!"

I introduce Chris. Tim Hayward was an airborne lieutenant colonel when I knew him in Yemen and Uganda, six and seven years ago. He is the most lethal specimen of warrior I have ever known. He ran the assassin's course at the School of the Americas; he has trained the SAS and the Spetsnaz in chemical and biological warfare. He can kill you with a heart attack, make you choke on a chicken bone, rig your brakes to fail at the exact moment you're highballing down a mountain pass. He also has a master's in international relations, five kids, and a gorgeous Belarusian wife who took silver in the biathlon at the 2014 Winter Olympics in Sochi.

"Come on," he says, "let's get your wounded outa here."

The CASEVAC bird, an extended-range War Hawk comes whooping in; Hayward and his troopers help Chutes, Q, and Junk get our engineer and the others aboard. Where is Salter? "You'll see him," says Hayward, "in sixty seconds." He leads us over to the video debrief rig, which is just an encryption cam mounted on the light bar of one of their trucks. The operator is just slating Chris and me, when we hear surface engines approaching from the west and see two rooster tails of dust emerge from behind the basalt ridge.

A pair of HSDs skim into view, moving fast and tracking toward us. The vehicles have no armor, no doors, and no windshields — just two aircraft-type seats slung between four all-terrain tires, with a light bar overhead and a roll cage tubed around. Materials are all superlight, stealth composite, even the 2.7-inch rocket clusters topside and finned-round autosights fore and aft. No vehicle that rolls on wheels can keep up with one of these speeders, and nothing that flies can zero its sights on them. I don't know what the military version costs, but the civilian type, made by Ford with a Rolls-Royce engine, goes for 2.1 mill.

The two HSDs slalom into the ravine and brake in a storm of sand and grit. Chris and I squint. Through the swirling alkali we see Salter dismount from the lead vehicle. He wears cargo trousers, a calf-length duster, and sand goggles. No helmet, no flak jacket. He pulls the goggles off over a peaked desert cap and beats the dust off both by swatting them against his right trouser leg. In a shoulder holster rides the M9 pistol that has been his trademark since Marine Corps days.

Two more CAAT vehicles and a surface-to-air missile truck come up behind Salter's vehicles, disperse into a perimeter, and stop, facing outboard. Hayward trots over. Salter, with Hayward and a couple of officers from the scout teams, mounts the ridge on foot, scanning the horizon to the east with binoculars. The force protecting him is, to put it kindly, underpowered. There's only one cloaking truck, no airborne security, and not another fighting vehicle as far as the eye can see.

"Far be it from me to criticize our commander," says Chris, "but what the fuck is Salter doing this far forward with nothing to protect him bigger than my nine-inch dick?"

"He leads from the front."

"I do too, bro. But I'm not the maraschino cherry on top of the hot fudge sundae."

Salter glances in our direction. Hayward is telling him something and pointing toward us. We can see Salter react with animation. He strides down the ridge. Chris and I move toward him, saluting.

"Stand easy, gentlemen!"

Salter comes up with his right hand extended. "Gent, you sonofabitch!"

He grabs my hand and embraces me warmly. He gives me shit about Abd el-Kadr and the Land Cruiser and makes a joke of times we nearly got killed in Yemen and East Africa. Such intimacy is one of Salter's gifts as a commander. It can't be faked. Though he is light-years beyond us, his junior commanders, in intellect and force of command, he makes us know that he loves us as brothers and as equals; we are his blood and he is ours. I feel with Salter now — as I have felt before, every time I have been in his presence — that unprovable but indelible certainty that he and I have known each other in earlier lifetimes and will know each other again.

I introduce Chris. "I know, I know," says Salter, indicating the satellite truck. "Hayward and I have been following you characters' getaway for the past three days."

Salter debriefs us himself. We deliver our assessments of Nazirabad, of Col. Achmed, of the sense of the situation. I present the engineers and hand over the document our team had been assigned to collect. I haven't looked at it; I have no idea what's in it. Salter passes the paper to his ADC, who stashes it at once in a locking briefcase. He starts to say something to the aide about delivering the report by hand and at once. Then an impulse seems to strike him. He glances to Hayward, then back to me.

"What division is your contract with, Gent?"

I tell him. He asks my pay grade. I tell him that.

"With your permission," he says, "I'm buying you out."

Salter indicates Chris, Chutes, Q, and the others. He asks if I'm happy with my team.

"The best there is."

"Acquire their contracts too," he instructs his aide.

Salter takes the locking briefcase from the ADC.

"Gent, I've got an assignment for you if you'll take it."

He hands me the case. I am to deliver it to a certain individual whom I know and about whose location "outside of theater" the aide will provide particulars and arrange all transport, cover, and compensation. I will complete the assignment as discreetly and expeditiously as possible, then turn around and get back to Salter in person as fast as I can. "After that," the general says, "I've got an important job for you and your team."

He glances to Hayward but says nothing. Chris listens; the others look on from their vehicles. Salter apologizes that he can't tell us more. He reminds us that our position, compensation-wise, is pretty cozy right now. We can play out the tail end of this campaign and fly home, each of us, with a quarter mill in the bank.

"This new job will triple that," Salter says. "But you may come back missing your ass."

"With respect, sir," says Chris. "My ass will take the money."

Salter regards me. "Will you go where I send you, Gent?"

I don't give a damn about the money. The mission is strictly secondary. What counts to me is the chance to fight alongside Chris and Chutes and the others. And the opportunity to serve again under Salter.

"Sir," I say, "I'll fly to hell if you tell me to."

4

CHAOS IN THE KINGDOM

I LAND AT AMMAN, JORDAN, at 1030 local, 20 August 2032, bound
for Inverness, Scotland—having flown out of Kuwait City an hour
and fifty minutes earlier on a private jet (no other passengers) leased
to Force Insertion. Queen Alia airport is bedlam. Status boards read

> FLIGHT CANCELLED
> FLIGHT CANCELLED
> FLIGHT CANCELLED

Loudspeakers broadcast in English, Chinese, and Arabic, as Asian
and Middle Eastern families and businessmen crisscross the floor,
pushing loads of luggage atop carts, or camping disconsolately in
recesses and alcoves. Even though I'm flying privately, Security has
required me to deplane; I have been searched three times and inter-
viewed twice. I wait with everyone else in the main terminal.

My assignment from Salter is to deliver the briefcase to Maggie Cole—Margaret Rucker Cole, the former first lady, widow of
the late president of the United States, Jack Cole. Mrs. Cole is stag

hunting in the highlands of Scotland. The plane will clear regional security here and continue on to Inverness.

In the terminal, TV news covers only two subjects — chaos in the Middle East and plummeting markets around the globe. Holo stalls broadcast bulletins and updates on the attempted coup in Saudi Arabia. The rising has been put down, say the Iranian news agencies FARS and IRNA, by mercenary troops commanded by Gen. James Salter and in the employ of the Saudi royal family. Al-Jazeera is reporting the exact opposite: Salter's troops, paid by sources unknown but suspected to be a cabal of young and disaffected princes, has overthrown the House of Saud. No one knows which report is true, if either. I certainly don't. What seems to be factual, at least according to Trump/CNN, Tass, and Ariel Caplan, the female combat correspondent from Agence France-Presse, is that chaos in the kingdom has touched off a regional territorial free-for-all. Russian and Turkish troops are clashing in the Caspian Basin; Iranian armored units, supported by the satellite and drone power of their Chinese allies, have emerged from their enclaves in Tehran and are sweeping south and west (the fore-wash of this wave is what swept me and my team out of Nazirabad), attempting to recapture the oil and gas fields that had been stolen from them, in their view, after the second Iraq-Iran war, by Lukoil, BP, Petrobras, DNO International, and ExxonMobil and their privately funded mercenary armies. Propaganda out of Persepolis is calling for the overthrow of all Sunni elements in Iraq and Saudi Arabia, which is all Sunni, even Wahhabi Sunni, except for parts of the Eastern Province. Iran's aim, reports Ms. Caplan, is the establishment of a "Shiite Crescent," which would extend from western Afghanistan across Iran and southern Iraq to the Arabian peninsula and whose boundaries would include the vast Rumayla, Umm Qasr, Zubayr, and Majnoon oil fields in southern Iraq and the supergiant Ghawar, Shaybah, and Khurais fields in Saudi Arabia—in other words, three-fifths of the world's known crude oil reserves.

Clearly in this scenario, not a single drop would flow to the United States.

Conventional U.S. and NATO ground forces have been gone from the Middle East for half a generation now, with power projection limited to "standoff" forces — the navy, including missile cruisers and destroyers, nuclear subs and naval aviation; satellite; and drone attack arms, both seaborne and land based in Qatar, Bahrain, and the UAE. The United States maintains two MEUs, Marine Expeditionary Units, shipborne out of Djibouti and Diego Garcia, but each of these comprises only a Battalion Combat Team. The only Western troops on the ground are Salter with his four armatures of Force Insertion mercs — and no one seems to know which side he is on, where his formations are, or even if they remain intact and unmassacred. Hysteria reigns on Capitol Hill, gas prices are setting new records, the Dow and the Nasdaq have gone over a cliff. Adding to the delirium, notes Fox/BBC, is the fact that this is an election year and the presidential primaries are in full swing.

I'm monitoring all this on civilian channels and also on my AKOP, the encrypted mil/net, which gets raw combat feeds, as well as my own bootleg satware that taps into the central database of the AFT, the All Force Tracker — the digital display and comm device onboard all merc aircraft, tanks, and combat vehicles, which links them and shows their locations, as well as those of the enemy.

At Queen Alia I wind up sharing a lounge alcove with a Lebanese businessman named Nabil al-Aftar, who is probably a spy, judging by the expansion of his irises when he gets a squint at this little beauty. We bond immediately and agree to swap secrets. He helps me log on to an outlet I've never been able to get aboard before — Arabic-language al-Manar, Hezbollah's mouthpiece out of Beirut. The site has footage, which it plays over and over, purporting to be the mass beheading of some forty Saudi rebels, supposedly in "chop-chop square" in Riyadh. It also has edited versions of public statements, with subtitles in Arabic, of both American presidential candidates, including the incumbent Murchison, denouncing the violence in Iran, Arabia, and the Caspian Basin, calling for restraint and moderation while simultaneously threatening nuclear Armageddon. Both candidates cite their "close personal ties" to Gen. Salter and declare, in the tone one reserves for talking a suicide-belt-wearing maniac down from a ledge, their confidence in his loyalty, stability, and self-restraint. "Let's go back," I tell my Lebanese friend, "to the beheadings."

According to al-Manar, two of the unlucky devils are West Point–trained generals in the Royal Saudi Air Force; a number of others are security force generals and colonels with pedigrees from Annapolis, Sandhurst, and St. Cyr. This intel is probably bogus — but try telling that to the true believers in Sana'a, Dushanbe, and Mogadishu, pumping it at high volume into their earbuds. I'm trying to read between the lines. Has there actually been a rising? Of whom? Against whom? With what aims and what second-generation consequences?

Do the contents of the briefcase I'm carrying have something to do with this? I have met Mrs. Cole in the past and have even shared with her what might be considered confidences. But that was years ago and under far different circumstances. Why have I been tasked to make this delivery to her now? What connection can the former first lady have to any of this?

My wife — I should say estranged wife — is a pretty famous new-media journalist. Her name is Adrienne Economides; you might have heard of her. She calls herself A.D. professionally because it sounds more like a man. I call her A.D. too. One of the more constructive habits I've acquired from her is the practice of due diligence. Research. A.D. is a scrupulous note taker and deep driller, as they say in the Nooz biz. She taught me about proprietary databases. Big outfits like the *New York Google Times* or Fox/BBC subscribe to these massive private search engines to the tune of five or ten million bucks a year. Authorized reporters get access. When A.D. and I split up, I gave her my Ford F-250 in trade for her two code-bars, which we still share. The conventional military also has a number of clearance-required databases — AKOP, Trident-V, and the Manassas Group being the most familiar to the general public. Private contractors have their own key-access sources as well. But the most reliable, comprehensive, and easiest to use are the two dedicated journalists' databases — Getty/Carolingian in London and al-Hamra in Dubai. The searchware used on both is called CPK, a.k.a. "cupcake." Among reporters, cupcake is a verb. You cupcake somebody. While I'm waiting in Amman, I cupcake Mrs. Cole. (There is also a "blind cupcake," which means your search is encrypted so that no one can trace who initiated the activity.)

Margaret Rucker "Maggie" Cole: widow of President Jack Cole (1960–2029), former two-term first lady. Bryn Mawr College, 1994, summa cum laude, English Literature; Yale Law School, 1997. Partner, Lowther Schapiro & Bloom LLP, 2006–2019.

I scan through a blizzard of blog posts, articles, photos, and videos. Few depict Mrs. Cole's family or professional life, which apparently she has guarded jealously. I have to run an enhanced search to learn that her father was James MacDowell Rucker who, according to an appreciation in *Oil and Gas Journal* upon his death in June 2019, "was a pioneer in 'rejuvenated extraction' from depleted fields using high-pressure nitrogen injection. He is credited with revitalizing the vast Ghawar field in Saudi Arabia, as well as Safaniya, also in Arabia, and el-Arish in Iran. He was the architect of the merger between ExxonMobil, Petróleos Mexicanos, and Brazil's Petrobras." A footnote tells me that Mrs. Cole served as counsel to this conglomerate for twenty-two years.

Most of the video of Maggie shows her as first lady. Jack Cole, as we all know, was a two-term governor of Virginia, chairman of the RNC, director of the Central Intelligence Agency, vice president under Jeremy Spruance, then president himself. The following is from politix.holo:

> After her husband's death, Mrs. Cole oversaw the design and construction of the Cole Presidential Library in Falls Church, Virginia, which she still directs, as well as founding and serving as CEO of the Institute for Strategic Analysis, an Alexandria-based think tank specializing in issues of energy policy and global politics.

My final cupcake is "intersect Gen. James Salter." Pickings are slim. I unearth only one tidbit that I had known before: that Margaret Rucker had been a sophomore at Bryn Mawr when James Salter was a first classman at Annapolis. I dig up a photo of the two of them together from June Week, the time of graduation balls and dances. Are they a couple? I can't tell. Maggie wears a gown and Salter is in dress whites, but there is no accompanying text or caption and the resolution is so poor that it breaks up into pixels when I try to enlarge it.

While I'm doing this a holo comes in from my estranged wife. She has tracked me via our shared cupcake code. Her call comes in with no greeting or salutation:

Y R U cpking M/Cole?

My reply:

Fine, thank you. How are you?

A.D.:

Cut the shit, Gent. What's up?

I try to block A.D.'s visual linkup so she can't grab any cues from the environment, but she catches just enough airport audio to get a glimmer before I toggle the camera icon off. "Where are you? Amman? Is that Gate 6?"

She's good, A.D. This is serious though. Revealing the tiniest clue will be enough for her to unspool an entire story; in ten minutes she'll know more about my assignment than I do and the saga will be all over the air, the Web, and the blogosphere.

My problem with A.D. is I have a weakness. I'm still in love with her. A.D. can get to me and she knows it. She starts asking how I am. Am I okay? She's been worrying about me, she says. What makes it worse is she means it.

Some women get to you with their bodies. A.D. does it with her voice. I can't describe it. It's not throaty or come-fuck-me seductive; if anything it's the opposite: cerebral and news-y. It has that rhythm to it. A.D. is quick. Nothing gets past her. She has a relentless curiosity that's childlike — and oddly arousing. I hear that voice and I have to hang on.

She makes me set up the holo where I can see her. That's another problem. Her face. I have a weakness for that, too. "You can't write anything about this, A.D."

"What'll you do, kill me?"

"Yes."

A.D. has been a finalist twice for Pulitzers. Along with Ariel Caplan of Agence France-Presse (who is A.D.'s best friend), she is one of the half-dozen most celebrated female journalists in the world, though you'd never know it to hear her talk. A.D. is tortured and insecure. That's one of the things that first attracted me to her. For years when I was with her, I tried to save her — to take away her self-torment, or at least ease the pain it caused her. Finally I realized that she didn't want to lose it. She needed it. It was the engine of her artist's soul.

I never knew a writer before I met A.D. Any time you have a writer, you have self-torture. Why? Because every one of them wants to be Shakespeare. And every American wants to write the Great American Novel. I don't care how many awards they get for journalism or movie-writing, they all want to be Hemingway. The women more than anybody. A.D. has four novels she's working on. I know them all by heart. She hasn't finished one. She's always going off to war. You can't help her. When I'd suggest that maybe journalism was her true calling, she'd cut me off for a month. I look at her now on the little, shimmering hologram. I hate that sick feeling in my heart but there it is.

"So," she says, "are you gonna get yourself waxed this time?"

"If I do, honey, you'll get the exclusive."

This is an old joke between us. A.D. asks if she's still in my will.

"Always, baby."

"How much do I get?"

I recite my line: "You'll never have to turn tricks again."

A.D. is half Greek, half South African. She speaks with a Johannesburg accent. On the occupation line of her passport, it says "war correspondent." A.D. is ambitious. She likes to quote Elvis:

Ambition is a dream with a V-8 engine.

I first met A.D. in East Africa in the late teens. We got married in Mombasa, at the Hotel Serena Beach, with Chutes as my best man and Rob Salter—then a 1LT with Force Recon—pouring the pineapple daiquiris. A.D. and I had a bayview suite for two nights that she got us comped for through Trump/CNN; the rate was $1,450 per. I was in the Marine Corps then (technically still married to my second wife, but who's counting?), a twenty-nine-year-old O-2 serving under Gen. James Salter.

I used to run into A.D. on flights. In Africa, to get anywhere, you have to travel by plane. Even if you're serving-military, you catch hops with whoever's going near where you've got to go; otherwise you wait around forever. A.D. was a correspondent for FaceTime and Trump/CNN, but she was filing stories as well on her own, through various mil/pol blogs and to her own site, *Line of Fire,* which was also the title of one of her unfinished novels. There was a gaggle of other hotshot female reporters in Africa then, all trying to be the next Christiane Amanpour. A.D. had bigger balls than any of them. In Somalia and Sudan she handled her own sound and uplink, traveling with just a cameraman and one big, strapping *kalash* (a different one on each assignment) to haul her drinking water and batt-paks. She used an Apple HD iCam with an encryption sync and a dejammer. A.D. dictated her stuff over the satellite or texted it from her handpod. *Kalash* comes from *Kalashnikov*; it's the ubiquitous African term for "young man." Whatever assistant A.D. had with her, she'd teach him to run the sound. If you want to puff up a black African, put a mike and a Nagra in his hand. These dudes would have leaped into a volcano for her.

A.D. is two years older than me. The first time she got word that she was a Pulitzer finalist was ten days after we got spliced. I remind her of that now. "I'm lucky for you."

"Yeah?" she says. "Did I win?"

A.D. is a politics junkie. She's up on every detail of the latest administration outrages. It's an article of faith with her that the United States under the last six presidents—Dems as well as GOP—has crossed what she calls the Augustan Point of No Return, meaning the date when Octavian took the name Caesar Augustus and the republic of Rome became the Roman Empire. She hates this. It's the passion of her life to make people see the parallels.

"I know Force Insertion hasn't pulled you out of Iran for fun, Gent. What kind of dark shit are you in on now?"

"Maybe I'm working for Human Rights Watch."

"Maybe you're working for Jim Salter."

A.D. asks if I still never read the news.

"I've seen it all before, darlin'."

I've told A.D. my vision of the ancient battlefield and my belief in previous lives. She regards both as humbug, which, I must say, pisses me off monumentally.

She fills me in now on the attempted overthrow of the Saudi monarchy. One report states that Western mercenary forces played a role in crushing the uprising; another says the mercs were part of the rebellion. A.D. believes both are fiction. "No one knows for sure because the peninsula has been shut down to news, even tighter than usual." Salter's in on this, she tells me. "I'm gonna get in somehow."

"Saudi Arabia. Is that where I'm going?"

"You don't even know, do you?"

A.D. knows more about Salter than anybody. A story she broke in East Africa in 2022 was instrumental in terminating his conventional-military career and propelling him into the under-world (as it was thought of then) of mercenary enterprise. A.D. ad-mires Salter as a warrior but believes his philosophy is founded upon a neocolonial, MacArthur-esque self-conception (I disagree; we've had more than one brawl on the subject) and that this drive is even more disquieting now, when Salter is a gun for hire, with no force to govern him except his own sense of honor.

"This is no joke, Gent. These fuckers are destroying the country." She launches into a rant about when corporations and government become one, it's called fascism. I say I have no problem with that if it keeps down the price of gas.

"You don't fool me, Gent. This shit bothers you, too."

When we were still living together, A.D. made it a ritual to give me a book each time I deployed. She continues the tradition now, crunching me the e-version of her current bedstand companion — Livy's *History of Rome.*

"A little light reading, sweetheart."

"I'll knock it off tonight."

She blows me a kiss. Her holo image sizzles off. I don't have to see her to know what she's doing: texting one editor after another, trying to snag a gig that'll get her a seat on the first jet to the kingdom.

I land at Inverness midafternoon. The city is socked in by the frigid, milky fog the Scots call *haar.* I can't see the runway lights till the plane is three hundred feet off the deck, but our pilot, Conrad Hilliaresse, sets the craft down as gently as a bee on a buttercup. Taxiing is more dangerous than landing; it takes us almost ten minutes, tiptoeing through the gloom behind a FOLLOW ME truck, before we reach the terminal and I've connected with my driver.

In the five hours since my chat with A.D., the situation in the Middle East has come into slightly clearer focus. Iranian armor has crossed the Iraqi border in Diyala and Sulaymaniyah Provinces but has not yet advanced beyond Baghdad to the south; it may have held up in place deliberately. The Chinese have contributed technical assistance to Iran but have shown no signs of dispatching ground troops; Russian and Turkish armor have checked their advances somewhere outside of Kirkuk and Mosul, respectively. A cease-fire has been proposed by the Syrians. UN negotiators are on the way.

Of Salter's four armatures on the ground in Iraq, one has taken up positions in the vicinity of the Diyala River, protecting the capital. I do not say "defensive positions," as it is part of Salter's philosophy that there is no such thing as defense. The other three have swept south at top speed. They remain intact, according to Reuters and al-Arabiya, and are taking possession of the oil fields at Rumayla and

Zubayr. Other elements are moving to secure Majnoon. Southern Iraq is being stabilized. Saudi Arabia for the moment appears calm.

My driver is a former SAS sergeant (in farmer-style civvies) who will not tell me his last name and claims to have no knowledge of who I am or why I'm here. All he knows is he has been instructed to deliver me to a certain country estate and wait to take me back to the airport. We speed north for half an hour along narrow, winding coast roads past Dornoch, Golspie, and Brora, then turn west, uphill into the interior. In no time the roads, which have been barely wide enough to hold two cars abreast, shrink to single lanes, then cart-width tracks. We're climbing through gorgeous, wild country without a tree or a bush taller than a man's waist. "How much longer till we reach the estate?" I ask.

"We've been on it for the past thirty minutes."

A manor house appears, grim and square and stony, set in the middle of absolutely nothing. We pass through an iron-gated strongpoint manned by a brace of dour-looking squaddies with bomb-sniffing Alsatian shepherds and see-through scanners, then proceed for another mile along an unpaved drive, through a second checkpoint, and finally beneath a portcullis-like security barrier and into an enclosed motor court paved with gravel. Two dark-green Land Rover Defenders squat before a sheltered entryway. It's August, full of sunshine, and the place is fucking freezing. I can hear hounds baying beyond a wall.

"Out you go, sir," says my SAS driver. Before my soles touch the deck, a gray-haired gentleman with the ruddiest cheeks I've ever seen scuttles from the manor house, introduces himself in an incomprehensible dialect, bundles me into one of the Defenders, and fires it up. He keeps mumbling, more to himself, it seems, than to me. I make out something about no time to dawdle, must beat the sunset. Apparently hunting stags in Scotland is a lot like hunting deer in Louisiana; the actual shoot happens at dawn or dusk, the only times of day that the prey shows itself. "If you don't mind, sir," says the guide, "we'll be ferrying two other gentlemen."

The right rear door of the Defender bangs open and in piles former U.S. secretary of state Juan-Esteban Echevarria, followed immediately by an extremely professional-looking security contractor who swings into the front seat, revealing a Sig Sauer P220 combat model in a shoulder holster beneath his coat and quilted vest. I have been prepped for none of this. The former secretary looks exactly like his photos — silver-gray goatee, Bolivian-dictator pompadour, hands the size of skillets. He goes 290 if he goes an ounce. He sits to my right in back; the Defender yaws to starboard. The secretary's bulk dominates the vehicle. He grasps my hand in a mitt as big as a Christmas ham.

"So you're Maggie's nephew," he says, introducing himself. "We've been waiting for you for two hours. The guides refused to take us out without you."

The Defender bucks and jounces out of the court; in ninety seconds we're on the moors, following rutted dirt trails that make the river tracks in Nangarhar look like Southern California freeways. Nephew? No one has alerted me to this cover story either— or given me the slightest warning that I'm going to be planted cheek by jowl with the former SecState (and winner of the Nobel Peace Prize) who singlehandedly, or almost so, destroyed Gen. Salter's conventional-military career.

The drive goes on forever, following back trails and sunken traces so as not to alert the game. It's eight in the evening and still not dusk. Our ruddy-cheeked driver, who apparently is a hunting guide or gamekeeper employed by the estate, wears a satcomm earpiece beneath his tweed cap. It squawks with staticy transmissions. "I'll ride ye as far for'ard as I can, gents," he says. "Then it's shank's mare for the lot of us."

He explains that four hunting parties are fanned out over a

number of miles, across the range of treeless vales ahead of us. Each party consists of a shooter and a guide. Mrs. Cole's is one of these. On a hunt, our driver reminds us, the guide has the final say in all matters. The radio transmissions are from the various guides ahead, navigating us in.

"The lady must be onto somethin', or her man wouldn'a shut down." He means that Mrs. Cole's guide, in the interest of stealth, is not responding to our driver's transmissions or allowing them to come through. "Stags can hear a mouse fart a mile away and pick up a Rover engine at five miles. They can smell the diesel thirty minutes after you shut the damn thing off."

He explains how the hunt, as twilight approaches, becomes a competition, even though the hunting parties are miles apart. "If one party fires, the hunt's over for aw th' others. Every animal within ten miles'll bolt."

We crest a rise and brake. The sun is finally setting. Our driver kills the engine. Before us in the failing light spreads a spectacular vista of dales and glens, receding into a smoky distance probably twenty miles away. "End of the line, lads." The driver springs down. "Let's have you!"

We advance on foot. The secretary is not happy. "How much farther?"

"We've only just started, haven't we, sir?"

I like our guide. He doesn't wear hunting togs; except for his shoes, which are rubber mud-sloggers, he's dressed in a gray houndstooth business suit with a tattersall shirt and a necktie with little Irish setters on it. He looks like a banker. The gear works, though I'm shivering in my North Face field jacket; he's toasty as a tick.

"What's your real name, Colonel?" Echevarria tramps beside me over the spongy, heather-carpeted turf pocked with patches of spiky, knee-high gorse. "Or do you go by rank in your outfit? Clearly you're nobody's nephew."

"I'm somebody's nephew."

"My guess is General Salter's."

Our guide hisses for silence. "If we molest the lady's hunt," he says, "she'll have all our bollocks, mine first."

We cross two ridge crests and start down a third. I'm scanning ahead. "There." The guide's hand stops us in place. He goes down on one knee. We do likewise.

"Where?" says the secretary. There's excitement in his voice.

The guide indicates a rocky promontory, well over a mile ahead. Daylight is going fast. It's hard to tell the rock from the dark furze and heather. The secretary squints through 10X pixel-aug binos. I'm straining with the naked eye.

"See the stag?"

I can barely make out a darkish blotch, perhaps three hundred yards below the outcrop, in a vale that must contain a spring or a burn, as the Scots call a creek. The blotch could be one animal or several. I can't see the first lady.

"Here, Colonel." Echevarria passes me his glasses. They're beauties: Special Forces optical-enhanced binos that deconstruct visible light and IR/UV into digital elements, then recombine and enhance these signals electronically. With the tap of a button, a full-color representation zooms into focus. I can see a guide, prone among rocks, and Maggie Cole on one knee beside him (apparently she needs the extra height to get a clear shot, given the down angle) with her rifle sling-braced around her left upper arm and forearm. She looks like a Marine on a rifle range.

"Why doesn't she shoot?" asks the secretary. The guide shooshes him. He snatches the glasses back. Maggie wants the trophy, the guide says, meaning she must go for a heart shot. She's waiting for the stag to turn his chest toward her.

I find myself calming my own breath and stilling my heart. This is serious shooting Mrs. Cole is doing. A deer rifle weighs twice as much as an M4–40 carbine and it only gives you one shot. The first lady must put a single round inside a circle no bigger than a fist at three hundred yards. If she fails and only wounds the stag, both our parties will be out here on foot in the dark tracking the poor creature to put him out of his agony.

The secretary peers through the binos. I see him react and, a second later, hear the report of the rifle. It's too dark now to see without glasses. "He's down!" cries the secretary.

"Bloody hell!" The guide slaps his thigh in celebration. We stand. The valley echoes with the rolling peal of the gunshot. Our escort hands me his own glasses; through them, I can see Maggie's guide stand. She herself has not moved, except to work her arm and shoulder free of the sling and to elevate the smoking barrel of her rifle.

My SAS driver is supposed to pull me out as soon as I deliver the briefcase. But by the time the motorcade of Land Rovers has delivered the hunting parties back to the manor house in the bone-rattling dark, Mrs. Cole won't let me go. She is still high from her trophy shot. She downs three sherries like water, though the cold may have something to do with that; when a serving man brings single malt in a decanter for the group, she signs for two fingers, then changes it to four. The gathering — whose numbers have swollen to nearly two dozen, counting the hunters, their assistants, and their aides — breaks up for an interval so that its members can bathe and change for dinner. There is no cold on earth like Scottish cold, and it's worse after dark in a drafty, vaulted, stone-founded hall. Not even a pair of walk-in fireplaces roaring with timber can take the edge off. "Now you see, Colonel," says Echevarria, setting a hand on my shoulder, "the evolution of 90-proof malt whisky."

The secretary is a bit of a bully. In front of his aides and the first members of the party returning from their tubs, he tries to provoke me. "Clearly our bearded 'nephew' is a soldier for hire and, judging by the scorches on his neck and brow has come to us straight from the fight. But which fight and for what purpose? What's in the briefcase? Something to do with petroleum, that's certain."

A part of me would love to pop the Secy right in his beautiful capped front teeth. But my orders are to exercise discretion. Then too, Echevarria — I know from his history — is a stand-up hombre. When he reaches stiff armed for a cigar offered by a serving man, I remember news photos of the suicide car bomb that killed his wife and daughter six years earlier in a motorcade in Oran; the secretary lost the sight in his left eye and suffered paralysis in that arm from the elbow down, but he never backed off or trimmed his rhetoric. His aides — if they're any good, and I'm sure they are — have acquired my identity hours ago and cupcaked me through half a dozen mil/pol databases in the time he and I have been away on the moors. Without doubt the secretary has been informed of my service under Salter in Mosul and Yemen and East Africa. It would not surprise me if he knows too the origin and ownership of the leased jet I flew into Inverness on.

"Do you admire General Salter, Colonel? Are you a loyal myrmidon or only a gun for hire?"

"Sir," I tell him, "I'm just here to see my aunt."

Maggie Cole returns. She descends the stone and hewn-timber staircase in boots and Western-cut jeans with a man-tailored white linen shirt and a quilted vest, crimson, with a silver stag pin at the collar. All conversation ceases. Maggie is fifty-nine. She looks sensational. She crosses toward one of the great fireplaces, greets the secretary and others, and comes up, smiling, to me.

"Gilbert, is Inquisitor Torquemada attempting to rack you on the wheel?"

"He's stretching my bones a bit, ma'am."

The secretary salutes Maggie with a crisp bow. The former first lady takes his arm. With a smile she steers the group and the conversation toward the vaulted stone dining hall. When I sign to her, as subtly as I can, that my orders are to get out of Dodge pronto, she dismisses this with effortless charm and motions me to keep close beside her. One of the guests — a Conservative MP named Sir Michael Lukich — asks Echevarria why he so dislikes Salter.

"I don't dislike him. I fear him."

And why, asks the MP, has the secretary himself trekked to this remote outpost, if he does not count himself among the general's admirers or adherents.

"I've come, sir," replies Echevarria, "for the same reason we all have: to collect my bounty. I believe the technical term is 'being co-opted.'"

Here the secretary turns to me, the outsider. He speaks as if for my edification, but in truth his oration is intended for the ears of all.

"A sum," he says, "that could only be described as munificent shall be donated by firms associated with General Salter to a charity dear to the hearts of my late wife and daughter. I shall accept this largesse, Colonel, as my fellow guests will claim their own respective emoluments, though perhaps I shall take mine with a bit more shame."

A murmur of indignation arises from the company. The secretary dismisses this with a gesture of contempt, aimed, it seems, at least partially at himself.

"Surely, Colonel, you have apprehended that these gentlemen, however impeccably turned out in field-and-stream attire, have not traveled all this distance to stalk wild bucks and harts. In truth, the only real hunter in this company is our hostess — and her aim is to bag far more substantial quarry."

I'm a Southerner; I can't let this pass. "With respect, Mr. Secretary, your tone is offensive, addressed to the former first lady."

Echevarria smiles. "Margaret, is this young man indeed your nephew?"

Mrs. Cole releases the secretary's arm and takes mine.

"He is now."

Dinner is game meat and whisky. The platters of venison, grouse, duck, and hare placed before the party, along with potatoes, beets, parsnips, and several vegetables I don't recognize, must total twelve thousand calories per man. I down it all and so does everyone else. The conversation steers clear of politics until the group repairs to ancient leather chairs in the sitting room. Cigars appear, and brandy. The MP asks Echevarria what act he fears Salter might take under the current circumstances that would prove injurious to Western interests.

"Sell Iraqi oil to the Russians or the Chinese."

"He can't do that."

"Why not?"

"Because it's not his."

"My young friend," the secretary says, "what's his and what's not his makes no difference to a man like Salter. If I had not pulled the plug on him nine years ago, these highlands you have tramped over so happily today would have been molten glass—"

"I beg your pardon."

This from Maggie Cole, in a tone like iron topped with honey. She is standing with a hand against the rolled leather back of an armchair; now she rises to her full height and turns toward Echevarria.

"First, Mr. Secretary, it was not you who 'pulled the plug' on General Salter nine years ago. It was my husband."

The secretary bridles, but swallows this. The face-off between Salter and President Cole in 2023 has been recounted a thousand times in books, films, and participants' memoirs. Other than the

Truman-MacArthur showdown in Korea in 1952, this incident was the only time that a serving military commander had defied the orders of his commander in chief and initiated actions that would have called the bluff of a nuclear-armed superpower, with world war potentially the consequence.

President Cole ordered Salter home and fired him.

"And second?" Secretary Echevarria asks.

"Let me ask you, J.E.," says Maggie to the secretary. "What would you do now, if you still held office?"

"The age of Great Powers has returned," says Echevarria. "In truth it has never left. What can be done, therefore, will be negotiated between and among these actors — not in the field and not compelled by the actions of armies, state sanctioned or otherwise. Too much is at stake."

While the secretary is speaking, a report comes via one of the guests' aides that Salter's forces have completed their seizure of the Rumayla, Zubayr, and Majnoon oil fields in southern Iraq. His mercs are, thus, the West's final line against whatever Iranian, Central Asian, or Chinese-backed forces wish to exploit the current chaos by pressing their advantage. It will be months before conventional U.S. or NATO reinforcements can deploy. Salter's privateers are the power on the ground for the foreseeable future.

The secretary, with an edge, asks me what I think of this. I answer that my role is to follow the orders of my superiors, not to question them. Maggie smiles.

"What the secretary means by 'Great Powers,' Gilbert, is that an accommodation will be reached between the United States and the People's Republic of China. By this undertaking, naval incursion into and about Indonesia's Strait of Malacca by the latter will no longer be considered provocation by the former. You realize of course that 59 percent of China's nondomestic oil is transported by supertanker from Africa and the Persian Gulf through that passage. In return for the United States' acquiescence to this new understanding, the Chinese government will invoke its influence upon its Iranian and Central Asian allies. It will induce them to back off. All nukes will stand down, all apocalyptic rhetoric be dialed back."

Maggie smiles again. "I see by your expression, Gilbert, that you're wondering how all this will happen. Let me tell you. No treaties will be signed, no measures placed before Congress. The Joint Chiefs will not be consulted. The electorate will not read of this accommodation in *FaceTime* or *Apple imPress,* nor will they learn of its existence via Fox/BBC, the Courtemanche Report, or ITV Huff-Post. It will be enacted by Letter of Instruction of the commander in chief and take the form of a two-line alteration in the Rules of Engagement. American naval and air commanders in the Western Pacific and Indian Oceans will be informed that certain confrontation scenarios, which formerly had been considered acts of war, will now be looked upon — how would you put it, Mr. Secretary? — more benignly."

Echevarria's eyes deny none of this. Apparently the scenario Mrs. Cole has just laid out is exactly what will happen.

"This accord will achieve its desired effect," Maggie says. "War will be averted; markets will stabilize; oil will flow." She pauses for the briefest instant. "And the United States will have backed down one further increment from her once-proud pinnacle of power."

The secretary snorts. "And what would *you* do in the circumstances, Mrs. Cole?"

"You know damn well what I'd do."

My car finally arrives. With it via the SAS sergeant comes a note from Salter, handwritten on a back cover torn from a paperback copy of *Lost Victories* by Field Marshal Erich von Manstein. It instructs me, using nicknames and terms that only I would understand, to fly to Cairo, recruit a certain individual, then return directly, via Conrad Hilliaresse's aircraft, to Salter himself. I bury the note in the coals of a brazier, pausing till the paper curls and crumbles into ash.

I hear the secretary addressing Maggie. "What, Mrs. Cole, was your second point concerning 'pulling the plug' on General Salter?"

"My point, Mr. Secretary, was that you — and my husband — were wrong."

Mrs. Cole walks me out to the fogbound court. The rush of the hunt and the whisky have left her. It's cold; she shivers.

"Whatever General Salter told you, it didn't prepare you for this, did it, Gilbert?"

"He never says much, ma'am."

"You did well. But then I would expect nothing less from a blood relation."

The first lady shakes my hand warmly and presents her cheek. I am not unaware that I am standing in the presence of royalty.

"Give my best to Jim when you see him. You shall stay with me on my farm, Gilbert, the next time you're in Virginia."

BOOK TWO

NILE

5

CLOSE TO ISLAM

I ARRIVE IN CAIRO at 0630 Zulu—eight thirty in the morning, local time—22 August 2032, seven hours after departing the highlands and five after wheels-up out of Inverness. Cairo is enormous, nineteen million people, bigger than New York, L.A., and Chicago combined. It's ugly. I've never seen an uglier city. And it's hell to get around. It takes three hours to clear Customs at Cairo International, followed by another ninety minutes of add-on security (hastily emplaced because of the Saudi crisis), complete with biometric scan, full body search, and polygraph interview. I emerge to sunlight at two in the afternoon. A traffic jam extends for twenty miles in every direction.

A car is waiting for me. "William" picks me up in a black-and-white '02 Opel with no meter and all the windows open. He's wearing a white cotton shirt, soaked through. In the Middle East, a passenger will often ride up front with the taxi driver as a sign of social solidarity. I get in back. William apologizes for the heat and the diesel fumes; it seems his A/C has crapped out just ten minutes earlier. William is not a real cab driver; he's a policeman moonlighting on a private contract. The first item I take note of in any vehicle is the fuel gauge. William's is on empty. "How far are we going, William?"

"Not far. Near." His accent is thick but penetrable.

I make him fill up. In Cairo every median and boulevard crossing is populated by boys selling a liquid they claim is gasoline, which they dispense from ten-gallon plastic jugs via a pouring funnel. Gas in the States has hit eight bucks a gallon; here it's $6.50 USD (42.5 Egyptian pounds) a liter. The juice is half kerosene but people pay because they're all driving around with the needle on E in cars so ancient that they don't dare top off for fear that the tank will outlive the vehicle.

Egypt, since the fall of Mubarak and the National Democratic Party, has transitioned, after an interval of freedom, from a secular police state to an Islamic police state. The trick to fueling in Cairo or in any part of the country, I've been forewarned, is to have either a police badge or a retina-scan card from the EST, the civil and humanitarian arm of the Muslim Brotherhood. EST has all the petrol, in service compounds behind fences topped with razor wire. Of course everybody carries a siphon. If a foreigner is foolish enough to park his car without passing out a little *baksheesh* to a pack of street urchins to stand sentry over it, his tank will be dry in five minutes, not to mention tires and wheel covers stripped, along with the alarm rig, the sealed-argon headlamps, and the nav and sound systems. If the thieves can get at the engine, they'll winch that out too, though every car hood in Cairo is double padlocked and booby-trapped with pepper spray. I was in Egypt briefly during the NDP's last days. One of the stunts the street kids worked then was to wait on the sidewalk outside a hotel for any European or Asian who was wearing a clean business suit. The little hoodlums would approach, holding out one hand empty, palm up, the other holding a thick black glob of shoe polish. You learned to dive into a cab fast.

I pay for the gas and slip two folded U.S. fifties into William's shirt pocket. We are instantly the best of buds. This is not entirely inauthentic. By recognizing his state of need and addressing it at once and without ceremony, I have proved myself a friend. Who else will do this for William? Not even his own brother, if he has one, who's for sure as tapped out as he is.

I am here in Egypt to contact and recruit a gentleman named Abu Hassan el-Masri. These are my orders from Salter. El-Masri is a generic name, the equivalent of Joe from Kokomo. It means "father of Hassan, the Egyptian." My man is not from Egypt. He's from Bergen, New Jersey.

I know el-Masri from Yemen in 2019 and from several contract assignments over the decade. El-Masri was a contractor flown in to Sana'a by Salter to act as an interpreter and disbursements adviser, meaning bagman. Before that, el-Masri had served as a sergeant in the Egyptian army and, earlier still, as an undercover agent of the Amn al-Dawla, the old regime's secret police. My instructions are to recruit him CDW — Can't Do Without. Americans are not permitted in Egypt since the rise of the Brotherhood, so I'm traveling on a Canadian passport.

El-Masri lives in Helwan, a prosperous suburb. William gets me there in about an hour, coming in down Uribe Street, by Sadat's tomb, then past the Citadel and through Maadi into a maze of streets choked with taxis and buses, minicabs, gharries, bicycles, and mopeds. I haven't been in an Arab country in over a year. It all comes back. The smell—which is a malodorous amalgam of diesel fumes, animal and human excrement, rotting fruit, dust, and body odor that is simultaneously revolting and romantic—triggers a full-body flashback.

"Do you have something for me, William?"

He indicates the cargo pouch behind the driver's seat. Inside an oiled rag I find a U.S. Army Colt .45 automatic, M1911A1, loaded, with three full clips in a wrapper. I see William smile in the rearview. "Beautiful," he says.

I agree.

I have traveled to Egypt without a weapon, knowing that Customs and the police at any hotel will go through everything I have.

"William, let's talk some shit."

I ask him who hired him and what he knows. The tone I take is agent to agent, peer to peer. Does he work for a specific agency or department that's part of an overall operation? No, he's freelance. He doesn't know who hired him; a broker he often works for phoned him with a job. Did the hiring agent say what the job was? To bring you to this address. William doesn't know who lives there.

"Then what?"

"Wait for you. Watch over you."

I ask if I'm in danger. He grins. "The blind are leading the blind, no?"

We inch forward in the gridlock. One of the things I do to kill time when I'm traveling is to cupcake A.D.'s byline. She never stops working. She's got contacts at every videomag, holozine, and network, mainstream or alternative, and at a hundred online and subscription journals. Sure enough, here she is now with an op-ed two hours old in the satfeed *Seattle Post-Intelligencer.* The piece is about Saudi Arabia and mercenary forces. It's about Salter. A.D. has pounded it out, I'm certain, within minutes of our holo call from Amman and placed it within hours after that.

"For those who fail to recall General Salter's résumé," A.D.'s second paragraph begins,

it includes the swift, violent, and extremely efficient takeover of the state of Zambia in East Africa during the famine and tribal genocide in the early twenties. With only two Marine Battalion Landing Teams and four squadrons of gunships, Salter stabilized a region the size of Kansas that was in the throes of one of the worst humanitarian crises of the new century. He also set himself up as that region's de facto dictator and confronted nuke for nuke the Chinese 9th Expeditionary Army based in Sudan, before being sacked by President Jack Cole and enduring before Congress a spectacular public defenestration. Where is Salter now? I know no one who can say for sure, but hints from certain well-placed sources make the screen on my GPS start calling up Saudi Arabia.

A.D.'s next two paragraphs recap Salter's career, post–Marine Corps. She names General Pietter van Arden, the legendary South African mercenary, and cites the 2018 acquisition by van Arden's company, AST Security, of Xe International, Titan, DynCorp, and half a dozen others to form the military-contracting superfirm, Force Insertion. Salter, A.D. writes, has been employed for almost a decade by this notoriously secretive enterprise. Where is he now? Why is none of this in the press? Why aren't we seeing satellite real times, Twitter feeds, or street-cam videos smuggled out of the kingdom? Who's putting the lid on this? "Our friend,"[2] A.D. reminds her readers, referring to Salter,

has in recent years accepted employment from such dubious entities as the West African Congress of Unity (which has failed to stop ethnic cleansing in at least three of its member states); from the dictators William Johnson Brown and Mbuke Egbunike; from forces on both sides of the conflict in Uzbekistan; and, to "advise" a regimental-size unit of Russian mercenaries, from no less a personage than Premier Evgeny Koverchenko. Salter is an American patriot but he could be more dangerous to U.S. security than any general of any sovereign foreign state. And this man is no mere military goon. His forces include highly trained civil affairs components — teachers and translators and

SysAdmin teams that he trains himself and are said to be the best in the world. He is an acknowledged master of tribal psychology and of operations within failed states. Probably no commander since Philip of Macedon has so skillfully employed bribery, intimidation, and co-optation to achieve his military and political ends. If they gave Ph.D.s in Taking Over Foreign Countries, Salter would be running his own school at Harvard. What is he up to? The American public needs to know.

A.D. is shrewd to write this as an op-ed. Because it's an opinion piece, it's not subject to strenuous fact-checking. She can speculate. But what she's really doing is angling for a gig. She wants some network or mega-zine to send her to Saudi Arabia. Stay tuned, I tell myself.

William breaks free of the traffic finally. Our taxi enters a neighborhood of quiet lanes lined with jacarandas and magnolias. Streets are paved, sidewalks shaded. On both sides of a fragrant way I glimpse gated enclosures, their pastel walls brightened by pots of geraniums and bougainvillea. William finds el-Masri's house. He parks across the street. I dismount. William is reaching for a girly magazine he keeps under the driver's seat.

"William, do something for me."

"Sure, boss."

"Take a post on that roof."

I indicate a tangerine-colored two-story house, kitty-corner from el-Masri's.

William squints unhappily. "People live in that house, sir!"

"Watch over me."

I hand him the .45. It would be an insult to el-Masri's hospitality to bring it into the house.

Affluent Eastern residences are often built around courts. You enter through a stronghold door in an exterior wall, in this case opened by el-Masri himself when I ring the copper bell. My old friend is reinforced by two bull-necked gentlemen, one of whom carries an S74U, the snub-nosed version of an AK-47. The other comes forward and pats me down. El-Masri greets me with a hug and a kiss on both cheeks. He has been eagerly awaiting me, he says.

"You are still trim, Gent!"

He beams and pats his own jelly roll. In we go. While a boy fetches iced drinks, the phone rings; it's the lady from the tangerine two-story, wondering why a strange man has just climbed onto her roof and inquiring whether this outrage has anything to do with the Englishman who has just entered el-Masri's court. The conversation is in Arabic but el-Masri, grinning and holding his palm over the receiver, translates.

"By the way," he asks me, "you're not here to kill me, are you?"

He apologizes to the lady, feeds her some story that she clearly doesn't buy, then sends his boy across the street to tell William to come down.

"Seriously, are you here to assassinate me?"

I tell el-Masri I'm not sure his stature merits the term "assassinate."

"Don't fuck with my head, Gent."

I'm a friend, I swear.

"I would not hold it against you . . ."

I repeat my denial.

" . . . in fact, I would respect Salter more if I knew he was operating with such prudence."

A spread of hummus, sliced tomatoes, onions, and olives appears, served by the bodyguards, whom el-Masri introduces as his brothers — "Jake" and "Harry." The pair either live here in the compound or are doing a hell of a job of faking it; one is barefoot, the other wears pajama bottoms.

"Brothers, we can learn much from our guest," says el-Masri.

"I have seen him take the head off a man, like this"—he panto-mimes two backhand hacking blows—"and blast an entire village down a mountainside into a river. He is a one-man wrecking crew, believe it!"

I assure el-Masri that I have come only to talk and to deliver an offer of employment. We sip John Collinses—the English version of a Tom Collins—on a shaded terrace that overlooks a court where el-Masri's two children play around a fountain. Temperature, I'm guessing, is 105. El-Masri speaks English with a New Jersey accent. He says "tie-yid" for "tired" and "ma-fack" for "matter of fact."

El-Masri tells me about tough times in Egypt. In place of his former profession in the Awn al-Dawla, the secret police, he (and his brothers) now work in the furniture business; they own a factory at a town called Damietta, which is the artisanal center of the country for hand-carved chairs, desks, cabinetry. "Ninety percent of our shit is for export, but with gas through the roof, we're fucked. Then the tariffs. Don't get me started!" He tells me he'd give anything to get back to Jersey.

"Go," I say. "You're an American citizen."

"Tell that to Homeland Security. Why do you think I was with you in Yemen in '19, Gent? Because my name came up on a list. The CIA promised they'd get me home after that hump. Guess what? I'm still here. I can't go near the States, me or my brothers." He waves as if to say, What are ya gonna do?

"Well," I say. "Maybe I can change that."

There's a festival in Egypt called the "Ascent," commemorating the overthrow of the secular state. The Islamic calendar is lunar; this year the date falls on August 7. But for those in government service who cannot celebrate at that time, there's a second feast called "Little Ascent" two weeks later. That's tonight. Before el-Masri can quiz me about Salter's proposition, or I can offer it, we must celebrate. Everyone in the clan shows up.

"I have fallen down in my faith," shouts el-Masri above the festive din, pouring me a normal-sized Red Label while supersizing one for himself. He has invited William in. William is more of a believer, but he doesn't turn down a drink either. There's a phrase you hear all the time in Afghanistan: "Close to Islam." A man who is proud and brave, honorable, generous to strangers but also humble and God-fearing is said to be close to Islam. I admire that.

The feasting room at el-Masri's is all men. The women do the cooking and serving, which comes through the kitchen door, so that you only see their hands as they pass the dishes in and out. As each course is served, a toast is offered. It's an insult not to drink. There must be at least thirty courses. I'm sitting next to el-Masri, on the carpet, with our backs against the wall. This is handy, he says, because if you pass out, you won't hurt yourself when you fall. As he drinks, he tells his life story.

"I was born in North Bergen in 1990. My father was an Egyptian immigrant, my Mom is Tajik from Afghanistan. The old man had his own dry cleaning business, plus he ran limos to the airport; we were doing good, or so he told me later when we landed back in Cairo begging on the street. The old man had fought in '67, the Jewish War, the Six-Day War. Israeli jets wiped out the Egyptian Air Force on the ground. This was al-Nakbah, 'the Disaster.' The Jews kicked the crap out of us, even though we had the newest and most advanced Soviet tanks and guns. Dayan took all of Sinai. My father bolted for the States, he was so ashamed. Then came '73, the Ramadan War—the Israelis call it the Yom Kippur War—which started out great but ended up even worse."

As soon as el-Masri and his sister were old enough to travel, in '96, their father packed up the clan and moved home to Cairo.

"We Egyptians are a proud people. We built the fucking pyramids. You cannot imagine the shame we felt. How could we be beaten by these Jews, who had been our slaves and who knew nothing, now, but how to eat shit and march into gas chambers like sheep? And how did *I* feel, landing back in the old country? I'm six years old and can't speak ten words of Arabic. Worse, I'm an American! My best friends, who I'm missing like hell, are Harvey Dinnerstein and Marshall Weiss. I hate this freakin' place."

The host's tale is being narrated to the entire room, whose denizens listen in various states of patriotism and inebriation.

Egypt in the aftermath of defeat, el-Masri says, split into two factions, each burning with shame and the passion to restore national honor—the pan-Arabists under President Gamal Abdel Nasser, who wanted more technology, more Westernization, more Russian MiGs and tanks; and the Islamists who saw this humiliation at the hands of the Hebrews as the justified punishment from God for straying from the path. This was the start of the Muslim Brotherhood, the dissident movement, which later, allied with al-Jihad after Nasser's death, was responsible for assassinating his successor, Anwar Sadat.

"I joined the Home Guard in '08," el-Masri said. "They put me in the military police. In those days the army was riddled with dissidents. Every other private soldier was either a member of the Brotherhood or a sympathizer. They had no power but they believed. God was on their side; they were not afraid to die. When you caught one, you couldn't make him talk. Arabs lie. Let me tell you this, Gent, if you don't know it already. We lie for fun, we lie for profit, we lie all the time, and we don't even know why.

"I became an interrogator. I have seen and done things that God will judge me for. And it got us nowhere. But once you are part of the secret police, you can't get out. It's like the Mob. The only way you can go is in deeper, which is what I did: I volunteered to work undercover. I had a commanding officer named Hani Salem, Colonel Salem. A shrewd fellow; he became my mentor. I was what, nineteen? My waist was twenty-eight inches!"

El-Masri is telling the story in English and Arabic, to me and his brothers and uncles. They interrupt, wanting to know who I am and how el-Masri knows me. "How did I buy this house?" he asks. "With money made from General Salter, chasing a certain motherfucker named Razaq into the mountains of Yemen in the company of my dear friend Gent! Is this true? I would not lie."

And he raises another toast and returns to the main saga.

"Colonel Salem said he would protect me. Any time I wanted out, I just had to whistle. Can you believe how stupid I was? I said yes. Charges were trumped up, I was thrown in jail, the big one at Saladin's Citadel where hundreds of the Brothers were being held. The last thing Colonel Salem promised me was that the guards would only pretend to torture me. But once I was behind bars, it became clear that this would not work. So they gave me the business, just like they did to the Brothers.

"I had read the Koran before but never studied it. Now I made friends among the Brothers who were going through the same hell as me. I have to tell you, it helped. The guards would tie us to doors set on the floor and beat the soles of our feet with iron rods. You cannot imagine what that pain is. We cried verses from God's Holy Book. They hung us by hooks, they electrocuted us; they poured acid onto our flesh, they burned us with cigarettes and with blowtorches; they strapped us over tables and raped us. Look around you, Gent. Many in this room have endured worse.

"When the guards got tired of beating us, they threw us back into our cells, which were not cells but large rooms with one concrete runway in the floor for piss and shit and no beds, not even pallets of straw. We tended each other. Will you believe me when I tell you this was the most joyous time of my life? Yes! For we were brothers, united in the holy cause. Death held no fear for us. We prayed for it. We slept in each other's arms as Jacob did with Esau and when our torturers came for us again, we cursed them and pitied them, devils that they were, while we were holy warriors, whose martyrdom would raise us to heaven. The human mind is a beautiful thing. For here I was at nineteen years old, sent in to spy upon these seditious fellows, and now I had become closer to them than to my own flesh. Friends who died, I still cannot speak of them. Love and faith flowed through our veins like the blood of the Prophet. What need had we to fill our bellies? We sustained ourselves upon God's holy writ, the succor of his verses, and on our own virtue, which we tested every day and which every day grew stronger.

"There was a boy in my cell named Qazi Ahmed Razaq. He was the closest to my age, only a couple of years younger. A guard named Ephur used to sodomize him every night, sometimes in a room they had for showers (though no one was ever permitted to shower there), sometimes in the corridor outside our cell, where we could hear the boy's screams and we shouted back through the wire mesh door, cursing this Ephur and vowing to murder him. Young Razaq was Tajik; I could speak the language, and I became his friend. He was a good kid, educated; he spoke English. His father was Habibullah Mohammed Razaq, who had been one of the legendary Afghan mujahideen during the fight against the Soviets. Why do I tell you this, brothers? Because this Razaq, like I said, is how I came to meet our American friend, Gent—and, I will bet, Razaq is also why Mr. Gent is here right now. But I am getting ahead of my story.

"In prison, there was a group called Takfir Wal Hejira. They were Salafists, hard as iron. *Takfir* means excommunication, *Hejira* means to leave, to depart in an exodus. I became a Takfiri, as did Razaq, who we called 'Razz.' To be Takfiri was to be purest of the pure, sternest of the stern. We declared this man a true Muslim and that man false. The false knew no protection. They were worse than Jews or Crusaders because they undermined the holy faith from within. Takfirism fell from grace years ago, but many in this room — sons and grandsons of men I knew in those days — many of them still believe."

El-Masri's friends rapped the tabletops and acclaimed him with the "koo-koo" sound that Egyptians make to signify approval.

"One night they came for me — the guard Ephur and two of his thugs. They knew I was Razz's friend; they knew we had declared them heretics and apostates. And they just wanted to fuck with me. They took me to the shower room. What they did to me I will never tell, except to say that worse has been suffered by many. The guards got tired and wandered off. Ephur never got tired. He was naked, with his trousers around his ankles. It was just him and me in the dark.

"I killed him with the faucet from a shower. I pulled the fitting off — a four-pronged hot-cold faucet — and ran at him with all my strength. His trousers made him tumble; I jammed the fitting-end of the faucet into his eye until blood gushed. He screamed and grabbed me with both arms as if to crush the life out of me, but we were both dripping wet and the tile floor was slippery. I got him facedown and dug my fingernails into the long hair around his ears; I beat his head into the floor until I felt his skull crack. The others heard the screams and came back. They beat me with clubs and kicked my ribs in with their boots. I was saved only by the chance of the morning detail being marched past. A sergeant who knew me made the beating stop.

"I was in the prison hospital for nine weeks. Colonel Salem kept the guards from murdering me. He got me out of there. Razz was released the same day as me. This was no accident. The police wanted me as a link to him. A black Mercury Navigator picked him up. He told me to come with him. We were given body armor and helmets. Two other vehicles in a convoy escorted us to a house on Gezira Island. I have tried to find that place again, more than once, and have never come close. It was a safe house operated by some arm of American intelligence. Waiting there was Razz's father. The old man wept as if his eyes were rivers. 'This is the one,' Razz said, meaning me. 'Not a hair on your head will be harmed,' the old warlord vowed to me, 'so long as I live.'

"A man, an American, handed me $3,000 in cash. I was given new clothes and papers and flown to the U.S. Naval Base at Bahrain; they kept me there for eighteen months, in language school and UW training—Unconventional Warfare. I was supposed to get a new American passport and be repatriated, with my family, to the States. Who was I kidding? I'm a Muslim carrying a gun. No way U.S. Homeland Security is gonna gimme an EZ-Pass to New Jersey. I wound up back in Damietta, a civilian again, with a new name and a crap job in the furniture business."

El-Masri grins at me.

"This was me at twenty-one, Gent. A long way from North Bergen."

My assignment is to get el-Masri on the plane that night if possible. But he and the house are on Arab time; by two in the morning, my prize is passed out on the carpet and I'm not far behind. Harry the brother wakes everyone for prayers at dawn. The festival lasts two days. No one is going home. When the day's heat has passed, the rite begins again. This time el-Masri's brothers and uncles tell their life stories. It goes on for hours. No one interrupts. The tales are of ghastly suffering endured with patience and a depth of faith that we in the West cannot conceive of.

Sometime around midnight, it's el-Masri's turn again. I'm texting Conrad, who's waiting with the plane at Cairo West. Chris Candelaria, Chutes, Junk, Q, the whole team is in place at our next destination. A message from Salter's number one, Pete Petrocelli, appears in my text window:

Got him?

I answer not yet.

Get him.

El-Masri washes; he daubs rosewater. He returns to the caucus as fresh as Minnesota Fats. The prior speaker, his uncle (it seems they're all his uncles), has finished with his own tale of striking back at the United States. This brings up 11/11 — the seaborne dirty bomb attack in 2019 on the port of Long Beach.

"Razz was behind this."

El-Masri seats himself cross-legged at my side.

"Behind it himself, or in possession of knowledge of who was. This brings us to our guest, Colonel Gent — and to General Salter, in whose name our friend has come now to visit us."

The brotherhood leans in, listening intently.

El-Masri picks up the timeline. Seven years have passed since he and Razz were released from prison. It's 2019. The youth Razaq is no longer the prince-in-waiting of an Afghan Tajik power family; he has become a force in his own right. With his father he controls half the transshipment routes for opium moving out of Afghanistan via Tajikistan, Uzbekistan, and Turkmenistan to Russia and Western Europe. He is worth tens of millions. His militia numbers twenty thousand. And he remains a rabid, U.S.-hating Takfiri.

6

CRAWLING MAN

"IN NORTHERN YEMEN, THEY have mountains," continues el-Masri. "That's what the Yemenis call them. They are more like tits. You could build mountains as big by hand. But they are steep and barren and without water; you have never seen no place like this. God himself will not go there. In Yemen when a man defeats an enemy, he cuts off his testicles and wears them on a cord around his neck. I have seen bandits do this more than once. Better, they believe, if the victim is still alive. You want him to see your knife and feel the weight of his balls coming off into your cupped palm." El-Masri glances to me. "Not like you Christians, who want only a man's money."

El-Masri retells the tale of 11/11, the 2019 dirty bomb attack on Long Beach and the frantic search in the aftermath for who was behind it. "Brothers, I will tell you something about the American people. You can fuck with them only so long and only so much. You remember Cairo then. The city emptied so fast you would think no one had never lived there. Everybody was waiting for the nukes to rain down. Tehran, too, and Islamabad and every town and village for a thousand miles except Mecca and Medina. I was here, at

Damietta. We stayed, my brothers and me, to protect the furniture factory. I was working then too for the UIV, the Upholders of Islamic Virtue, which was the Brotherhood's most secret arm of internal security. The phones were ringing like crazy from the Americans. Every secret police officer, old or new, was called in for his contacts. My name came up, linked to Razz. The Americans had reports that he was the money behind the bomb, or if he wasn't, he knew who was. A car came for me. Three hours later I'm getting off a plane at El Rehaba airport in Sana'a, being picked up by three U.S. Marines in a ragged-ass, twenty-year-old Humvee with a .50 caliber up top and three racks of jerry fuel cans. The team leader is Gent. I had never met him before. He did not look happy to see me." El-Masri turns to me now grinning. "What did they tell you about me, Gent?"

Only, I say, that my team had forty-eight hours to track down Razz before the entire Middle East was nuked into molten glass—and that el-Masri was the only man in the world that Razz would talk to.

"And I was!" The Egyptian laughs, remembering. "Who was on that team? The tall one with the parachute pants . . . 'Chutes!' Yes! And Junk and Q and that Hindu from Sri Lanka . . ."

"Tony."

"Yes. And Salter. He was our boss."

El-Masri sketches a quick map on the tabletop—of the tribal Houthi north of Yemen. There is a town called Abada, the last outpost before you enter the Vale of Sinn; my team and two others were flown in aboard a KC-130. The teams were part of TacOps, short for Tactical Operations. This was an experimental program, later discontinued, which operated under MARSOCOM, Marine Special Operations Command, which itself was an experiment under SOCOM, Special Operations Command. The teams were hybrids, meaning they included CIA field operators, Yemeni Special Forces, and private contractors.

I was still a Marine then; this was the first time I had worked with soldiers for hire. They were impressive. Former Special Forces, Navy SEALS, NSA—we had four on our team; the youngest was forty-two; the oldest was sixty. They were tribal warfare experts and intelligence specialists. They had lived with the tribes; they spoke the languages. This was their life. They got home once every eighteen months and turned around and came right back. The mercs' overall contract was with Lockheed, but their direct employers were private intel agencies—Strategic Modalities Corporation, American Intelligence Security, Actionable Analysis International. I had never heard of any of these. The contractors wouldn't tell us how much they were being paid, but it was clear that the decimal point in their checks was a lot farther east than in ours.

El-Masri's contract was with StratCorp, a Cairo-based intelligence outfit, but he had been recruited at Salter's by-name request through the Egyptian Islamic Police. He came in with a CIA field operator, "Monty." Monty was the bagman. We never knew how much payoff cash Monty was carrying, but it was well over a million and he was cleared to come up with millions more. Monty and el-Masri's job was to get to Razz with greenbacks if the rest of the team couldn't do it with bare knuckles.

At that time, less than twenty-four hours after the Long Beach blast, the U.S. public was screaming for nuclear payback. But against whom? Our team, though we didn't know it at the time, was one of over sixty operations on every continent but Antarctica, chasing down leads.

From Sana'a, the capital of Yemen, three other teams were already on Razz's trail; they had pursued him by helicopter, truck, and even horseback north through Huth and Sa'da and were closing in on him approaching the Saudi border.

My team, with el-Masri, Monty, and two others, took off after them. Salter himself was already at Najran, across the frontier, with five twelve-man TacOps teams and a detachment of Black Hawks from the 160th SOAR, Special Operations Aviation Regiment. His was the blocking force. The task of our three teams and the three ahead of us was to drive Razz and the tribal fighters who were protecting him into this force. Razz was to be taken alive, no matter what the cost, because he could tell us who was behind the bomb.

"In these mountains in Yemen," el-Masri continues his recitation, "there are no roads, only tracks and washouts from the winter floods. Tracks mean ambushes. You are driving through potholes bigger than your truck, with high ambush-ground on one side always and sometimes on both. We have chased Razz for thirty-six hours now. No sleep. Many of you brothers have fought in such country. You know how easy it is to lose an enemy in terrain so vast, with no maps worth a shit, where you don't know where the hell you are but the enemy does. It is like chasing a rat through a maze. Still we are on Razz's ass.

"At the mouth of the Vale, Salter lands and joins us. This is crazy. A freaking two-star general in the dirt with TacOps teams — but this is how he rolls. Meanwhile two sandstorms in a row have whipped through. All drones have crashed. We're blind. It's November.

"To make a long story short, Razz and his men hit us at a T in the trail with four IEDs daisy-chained together. The first knocked out the lead Humvee, which was Gent's guys Chutes, Q, and Junk. The second two vehicles were trapped; then the fourth, a 7-ton truck, got blown too. Now all four are fucked. Gent and me are in number five, which is still outside the killing zone. The ambush is now twenty seconds old. The enemy is firing from high ground on the right and behind. They have AKs, two light machine guns, and one motherfucker Russian Dishka, which is tearing the hell out of the vehicles in the kill box. Worse, we can see Houthi fighters scrambling down the hillside with RPGs, trying to get close enough to finish the job.

"I turn to Gent, who says to me, 'Hang on.' He is in the commander's seat on the right, Tony from Sri Lanka is driving; the third man, Mac, is up top on the .50 caliber. The way Americans fight is fire suppression. They have IADs, Immediate Action Drills. They turn toward the enemy and give them hell. But this don't work now, because Razz and his muj have hit them too hard too fast. The bad guys have fire superiority. Americans fight from what they call the PofA, Point of Action. They always go where the shit is hottest. I studied this and even taught it at Bahrain, but I had never seen it. This is some crazy shit.

"Gent's Humvee is rolling now, downhill, no road, firing like sons-ofbitches. I hear him shouting into his headset. He is trying to save Salter. Salter is down, in vehicle number three.

"In that high clear air you can see the streaks made by the bullets as they fly. Every American vehicle is on fire, every tire is shredded; the men who ain't hit have dived behind boulders or into creases, any microterrain crack they can find. They are returning fire, but when they jumped from their vehicles, the only weapons they took were the M4-40s and SAW light machine guns in their hands, and the only mags or belts they have are what they jumped with. Meanwhile Razz's tribesmen are scrambling to flank the T-end of the ambush, where they can get direct fire onto the Americans. I'm with Gent, bouncing downhill over boulders with AK rounds zinging all around us.

"Suddenly we see Salter stand up and run to the shot-up 7-ton. This is the truck that got blown over sideways. It's on fire; rounds are cooking off. Salter plunges into the truckbed, then pops back out, with his vest burning. He's carrying in his hands four metal cans of 5.56 ammo with two big belts of NATO 7.62 rounds over his shoulders. When the Houthi see him, every weapon on the hillside leaves what it is shooting at and concentrates on Salter.

"It's like a movie. You see it but you don't believe it. Gent is shouting into his headset, telling Salter to get down, we're coming for him. He is a general, man! He's fifty fucking years old . . . he ain't supposed to be doing this. I can see Salter fling himself into a trench between boulders. His vest and trousers are on fire; he's beating the flames out with his bare hands. The muj are plastering this hideout with so much fire that a cloud of dust blows up as big as a house. They think they've killed him. We can hear them whooping.

"But Salter gets up again. He's trying to get to the men up front, to bring them ammo. We can see them—Chutes and Q and Junk— waving at him to go back. He's alone, Salter, on his belly now, crawling toward vehicle number one. The truck is about fifty yards away. This is like saying fifty miles. Every shooter in the ambush is now zeroed on him. They forget us coming down the hill. They forget everything. Every one of those bastards wants to do one thing: kill the Crawling Man.

"Salter stands up and runs into the open. You can't believe the volume of fire that pours onto him. The muj are getting pissed now. They are yelling. The Americans are yelling. Salter can't survive. No one can, under such fire. But somehow these bastards can't hit him. There is something about his courage. It is not emotion; it's not crazy or frantic. You can feel his will. He won't quit. He is spitting in the face of death. This fills the valley. He means to save his men and he will let nothing stop him.

"Suddenly the craziest thing happens. The muj stop firing. They stand up. First one, then another. It's only a moment. To this day, I can't say for sure what it meant. Gent's truck has almost reached Salter now. I see Gent leap down and race toward him. I'm expecting Razz's men to tear them apart. But when we look up, they're gone. It's the most amazing fucking thing I ever saw."

The room is silent as el-Masri finishes. He is shaking his head, remembering.

"But this is not the end of the story, brothers. Gent hauls Salter to safety behind our Humvee. Salter is bleeding from everywhere, but he won't go down. The Humvee is up front at the T-end of the ambush, with Chutes and the others rushing toward us. I look up the hill and there is fucking Razz — fifty feet above us with a dozen Houthis and AQ motherfuckers. All I see is RPGs and AKs. It is that moment when you say to yourself, 'So this is how it ends.' Our guys are all looking up too. We are dead meat and we know it.

"Then Razz sees me. His eyes get big. I'm thinking, I got one-tenth of a second to come up with something. I raise my arm and point straight at him. 'You owe me,' I say. I don't know where the fuck this comes from. It is like somebody else is saying it. And I don't shout it neither. I just say it calm, like I'm speaking here right now.

"Razz looks at me. He looks at Salter. He has no clue who Salter is, but he knows he's somebody big because he's fifty fucking years old. All this is happening in slow motion. I see Razz raise his hands. The Houthi put up their guns. In the distance we can hear the sound of Black Hawks approaching. Razz makes a sign; his guys melt away up the slope. He looks at me and says, in English, 'This is a card you can play only one time.' Then he vanishes too."

Two in the morning: I'm in el-Masri's kitchen, washing my face in the sink, when he comes downstairs, carrying his holdall. The plane is waiting. We're ready to roll.

"Gent," he says, "we must ask for more money."

He wants the code to contact Salter. This is business, he says.

I balk. My compensation, I tell el-Masri, is more than generous. I'm not in this to milk Salter. "Besides," I say, "how do you know he'll pay it?"

"Because you and me are indispensable to his enterprise."

"How do you know?"

"Because he is telling us *bubkes*. In my business when we keep someone in the dark, it is so he can't talk if he's captured. And why don't we want him to talk? Because whatever he's doing for us is so fucking important we can't take a chance. That's you and me, my friend. I'm asking for double."

I tell him to include me out.

"Gent, my friend. With that attitude, you will never get ahead in life."

I won't give him Salter's code. El-Masri gets through anyway. Later, on the plane, he tells me. I ask if he got the money he wanted. He winks. "I always get it."

While we're at it, I ask el-Masri for his take on the attempted coup in Saudi Arabia. If anyone can dope out the inside story, it's him.

"Let me tell you something, my friend. The Saudi royal family exists in a state of nonstop terror. They are sitting on the wealth of the world and they have no balls. They pay off everyone not to murder them in their sleep; this is how they live. Well, now King Nayif and his brothers have grown a sack. They won't beg no more, not to the U.S. — and not to the Chinese or the Russians. Who started this uprising? They did. Why? To clean house in the army. And to throw a world-class scare into the oil markets."

To what end, I ask. Gas in the States is already eight bucks a gallon. Prices can't go any higher without the global economy collapsing.

"I don't know, my friend, but I will tell you this. Whatever pie these princes are baking, if you lift the crust, you will find our benefactor."

"You mean Salter?

El-Masri smiles. "Grinning like a fox."

BOOK
THREE

THE EMPTY QUARTER

7

PSAB

WE ARE BOUND — EL-MASRI and I — for an area in Saudi Arabia's Eastern Province called the Empty Quarter. It's noon; the Egyptian and I are the only passengers on the Gulfstream 450. Conrad Hilliaresse is our pilot; he has his second officer and a comm chief forward behind a partition that they keep sealed. Aft is a lavatory and a stand-up galley with Cokes, chips, and sandwiches. El-Masri and I have the main cabin to ourselves — two facing seats down one side of a narrow aisle, with fold-down tables between, and banquette/bunks down the other. The Egyptian's lower back has gone into spasm; he lies in the aisle, stretching his hamstrings.

"Gent, are you still plowing that bitch from South Africa?"

"You mean my wife?"

"Your lovely wife."

El-Masri talks like a street mook from Newark but he's actually quite educated. He has a degree in Islamic philosophy from Anwar al-Saad University in Cairo. He considers himself a romantic.

"Do you ever think about your own death, my friend?"

"No, but I think about yours."

El-Masri creaks upright. "All soldiers are romantics, Gent. The worst are us so-called mercenaries, for we have come to fight for hire only after having our hearts broken fighting for a flag. And you, my brother, you don't fool me. You act hard-core, but underneath you are a cream puff."

I like el-Masri. I owe him my life from Yemen and may owe it to him again before the next week is up. I ask him what he knows about the Empty Quarter.

"I know it is not empty."

We're over the Eastern Province now. I look down on the fields and pipelines, pumping stations, storage tanks, and processing complexes of the massive Ghawar and Khurais facilities. All are humming as industriously as ever. I see no sign of the uprising that has dominated the news for the past eight days. Supply routes are clear; no checkpoints, no barriers. Another twenty minutes and there's the airfield. El-Masri suits up in Kev-lite vest, M4-40 with mags, and wraparound Oakleys; he brings me two liters of Solaire bottled water and stows two for himself.

The Empty Quarter, as el-Masri has predicted, is anything but empty. Our plane touches down at 1300 local time into a facility as sprawling as Disneyland and as packed with troops and transport as D-Day at Normandy. The place is called PSAB, Prince Sultan Air Base. It's eight thousand acres in the middle of absolutely nothing, seventy-five miles southeast of Riyadh.

The Egyptian and I step down onto concrete so hot it blisters your feet right through your boots. Chris Candelaria is waiting for us in a '23 Chevy Simoom bulletproof with a cooler of iced Rolling Rock. Salter has acquired his contract, he confirms for me, along with those of my entire Iran team, plus several ex-UAE Special Forces operators and a former SAS captain named Coombs, whom I will meet as soon as we get back to the converted hangar that the team has turned into our temporary home. Chris gives me an orders packet from Salter (actually from his aide Pete Petrocelli) and Pete's secure number on-base, which I am to call ASAP. Chris brings us up to speed as we drive. PSAB was an active U.S. base in the '90s. The air force flew combat sorties out of here in the post–Desert Storm days of the no-fly zone and Saddam Hussein. It was used again as a support facility in '01, during Operation Anaconda, and throughout OIF and the campaign in Afghanistan. The Saudis shut the base down in '16, following the Ramadan coup attempt that supposedly originated from the site. It's been sitting empty ever since.

No longer. Financed by God knows who, the place has been brought back to roaring life. Transport planes are coming and going. Lines of troops in full kit snake across the tarmac, boarding C-130s, An-225s, and converted civilian 747s. A sand berm thirty feet high, topped with razor wire and studded with security towers, rings the expanse. I get on the horn to Petrocelli, whom I've known since East Africa in '22.

"What's up, Pete? Where are we going?"

"Couldn't tell you, Gent, even if I knew. Did you get your OP?" He tells me to disregard everything except the top sheet; plans have changed.

"Iraq?" I ask. "Back to Iran?"

Pete can't say. "Tim Hayward's on his way. You're gonna be working with him again."

"Is Salter here? What the fuck's going on?"

Salter's flying in from Basra right now, says Pete; he wants to brief you and your team tonight. "Chow with the boss, I'll get back to you with time and place." He laughs. "Welcome to history, cowboy!"

El-Masri has already sussed out the drill. "This is Saudi money," he says. "I got to give them credit, the princes have grown gonads at last." Salter, he says, holds the fields of southern Iraq. "That's where these troops are going; they can't be heading nowhere else."

Chris agrees. The mobilization's aim is to hold Iraq, to prevent the Iranians' move to establish a Shiite Crescent. PSAB is wall to wall with aircraft and armor. On the tarmac and inside Mahaffey and CoStruct hangars sit scores of big-bellied C-130s and C-17s, even a massive C-5 Galaxy. More jumbos squat in the sunblast a mile away across the field. We pass two EC-130s and one 130H—jammer craft that can broadcast TV and radio and interdict enemy transmissions. Behind Hesco revetments squat row after row of recycled transport choppers—Sikorsky D-12s, Army Chinooks, and Marine Super Stallions—plus scores of Iraq-era Cobra gunships, Apache attack helicopters, and the new Chinese drone Wasps, which are basically pilotless missiles. Out on the runways, ancient Ilyushins and Andropovs land and take off in steady succession. This fleet can only be Alessandro Martini's Regia Aeronautica and Teddy Ostrofsky's Air Martiale (or whatever names these notorious arms merchants are using currently to identify their private air forces out of Iran, Angola, Sierra Leone, Sharjah in the UAE, and Burgas in Bulgaria). The whole armada is protected from aerial and drone attack by hundreds of Chinese I-SAM rocket trucks and cloaked from satellite surveillance by Tata/Hewlett-Packard masking stations. Everything is private enterprise. Ground transport is KBR, Pilot, Acacia, Overnite, or owner-operators from Bulgaria and the Czech Republic, Serbia, Macedonia, Turkey, Pakistan, Jordan, and Egypt, all independent contractors with their names and home ports on the truck-cab doors. No vehicles bear the American flag or the banner of any nation. You see the logos of Force Insertion, Trans-Asia, Iramco, Neilson, Moxie, ZORX, AmmasaUniv, and the ubiquitous Roman helmet insignia of the Legion.

The scale of the mobilization is beyond anything I've seen short of full-bore invasion. It's incredible how far the merc biz has come in only twenty or twenty-five years.

In the original Iraq and AfPak eras a generation ago, military contractors were hired individually and assigned to teams of varying size and specialty. Primary missions back then were to provide security for VIPs, diplomats, press, aid and humanitarian workers, and civilian staffs of various NGOs; detention, prisoner interrogation, and so forth; as well as force protection—guarding bases and troop concentrations. That was the low end. At the other extremity you had elite teams of highly skilled operators undertaking such business as in-country and cross-border direct action and sensitive site exploitation—assassinations and raids. In such capacities, contractors usually worked in conjunction with, and under command and control of, conventional military or special forces, as the hybrid teams did in Iraq and Afghanistan, Yemen, Somalia, Pakistan, Uzbekistan, and Tajikistan. Some of these operations were spectacularly successful. Few, if any, made the evening news.

Gen. Pietter van Arden, the iconic South African commando, was the first to organize, train, and equip full-scale private combat formations and put them out for hire as units. In the profession in those days, the late teens and into 2020, there was no such thing as a standing force. An individual operator was either CS—Core Service, meaning command cadre—or TA, Time Available, meaning on call. Mercs were either working or waiting to work. This system functioned well as long as the jobs didn't get too big. Company- and even battalion-sized formations could be put together with a six-month train-up, with their logistical tail outsourced and the employer fronting the funding in cash.

But when the first legions and armatures were put together in 2021—meaning brigade- and division-sized airmobile fighting units—under van Arden and, later, under Salter, it became necessary to have basing, manning, and staffing of a far more professional and permanent basis. Intelligence, communications, and logistics arms were added—outsourced but full-time—along with artillery and antiarmor, medical, air defense, satellite, drone elements, and so on. A command and logistical architecture evolved, based loosely on a Marine Expeditionary Force — in other words a force designed to project power across oceans, into theaters in which basing and resupply could not be counted upon.

An armature was constituted of three primary maneuver elements, called legions, each roughly the size of an army brigade or a Marine Regimental Combat Team. These were commanded not by colonels, as a conventional formation of that size would be, but by former one- and even two-star generals. The saying in the profession was "Step up in pay, step down in rank." Within the mercenary corps, the billet of sergeant was filled by a former staff or gunnery sergeant; captains served in lieutenants' posts; if you had been a lieutenant colonel, you stepped down to major.

Each legion was constituted of three battalions — two infantry and one weapons. Battalions were divided into three centuries — the equivalent of reinforced companies — and platoons. Each legion was supported by its own armored brigade, called a maniple; its own artillery arm, called a ballista; and a dedicated air wing called a corvo, or crow. The air wings were unique in that their command and control elements beneath armature staff level, as well as equipment, organization, training, and operation, were outsourced to private contractors. This was Wild West Central. Individual aircraft and crews were brought on board in one of three ways — as OOs, owner-operators (in which the pilot himself or a syndicate of investors supplied its own plane or helicopter and hired it directly to the company); straight hire (where the company itself owned or leased the plane and contracted with the pilots and crew to fly it); or the "sillidar" system, in which a single firm or investor supplied a number of planes and leased them to the contracting company as units — with or without flight teams.

Service crews and equipment maintenance were also outsourced. What made the system even more colorful was the manifestation — overnight, it seemed — of a middleman apparatus of hiring reps and lawyers, many of whom were female and at least half of whom were either married to or sleeping with the individual contractors whose deals they were negotiating. The verb was "bitch." "Who's bitching you?" meant "Who's your hiring agent?" To be "bitched over" was to get double-crossed or screwed. By and large, the reps were honest and they worked hard. Standard commission was 15 percent for an individual and 10 percent for a package, meaning a team that signed up collectively, as a unit, with 20 percent for bonuses and incentive pay. Some reps would work free for the individual contractor, taking their commission from the hiring entity or its employer. There were other firms, called "slop shops," run by paunchy ex-campaigners working out of their basements that scoured the docket for cheap and last-minute openings. The system sounds nuts, I know. But in Georgia and in San Tome and Principe in '21 and in Yemen and Angola in '22, these jury-rigged schemes were put to the test and passed with all banners flying.

As with most technical revolutions, the rise of mercenary forces came about with virtually no legislative or regulatory oversight. The world woke up one day and merc armies were everywhere. Force Insertion quelled one revolt in Nigeria, then another in Mali. The company did it with half-brigade-sized forces that were in and out in ninety days. By August of 2023, I myself had signed up for a tour. My first check was $92,500 for 110 days in the Pankisi gorge in Georgia, protecting the Baku-Ceyhan pipeline. The employer was a consortium of energy companies, including BP, ChevronTexaco, and ConocoPhillips, as well as the governments of Turkey and Azerbaijan, but the actual check came from Force Insertion, drawn on the National Bank of Capetown. You signed a contract two pages long that said you had never been a Communist, Fascist, or Islamist; you waived all rights to compensation for death or dismemberment and repatriation of remains to your country of origin, and you indemnified and held blameless Force Insertion for any acts committed by you or contractors serving beneath you, which might render Force Insertion liable to prosecution before a state-founded or transnational court of law. You had to buy your own clothing, gear, and weapons and provide your own transportation to and from the front. In-theater you received the same medical care as Force Insertion's highest operatives (which was outstanding), but once you got home you were on your own.

It worked. The pipeline stayed safe; the gas went through.

Legal and ethical objections were raised, as they should have been. But the shit worked. No one could argue with it. When the crisis in Guinea broke out in '26, the solution was a no-brainer. U.S. DoD, with the approval of the president and Congress, contracted with Force Insertion for a one-year fee of $11.7 billion to "secure, stabilize, and pacify" the northern four provinces and to "dismantle and disarm" the Amal tribal and AQWA , al-Qaeda in West Africa, and related militias operating with them. Aerial, satellite, and drone battlespaces were owned by the appropriate arms of the conventional military. The dirt belonged to the mercs.

Salter commanded. What made these merc forces so effective? In the conventional military, three of the four most dysfunctional operational elements are OPCON, OPFUND, and ROE — Operational Concept, Operational Funding, and Rules of Engagement. The fourth element, OPTEMPO — meaning the speed with which a field unit can execute an operation once it conceives it — is a product of the other three. Force Insertion streamlined all four and made them work. Gone were the eleven levels of clearance that a captain or lieutenant on the ground had to negotiate before he could pull the trigger. One phone call brought the green light — and brought close air support and drone or ground-based fires. Better yet, the definition of an engageable target expanded dramatically. If a suspected enemy stuck his head up, you were cleared to blow it off — man, woman, or child; armed or unarmed. In the realm of funding, Force Insertion operators were supplied with bags of cash and given the latitude to spread it around. Commanders had Lexuses and Range Rovers to pass out as gifts of honor; we could send tribal chieftains' sons to Atlanta and Houston for surgical operations, get their daughters into Florida State, or set their wives up in condos in Dubai or Miami Beach.

On the home front, the single most powerful attraction tool for Force Insertion was the lump-sum million-dollar payout for CDD, Combat Death and Dismemberment. At one stroke, this grant eradicated 99 percent of all family-based risk aversion — and it cut out the weeping widow shot on the evening news. When the conventional military used nukes on Natanz, Kashan, and Anarak in Iran in 2019 in retaliation for the 11/11 dirty-bombing of Long Beach (for which the Iranian Revolutionary Guard supposedly supplied the radioactive bomb-wrapping material), casualty aversion made it impossible to send regular U.S. troops tramping through the contaminated dust of the No-Go Zone. Force Insertion put two centuries on the ground in forty-eight hours. The mercs didn't care if their nutsacks glowed in the dark; they lined up by the hundreds for the bonuses and incentive pay.

Long Beach and the nuclear counterstrike against Iran were what finally made mercenary forces preeminent. After that horror show (and the massive anti-American riots and demonstrations that were ignited in response around the globe), the conventional U.S. military withdrew all but token forces from the Middle East and Central Asia. Homeland defense became the new Core Mission. A hybrid strategy of counterterrorism (much of it outsourced) and "stand-off containment" replaced counterinsurgency, nation building, and all expeditionary or occupational adventures. The American public had had a bellyful. From now on, power would be projected by naval, air, satellite, and drone technology. The troops would stay home.

Into this vacuum flowed mercenary forces. Ground occupation became outsourced, funded at first by DoD in the interest of national security but before long by corporations or consortiums seeking to secure their investments, exploit contracted-for resources, or protect their personnel and infrastructure. Rates of pay became market driven; overnight, salaries shot to double and triple those of the conventional military. Incentives and bonuses made the sign-up packages even more attractive. The exodus from the army, navy, and Marines was spectacular. Applicants queued by the thousands. And these were quality troops—Airborne, Special Forces, SEALs, Rangers, the cream. Average age was thirty-two. Majors were competing for postings as O-2s. Nor was this groundswell limited to grunts and trigger pullers; staff officers, planners, intelligence, tech, and logistics specialists were throwing elbows, greedy to get in the door.

Merc had ceased to be a four-letter word. In those most overextended, underresourced, and grimly anti-American times, the president and Congress had at last found a means of projecting U.S. power that was (a) mission-effective, (b) cost-effective, and (c) did not run afoul of the extreme risk aversion of the American people.

Were these new for-hire forces alien, treacherous, or unreliable? Hell, no—they were just our same guys, in upgraded uniforms, finally getting paid what they deserved.

The final stroke that made the idea of mercenary forces acceptable to the American public was the inclusion of foreign volunteers. The Probst-Avenal Act of 2021, which provided a path to U.S. citizenship for overseas nationals who had served thirty-six months in for-hire combat billets, brought in the cream of veteran warriors from every army on the globe and meant that homegrown U.S. casualties would remain low low low.

How good were these contracted forces? Could a mercenary army hold its own in a straight-up fight with the conventional U.S. military? Never. Force Insertion, for all its quality of personnel and latitude of maneuver, couldn't begin to match the technology and transport; the aerial, naval, satellite, and drone capabilities; the intelligence apparatus or the heavy (read, nuclear) weapons systems that could only be funded by entities on the scale of nation-states. Head to head, a private versus national army clash was a no-go. But in certain arenas, in failed-state warfare, in tribal and ethnic conflicts, in contests where restrictive rules of engagement hamstrung conventional operations . . . in these areas, a merc force could shine. And since these were the areas an empire needed, pay-to-play forces came to be seen in a fresh, new light. The idea of mercs achieved respectability.

But what of my team now? What's our mission? Chow time comes and goes. A call from Petrocelli informs us that Salter has been delayed. Ten minutes later a text says he won't get here for two more days. Patience is the prime virtue of the warrior. Still, my guys are hot for action. They want to know what our job is. Will we reinforce Salter's armatures in southern Iraq? If so, in what capacity? Where? When? Why has Salter specified this particular crew, in these numbers, under this leadership, in this configuration? And what's the connection to Tim Hayward?

The two days pass; Salter's still hung up in Basra and Umm Qasr. A third day. Still no orders. More troops fly out of PSAB. Thousands more fly in.

We train. Fourteen hours a day I rehearse the team and myself. The men are eager and ready. Everyone is excited. Salter has left one top sheet for me — a hand-scrawled Concept of Operation that lists the evolutions he wants us to train in.

> Helo infil and exfil
> SSE day/night
> DA
> Use of AT-7, C-6, Chinese RRM
> SERE, mounted and dismounted
> Night/mt/winter/riverine

SSE is sensitive site exploitation. Raids. DA is direct action. Snatch-and-grabs and assassinations. SERE is escape and evasion. An AT-7 is a shoulder-fired antitank missile; C-6 is a new, superpowerful explosive; an RRM is the latest generation of portable surface-to-air missile.

Fourteen hours a day become sixteen and eighteen for me. It is no easy chore to mold a unit, even of mature, proven professionals. I do it the only way I know how: by working twice as hard as everyone else. I'm awake before the first team member opens his eyes, and I don't knock off till the last one gets his head down. I know every man's weapons, IADs, SOPs, and TTPs more thoroughly than he does; I can do every job as well as or better than the man assigned to it—and he knows it. Every operator except the Englishman Coombs, Chris Candelaria, and the UAE Special Forces guys has served with me on multiple deployments. They know I will eat my own liver before I will let them down, and they know I will eat *their* livers if they give me or the team any less than their high-end max. I love them and I tell them. I tell them over and over.

In a war zone, even a staging area like this, I can never sleep. I need pills to close my eyes and pills to pry them open; I gobble tabs to shit and capsules to stop shitting. I take steroids. I drink. The cargo pockets of my trousers are a one-man Walgreen's. I'm stocked with Percocet, Vicodin, Demerol, OxyContin; Dexedrine, Methedrine, Ritalin. I've got reds, white, blacks; Ambien, ephedrine, and a cocktail of my own—Valium, Inderal, and atropine: the first keeps you calm, the second blocks adrenaline to the heart, the third keeps your hands from sweating; you're so calm, you can cruise a lie detector test. Quality liquor is wasted in a combat zone. My body likes the cheap stuff anyway. Early Times, Carstairs, any kind of rye or Irish whisky. I shower in it. I brush my teeth with it. We all do.

How do you motivate warriors for hire? You don't. They're geeked already. They fight for pay, yeah—but in the shit, money means nothing. They've gone way beyond that—past country, past pride, beyond even love for their brothers. They have reached the place, these play-for-pay-ers, where they don't give a damn about anything and they still give their all.

A civilian might ask, Why do you need to train? Aren't these professionals prepared already? Yes, they are, but still a thousand and one mission-specific skills and individual and team procedures must be defined and rehearsed. Remember, we are no longer U.S. military with unlimited resources and standardized protocols. We're privateers, we're gunslingers. What gear do we have for night operations, for land navigation, for IPB (Intelligence Preparation of the Battlespace), for communication by FM, VHF, low satellite and high; for ordnance use and disposal? What weapons, rations, medical gear? What's our casualty treatment and evacuation scheme? If heliborne CASEVAC is out of the question where we're going (and it probably is), what are our scenarios for mass casualties, for severely wounded individuals, for dead? Communications. Will we have American comm gear or Chinese or Bulgarian or some shit we've never heard of? Iridium phones, supersats, IMBTTRs, PSC-8s, and PRC-220s? Task organization. Timeline planning. Under-fire TTP—Tactics, Techniques, and Procedures.

The team and every member have to master drills for Driver Down, Team Leader Down, Break Contact drills, Close Quarters Battle drills, Emergency Assault drills. What tech gear have we got? Will we be supported by drones, Ravens, Dragonflies? Have we got handheld BF Trackers, "confetti" surveillance pods, Falconview imagery software to plan our missions? What's our flyaway package? What's the equipment? What are the protocols? What host nation units or individuals will we be working with? What indirect fires can we call on, if any? What air assets? Who brings us in, who gets us out, where the hell are we going in the first place, how do we find it, day or night, and what do we need to know once we get there?

Mission planning: what's our primary scenario, alternate, contingency, and emergency? What weapons will we have? These all need to be zeroed, laser PESQ-3s and -7s locked down, and the same for night and thermal sights and surveillance gear. What about foreign weapons? Is every team member up to speed on Soviet-era RPKs, PKMs, AKs, and anything else we might stumble onto and have to use? Will we be crossing rivers, deserts, mountains? Mounted or dismounted? Will we be conducting reconnaissance, assaults, or assassinations? Will we be breaching fortified compounds? Will we need greenbacks, gold, interpreters? And when we've finally trained for every contingency, what happens when the shit hits the fan and we're on to Plan B, Plan C, and Plan Z? Combat is a team sport. We have to drill. We have to practice. We have to rehearse.

The final factor we train for is the unexpected. What if we're snugged down in a hide and innocent children or shepherds stumble onto us? This ethical nightmare has screwed special operators again and again. What if we hook up with our host-country nationals and they turn against us? What if they test us, demand money or the performance of some abhorrent act? What if some grinning, gap-toothed chief puts a pistol in our hands and demands that we execute a luckless local that the leader claims is a traitor? What if he insists that we compromise our security? Leave one of our men with him alone? What if an HC entity tries to make us take some of its booger eaters as part of our team? What if we consent and one is wounded or killed? If we're captured ourselves, what's our story?

The team comes together fast. They're like thoroughbreds at the gate. My only concern is delay. Day seven: the group has reached fighting pitch. I e-mail Salter. He'd better use us fast before we start going dull or worse.

Salter always answers promptly.

See you next stage, w/in 72 hrs. S.

BOOK FOUR

LORD JIM

8

HORN OF AFRICA

THREE MINUTES AFTER THIS text from Salter, a video link comes in from A.D. I click it. Up pops a SkyNews clip of her doing a stand-up on Route 80 north of Kuwait City. Columns of merc transport stream past in the background, heading for Safwan and the border of southern Iraq. The clip is what they call in the news biz a "tail" — an outtake, recorded after the real broadcast piece. Tails are full of profanity and mockery. My estranged bride grins into camera: Eat your heart out, Gent.

She signs "Call me" and "love," our traditional code.

A follow-up text comes in near midnight. A.D. is safe, rolling north with the troops. She has run into Dimitri and Dimitri, "the Brothers Karamazov" — Russian pilots we knew in East Africa. The pair is flying for Kiril Pachenko, the gunrunner, under contract to Force Insertion. No sign of Salter, says A.D., but she has an interview scheduled tomorrow with Juan-Esteban Echeverria, the former secretary of state whom I met in Scotland. Why is he here? Can I tell her anything? She slates a time for us to talk and signs off.

Dimitri and Dimitri.

I toss on my cot, remembering them—and the first time I met A.D. For some reason, the sight of her in-theater has upset me. This is her job; I understand that. She's great at it. But war is no place for a woman; I don't care what you say. I worry about her, and I'm furious at her for making me worry. I blame myself. She should be at home in our kitchen, fat and pregnant.

I take two Ambien.

Outside our hangar, a KC-130 taxis past with its big turbo-props droning. I close my eyes and I'm back in "the Horn" . . .

East Africa, 2022.

I was still in the Marine Corps then.

The thing about East Africa is there are no roads. You fly everywhere. Pilots are as common as cockroaches in Africa. Every white man, it seems, owns his own small plane or chopper. It's like having a car in the States.

In Africa you see a lot of Eastern-bloc crews, Soviet-era pilots who left home and wound up working for Alex Martini, Kiril Pachenko, or Teddy Ostrofsky. No pilot in Africa wears a uniform. It's shorts and shirts. The best you can hope for is the odd flight suit or bomber jacket that the flier wears to keep warm at altitude.

Above the African plains, the number one hazard is birds—pterodactyl-sized vultures that go zinging around like air-to-air missiles. Landing, the peril is wildebeest and zebra migrating across the airstrips. There's no radio at half the sites, and the weather changes minute by minute.

Every big plane you see in Africa, if it's not Lufthansa or BEA, belongs to an arms merchant. They're all flying guns. Most of the planes are antiques from the Soviet days—Ilyushins, Andropovs, and Antonovs that were obsolete before I was born. I can't begin to guess when the last spare parts for them were manufactured, but it certainly wasn't in this century. That was when I met Conrad Hilliaresse. He was one of the few non-Russians flying, and the only nondrunk. He took me on a walkaround of his plane one time, explaining that even these ancient Ilyushins had redundant systems for everything, sometimes four and five contingencies deep. Yes, he acknowledged, those four or five were now defunct, if not absent entirely, but the basic flying platform remained functional. This particular aircraft, he told me, was using orange juice in place of hydraulic fluid.

"Conrad, if you're not worried, I'm not."

"Just to be on the safe side though, I shan't retract the landing gear."

The way you fly in Africa, as I said, is by hitching rides. Schedules don't exist. The pilots, no matter how broke they are, won't let you pay. There's no pressurization on these aircraft and certainly no heat. And forget talking. The interiors are louder than Super Stallions and the fuselages are so riddled with bullet holes, patched and unpatched, that a gale howls fore to aft like a wind tunnel. On one flight with some Aussie Special Forces, I was watching a black African crewman shouting back and forth to the pilots, in KiSwahili, as he, the African, climbed up and down on cargo boxes tugging on wire cables that ran along the inboard flanks of the fuselage. One of the Aussies piped up. "What the fack ya doin', mate?"

The African shouted back: "Working the rudder."

I met Dimitri and Dimitri on a flight like that, from Princeville in Zamibia to Nairobi, on an errand for Salter. The Russians were flying a Tupolev Tu-114, which was the civilian cargo version of the Tu-95 bomber. I don't know how old that thing was, but it had propellers. I remember in jump school at Fort Benning, guys who got airsick would puke inside their own shirts rather than soil the beautiful clean deck of the army's C-130s. Nothing like that on this Tupolev; the underfoot was like the floor of a barn. I got so sick on this flight that they let me go up into the cockpit so I could see the horizon to settle my stomach. The pilots were both about fifty and both drunk as polecats. To navigate they had little tin boxes the size of iPods on the dashboard with a three-by-three window cut into them, like a TV screen, and a long strip of map paper scrolling on the inside. The paper was from a road map, like you'd buy in a gas station. I'm not making this up. The pilots scrolled the map by turning a little knob on the side of the box; they navigated by following the rivers and occasional dirt roads. I asked if they wanted to use my GPS. They said it would only confuse them.

I was feeling better now that I could see the horizon. I introduced myself and they did the same; when I couldn't pronounce their names, they just said, "I'm Dimitri," and "Me, too." They were drinking Early Times straight from the bottle; they offered me some, which I took. I asked them what ranks they had held in the Russian air force. "I was a corporal," said Dimitri who was flying the plane. He had to shout over the wind screaming through the cracks in the superstructure. Dimitri the copilot said he had been a private first class. My face must have gone white because they started howling.

"We're jerking your chain, dude," said Dimitri the pilot. "I was a major. He was a lieutenant colonel." I asked why they were flying in Africa. "We couldn't get visas to America," said Dimitri the copilot. "Why else? We're not crazy!"

I had thought of myself as a pretty good drinker till I met my first Russians. These characters are freaks of nature; the human liver must have evolved to some supernormal level north and east of the Ukraine. Black Africans are worse, except they don't drink distilled spirits; their booze of choice is *kishar*, fermented cow's or goat's milk, and other poisonous brews made from melons and sugar cane. This stuff is *living*. It's not antiseptic like vodka; you can't sterilize a wound with it. It's like compost; it's organic. The Western gut can't take this stuff. But these black Africans, even children, pour it down by the bucketful. They can live on it.

Africans don't really get drunk. Instead they achieve a state of detachment, a species of walking oblivion, and they stay in it. Many can do it without alcohol. It's a state of mind. The level of misery in some of these places is so intolerable that a sentient being can't endure it without some means of leaving his body. In the West we have hope; that's our drug of choice. The tribal African harbors no such illusions. The city African does, unfortunately for him. He's got a little education; he's seen movies and read books, studied the Bible or better yet the Koran. This is where suicide bombers come from: the hopeless who have been given hope. Some well-meaning Westerner gave it to them, probably a woman and probably as brave as she is clueless. When the bubble bursts, the city Africans can't take it. Hope has softened their skins; they're vulnerable now.

In place of hope arises hate.

We should leave them without hope. They're happier that way. The little kids with smiles on their faces and flies crawling across their eyeballs. That's their life. What's wrong with it? Who told us we had the right to mess with it?

I used to see A.D. on those flights. I ran into her once at Jomo Kenyatta Airport in Nairobi and another time at Dar es Salaam in Tanzania. We became friends before we were lovers. A.D. was back and forth to Sudan and Darfur all the time then, when both of those places were so hot not even the Chinese went in. She would catch rides on helicopters and small planes; I'd see her bundling across the tarmac packing sixty pounds of kit, then reaching up to be hauled aboard as the aircraft taxied down the runway.

A.D. at that time was not above donating her college-educated booty if she thought it would help her get a story. She slept with Pierre Mboku, the P.M. of Zaire. She was in Hans Klekker's bed, the UN chief inspector, as well as Colonel Karl-Jurgen Pedersen of Southwestern Mobe. I picked her up for breakfast once as she was tucking her blouse in, leaving the presidential palace at Harare.

It was A.D. who first made me aware of ambition. When I was courting her, I asked why she risked her privileged white bacon traveling to these crazy-ass places.

"Blond ambition."

A.D. had a philosophy about it.

"I come from a good family, Gent. My mum's a college administrator, my dad's a justice on the South African Supreme Court. I was raised never to strive for any object too conspicuously. Bad form. One was permitted to grind for grades, but only so she could marry well. I was raised to be a high-class brood mare."

A.D. was telling me this on another of those vulture-dodging flights. At least once on those jaunts, the plane would drop four hundred feet in one sudden, unanticipated plunge. A.D. used to confess all kinds of shit to me in those moments.

"Then one morning I woke up and I realized, I'm ambitious! I want to succeed! I want to be famous, I want to make a name for myself. It was like some great weight had been lifted off me. I felt like myself for the first time. I walked around that whole day, going over in my mind all the times growing up when I had felt crazy and wrong and different, in a bad way, from everyone else. I realized that they were all moments of ambition — and that what had made me disown my true feelings was that I had internalized this upper-class inhibition against manifest aspiration, against wanting anything in too unseemly a manner, or making a spectacle of myself by striving and failing." She smiled. "I packed my kit and got out the next day."

Why did A.D. cover war zones? "Because it's a fast way to get recognized and because there're only a few other women doing it. And I'm curious. I love train wrecks. They're horrible but one can't look away. I want to know what the human heart is capable of, the evil and the good."

What A.D. said made sense. I began to realize that I was ambitious too. I had an ego. I looked around at the guys in TacOps and it was clear they did too. It seemed that just about everyone in an elite, all-volunteer unit had some vaguely defined but nonetheless tangible aspiration, which was usually not fame or wealth so much as the desire to be *present at the center of events.*

We wanted to see what was going on.

We wanted to be part of it.

"You're no different from me, Gent. You want to see your name in the paper."

A.D. is a Jew. She doesn't have the drinking gene. I made it a point to stick with her when she was partying, to make sure nobody took advantage of her. One night we were in a corrugated-tin dive called the Coconut Club in a UN compound outside Djembe, West Congo, and A.D. had to pee; I walked her outside (the loo was unusable) and stood discreetly by while she squatted on some palm fronds in the warm rain.

"What the hell am I doing here? I should be home writing my novel."

When A.D. got down on herself, she hated everything, mostly herself.

"I gotta get out of here. I'm wasting my life."

She declared that journalism for her was a distraction, an excuse to avoid her real work. "Thrill seeking," she said. "I'm jerking myself off."

A.D. was the one who blew the whistle on Salter in East Africa. It ended his career and made hers.

9

BROWN BOMBERS

ZAMIBIA WAS A BREAKAWAY republic on the east coast of Africa, on the Indian Ocean.

The nation doesn't exist anymore; its territory has been re-absorbed as provinces into Somalia and Kenya. Its northeast border, when the state was sovereign, was marked by the tiny port of Sainte-Therese, which abutted the capital, Princeville. Refugees fleeing tribal wars in Somalia, and even Darfur, had been a problem there for thirty years; there were camps all along the border, with UN peacekeepers manning a supposedly demilitarized corridor called the Agarua, which means "Broomstick."

The president of Zamibia was a former Olympic sprinter named Innocent Mbana. He and his soldiers had left the poor people in the villages alone as long as they had nothing. But in the summer of 2022, a major push by U.S., Swedish, and Dutch NGOs brought in tons of humanitarian and medical supplies, along with rice, corn and barley meal, flour, and oil. A convoy of forty trucks, manned by KBR and Advance Systems drivers, left the port protected by a few Force Insertion mercs and locally hired security contractors, traveling under a guarantee of safe passage from Mbana. He broke it. The president found out how much the drugs were worth. To make a long story short, a massacre ensued. Cell-phone video got out. The images showed drivers and contractors being dragged out of their vehicles and shot or burned alive while Mbana's soldiers danced over them in glee.

The U.S. Navy and Marine Corps keep two Amphibious Ready Groups, ARGs, at sea at all times. One comes out of the East Coast, the Second Marine Division at Camp Lejeune; the other is from the West Coast, the First Marine Division at Pendleton. Each ARG carries a battalion-sized MEU(SOC), a Marine Expeditionary Unit, Special Operations Capable. There are other MEUs in reserve but in this case we had two together, the Eleventh MEU and the Twenty-Ninth, to form Task Force 68. Salter was its commander. He was a brand-new three-star. This was August 2022, right after AfPak II and the end of the second Iran-Iraq war.

In Zamibia at that time there were about two hundred American, Canadian, and European civilians, mostly pipeline engineers, doctors, missionaries, and humanitarian workers. The State Department, then under Secretary Echevarria serving President Jack Cole, had ordered them evacuated. Our job was to make sure they got out okay.

Salter called our teams together aboard the flagship, the USS *Peleliu*. Before Marines go ashore anywhere, Force Recon teams (or, at that time, TacOps) are sent in to seize and prepare HLZs — Helicopter Landing Zones — or ALGs, Amphibious Landing Grounds. That was us. Capt. Jack Stettenpohl ran the first team, Hellboy One; he was in overall command of the three-team section. My team was Hellboy Three. Two was Captain Robert Salter's, the general's son. We gathered around our commander on a platform overlooking the *Peleliu*'s well deck. This is a huge, cavernous space that can be flooded from the sea; the ship launches and recovers her landing craft from there.

Time was about midnight; the place was deafening with engine noise and reeking of salt water and diesel fumes. Col. Mattoon and his S2, Maj. Cam Holland, gave the briefing.

Holland told us that a full-on revolution had broken out ashore. He showed us UAV video from two hours prior. Buildings were burning; mobs roamed the streets. Salter let Holland and Mattoon finish, then he stepped forward.

"I'm expecting a total goatfuck, gentlemen. You'll see shit happening that you never saw on the worst days of AfPakI or II, Iraq, or Yemen. Keep a cool head. Do not react out of emotion. Your job is to locate and secure LZs for the main force, nothing more. Keep out of the way of Mbana's soldiers. Do not light anyone up without clearing it with higher, and when I say higher, I mean me."

Salter shook each of our hands. Our Super Stallions were cranking up on the flight deck. "You and your Marines represent the United States of America." That was all Salter said. He looked into our eyes, rapped each of us on the shoulder, and we took off.

The advance teams went in fast and encountered no resistance. Streets were empty; the city was calm. Mbana's troops had restored order. They welcomed us.

When I say troops, I use the word in its loosest possible meaning. Most were untrained, illiterate *kalashes,* nineteen to twenty-four years old, fresh in from the villages or off the streets of the shanty-towns and squatters' camps — commanded by thirty-year-old "captains" who couldn't read or write and were, like their subordinates, whacked out on crystal meth, double-dope (dopamine-enhanced crack), "brown-brown" (a mixture of cocaine and gunpowder), and khat, an African narcotic that you dip like snuff and that's cheap as air. The soldiers were called Brown Bombers from the color of the berets they wore.

The status symbol for these thugs was a video camera. Squad leaders wore plastic Chinese SolarShooters on lanyards around their necks. The cameras were used to take pictures of any civilian that the soldiers intended to rape or murder later on. The locals were terrified of these cameras. The Brown Bombers' weapons were AK-47s; their uniforms were surplus Albanian and Bulgarian cammies acquired from Teddy Ostrofsky or one of the other Eastern-bloc gunrunners, who also supplied the thirty-year-old Chinese 7.62 mm ammunition that was so moldy and rotten you could snap off the slug from the cartridge case with two fingers. The way you could tell an officer was he had boots. Everyone else wore flip-flops or went barefoot. The amazing thing was they all spoke English, pretty good English. They got it from TV.

Zamibia at the time, for all its troubles, had a lot of native charm. The architecture of the capital Princeville was colonial French, with Victor Hugo-esque manses built around courtyards and boulevards shaded by tall, leafy magnolias; cottages at the beach had palm-sheltered drives and big mahogany louvers built into the doors and windows for ventilation and shade. If a divorced woman or a widow wished to announce her availability, she left the shades open. Street vendors gave you oranges and coconut shavings for free, but shoppers voluntarily kicked in a few coins for the little paper umbrella, called a "flute," that came with the treat. The custom of "lagniappe," where merchants donate a little something extra for free, was practiced throughout the city. It lent a grace note to everything, as did certain endearing turns of phrase. When road crews shut down a street for repairs, the sign said

LANE ASLEEP

All married females were called "mamas," and those of marriageable age but not yet wed, "pretty mamas." If you greeted a mama as "pretty mama," you would always get a smile.

The soldiers who preyed upon these people were, in Zamibia as elsewhere in Africa, the scourges of their defenseless compatriots. But in truth, it was they who had been betrayed and swindled by their own elders. Any half-assed Western sergeant could've whipped three hundred of these young men into a solid, disciplined company and they would have thrived on it. But there were no trained NCOs in Mbana's cadre. Instead the youths ran riot. The energy of one fed on and inflamed the hot-blood emotion of every other. When their pay came late, which it invariably did, the mob got meaner and more dangerous. Mbana wanted it that way. He wanted his men to bully and intimidate the populace; it kept the people cowed and docile.

Mbana's army was so destitute it didn't even have insignia of rank. Corporals and sergeants used any sparkly geegaw they could pluck off a trash pile. They had Nike swooshes and Chinese red stars (the People's Republic had twenty thousand troops and over one hundred thousand laborers in neighboring Ethiopia) sewn onto their collars and pinned to their berets. Fire discipline was unheard of. When the Bombers cut loose with their weapons, it was in "death blossoms" — pull the trigger and spray the planet. As a collective entity, these troops didn't even rate the name of gang, which at least would have possessed a code of shame to hold its members to a standard of behavior. They were a rabble. They went from friendly to lethal in two seconds with no visible sign or warning. They were as nodded out as junkies and as murderous as a riverful of piranha.

These troops were illiterate and untrained, but they were not stupid. There was a subtlety to the way they operated that took us days to appreciate. They knew how to enter a street in a convoy of trucks and, without a word or a shot, instill utter terror into the populace. Their technique for neutralizing us Marines was to swarm our position, smiling. It worked at first, because part of our mission orders was to "establish rapport with indigenous elements."

A typical street encounter would go like this: a cabinet minister or general would come zipping up in a Mercedes or Land Rover, preceded by two "technicals"—Toyota pickups packing PKMs or Vietnam-era M60s—followed immediately by two truckloads of troops, who would dismount in a mob and surround us, beaming and jabbering about Cadillac Escalades, LeBron James, and American pussy. It worked. The Bombers were able to shunt us away from precincts of the city that President Mbana didn't want us to patrol and from sights that he didn't want us to see.

Where were our battalions from the MEUs? They were being held up offshore by the suddenly incendiary situation in Taiwan. Onshore we had no TVs and only military laptops; I missed half the crisis, catching scraps on my handheld. The one thing I remember was Chutes logging on to Fox/BBC and the rest of us gathered around, hearing how Beijing was pulling America's paper, firing a Chinese New Year's candle up Wall Street's ass, while the life savings of all of us were being swept away like the trash trading slips that used to be left each night on the floor of the New York Stock Exchange. Three days went by, then six. When I'd report each hour to Salter's command center with the flotilla, the final conversation was always with his aide, Pete Petrocelli, on the subject of the extraction of my team, Capt. Stettenpohl's, and Robert Salter's, should Task Force 68 suddenly be ordered to the South China Sea.

Zamibia is divided along an east-west axis by the Riviere Saint-Jerome, which splits in two at Princeville and runs to the Indian Ocean like an east-facing V. North is rice and maize country; south is diamonds and coca. In the V lies the built-up swamp where the French administrative capital had been sited in the colonial era and where President Mbana's palace and barracks, the Villa Zamibia, stood. Zamibia had broken away from Somalia and Kenya in '13 to become the East African Republic, was reabsorbed in '14, then seceded again in '16 under Mbana, to assume its current political form in January 2017.

In the intervening fifteen months, Mbana had driven the country into destitution while he and his posse preyed on the living corpse. The government taxed everything—bread, water, medical services. Bicycles were licensed, as were farm animals down to individual chickens. There was a tax to be married and a tax to be divorced, a tax to be born and a tax to die. Of course none of these tariffs were written down; the police decided them on the spot. A.D. had been there in '19; she wrote a story about Mbana's "poon safaris." The president would cruise through neighborhoods and shantytowns in his white 1966 Fleetwood convertible with three technicals packed with Bombers and two empty army trucks behind. Any girl who struck Mbana's fancy, his soldiers chucked in back and took away. If a husband or brother protested, he was tied to a tree, beaten with fan belts or barbed wire, his bones broken with clubs, and, if he was lucky, left for dead. A rebel force arose, which Mbana crushed, flaying captives alive, then dousing them with gasoline and setting them afire.

When Task Force 68 arrived, Mbana had just instituted what the opposition press (which was one hand-produced newspaper, published by an incredibly courageous black African editor named Alistair Finlay) described as a "Jesus tax." This levy was to serve as "penance"—Mbana's term—for the populace for allowing the uprising to happen in the first place. It was to be paid on Christmas Day. The tax was 33⅓ percent of the wealth and possessions of every man, woman, and child. Mbana's troops set up collection centers in the six district capitals, which were just poor market towns along the river or near a road that was passable for part of the year. From these camps, the soldiers raided at will. They would enter a village and obliterate it. They murdered men by hammering nails into their skulls. They raped women and girls, then shot them and dragged their bodies behind their trucks. If a male of military age resisted, the Brown Bombers cut off one or both of his arms, sometimes hacking them with machetes, other times chewing them off with power saws. Below the elbow was called "long-sleeving," above it "short-sleeving."

The third day we were in-country, my team and Jack Stettenpohl's received a hot wire—an emergency transmission—from Robert Salter, whose team was operating in a ville called Finisterre on the north side of the city. We found them in a park above the river. The rainy season had just started; temperature was about 110 with 100 percent humidity. Mbana's Bombers had stuffed three freight containers with "sinners"—his name for anyone who resisted or defied his orders—and padlocked them in. A throng of wailing, shrieking locals, nine-tenths women and children, surrounded these troops, pleading with them to release the captives. Rob Salter's team had been summoned by frantic friends and relatives. He had rushed to the site, only to be forbidden by higher command to intervene. Now my team arrived. Stettenpohl's had been ordered to stay where it was.

A hundred Brown Bombers ringed the containers. You couldn't hear the screams coming from inside; all sound was drowned by the clamor of the mob and din of the downpour. But you could see the containers rocking.

Rob Salter was up front, trying to negotiate with the Bomber commander. I joined him. There were two Belgian women from the UNHCR, the United Nations High Commission for Refugees, and two men, one a black professor, from Oxfam and Human Rights Watch.

If it's possible to have rain in hell, that's what the scene looked like. The park grounds were mud; the women's long colorful dresses and turban head wraps were soaked through. A Land Rover came up with MÉDECINS SANS FRONTIÉRES on the side; a Belgian doctor got out and added his appeal for the prisoners' release. While Rob was on the horn to his father on the flagship, begging for permission to intervene, a phalanx of mothers could no longer contain their desperation; they rushed Mbana's troops, attacking with umbrellas and stones and bare hands. The Bombers opened fire. No warning shots, no volleys over the women's heads. The troops unloaded on full auto straight into the front rank of the wives and mothers. I've seen a lot of shit in my day, but I had never witnessed anything like that.

We had two African Americans — Pope and Harvey — on Robert Salter's team and mine. Pope was a sergeant, Harvey a staff sergeant; they were both solid, disciplined Marines and consummate professionals. But when they saw soldiers gunning down unarmed women, they lost all self-command. Chutes and Q had to disarm Harvey. I couldn't see Pope, so berserk was the pandemonium that had broken out across the entire park, but I heard later that he had had to be wrestled to the ground and zip-stripped. It was axiomatic that African American troops had the greatest difficulty dealing with black African savagery. They took it too personally.

Mbana's troops had closed ranks now. They had configured themselves into a perimeter protecting the containers. Their eyes were big as headlamps. As for the women, about a dozen lay on the ground, swarmed by hundreds more, all wailing and screaming. For us, the immediate imperatives were to care for the wounded and to prevent the situation from getting even further out of hand. Every TacOps team has two hospital corpsmen. These were now rushing to aid the mamas. I had Chutes calling for CASEVAC. I could hear Rob Salter on the horn to his father. Rob was saying, "Yes sir . . . yes sir," in a voice that was an octave higher than normal. Clearly Gen. Salter was telling him to keep his head and keep his Marines' fingers off their triggers. Mbana's troops would not leave and would not relent.

We should have killed them. We should have cut them down where they stood. I know AFRICOM's fear was of an international incident. The generals in Kelley Barracks, Stuttgart, were seeing headlines — "Marines Massacre Africans." But what was the alternative? How could we stand there, bringing in choppers to take out the gut-shot mothers, while every living soul inside the boxes asphyxiated and died?

Twenty minutes later, the containers stopped rocking.

The Bombers melted away. The crowd drove us off the field with stones and curses. They hated us worse than Mbana's murderers because they knew we understood right from wrong, but we had stood by and done nothing.

Still the MEU battalions did not come ashore. The crisis in Taiwan had tied up everything. My team and Rob Salter's worked around the clock evacuating the American, Canadian, and European civilians. This was a clusterfuck in its own right. Most of the whites in the capital were humanitarian aid workers or human rights activists, who were as dedicated as Mother Teresa and who felt that now, more than ever, they could not pull out. They refused to report to the embassy or the other stations that had been designated as evacuation points. We had to hunt them down. Again our TacOps teams were put in an impossible situation. We were physically carrying nurses out of hospitals, while their patients surrounded us, weeping and pleading.

The third day Rob's team and mine were driving to a Doctors Without Borders hospital in Dingale, a village and refugee camp west of the Princeville "V." We were on a dirt stretch among acacia trees, when a young boy came running up to us, begging us to follow him and help. He was so frantic he couldn't speak; he opened his mouth but only a soundless croak came out. I took him up front with me on one Humvee with our two others following at three-hundred-yard intervals in case of treachery. Before we'd gone a mile, we smelled fire.

A tiny, tin-roofed house was blazing in the noon sun. The boy's family was inside. Chutes, Junk, and Q kicked down one of the flimsy walls and pushed through, enough to find what turned out to be a grandmother (though she looked to be only about thirty-five) and two babies, the boy's sisters. All had had their throats slit. On the side, in a still-burning lean-to, lay a young mama, still alive but charred horribly, whose throat had been hacked through in the same manner. A kitchen cleaver lay in the dirt. A crowd of hundreds ringed the scene, women and children, wailing like nothing I've ever heard. Ortiz, one of our corpsmen, made a show of trying to save the young woman but it was clear there was no hope.

From bystanders the story spilled out. Mbana's soldiers had a camp a mile off in the bush. The young woman had been ordered to report every morning, which she did, whereupon she was raped by whoever wanted her. There were fifteen or twenty such women in the surrounding villages who had been compelled to perform the same service. The soldiers said they would butcher the families if any of them resisted. "How long has this been going on?" I asked one of the mamas. She flashed ten fingers four times. This particular girl, she said, had been driven mad. She had slaughtered her own family with the kitchen cleaver, then lit the house on fire and hacked through her own throat.

Our onshore parties, as I said, were under strict orders to intervene in no local affairs other than those covered by specific orders. We buried the girl and her family. The crisis in Taiwan was approaching its climax. A brigade from the People's Republic Ninth Expeditionary Army (Nuclear Capable) had been deployed into the demilitarized corridor, only forty miles away. As we were gathering stones to mark the family's graves, a transmission came in from the *Peleliu*. It instructed us to move our camp south of the river, to the administrative area of the port, and establish a compound from which we could be extracted in a hurry if necessary.

We did this.

That night soldiers from Mbana's camp returned to the village. With machetes, they slaughtered every member of the young woman's extended family, including the small boy who had run to us for aid.

You can imagine our Marines' state of mind when they learned this.

We should have been there. We should never have left the village. Our two African Americans, Sgt. Pope and SSgt. Harvey, took it hard. I think they felt ashamed for their people. How could human beings commit such acts of barbarity? They came to me and Rob Salter together, both in tears. They wanted to hit the Bombers' camp.

Pope and Harvey were not gangbanging street thugs. Pope had two years at UC Berkeley; he had been an All-Pac-12 lacrosse player. Harvey was thirty years old, the father of three boys. I got on the radio to Col. Mattoon offshore, urgently requesting to get both these guys relieved at once and given counseling. That was my official position. Between Col. Mattoon and me, I told him I sided with Pope and Harvey.

"Gent, I didn't hear that."

"Then let me repeat it, sir."

"You'll do no such thing." Col. Mattoon ordered me to get a hold of myself. If I couldn't do it, he said, he'd find another officer who could.

The atrocities continued. I ordered my team not to engage in conversation with any innocents, don't buy a Coke, don't even say hello. I didn't want interaction with us to be the pretext for any further reprisals. Mbana's soldiers patrolled the villages with their Chinese cameras. The locals were petrified.

Meanwhile the country had plunged into an orgy of hyperinflation. Mbana's government was printing notes in denominations of millions. A new issue came out twice a day. Ten million was worth one

American dollar. A beer was five million bucks. Bank lines wrapped around blocks. People would come twice a day to take out whatever they could (the government only allowed them to withdraw so much each time) just so they could buy dinner. And everywhere the soldiers cruised with their AKs, their machetes, and their cameras.

The third noon we went back to the village. The soldiers were still making the women come to their camp. We would see the girls trudging along the road as if they were marching to the executioner. Back in town, we ran into a gang of Mbana's soldiers. They were in open-top, highback trucks, stoned on something. I was with Jack Stettenpohl; we were just coming out of the government printing office, where the operators had given up on churning out bank notes and gone to gas and ration coupons. Mbana's soldiers spotted our teams, waiting beside their Humvees on the street; they swarmed around them, all smiles. The soldiers knew we had been present during and after three separate massacres. In their minds, that meant we were with them. When I arrived, half a dozen Bombers had crowded around Pope and a gunnery sergeant from Stettenpohl's team named Larson, who was also black. They wanted to get their pictures taken with them. Suddenly Larson coldcocked one of them. The dude dropped like a stone. Stettenpohl and I plunged between the groups, ordering everyone to chill. The Africans were laughing; they thought it was a great joke. Even the guy Larson had slugged was smiling. Good friends, yes? Good.

That night another massacre took place. Of men, this time. The soldiers hit the first village and two others. I won't tell what they did except to say that if Lucifer himself had flown in from hell, he would've turned around and gone back to where it was civilized.

It wasn't Pope, Harvey, or Larson who initiated the call for payback. My squad radio beeped. "Gent, it's Rob. Meet me by the ball field."

We came together just before sunset, in the field adjacent to the soccer stadium. Jack Stettenpohl was there already. The grass was filled with displaced women and children under tents and lean-tos. Rob Salter led Jack and me to his Humvee. On the hood he had taped a mission plan, scrawled on a panel cut from a cardboard MRE box. In black lines drawn with a Sharpie, Rob had sketched the river, the Bomber compound, and three routes of approach and egress.

"Here's their camp," he said. "Are you with me or not?"

10

CHARLIE MIKE

"WHO'S THIS FROM?" JACK confronted Rob. He meant: Have you cleared this with higher? Has this been ordered by your father?

Rob said no.

"Have you even told him?"

"I'll tell him when it's over."

I'm out, Jack said. He made the case, which he declared was self-evident, that a stunt like this, if it got out in the press, would destroy not only Gen. Salter's career and our own, but also would blow up into an international moral catastrophe for the United States and for the Marine Corps. More to the point, Jack said, it was wrong. "They've got a name for this, Rob. It's called a war crime."

I have never seen a look like the one on Robert Salter's face. "And what is it," he said, "when these motherfuckers pour battery acid down the throats of eight-year-old girls?"

"It's evil," said Jack. "But it's not our business. We have orders and we've sworn to obey them."

Rob turned on his heel and ordered his men to start their trucks. They did. Plainly he had briefed them and they were all for it. I could see Sgt. Pope with Rob and Harvey and my own guys heading my way.

Stettenpohl turned to his radio operator. "Get General Salter."

But the task force commander couldn't be reached. He had flown to Bahrain that morning to confer on the Taiwan crisis. Col. Mattoon was with him. Next down the chain was our group commander, whom I'll call Major T. I could hear his voice through Jack's handset. "What do you want from me, Captain? To countermand my boss's son?"

Jack turned to me. "Don't tell me you're down for this, Gent."

"You're doing the right thing, Jack. Somebody's gotta keep clean."

I called my guys to circle up. This was beneath a grove of jacaranda trees beside the creek that flows through the stadium part of the park. Rob Salter had just finished briefing us on the site of the Bombers' camp and his idea of how to hit it and get out. I put in my two cents and we brought the plan into a shape we could all get behind.

Then I spoke to my guys alone. This is a life-changing moment, I said. I won't order any man to strap up. Do it or don't, but let no one take this decision lightly. The actions we take here tonight, we'll have to live with for the rest of our lives.

"We're not going in as Marines," I said. "Take off everything that says USMC, dog tags, everything."

"What about tattoos?" said Germain, our youngest. That produced a laugh.

A couple of years later I chanced to read a paper by a professor from Tulane, whose daughter I knew from back home. It was a study of clans and tribes in East Africa. The paper said that the typical black African despot did not see himself as a criminal. Quite the contrary. In his own eyes, he was acting under the honorable imperatives imposed upon him as a clan and tribal champion, that is, to take everything he possibly could from people who were not of his blood and either keep it for himself or dispense it in the form of patronage and gifts of influence to members of his own family, clan, and tribe. In Mbana's eyes the country of Zamibia was not a nation or a people over which he ruled as steward, but a fat sow for him and his buddies to feast on. I could understand that. It was like Iraq. It was like Afghanistan.

I held out my hand, palm down. Every man put his on top. Stettenpohl had vacated. He was a good man, a Dartmouth grad, father of two, with a future as promising as Rob Salter's.

Rob came back; we went over protocols and recognition signals one last time. "No phones, no radios. Don't even talk. Hand signals only." He was so calm it was spooky.

There was a crossroads in the bush a few miles south of the Bombers' camp. That would be our Vehicle Drop Off. The teams would travel separately to that site. We would stash the trucks in the treeline and go on dismounted.

0215, my trucks idled up to the VDO. Robert Salter's vehicles were already hidden in the trees. He came forward with his men in their night-vision goggles. Then we heard other steps.

Jack Stettenpohl came up out of the dark. His face was blacked; he carried an H&K 416, a modified M4–40 with ACOG infrared sights and an M203 grenade launcher underslung. He had twelve 30-round mags on his vest and one 20-rounder in the weapon. He didn't say anything. His guys were with him. Rob Salter was the senior captain; he had only one order: "Charlie Mike."

Continue Mission.

We came in from the landward side, trapping the Bombers against the river. My element and Robert Salter's entered the camp on a skirmish line fifty meters across and dressed at a double arm's interval. We wore NVGs. With the laser sights on our M4–40s, where you put the red dot is where the round goes. Stettenpohl's team had set up on a sandbar that ran about forty meters out into the river. They were prone, on line, with four SAWs, two AA-12s (automatic shotguns that fire Frag-12 explosive shells), and every other man's M4 on automatic.

Mbana's soldiers were bivouacked in about forty shelters and tents, spread over an area half the size of a football field. There was no security. We slung ICs into each hooch. These are mixtures of C-4 plastic explosive, flammable oil, and incendiary thermite; they blow with a sharp bang that coats everything with flaming jelly like napalm. After the first flash we didn't need goggles. The soldiers came out on fire. There's a tendency to shoot high in situations like that. The recoil of the weapon, fired in a burst, throws the muzzle up. I signed to our men to aim for knees and bellies. We came through in line abreast with no gaps. I stayed four or five paces to the rear, dressing the line and directing fire.

The massacre was over in less than three minutes. Probably half the Bombers were cut down in the river. They were highballing, naked and unarmed, or if they had retained the presence of mind to grab their AKs, they flung them away now so they could run faster. Stettenpohl's gunners tore them up from the flank. The soldiers that reached the far shore, he blew away with claymores his men had planted. A few got away into the bush. We didn't chase them. Our trucks came up; we collected all the camp's weapons and loaded them aboard. We policed up all our own brass, wires, and whatever scraps of primers or detonators we could find strewn around from the cannisters. There were a few wounded Bombers on the ground, crying and moaning or trying to crawl away into the dark. We left them.

It was four in the morning when my team got back to its own camp at the southern end of the city park. The three teams had split up at the crossroads after the action. Each unit had returned to its Area of Operations. The plan was to resume our stations and carry on as if we knew nothing. Privately I was concerned; we had to take seriously the possibility of payback. The soldiers who got away would bolt straight to other units. What would I do if I were them? I'd sure as hell come after us.

My team's perimeter was an oblong under acacias at the south end of the park. It was on a rise with good fields of fire on all sides. We had camo nets rigged low over slit trenches that linked all positions. Razor wire protected the perimeter; we had a fortified vehicle-entry behind sandbags. I had left one man on guard; he reported no activity. I sent in Chutes and Quinones to get water bottles and stuff to clean up with. We intended to remain on alert till dawn outside the wire, in a new perimeter about two hundred yards west in a denser grove of acacias. Suddenly we heard Chutes cursing, or what sounded like cursing. He reappeared at the wire, waving me and Sgt. Kean, our weapons specialist, forward. "You ain't gonna believe this, Skipper."

We crept up to Chutes's hooch, which was just two sleeping mats behind a low row of sandbags. We had to go in on our knees under the camo net. "What's that smell?" Kean said. Something light and oily had been spread over the bedding. Chutes was laughing. "Touch it," he said.

It was flowers. Petals. Thousands of them.

Chutes tugged Kean and me to the side of the position, which was stacked with Chutes's water bottles and MRE boxes. We could see half a dozen straw baskets set down like an offering. "Check this shit out," Chutes said. "It's papayas and mangoes." He held one up. "This is a fucking guava!"

By dawn the capital knew everything. Word had spread to the entire province. I was in camp, boiling water for our morning mud when a seventy-year-old African woman materialized out of the mist and handed me a hot bowl of the best coffee I'd tasted since I left Louisiana. Another lady was taking down my shirt and socks, which were drying on a line. How these women got inside our wire, I will never know. Girls and grown females glided through the camp, collecting dirty laundry. Their smiles were as shy as virgins'.

Downtown when we went for breakfast, no one would let us pay. The mood was sober. No one high-fived us. Nobody clapped our backs or shook our hands. But grandmothers and young girls would come up and slip us colored scraps of paper. On them was written "Merci" or "God bless USA."

No word appeared in the paper or on TV. It was as if nothing had happened. I asked an old man named Emile who sold us phone cards. "There is a proverb here in East Africa: 'Do not follow the footsteps of the morning.' It meant things change. What has happened is not what is to be."

All that day, the mood was like nothing I, or any of us, had ever experienced. Trucks and minibuses had begun fleeing the city—Bombers and their families. As soon as dark came, the people would butcher them. The women would do the killing. They would use machetes. In East Africa, as in all tribal societies, no crime or outrage is ever forgotten. The name and face of every transgressor is known. The victims, whose turn it was now to take vengeance, knew to which districts their tormentors would flee and among whose clan and family they would try to hide.

Next morning, Marine landing parties came ashore from the flotilla. Throngs lined the beaches, cheering the amtracks as they landed. More thousands ringed the soccer stadium to greet the CH-53s whoomp-whoomping in. Gen. Salter flew in on a Cobra from the *Peleliu* and set down on the lawn of the presidential palace. When the tracked vehicles rolled into downtown, Marines on top were inundated by delirious mobs of women and young boys, who climbed aboard and hung off every kit rail and porthole.

Mbana had made his bird, as Vietnam-era Marines would have said. His private jet had taken off without running lights in the middle of the night. A second plane followed, carrying Mbana's women and his gold. The neighborhood of the presidential palace, when Salter's Cobra set down on the lawn, rocked like the Vieux Carré on the final night of Mardi Gras. Everyone was dressed in bright orange and hot pink, purple and tangerine. In East Africa when women are happy, they wrap their heads in bright turbans called *akeeshas*. That was all you saw, bobbing and bouncing, an ecstatic ocean as colorful as a crayon box.

Salter took over the country as efficiently as Alexander the Great, whose campaigns he had studied in detail. The two onshore battalions assumed their AOs — 3/7 south of the river as far as the second-largest city, Amintra; 5/9 in the capital where we were. A third and fourth Battalion Landing Team of the Fourteenth MEU remained offshore as a reserve and Quick Reaction Force.

I wasn't there when Salter took possession of the palace but I heard that his first official act was to run up the black-and-green flag of Zamibia and salute it, along with every member of his staff and combat team, standing at attention, while Mbana's military band played the national anthem — theirs, not ours.

His second act was to bring in the ministers of every governmental agency and have them publicly swear allegiance to the flag of their country. Normal life would resume, Salter announced. Power and water would be restored; fuel would be rationed but available. Disorder would not be tolerated. Thieves would be delivered to justice; looters would be shot on sight. Any merchant charged with profiteering would answer to a jury of those he had attempted to exploit. Marine patrols would guard residential neighborhoods and stand sentry at private businesses, hospitals, and government offices. This was a Saturday. Today and Sunday, Salter declared, would be a national holiday. Monday everyone would return to work and to school. Banks would open. Public ministries would be staffed. Salaries would be paid.

A Marine Expeditionary Unit carries with it twenty million in Uncle Sam's greenbacks, secured in the commodore's spaces aboard the flagship. That night Salter had the lump sum from both task forces flown ashore. The cash was in hundred-dollar bills, in eight brushed-aluminum caskets. He went on the civilian TV channel, not a military one, and declared that these funds now constituted the financial reserve of the country. They were backed by the government of the United States. It seemed a ridiculously tiny amount to serve as the currency reserve of an entire nation, but then again, trust is everything with money—and the people trusted Salter. They trusted the Marines. I was watching the general's speech, with Rob Salter and Jack Stettenpohl and the rest of our teams, on a satlink parked on the hood of a Bedford truck in the middle of a village street with electric lights running off a diesel generator and about a thousand men, women, and kids packed around so tight you couldn't lift your arms from your sides and if you did, you couldn't get them back down. The people couldn't hear a word and neither could we, but they never stopped cheering.

By next morning, villagers started showing up carrying "stars." This was the temporary unofficial new currency. It was nothing but scraps of colored paper with Salter's personal three-star stencil stamped on them. Each "star" was worth a buck. Any kid with a copy machine could counterfeit them, but nobody did. The stunt worked. We Marines used the stars too. In fact, the only problem with this tender was that the locals held it in such awe and viewed it as imbued with such good juju that they squirreled the bills away for luck and didn't even spend them.

I had never taken over a country before. Who had? The people adored you. If you were a Marine, you were everyone's number one son. We became the Peace Corps. We patrolled the streets, we repaired sewers and power lines, we delivered babies.

The onshore force was cut off from TV. None of us had time. We gleaned only snatches about the crisis over Taiwan or even of the mounting threat to our own position from nuclear-capable Chinese forces massing along the demilitarized corridor. The only thing we knew for sure, because we could see it happening from the hills above the harbor, was that we had lost our own carrier group, Adm. Spence's. Under orders from President Cole, the battle group was steaming right now for the Strait of Malacca, where U.S. and Chinese subs were facing off and the world was holding its collective breath over this potential nuclear showdown.

In-country, reprisals continued. Elements of Mbana's soldiers had rallied into raiding parties and taken to the bush. They still resisted. They still terrorized. The natives went after them.

Any individual who had collaborated with the army—informants, girlfriends, merchants who had supplied the Bombers or relatives who had harbored them—was fair game. We talked to people. They told us how things worked.

The word for shame in local dialect is *imare*. There are twenty-two words for shame in Swahili and Gozen. There's a word for the shame associated with failure to extend hospitality when it is called for, and another term for the shame of neglecting a parent or grandparent. *Imare* is the shame of failing to stand up to an oppressor. This is the worst shame of all. It can be made whole only by blood and only within a ritual called *inagama hura*. *Inagama* means "sever"; *hura* is "soul." The malefactor must be dispatched in such a way that not only his body dies, but his spirit, too. The skull must be severed from the body and all four limbs detached and scattered. Inagama cannot be enacted individually; it must be performed in a ritual group, called a *gangara*, which has been purified beforehand.

There is another type of shame, which I could never pronounce and could never find anyone to write down for me. It's something like *urchita nambe,* with the "ch" sounding guttural and the "b" in nambe spoken singsongy at the top of the throat. *Urchita nambe* is the shame of women. Not the shame of men who have failed to protect their women, but the shame of women whose souls have been violated. This is the shame that made our young girl take her own life and the lives of her family that first day. This woman's act, we learned, was no aberration. It was mandated by tribal law. By such a slaughter, she had saved her own soul and the spirits of her family from the pollution inflicted on her by the soldiers. In East Africa, we were told, rape was an expression of manhood. When a man took a woman by force, he acquired her power. He stole a piece of her soul, which made him stronger and more virile, while degrading and shaming her. Again, the stain of this infamy could be washed clean only by blood.

When we Marines landed, our presence took the lid off this shame and the emotion that accompanied it. This was not rage. You could see it. It was deeper; it was at the level of the soul.

What it meant in effect was that the entire population of wronged villages, male and female, packed up and set off into the bush, armed with clubs, spears, and machetes, tracking down those who had shamed them. After Salter's initial takeover of the capital, as I said, raids continued by the Brown Bombers in the outlying regions and in the townships and shantytowns. Salter immediately dispatched platoon- and company-sized response teams to hunt them down. Vehicle chases would take place across hundreds of miles, in Humvees and requisitioned "technicals" and jingle trucks, with Cobra gunships overhead and Crow and Raven thermal-sensor drones quartering above the bush, zeroing even on bodies that hid themselves in rivers or slathered themselves head to toe with mud. Salter had pledged to protect any Mbana soldier who surrendered.

The detainees must face justice, but they would have a fair chance to defend themselves.

The problem had become the *gangaras,* the ritual vigilantes. The Marines were in a race with them to get to the bad guys first.

By now, reporters had started showing up. Not the mainstream media; they had their hands full with Taiwan and a collateral crisis in Egypt. We got the freelancers, the wild Aussies and Germans and South Africans with their handhelds and their nCryptor uplinks. They were like paparazzi. They had unbelievable guts; they would do anything for a shot or a piece of sensational video.

A.D. came in with them. She was the only legitimate journalist, other than Ariel Caplan, who brought a camera crew from Agence France-Press TV, and John Milnes, the two-time Pulitzer Prize–winning war correspondent from Fox/BBC, who traveled alone except for his valet, Whittaker, who cooked his meals and boiled his shirts and whom he paid out of his own pocket. By now the machete reprisals had become a serious PR problem for Salter. The gonzos wanted footage. None except A.D., Caplan, and Milnes was covering Salter's restoration of the courts of justice or his reactivation of the water treatment plant. The freelancers wanted video of black Africans hacking the heads off other black Africans or, even better, black African women and children doing the hacking, which was in fact how the honor imperative worked. It became the Marines' full-time job to keep these journo vultures in their hotels or inside the wire on our bases.

You had to feel for the locals. I've served in a gaggle of these ass-fucked countries and it's the same in every one. First, there's no indigenous economy. There's no entrepreneurial class, no middle class, no capital, no respect for property rights. There are no businesses other than roll-up storefronts selling rice and cement — or the odd mom-and-pop Chiclets and T-shirt stand. The only enterprising capitalists are criminals. Government exists in external form only, a travesty of legitimate governance, with tribal thugs and gangsters occupying the ministries and looting for themselves and their families whatever revenue or matériel is extracted from the earth or flows in from outside the borders.

What enterprise exists is either subsistence farming or narcotics. Cash comes in from outside, not as capital investment — because no First World bank or corporation is reckless enough to take such a risk — but in the form of humanitarian aid, military support, or poison-pill loans from the IMF and the World Bank to fund well-intentioned but artificial projects such as infrastructure construction and rehabilitation — roads and wells, power stations and water purification plants that look great on paper but on the ground are nothing but sinkholes of corruption, with the outside cash flowing into the pockets of whatever tribal or criminal despot lords it over the region. The infrastructure project itself is abandoned halfway through, when the foreign workers bolt because they can't stand conditions any longer, with only the shell left standing after every item of value has been looted by the locals.

These countries are often called "failed states," but the truth is they're not states at all. There's no source of revenue sufficient for the central government to pay for police or security forces (if these could even be created, which they can't) to protect the simple, hardworking villagers in the provinces. So the warlords do it, as they have for the last ten thousand years, by extorting money from the locals and shaking down any outside entity via tolls or road or river taxes (and nowadays pipelines), either in the form of institutionalized patronage from whatever Western or Asian buccaneering entity is ripping off the natural resources, or informally by checkpoints and roadblocks at the muzzle end of AK-47s. The regional lords extract protection money from the narco traffickers (most in fact are indistinguishable from narco traffickers) and use this revenue to recruit and fund their militias. The real currency of the nation is hopelessness. If a young man of courage and vision arises, he has two choices: join the gangs or bolt the country. The rare honest man, the stand-up politician, the crusading editor gets his few column inches in the Western press and then is shot, hanged, poisoned, or "detained for his own protection" and never heard from again.

That's what you see in these countries. And you see something else: the long-suffering, brave, generous, God-fearing, patient, kind, and, against all odds, cheerful wives, husbands, and children of the villages and cities. That's what we Marines saw and that's what Salter saw.

There are three primary tribes in Zamibia—the Zamibs, the Nahallawit, and the Koros. Mbana was a Zamib. These were the majority, constituting about 60 percent of the populace; the other two tribes composed 30 percent, with the final ten made up of smaller tributary tribes. When Mbana was in power, his tribesmen persecuted the others. All the judges and ministers were either Zamibs or tokens. When the Marines took over, the minority tribes didn't trust the courts because the justices were still essentially Mbana's cronies. Salter had to have his platoon and company commanders dispense justice themselves, in person, at least temporarily. The problem was the East African mind is so tribal and so finely attuned to distinctions in rank that any man of substance, which was everybody above the age of thirty, refused to have his case adjudicated by these young lieutenants and captains who were perceived by these tribesmen as the "sons" of Salter. The petitioners wanted the real deal. They demanded the man himself.

Salter began hearing grievances. He conducted these proceedings outdoors, first on the palace grounds, then in a quadrant of the soccer stadium—partly because these were the only sites big enough to contain the multitude of plaintiffs, and partly for the transparency of the venue, to let the people see that business was being conducted in the open and nobody was selling them out behind closed doors.

In East Africa, no public act can be taken in the capital without report of it flying on wings to every village and crossroads of the interior. A wise judgment is commended. Two in a row are acclaimed. Three and they're writing songs about you. Salter dispensed justice like a Marine. What counted to him was the group; every judgment he handed down had as its aim the strengthening of the bonds within the community — and the swift kicking in the ass of anyone who tried to fuck with those bonds. He might let a bad actor slide once, but he'd hang the sonofabitch by his nuts the second time. He couldn't be bought, he couldn't be bribed, he couldn't be manipulated. The people loved him. He became, in the popular imagination, a cross between Solomon and Atticus Finch. The badge of office worn by a native justice is a scarlet sash called an *inguro*. Salter resisted wearing one at first. He appeared only in uniform. But after a week, he relented.

A Westerner seeking to restore stability to a tribal society inevitably finds himself in an ethical bind. Does he go along with the native customs, which are usually barbarous but effective, or does he attempt to impose "civilized" standards, which the natives consider at best quaint and at worst inscrutable, and which in the end only make matters worse?

In the bush, the machete massacres continued. Official MEU policy, as articulated by Salter in his Orders of the Day, was to prevent these outrages by all means necessary. A typical day had half our battalions in the air, in platoon-sized security-and-stability elements, following up reports of potentially inflammatory gatherings or of out-and-out violence. I was present for several incidents where Marine forces actually intervened. This was wildly unpopular. The women would wail and lacerate their scalps till blood was sheeting down their faces. They wanted justice. They cried Salter's name, or the name he had come to be called, *Ero Horo* — "The Man with the Clock" — because of the big Bulova he kept on his desk during the petition hearings. Ero Horo would never order his Marines to prevent justice! Ero Horo understood! He was one of us!

The problem of course was the evidence of the massacres. It was too grisly, too visual — and there were too many cell-phone cameras. Finally, what everyone feared would happen, did happen.

Second Platoon of Kilo Company 3/7 was on a heliborne sweep at the south end of the delta when they came upon a *gangara* in progress. The date was 11 September 2022, the twenty-first anniversary of the fall of the Twin Towers. Col. Mattoon was in charge of the Joint Operations Center when the call came in. I don't know what factors influenced his decision. Maybe the violence on-site had gone too far already; maybe to intervene at that stage would only have risked more lives. Maybe second platoon's commander indicated that he lacked the force to influence the outcome. Maybe Mattoon was simply acknowledging political reality: that what gave Salter his influence over the population (the solitary element, in fact, that kept the country from descending into chaos) was that he was perceived as being the lone Westerner who understood the locals' concept of honor and possessed the courage to stand up for their vision of justice. Whatever the reasons, Mattoon ordered 2nd Platoon to RTB — Return to Base — which they did.

In other words, he let the massacre continue.

Someone had a satphone camera.

Three hours later, the video was all over the Web.

The first reporters on the scene were a couple of freelance South Africans. I knew them; they were decent guys. They were actually going to pass up the payday because they knew what a shitstorm it would unleash. But then a take-no-prisoners Dutch journalist named Ditman Kroon appeared, and a couple of Americans who the South Africans knew would never sit on so hot a story. So they went for it.

The press crucified Mattoon first. Then the Marines on the ground. Then Salter. Of all the written pieces, A.D.'s was the most even-handed in its tone and balance. It at least gave Salter credit for good intentions and articulated the moral dilemma he found himself in. But her piece was the one with the widest circulation, being published by the London mega-zine *Topix,* whose high-def version featured—and hyped sensationally—the raw, uncensored head-lopping video. And *Topix* was the first to use the phrase "Lord Jim" to describe Salter.

That did it.

The line was too good.

A.D.'s editors at *Topix* rewrote her original, scrupulously factual draft, tarted it up with unsourced allegations, rumor, and sensationalized hearsay; threw in a four-page spread of photoshopped atrocity pix; and capped it off for the magazine cover with a photo of Salter wearing his tribal *inguro* sash, which made him look like a gone-native megalomaniac out of Joseph Conrad. In the press, Salter was already the "Crawling Man" hero from Yemen, a Marine's Marine, the kind of old-school, Chesty Puller–style jarhead that the media lionizes when he's riding high and attacks like a pack of hyenas the instant he stumbles.

Now the Chinese entered the picture. Zamibia has oil. The Ninth Expeditionary Army was in East Africa for one reason only. It massed along "the Broomstick," the demilitarized corridor. The pretext for invasion was humanitarian: U.S. Marines had run amok. The Chinese brought up tactical nuke artillery that could not only annihilate our land forces but also take out the support vessels at sea. Was there a connection to the crisis in Taiwan? I'll leave that to the *Wiki Washington Post.* Bottom line: the People's Republic had Uncle Sam down, and they were about to carve a steak out of his ass.

Salter's response was aggressive and audacious. He struck cross-border by night with two reinforced rifle companies, seizing a high ground called the "Mons Orientale," which compelled the

Chinese to withdraw. He ordered up his own tactical nukes. (They never actually got ashore, but the ordering was enough.)

A Chinese Jin-class nuclear submarine was reported on its way, to augment the two Song class boats already within missile-launch range. President Cole was compelled to respond. He ordered the *Abraham Lincoln* with its battle group back from the Strait of Malacca. This was at the peak of the crisis in that theater. We watched on our handhelds. Marines were Sharpie-ing "WWIII or Bust" on their helmet covers.

Salter didn't back off for a second. Nor was he shy about inserting himself into it personally. He appeared via satellite on *Beltway Overnight* and, next week, on *Face the Nation* — both times without clearing it with higher. When the White House furiously ordered him to cease, he obeyed but he continued to blog and tweet. The public saw him on HoloTube, tramping frontier CPs in a flak jacket with no helmet, quoting Livy, Thucydides, and Hobbes as he pointed across the border at the Chinese forward positions in the Broomstick, explaining what would happen to the helpless citizens of Zamibia when "those bastards" crossed the line. His Marines loved it. Amazingly, so did vast segments of the American electorate. Pete Petrocelli told me later that his in-box crashed from the volume of traffic — favorable, nine to one — which included contribution offers totaling well into eight figures and public support from the loftiest spheres of government and commerce.

President Cole ordered Salter to withdraw all troops from forward positions, to disarm all tactical nuclear warheads, and to redeploy out of range of the Chinese all systems capable of delivering such ordnance.

Salter refused.

By this time, anchor-level news crews had arrived from Trump/CNN, WSJ/CBS, SkyNet, and al-Jazeera. Salter called the teams together, along with A.D., Ariel Caplan of Agence France-Presse, and

John Milnes of Fox/BBC who were already in-country. What he did then was not as crazy as it was later portrayed to be.

I have this account from Rob Salter, who was present front and center. The occasion was a walk-and-talk near one of the forward observation posts along the border. Salter was responding to questions about why he had refused to stand down his nukes. He answered that he was prepared to do so (in fact, orders were already in the pipeline), but first he wished to speak with the president, the secretary of defense, and the chairman of the Joint Chiefs; VTC—video teleconferencing—was slated to take place in two hours.

Salter felt certain, he told the reporters, that he could convince his superiors of the inadvisability of their directive. The United States was not vulnerable, Salter declared. It was the Chinese who had overplayed their hand. With one strike he, Gen. Salter, could topple, not only the Asian despots' decades-long effort to control African oil, but he could "make their whole house of cards collapse." Taiwan could be saved—and that was only the beginning.

"Isn't such strategizing, General, a few levels above your pay grade?"

This question came from Ariel Caplan, A.D.'s friend, who was at that time the most widely watched TV journalist in Europe. Salter responded by asking the news producers if their networks would be interested in carrying him live to "address the nation." As I said, Rob was there. He heard this. He swears his father's tone was joking.

Perhaps this was lost in translation. Maybe the story was just too juicy to let pass. Whatever the cause, two hours later, that remark—in garbled video, shot from behind Salter so the expression on his face was not visible—was leading every news broadcast on the planet, and Salter was being portrayed as MacArthur in Korea, Caesar in Gaul, and Alcibiades in Sparta.

President Cole fired him and called him home.

Salter was pilloried in absentia while Task Force 68 was still in East Africa. We watched on our handhelds. The experience was surreal. As Salter on television was being portrayed as Marlon Brando in *Apocalypse Now,* Salter in real life was standing tall like Martin Luther King at Selma.

He had been relieved of command. Technically he was under arrest. Nobody in Zambia gave a damn. To the working folk of Princeville and the provinces, Salter was the nation's savior. The people begged him to stay. Candlelight vigils ringed his CP. The natives knew that Salter and his Marines were the only forces holding back chaos, the next tribal bloodbath, not to mention a Chinese invasion.

The task force's orders were to embark for home. UN peacekeepers from Burundi and Zaire would take our place.

We were to leave the country to its fate.

Adm. Spence returned and took over. He instructed the commanders of both MEUs to pull out their onshore elements in darkness. He didn't want a spectacle. The Marines refused. I had never seen anything like it. "Mechanical breakdowns" occurred; communications crashed; schedules fell behind. The troops were supposed to be transported to the harbor by 7-ton MTVR trucks. Instead they marched on foot. The hour of departure was slated for predawn; instead the march-out kicked off at eleven in the morning. The entire city lined the parade route. The Marines marched out by platoons. Women swamped them, weeping. The mamas couldn't understand why we had to go. They knew Salter had been disgraced but they couldn't figure out why.

Task Force 68 was not sent directly home. Taiwan was still too hot. We were sent to Diego Garcia in the Indian Ocean, then to Jakarta and finally Osaka, Japan.

Salter had been flown home, first to Camp Lejeune, along with Col. Mattoon, to face an in-service inquiry. We got updates every day from Pete Petrocelli—Jack Stettenpohl and me, and of course Rob. Orders came for the three of us. Jack's remaining term of enlistment was only three months; he was given a speeded-up honorable discharge and enrolled, like all officers following their service on active duty, in the Active Reserve. Rob was granted the assignment he had been campaigning for for six months: command of a TacOps section—three twelve-man teams—in Paktia Province, on the Afghanistan-Pakistan border. The billet came with a promotion to major. I was returned to Quantico as an instructor at TBS, The Basic School. The story of the massacre of the Brown Bombers was all over the Marine Corps by then, but the unspoken code of Loose Lips Sink Ships kept all jaws locked. If the press ever got wind of that debacle, the Corps's image, already in tatters from Salter's public firing, would suffer a blow from which it might never recover. Rob, Jack, and I parted with vows of silence sealed in blood.

By then, Salter was testifying before Congress.

In stress situations like that, my response is always to train. I was running seven miles a day and swimming two. Jack Stettenpohl was back in the D.C. area too. He was keeping as low a profile as I was, working privately for a friend from Dartmouth, another Marine, who was running for Congress. One night we met at a bar in Georgetown. Jack showed me a bunch of poll figures and other data about his friend. Then he leaned in closer. "But here's the really interesting part."

Jack riffed through a sheaf of documents. Sometimes in surveys, he said, the pollsters will throw in what they call "rogue questions." These have nothing to do with the issue under investigation; they're inserted just to see if the respondent is paying attention and answering honestly. The rogue question was:

> If the presidential election were held today, which one of the following candidates would you vote for?

The choices, Jack showed me, were the expected ones, headed by President Murchison, the Democratic incumbent. I followed Jack's finger down the columns. "Now," he said, "look at the write-ins."

Gen. James Salter   23.7%

"The figure for write-ins typically doubles in an election when the candidate's name is actually on the ballot — meaning when voters don't have to go to the trouble of thinking, remembering, and actually writing it in."

"In other words . . ."

Jack indicated Murchison's figure of 26.4 percent and that of Senator Dodd, his Republican challenger, at 29.4 percent. "In other words, our ex-boss is roughly twice as popular as the president of the United States."

Jack ordered another round.

"But the significance of these figures," he said, "goes way beyond Salter. It's the American people and their state of rage and fear. Our fellow citizens are pretty fucking pissed off. Think about it, Gent. A maverick jarhead who has just risked nuclear Armageddon — and Mom and Pop in Peoria are standing by, unprompted, to make him Man of the Year. This is some shit, bro!"

The spectacle of Salter's congressional testimony set new records for television and Web viewership. The general had never cultivated political partisans or put himself forward for office, yet thousands of placard-wielding supporters demonstrated on his behalf outside Congress, with adherents including two senators and half a dozen congressmen urging that he be taken seriously as a candidate for president.

Salter was the kind of warrior-statesman, Senator Groomes of Montana declared, that this country had once possessed in Patton and MacArthur — and whose fearless leadership it desperately needed right now. Salter's partisans revered him because he wasn't afraid to speak the truth or to kick our enemies in the ass. Salter would have nuked Tehran after 11/11, or Islamabad or both, they believed (I didn't share their opinion)—and that was all right with them.

Against these campaigners marched equally rabid prosecutors who declared Salter the updated counterpart of the Burt Lancaster character in *Seven Days in May* and who swore that hip-shooting buckaroos like him were the reason the world had come to fear and despise the United States in the first place.

There was never any doubt, legally speaking, that Salter in East Africa had ignored protocols, violated rules of engagement, and disobeyed direct orders.

On the stand he would not back down. "If you're asking me to recant, Senator," he told Avery Drummond of Colorado, "you and this committee can go straight to hell."

The story consumed the air, the Web, and the satfeeds for weeks. Salter was depicted by his admirers as a twenty-first-century Caesar, dwarfing his contemporaries. His enemies called him "a wannabe Caligula" and "Napoleon in a Crackerjack box." Throughout this fortnight of folly (Ariel Caplan's phrase), Salter refused to pander or apologize. The online *New York Post* ran a cartoon of him crucified with spikes made of his own quotes: "I was obeying a more ancient law" and "Name the price and I'll pay it."

His most notorious quote, which was replayed endlessly on TV and the Web and handhelds everywhere, was his call for universal service. A draft.

"If you don't want men like me taking affairs into our own hands, then step up and put this country's youth in harm's way—not 1 percent as the case stands now, but 100 percent. No exceptions. Blind. Paraplegic. Everybody. Does the nation have vital overseas interests? Then, godammit, defend them! When you do, I'll shut up and you'll never hear from me again."

Before the Senate committee Salter asked rhetorically how many infantry lieutenants and captains from Ivy League schools were currently serving in the Marine Corps. "Seven," he said. "We should have seventy. We should have seven hundred."

How many sons and daughters of congressmen are serving now in combat billets? "Four—and three of those are from one family. I call that a national disgrace. Don't stick me and my warriors alone on an island, then pillory us for acting like warriors."

The usual hawks and red-staters rallied to Salter's cause. But those in shades of pink found something to like too. Even along the Hudson, Trotskyite Westsiders were lining up behind the general.

John Milnes, in a piece for Fox/BBC, wrote this:

What has been lost amidst the histrionics of this Beltway lynching is the fact that General Salter's actions in East Africa, while they may have been unorthodox, even brutal, when judged by the parlor-room standards of Georgetown or the East Side of Manhattan, were in fact measured, practical and above all effective. They worked. They saved lives. They brought order out of chaos. Salter demonstrated no personal agenda and no private ambitions for himself, the Marine Corps, or the United States. He was trying to help the people and, in my opinion, doing a damn outstanding job.

For a moment it looked as if Salter's charisma and the sudden groundswell of support might actually pluck his chestnuts from the fire. Then came the bombshell on CyberLeaks and the mil/blog, the Courtemanche Report.

Both sites broke the story of the massacre of the Brown Bombers. Somehow DeMartin White, the CyberLeaks CEO, and Eric Lavalle Courtemanche, the radical blogger, had gotten their hands on a draft of an internal Marine Corps report. The document named Rob Salter as the initiator of the outrage. For some reason, Jack Stettenpohl's name and mine either did not appear or had been redacted. The leakers weren't after us, or even Rob. Their target was Gen. Salter.

The story exploded. Salter came forward at once and took responsibility for issuing the orders that led to the massacre.

It was too late. The cause was picked up by the fire-breathing congressman from Montana, Jake Fallon. He led the torch-and-pitchfork brigade. Rob's career was finished. His life was ruined. He faced prosecution for war crimes. He could go to prison or even face a firing squad.

There's an unofficial military communications channel, as I mentioned before, called AKOP. The system had been put in place in the early teens to expedite resupply of forward units from bases in the States, but various geeks and gamers had figured out how to hack into and tweak it so that one serviceman could contact another, by text in the notepad section, through their All Force Trackers.

I jumped on this channel now, straight to Rob. It was eleven in the morning in Quantico, where I was—twelve thirty at night (with the half-hour drop east of Kabul) in Paktia. Rob had seen enough of the news to reckon the scale of the catastrophe; he had talked to his dad; he knew how bad it was, not only for himself and his father but for the Marine Corps and for the whole country. No one from higher, he told me, had contacted him yet; he still commanded his three TacOps teams. "What's next?" I typed.

"Fuck 'em." Rob's text ticked back in real time. "I got a job to do and I'm gonna do it."

An army COP, a combat outpost on the Pakistani border, was under attack at that moment. Rob took two of his teams and went in.

The Bomber fiasco had turned my life and A.D.'s upside down too. I prepared a letter confessing my role. My wife begged me not to send it. I'd be taking down not only myself but Jack Stettenpohl and his wife, not to mention further opening the can of worms that led to every other Marine who had taken part that night. Besides,

A.D. said, she smelled a deeper story, a giant rat of a story, in the leaking of the report and then, twenty-four hours later, its mysterious deletion from all Marine Corps databases. She wanted that story.

We fought. I hated myself. I hated being safe in Quantico. I should be with Rob in Paktia. I should be backing up Gen. Salter before Congress.

A.D. and I kept fighting. Three nights after my AKOP talk with Rob, she and I got into a real wall-banger. At the height of emotion, the phone rang. I picked it up, ready to unload on whoever was calling.

A female voice identified herself as a journalist for the Associated Press. Did I have a comment on the death of Robert Salter?

"What?"

Major Robert Enslow Salter, the reporter said, had been killed in Pakistan twelve hours earlier, apparently in an unauthorized cross-border raid. His body—or what militants claimed was his body—was, in the enemy's words, "in the hands of the innocents he and his gang of murderers had attacked" and would be put on video display within the next twenty-four hours.

I got off the phone and started AKOPing everyone I knew. Had Gen. Salter heard? What would he do? I phoned Jack Stettenpohl but couldn't find him. Online and by satellite I connected with other friends who had known Rob in East Africa and Yemen. More kept breaking in. I'd have one Marine on the land line, one on text, another on cell, and a fourth on Skype. Around nine I picked up probably the thirtieth call of the night.

"Captain Gilbert Gentilhomme?"

The voice was southern and female and pronounced my name correctly.

"Yes, ma'am."

"This is Maggie Cole. I apologize for phoning you at such an hour, but I must speak with you on a matter of some urgency."

"Maggie Cole?" I said. "Margaret Rucker Cole?"

"It's about General Salter, Captain. Will you help me? What I'm about to ask must be kept in the strictest of confidence."

Forty minutes later, I was speeding into Delta's Short Term Lot at Richmond International Airport, having cinched my divorce from A.D. by refusing to let her ride with me.

This was my introduction to Margaret Rucker Cole. She was then the wife of the president of the United States. The first lady. She was also, I was beginning to understand, a longtime friend of Gen. Salter. While I was racing to Richmond International, A.D. was keeping up a running commentary via Bluetooth. She was scouring her databases. She came up with half a dozen TPIs, time-and-place intersects, between Salter's stations of duty and Maggie Cole's former addresses.

Salter, Mrs. Cole had told me, had booked a flight to Pakistan. He was defying his congressional subpoena. He didn't give a damn what anyone did to him; he had to try to get Rob's body back. Mrs. Cole had been unable to stop him. Salter's transatlantic flight connected at Richmond. My job was to intercept him and keep him off that plane, even if I had to physically overpower him. These were Margaret Cole's instructions. She would connect with me in person as quickly as she could. Two teams of "security specialists" were at RIC already, primed to stop Salter. But Mrs. Cole wanted to employ such impersonal means only as a last resort.

"You must bring him back, Gilbert, as a friend."

Baggage claim was packed with late travelers. Businessmen and sales guys were snatching their bags and rolling away to the taxi stands and rental car counters. I was scanning the crowd when I noted one pale old dude struggling with two heavy nylon flight bags, the old-fashioned kind without wheels. I was thinking, *Man, I hope I never get that old.*

Then I realized it was Salter.

I dashed around the carousel, straight up to the general.

"Sir, let me take those."

I grabbed one bag, but Salter fought me for the other. He looked like death. "Gent?" he said.

"Godammit, sir, gimme the fucking bag."

I took him straight home to the apartment A.D. and I were renting in Alexandria. Mrs. Cole had sent a doctor over. Salter strode right past him. He and I wound up killing a fifth of Black Label at a table in the apartment's galley-sized kitchen. A.D. had diplomatically cleared out.

Twenty-four hours passed. The first lady couldn't get away; the gossip sphere would run wild if she were spotted with Salter. But she managed to phone midday on a White House secure line; she and the general talked for ninety minutes. Salter had switched from Scotch to coffee. Then, that midnight, he and I were watching English-language DAWN-TV out of Islamabad, when a grainy, handheld video came on, showing a young Western male's naked, mutilated corpse, strung upside down in a Pakistani mountain village. Jubilant mujahideen posed beside it. The body, the newscast said, was that of an American.

Salter stood up.

His eyes were the color of blood; his neck had blown up to twice its size. I made him sit. He couldn't speak. I was afraid his heart would explode right in his chest.

The phone rang. It was Maggie; she was downstairs. The story had hit all over. She came up. Two agents of her Secret Service detail came with her; others waited outside. They would protect us, Maggie said. No one would breathe a word. We drove to Baileys Crossroads, so Salter could get some air. Already I knew what I was going to do and how I was going to do it.

Salter and Maggie started walking. It was one in the morning and raining. I caught up with them outside an Amazon bookstore. The place was totally deserted.

Salter was telling Maggie he would get on a plane for Pakistan tonight; she was clutching his shoulders in both hands, rattling off all the reasons why he couldn't. I came up beside them.

"I need a million bucks for expenses," I said, "and a team of ten to twelve men that I'll request by name."

Salter and Maggie turned toward me. I told them I'd need air and ground transport, weapons, papers and IDs, overflight clearances — and another three million, in cash or electronic equivalent, on call if I needed it.

"What," Maggie said, "are you talking about?"

"I can be in Peshawar in two days and on the border in four. I'll have Rob's body back in a week."

11

C-6

THE STRIKE TEAM WENT in from the Pakistan side, across the mountains, using the same ratlines that Saudi volunteers, Syrian martyr-wannabes, and Haqqani and Peshawar Taliban used to infiltrate into Regional Command East via the passes through the Zazi Valley. The place was like the Ho Chi Minh trail; after dark, the footpaths were so crowded with infiltrators, you could find your way simply by the dust and the trash of the mob ahead of you.

We were twelve men in one team—me; Tim Hayward; el-Masri (who was fluent in Dari and Pashto but had brought along a second interpreter who knew the local dialect); Chutes, Junk, and Q; three Afghan Moumand tribesmen of the Konar who had been trained by U.S. Special Forces; an American TAC—tactical air controller—to handle helo extraction and emergency CAS—close air support, and an Israeli demolitions expert, Avigdor "Avi" Donen (son of the famous general Levi "Lebo" Donen), to instruct the team and supervise its use of C-6 molecular explosive.

This package had come together not via the conventional military, but financed by and under the personal sponsorship of the mercenary general Pietter van Arden. One phone call to him and all doors opened. Van Arden (who was fatally ill, with less than a year to live) had his own agenda. He had labored for decades to build Force Insertion into a credible warfighting entity. The enterprise had lacked only one element — a charismatic field commander on the level of a James Salter. There was more to it, of course. Van Arden had known Rob Salter for years and had mentored him since he was a boy. The men respected and loved each other.

Team personnel came together fast, with no individual hesitating and no element asking questions. I learned later that the behind-the-scenes support team for this strike totaled 232 people in twenty-seven countries. Intel, supply, and transport came from the United States and England, South Africa, Israel, Australia, New Zealand, Canada, Egypt, and Saudi Arabia, with in-country aid and backup coming from all these plus the British SAS, UAE Special Forces, and Special Operations commands from the Netherlands, Germany, and Turkey. We even got help from the Pakistani army and the ISI (Inter-Services Intelligence).

The village that held Rob's body was called Tel Amal. By midnight, seventy-two hours after assembly at Bahrain in the Persian Gulf, the team had reached the ridge overstanding the site. Everyone wore beards and hajji-flage. By tribal courier, from the related Pashtun kin groups across the border in Ali Khel, an offer of three million dollars cash had been tendered for the return of Rob Salter's body. This had been refused. If an attempt was made to retrieve the body by force, the defenders of the fastness vowed, those criminals caught or captured would pray to heaven that their mothers had never given them birth.

We found a vantage and scoped the village, or that portion we could see from a hundred feet above the trail. The colony clung to the mountainside, snaking up from a river gorge several hundred feet below along lanes so narrow that two men could barely pass abreast. Houses were unmortared stone and shingle, stacked atop one another so that one family's roof was the next household's entry court and set back against the mountainside like a Zuni pueblo. The stonework was spectacular. Each house was an impregnable redoubt. The village as a whole constituted a masterfully articulated fortress, with ascending and reinforcing platforms of defense and interlocking fields of fire. The place could've withstood Alexander in 333 B.C. It could certainly stand off American drone strikes and thousand-pound JDAMs today.

I called the team up. Avi Donen, our ex-Israeli Defense Forces demolitions expert, had given us a hurry-up class back at Bahrain. "C-6 is C-4 squared." It was molecular explosive, he explained, that was armed with dime-sized, wireless, push-in detonators called "thumbtacks." As many as twenty bricks could be daisy-chained together and set for individual, simultaneous, or sequential explosions. The trigger was a cell phone with an app. "Four squares the size of Hershey bars," Avi said, "are the equivalent of a thousand-pound bomb." He told us that his demolition team in Israel had once set four charges at the corners of a half-acre orange orchard. "After we blew it, there was nothing left but ash. Not a stump, not a leaf."

In Bahrain, our own team had not had access to a demo range, so none of us had used the stuff yet or seen with our own eyes what it could do.

Avi warned us now. "Plant the charges low, at the centerline of the buildings. We'll blow 'em individually from the bottom of the village up. When you hear 'Fire in the hole!,' get behind something as fast as you can. Don't count on your plugs or your headset to protect your ears. Cover your eyes and open your mouth. If you don't, the disparity between internal and external pressure from the concussion will bust up your insides. After my team blew that orchard, I was pissing blood for ten days. If you can't get on the ground or behind cover, get the fuck away from any drop-offs because, believe me, this stuff will pick you up and lay you down. Hang on to your composure. The power of C-6 is that it scares the shit out of you. Human senses can't stand the violence of it; it's too extreme. That's why it's never used in the IDF by troops, only by demolition engineers."

Questions. "Dogs?"

"Silence 'em."

"Kids?"

"Chase 'em."

"Muj?"

"Kill 'em."

We went in fast in two teams of four and one team of three, with our air controller topside keeping contact with the bird that, we hoped, would haul us out when this was over. In five minutes, twelve charges had been laid. The teams rallied on a stone square at the top of the village. Two firefights had already erupted, from which our guys had broken contact. Alarm bells were ringing all over the village. AK-armed forms darted in the shadows. We had seconds, not minutes, to make this work.

El-Masri's partner, Ajmal, bellowed through a bullhorn in Pashto: "Bring us the body of the American!" Avi hissed into his headset mike. The first blast went up at the foot of the slope. The concussion equaled four thousand-pound bombs. It felt like the whole mountain had exploded. In seconds, massive clouds of black dust engulfed the gorge. Shingle was raining like shrapnel. I could hear women screaming and goats bleating.

"Bring us the body of the American!"

I waited twenty seconds, then nodded to Avi. The second blast made my brain rattle in its pan. I spit blood. A roar that felt like thunder times ten rolled upslope from the gorge. Stone houses, scores of tons, were plunging into the river.

Avi was right; the violence of the explosions was more than human senses could endure. The concussion unmanned you at the cellular level. Our team was two hundred yards uphill from the blast site, shielded by blockwall upon blockwall of megatonnage stone, and still our internal organs felt bruised and battered.

"Bring us the body of the American!"

Armed shapes appeared upslope from the square. I saw muzzles flash. I dove for cover.

Avi detonated the third charge. We all plunged behind walls. Slides started on the west end of the village; half the mountain was coming down. The firing from upslope stopped. El-Masri, Tim Hayward, and I peered cautiously from our hides.

A form stepped forward.

A tribesman — an elder, about fifty — appeared across the stone square. On one side of the site was the mountain, climbing straight up for a thousand feet; on the other three sides squatted the as-yet-undestroyed upper houses of the village. Ajmal shouted to the man to give us the American's body. Our Pashtuns scurried forward, reinforcing me and el-Masri. More armed tribesmen appeared in the shadows.

The chief started toward me, hands above his head. I set my M4–40 on the ground and did the same. "What's he saying?" I was shouting into my headset.

El-Masri: "Loosely translated: 'Eat shit and die.' "

I closed to ten feet from the chief. From its sheath behind my shoulder, I drew an East Indian planter's knife, the kind used to cut sugar cane. The weapon was two-thirds the size of a machete and as sharp as a surgeon's scalpel. With one swipe, I opened the chief's throat from ear to ear. I snatched him by the beard, to keep his weight from plunging. Howls of shock and horror pealed from the muj. With two backhand blows, I hacked off the chief's head. Blood spurted from the void of his neck, painting the front of my *shalwar kameez* trousers.

Avi hit the next trigger.

What was our plan? To create terror. Visceral, cellular terror. No lesser force could compel these proud, primordial tribal warriors. Death meant nothing to them; they would send themselves and everyone they loved to hell in the name of pride and honor.

Evil, unholy, animal terror. Only that would make them crack.

Avi's fourth blast blew me sideways into a stone wall. The chief's head vanished; I never saw it or his body again. I felt as if my shoulders had been wrenched from their sockets. My knees were jelly. I couldn't see or hear or think.

Somehow I got to my feet. Chutes and Tim Hayward were lifting me. Two boys of the village, naked and burned black, were crawling toward us upslope across the square. Blood was sheeting from their ears, eyes, and mouths. Their hands, raw as pulped meat, pled for mercy.

They were dragging a plastic sack.

In the sack was Rob's body.

El-Masri and one of our Pashtuns took it; they peered inside. "Where's the head, you sons of whores?" The boys staggered back down the slope; they returned in moments with a skull. The rest of the bag was bones. Later, on the outmarch, I carried this parcel myself. Its weight was that of a doll.

Our air controller was pumping his fist up and down, meaning hurry, he's got our chopper on the way to take us out.

Avi came up beside me.

"How many charges left?" I asked.

Eight, he said. His expression asked, *What should I do?*

"Blow down the whole mountain."

BOOK FIVE

SHIASTAN

12

SUGAR MEN

2145Z 3 SEPTEMBER 2032, a warning order comes from Pete Petrocelli. Our group — now officially Team Bravo — is to be ready to
move out from PSAB in six hours. Aircraft and pilots have been assigned to us; we will not wait for rotation or for force availability;
we'll have our own birds and our own flyers. With Coombs, Chutes,
and el-Masri, I spend till 0400 staging our gear in the hangar we've
taken for our own and the rest of the night in the Air Control Center,
going over plans and contingencies with the rotary- and fixed-wing
pilots who will take us out of Prince Sultan and to our destination,
which, we are told, could be any of four different sites requiring six
different insertion schemes — nor have we been informed of the real
geo location of the landing zones; we are given only sector maps with
Americanized overlay code names (MSR Miami, Hill 321). We still
don't know what country, or even what region, we're dropping into.

This is Salter's doing. He has become, since Rob's death and the
Senate hearings nine years ago, a chess player on levels beyond those
customarily occupied by military commanders. He lets others know
the minimum necessary to perform their missions, nothing more.

Every scrap of information is meted out with multiple objects in mind—and for the eyes and ears of multiple audiences. Salter has taught himself how to leak and how to conceal, how to let specific individuals find out what he wants them to know when he wants them to know it, and how to keep them in the dark until a moment of his own choosing—all for his own purposes, which he reveals to no one.

He never speaks of Rob again. He attends the funeral alone. I'm not there. I'm with Tim Hayward, Chutes, and Q in the military hospital of the Israeli air base at Ramat David, losing three toes to frostbite and part of a lung to complications from pneumonia. I have lost twenty-seven pounds in eleven days. El-Masri and two of our Pashtuns are recovering in a separate ward from exposure, dehydration, and dysentery. Escape has taken not four hours as planned, but most of two weeks, on the ground, fighting all the way. I'm still in hospital—the Fifteenth Scottish General, in Gibraltar, by then—when Rob's body finally arrives home.

The funeral is at Arlington. Rob is a Silver Star recipient, along with three Bronze Stars with combat Vs and two Purple Hearts. That rates full military honors. Gen. Salter attends in civilian clothes. A.D. covers the event for *Topix,* the London mega-zine. The day is overcast with snow flurries and an icy wind off the Potomac. Mrs. Cole arrives early, alone. Two ex-senators (but no current ones) and four congressmen stand in the ranks. The remaining mourners are friends, family, and military. Reporters—of whom there are no fewer than fifty—are kept at a discreet distance by a Marine guard detachment.

Salter reads a single passage from Marcus Aurelius. He speaks not a word to the press. Maggie Cole comes no nearer to Salter than fifty feet. The pair makes no eye contact, nor does any intermediary pass a note or verbally convey a sentiment. Mrs. Cole leaves, driving her own gray Land Rover. Salter departs in a chauffeur-driven Lincoln town car, which spirits him directly to Dulles, where he boards a private jet—all this is A.D.'s reporting—with flight documents filed for Stensted, London. The aircraft is leased to Force Insertion.

When I return to the States in late February, a package is waiting for me. Inside are two Naval Academy rings—one from 1992, Salter's; and one from 2016, Rob's. A note in Salter's handwriting says this only: *In a hundred lifetimes, I can never repay you.*

A.D. has a second envelope for me with a return address from Lausanne, Switzerland. Two mornings later, a man flies in from that city to take me to breakfast. When he flies out, I have become the holder of an account in which resides $2.7 million.

Mrs. Cole sends a car to bring me for dinner, alone, at her farm in Middleburg, Virginia. She has two long letters from Salter, portions of which she allows me to read. She's emotional. Rob's death and its cynical exploitation by Salter's enemies, along with Salter's own departure under such conditions of disgrace, have devastated her.

Salter, she tells me, is in London. He has assumed command of all Force Insertion field units.

He has become a mercenary.

I remember at that time feeling sorry for Salter. What species of "assignment" was he likely to be honchoing for Force Insertion in some third world cesspit? Supporting the Spetsnaz on cross-border assaults into Kyrgyzstan? Protecting platinum extraction sites in Central Africa? Salter was a Marine; this shit must be hell to him.

But when I'd run into Salter in the field—by 2024 I was working these merc gigs myself—he looked lean and hard and even more charismatic as a privateer than he had been as a USMC three-star. He was a man on a mission, Chutes said once, though none of us could say exactly what the mission was. Salter moved like a deposed heavyweight champ, who trains and trains in his private camp in the mountains, waiting for a return shot at the title, which he knows will come again and which, this time, he'll be ready for.

I flew a dust-off with him one morning over Khartoum, in the middle of the north-south secession struggle in '23, when John Milnes of Fox/BBC wrote that "the confluence of the Blue and White Nile has become the Red Nile, incarnadined with the blood of innocents." Salter's old Jump CP — his mobile command post — remained intact, with Gunny Dainty and other vets now serving as contractors pulling down half a mill apiece. But there was an additional unit that none of us had seen before. The troops called them "sugar men." They brought the money. They were civilians — Yanks and Brits, but also Germans and Russians, Japanese, Indians, South Koreans, and Chinese. They had Salter's ear when the rest of us couldn't get near him.

I never asked where the $2.7 million came from that wound up in my bank account. But you had to wonder: if that much cash is flowing to me, how much more is being lavished on players in the echelons above? And since when did former Marine generals own the savvy to stash cash in numbered accounts in Geneva and Lausanne? Me, I'd never even heard of these fucking places.

Salter turned to the sugar men; they wrote the checks. Was all this *dinero* coming from just our employers? Nobody asked, least of all me.

Force Insertion's field strength at that time was six armatures with all supporting arms: sixty-seven thousand soldiers for hire. Elements were under assignment across seventeen separate theaters, employed by state, corporate, and humanitarian entities (including five for the UN) on every continent except North America and Antarctica. Overall direction of the firm remained, then, in the hands of its founder, Gen. Pietter van Arden. When the eighty-one-year-old visionary died twelve months later of pancreatic cancer, F.I.'s board put Salter in charge of the whole show.

That's where he remains now, a decade later, as Team Bravo — with me and el-Masri reunited — at last boards its first-leg transport craft, a leased Air Martiale C-130, and trundles down the runway at PSAB, eager to connect with its commander and be briefed by him on its assignment.

The flight is supposed to take us directly to Basra, a staging point en route to our ultimate destination, but halfway there something goes wrong up ahead. We're rerouted to Kuwait City. When we get there, the tower won't let us land. The pilots take us out over the gulf and start circling. "What the fuck's going on?" says Chutes.

We're all thinking: Salter's armatures control Basra and the southern Iraqi oil fields; what's the problem?

A C-130 is a lumbering, big-bellied turboprop. Our team of twelve is crowded forward, on canvas seats along the port bulkhead, just aft of the ladder that mounts to the flight deck. The rest of the cargo bay is taken up by a single 7-ton truck, two bladders of fuel, and a dozen pallets of ammunition, rations, and Solaire spring water — not for us, for delivery in Basra. While Chutes climbs to the cockpit to get the latest skinny, the team collects around Iranian FARS-TV, which Coombs is bringing in on his handheld. FARS is playing cell-phone and skycam video of street carnage in the Shatt al-Arab section of Basra. Force Insertion's assault elements are leveling the area, block by block, against fierce resistance by fighters that FARS and English-language al-Jazeera (we're switching back and forth) identify as local militias, possibly Fadhila; possibly JAM, Jaysh al-Mahdi, the old Madhi Army.

"I thought the fix was in," says Q, impressed by the fury of the resistance. "Who told these assholes to put up a fight?"

Nobody knows. I try to reach Pete Petrocelli. I even try Jack Stettenpohl. No one's reachable. What I know — what we all know — is that Iraq, since the close of the second Iran-Iraq war, has been the bulwark of stability in the Middle East. Oil is why. Big-time fields have come online or been revitalized down south: West and East Qurna, Zubayr, the colossal Majnoon field with thirteen billion barrels, the Halfaya field. By 2029, three years ago, southern Iraq was producing fourteen million barrels a day, equal to Saudi Arabia, even with its own two monster new fields at Shaybah and Khurais. The country had stabilized. Royal Dutch Shell is heavily invested, along with Malaysia's Petronas, Kogas from South Korea, Occidental, Italy's Eni conglomerate, and Norway's Statoil. I know these because our contracts are with them.

Originally, soldiers for hire only signed with the military contractor—Force Insertion, the Legion, DynCorp, whatever—which itself held the underlying contract with the end employer, the EE. But after the 2024 DynCorp mutiny at Khartoum, that changed. EEs began requiring individual mercs to sign contracts with them as well, including the infamous "forfeiture of all shares" clause. The second thing they insisted on was that contractors be paid only a tenth of their fee in cash; the rest was in stock or incentive bonuses, in contracts of marque or what we called "spec jobs," meaning you got what you could get in the form of resources—diamonds, oil, platinum—from the country itself.

As I'm thinking this, I hear Chutes return from topside and, crossing to Coombs's screen, key in a channel change. "Yo, Gent! Ain't this your old lady?" He passes me the tablet. Sure enough, center screen is A.D., ducking bullets on a smoke- and dust-obscured boulevard. The caption says AL-HUSAYN, BASRA.

My bride is crouched behind a concrete Texas barricade, wearing cargo pants, a dark blue flak jacket with helmet, and speaking into a Trump/CNN mike:

> . . . General Salter's plan appears to be to seize and break away from the central government of Iraq its six southern provinces—with these provinces' willing and even eager participation—so that this

entity can declare its political independence and found an entirely new state: the nation of Shiastan.

Shiastan, A.D. explains with the rattle of machine-gun fire in the background, is the ethnic and tribal "nation" constituted of the southern governorates of Najaf, Qadisiyah, Missan, Thi-Qar, Muthanna, and Basra, including the lands of the Marsh Arabs. It possesses 15 percent of the world's known reserves and is second in oil wealth only to Saudi Arabia.

Sources have hinted that Saudi billions may be behind this incursion. The aim is to block nuclear Iran from achieving its goal of establishing a "Shiite Crescent" that would extend from western Afghanistan through Iran and Iraq and into the oil-rich Eastern Province of Saudi Arabia. The Saudis have hired Gen. Salter and his 31,000 in-country mercenaries, these sources say. Once this region breaks away and is recognized by the community of nations, the new Islamic Republic of Shiastan will no doubt make long-term deals for said reserves with Salter's employers, whoever they may be.

None of this explains what's going on in Basra.

"Bank on this," says el-Masri. "The Saudis have lost their balls. They have turned off the spigot and now every Shia mob is greedy to fight."

I key my own holo and hit A.D. on the speed dial.

Baby, keep your head down.

When my message box lights up right away, I know the video on TV is a postfeed.

Where R U?

Above your head.

Craning around in my canvas seat, I can see Kuwait City below to the east. Our aircraft comes out of a bank and levels off, heading north. The crew chief has come over, with his thigh-holster 9 mm and his headset tethered to the comm panel. "Feet dry!" he grins and flashes us the thumbs-up.

Gimme something, Gent.

You know more than me, honey.

Bollocks.

While I'm pecking out this exchange with A.D., Chris Candelaria gets on the horn to one of his DSF buds from Nazirabad, who is on the ground at Shatt al-Basra. The worst of the fighting is over, the friend tells Chris. The video we're seeing on FARS and al-Jazeera is two hours old. Everything's cool. Aside from this one hot spot, Basra and the southern provinces are still with the program. In fact, just as Chris's friend's text rolls in, FARS-TV begins broadcasting, live, from Highway 6 against the smoking backdrop of what used to be a slum called al-Hyanniyah, a spokesman for the Waeli syndicate, the politico/religious gangsters who run the region. The dude is in a bloodied white dishdasha, speaking Arabic. There's no translation but among Coombs, Chutes, and me, we piece it together. "Authorities now have the city under control . . . an uprising of militants has been put down. We'll have more for you shortly."

I tell Chris to ask his friend what he believes is going on. We thought the deal had been sealed. Why is the city resisting?

Saudis pulled the plug.

The friend has to go. I get back to A.D.

You know something, Gent. I can feel it.

Darlin', stay safe.

I hate you!

In minutes we're over the city. El-Masri, Chris, Chutes, and the others grab their TNVGs—thermal night-vision goggles—and crane around in their seats to peer out the ports.

Basra lies below in the dark.

"Where's the smoke?" says Chutes.

The city looks untouched.

"There!" Q points.

Thermal vision goggles don't just magnify ambient light like the old Iraq-era NVGs; they pick up heat signatures and digitally reconstruct them. In their crimson cast, we can see one sector along the Shatt waterway that looks like it's been cleaned out by a five-kiloton blast. For what appears to be a square mile, not a stick remains standing. The place is smoking, a leveled plot of wild-cherry-tinted rubble.

"I don't get it," Quinones says. "The city looks cool except for that one Black Hole."

El-Masri eyes the moonscape. "Welcome to Shiastan."

There's a desert airstrip north of Basra called Hantush. It has no tower, not even a radio shack. But it does possess two full-length hardened runways, crossing in a shallow X. Corporate jets of Royal Dutch Shell, BP, and Petronas used the site in the '20s, as did the Third Marine Air Wing during Operation Iraqi Freedom in '03 and

Saddam Hussein in his day before that. Our C-130 sets down in pitch darkness, the pilots using TNVGs and riding the glide path set up by a laser comm team on the ground. The field itself appears slightly more hospitable when we waddle off the rear ramp and hump our 120 pounds of gear per man. A line of fire barrels can be glimpsed to the east side of the runway, with at least thirty vehicles, mostly Suburbans, Kodiaks, and Land Rovers, beside them — and a front of chemlight-illuminated tie-downs paralleling the tarmac, with the dark shapes of a half-dozen Black Hawks and Sea Stallions visible in a row. Port and starboard lies raw desert. A ground chief greets me, confirms my identity by three different parameters, including retinal scan, then leads our team on foot toward two parked War Hawks across the sand, on a separate hardstand. "Who's the company?" I shout over the taxiing 130's prop wash, indicating the line of civilian vehicles.

"Sugar men," says the chief. "Waiting for the boss."

We hear something huge and loud approaching. Out of the black drops a Lockheed C-5 Galaxy, massive as a Safeway.

"Salter," the chief says.

The plane touches down and rolls fast past our position, toward the north end of the runway. An on-ground combat team protects the aircraft; as soon as the jet's wheels touch down, three up-armored Humvees, a surface-to-air I-SAM truck and a CAAT antiarmor team roll out to protect it. I see Dainty, Salter's old security chief from Mosul, and an underaged buck colonel named Klugh, whom I don't know. I give Dainty a high five, but the colonel stiff-arms me.

"Hey, fucker," I tell him, "I was with Salter when you were popping pimples in junior high."

"Yeah?" he says. "Well, you ain't with Salter now."

As the security team rolls out, Dainty tries to smooth things over. "Don't mind Klugh, he can be a bit of hard-on, but he's aces in a scrap."

Team Bravo has reached the tie-downs now. Our War Hawk pilot, Maj. Mark Kelly, whom we know well from briefings at PSAB, comes up, shaking his head.

"Fucked again, Gent," he shouts over a rising wind.

"What?"

"Show's off."

Chris, Chutes, and Coombs hurry up.

The operation has been scratched, says Kelly.

"Just us?"

"Everything."

Kelly tells us the Saudis — our employers, apparently — have gotten cold feet. That's what went wrong in Basra, that's why the fighting. He points to the lineup of Suburbans, Kodiaks, and Simooms. "That's why all these low-rise motherfuckers are here."

I've heard shit like this so many times that I don't believe anything anymore.

Good or bad, nothing is real till it happens or it doesn't. I convey this to my team in no uncertain terms.

Everyone, keep your head in the game.

I make them eat. I make them hydrate. I make them look to their weapons. My cargo pockets hold a cache of airline-mini Johnnie Blacks; I pass them out like Tootsie Rolls. It helps.

The team stages its gear on the hardstand; Kelly's crew chief and door gunners are lashing their rotors to little steel X's countersunk into the tarmac. The flaps of our rucks are snapping in the rising gale. We can see Salter's Galaxy coming about at the extremity of the runway; already half a dozen VIP motorcades are maneuvering to intercept him as the plane taxis back.

"Who are these black shoes?" asks Q.

"Bankers." Chris Candelaria watches, paintbrushing sand from the receiver of his H&K Q6 over/under. "Each one of those bulletproofs is packing dudes with investments of 5B minimum."

"What are they here for?"

"To make sure Salter doesn't piss it away."

"Saddle up," I say. "We're getting in line too."

Salter's C-5 taxis back and comes to a stop. The sugar men's Sub-urbans and Kodiaks press around it. I lead our team up too, on foot, bringing Chris and el-Masri and Capt. Coombs, hoping one of us knows somebody who can get us aboard. The Galaxy's massive nose elevates and its rear doors swing wide, revealing a cavernous interior bathed in red night-vision lights. Salter emerges like he always does—no entourage, just him and his longtime aide, Pete Petrocelli. He wears an M9 pistol in a shoulder holster, in night camo with desert boots and no hat. He looks fit and trim. His hair is cut as high and tight as it was when he was a Marine.

I try to flag Pete down but it's impossible. The big shots sweep forward. In moments Salter and Petrocelli are pulled away.

I'm wriggling through the crush. El-Masri is at my shoulder. Suddenly I spot a familiar profile.

"Jack!"

It's Stettenpohl. In civvies. He's a third-term congressman now, ranking Democrat on the Armed Services Committee—and already being mentioned as a possible VP.

We embrace like brothers. I introduce him to el-Masri, to Chris, and to Coombs. He knows Chutes from East Africa. I point out Q, Junk, Mac, and Tony back outside the aft doors. "What are you doing here, man?"

"Same as you, Gent. Making money!"

Jack gets us aboard. He has been with Salter, he says, for the past ninety-six hours, through the meat of the whole Saudi-SoIraq fiasco. Our team shuffles up the massive steel boarding ramp to a galley aft; Chutes, Q, Mac, Junk, and our UAE troopers help themselves to Red Bulls, sandwiches, and microwave pizza. The C-5's scale is colossal, more like a ship than a plane.

Around the chow trough hovers a flock of youngish, executive-looking Yanks, Brits, Germans, and East Indians, wearing desert boots and sports jackets, several topped with cammie IBAs, individual body armor. Stettenpohl introduces us. These sprouts are hotshot VPs from investment banks and sovereign wealth funds, come to bird-dog their bosses' money. Chris recognizes two from Credit Suisse; another comes up from Jadwa Investing in Riyadh. We start shaking hands. There are reps from French Total, Menatep Bank in Russia, Onexim, Yukos, and Rossiisky Credit Bank. A guy hands me his card in German: Dresdener Kleinwort Wasserstein.

Topside on the command deck, the hatch to Salter's conference cubby is opening. Who emerges but my old buddy from the Highlands, former secretary of state Juan-Esteban Echevarria. He looks old and fat, sweating like a hog in the yards of material that make up his business suit. I have no inclination whatever to catch his eye or speak a word. Let his security team hand him down to his motorcade; I take a step back into shadow so he won't see me.

But a few minutes later I glance across the cargo deck and spot the secretary again, slumped against the aft bulkhead in obvious distress, with his team clustered around him.

He's sick. His detail is calling for a medical officer. I feel my secret self come forward. I stand and cross straight to Echevarria. The security men block me at first but a quick exchange and the Secy remembers me. "Colonel!" He waves me through.

"It's dust," I say, indicating the rising sandstorm outside. "It fucks everybody up."

I pull off my kerchief and douse it with water from a Solaire bottle; I make the secretary press it over his nose and mouth and breathe through it. "In thirty seconds, you'll be fine."

I sit beside him and talk him through it. He's scared, that's all. His ass is so wide, it takes up two seats; he's so heavy that his heart and lungs are overwhelmed in this heat and dust. I pluck the last airline-size Jack Daniel's from the cargo pocket of my trousers. The Secy takes it down in one snort; by the time the doc arrives, Echevarria is fine. He's grateful. I soak the rag again and make him press it to his forehead.

"So, Colonel, are you still undyingly loyal to your commander?"

"Will I disappoint you if I say yes?"

The secretary's breath is coming easier now. His color returns. "I must tell you," he says, "I felt for him. The loss of his son — and in such a grisly manner. But by God, he has caught the world by the balls since then!"

Topside, another group is exiting Salter's conference compartment. I ask Echevarria what errand has brought him here, to the middle of the desert in the middle of the night. "Not to collect money for another charity?"

The secretary smiles. "Colonel, I understand that you're something of an authority on tribes and tribal warfare. You know, then, how the sheikhs and *maliks* make sure to plant their own trusted men within the power structures of the enemy. That way, no matter who wins, their own and their tribe's interests are protected." Echevarria observes that Washington, D.C., is no different. "Such mischief, as I'm sure you were aware, was very much afoot in that hunting lodge where you and I first met. But you have no idea," he says, "of its daring or its depth."

How daring, I ask. How deep? The secretary leans closer.

"The hour shall come in America, as it has for all empires, when the franchise passes officially from the Many to the Few."

"The franchise? You mean the right to vote?"

"You're an educated man, Colonel. You've read of 'the Four Hundred' at Athens. And 'the Thirty' under Critias."

I stare at the secretary. Is he joking?

"I've trekked here to treat with Salter, Colonel, as Cicero once appealed to Caesar—to make the case that, when this Catalog of the Elect shall be compiled, my name will appear thereupon."

Can this be true? Overseas—and by that I mean any place where combat is imminent and the home turf belongs to the enemy—you hear crazier shit than you ever heard in your life. Every dude has a story; 99.9 percent are bullshit. You listen, you shake your head, you keep trucking.

How else can I take this? A former secretary of state (whom I have no reason to disbelieve) has just told me that a plan exists to heave the democracy of the United States into the shitcan. Yeah thanks, Mister Secretary. Now, if you'll excuse me, I've got real business to take care of.

Topside, another delegation is lining up to see Salter. I stand and extend my hand to Echevarria. Don't breathe outside in this dust, I tell him. Keep a wet rag over your nose and mouth. "And send your boys to scout up a few more Jack Daniel's!"

I won't let the secretary rise to shake my hand; he's still too wobbly. But as his ham-sized fist reaches up to take mine, I find myself feeling surprising affection for the old gaffer.

"Take care of yourself, Colonel. I hope we can resume our new friendship under more civilized circumstances."

Back at the chow trough, Chris and Jack Stettenpohl have hit it off like lifetime chums. They're talking finance. Meanwhile Coombs has run into a mate from Cambridge, which is apparently a hotbed of recruitment for the SAS, at least for a certain type of adventure-craving blue-blooded undergraduate.

My concern as team leader is to get to Salter ASAP and not let any of this extraneous bullshit bleed away our focus or resolve. It's impossible of course. We're stuck at a cocktail party and the gossip is flying.

How did this Iraq/Arabia operation get going in the first place? Coombs's Cambridge mate, Gillie, puts us in the picture.

"The whole stunt," says our new pal, whose full name is Fothergill, "was initiated a decade ago by a single individual—an Iraqi expatriate named Hussein Sayyid Assami. It was his idea to break Shiastan off from Iraq and take it public."

Fothergill explains how this expat made the rounds of wealthy investors in London, Riyadh, Dallas, Beijing, and twenty other petrocentric enclaves. "He positioned himself as a Western-friendly businessman—which he was—who possessed the tribal and political connections to broker a deal for the new al-Arish field, as well as taking a shot at Majnoon, Umm Qasr, and Rumayla. At the time these were badly underproducing, but Assami produced substrata projections that showed the fields were prime candidates for HPNI, high-pressure nitrogen injection. Assami was a petroleum engineer as well as an investment banker. When he talked, you were mesmerized. My uncle hosted an evening for him at the Chelsea Club. Assami made no attempt to disguise his ambition; he wanted to be the Man in southern Iraq."

Jack Stettenpohl confirms this. Assami put together over half a billion from various players to create an enterprise that would exploit these fields toward his own advantage. The deal was hot. In came the heavies—Goldman Sachs, Passport, Carlyle, CIC, and others. Chris backs this up. "I was working at Carlyle then; they recruited me because I had been here on the ground as a SEAL. Half a billion became two, then five. Then came the backstabbing, the inevitable revelations of fraud, self-dealing, and so forth. Soon the lawsuits started flying."

"By this time," Coombs's friend continues, "Sayyid Assami was history. The big guns didn't need him anymore. By now, a boatload of global banks and sovereign wealth funds had come on board, not to mention the energy conglomerates. Italian Eni was in for 4 billion,

Kogas put up 3.2; Petronas and Royal Dutch Shell were already operating the supergiant Majnoon field, but now they added 3.6 billion for HPNI; Occidental had 2 billion sunk in West Qurna. Statoil jumped in from Norway, with OAO and Lukoil, as well as the Iraqi government itself with South Oil and Missan Oil."

El-Masri squints around. "No wonder Salter can afford this battleship."

Force Insertion had been hired originally only to provide field and pipeline security. "Then," says Jack, "the Saudis got into the mix. With their cash, a whole army could be put into the field. The show went from an oil deal to a freaking invasion."

Everyone on the aircraft is waiting for Salter. We watch one frenetic party shuttle into his conference room on the third deck. "The Iranian foreign minister," says my new pal from Dresden. Two Slavic-looking groups follow, recognized by no one—Poles maybe, or Russians.

Finally Petrocelli tramps down. He's smoking, something I've never seen him do.

"Gent, can you hang for a few more? The boss is dying to get you topside."

He turns to speak to another group; I catch his sleeve.

"What's going on, Pete?"

"Cold feet."

I ask what that means.

"The money people behind this show. They just bailed."

"The Saudis," says el-Masri. "I told you they would turn pussy."

We wait. Topside in the tech bays, comm boards are lit up like New Year's. Kodiaks and Yukons keep rolling up outside in the dark, discharging fresh bods in various stages of hysteria. Chris comes back from palavering with a clique of his high-finance homies.

Indeed, he reports, the Saudis have yielded to world pressure.

"What's happening now," says Chris, "is every oil player on the planet is having a near-death experience. The lines are ringing off the hooks in Riyadh and London and Abu Dhabi. In Moscow, Koverchenko's head just exploded. Every satellite feed on the globe has some governmental spokesperson condemning 'this act of naked aggression' and demanding that the Saudis—meaning Salter—roll back every inch of real estate they've taken, like the Israelis did with the Sinai in '73."

"Will we?" Chutes asks.

"Beats the shit outa me," says Chris. "It's Salter's call."

For two hours, our team does nothing but knock back Red Bulls and monitor combat feeds. Scattered fighting is still going on—not between Force Insertion and the southern Iraqis, as the press is reporting, but between F.I. elements allied with the southern Iraqis against Iranian units, main force and fedayeen, which have crossed the border. It's no contest. The Waeli brothers have appeared on Fox/BBC, al-Jazeera, Trump/CNN, and Al-Arabiya declaring the independence of the sovereign Islamic Republic of Shiastan. Within ninety minutes, twenty-one oil-ravenous states have recognized the new nation.

I'm starting to get it. The key players behind these Big Oil and Big Bucks machinations are apparently a confederation of disenchanted Saudi royals—the young princes. The rising against the crown began with them. Their goal was power, not for their own advantage, but to preserve the kingdom and the House of Saud, which in their view was being sold down the river by the geriatric generation, who did not grasp or appreciate the threat from nuclear-armed Iran and its allies, including China and Russia, for whom the establishment of a Shiite Crescent composed of Iran, a Shia-dominated Iraq, Syria, and others was a desired end-state to counter the Saudi/U.S. alliance that had stood since the end of

World War II but that increasingly, from the Saudi perspective, was becoming a liability.

The princes were desperate to stop Iran. They couldn't employ force themselves; they had no real army and no authentic commander. But they saw a chance, by employing Salter and Force Insertion's four in-country armatures, to piggyback onto an existing operation and turn it into a miniblitz that would simultaneously thwart Iran, bring the world's second-largest oil reserves under Saudi control, and outflank their own brain-dead elders. It seemed like a good idea at the time. But now, in the face of blistering outrage from the world's military and financial powers, the princes have found themselves isolated and alone.

They are caving.

Instructions, apparently, are coming in right now over Salter's encrypted comm terminals, ordering him to stand down, back off, lie down, and die.

"We will learn now," says el-Masri, "what size balls our friend Salter possesses."

On this cue, Petrocelli appears topside along the rail. He waves us up.

The aircraft is configured into three levels; you climb up by a ladderwell. Level Three has two conference rooms, with a full kitchen, showers, and sleeping cubbies.

Salter appears. With him is Tim Hayward. Salter greets Coombs first, then Chris. El-Masri and I are the trailers.

"At last," he says, "my bandits."

Salter embraces us like a father. "Godammit, Gent, this whole fucking circus is worth it, just to work with you again."

He takes my hand and el-Masri's. He's thinking of Rob, I see it in his eyes. I ask him what's going on. Has the plug been pulled? Is our mission scrubbed?

"Fuck no, bro," he says. "You're going."

13

COMMANDER'S INTENT

THE MISSION, SALTER TELLS us, is a snatch-and-grab of the next head of state of Tajikistan.

Two teams. Alpha, under Tim Hayward, will eliminate the old boss. Bravo—my team—will install the new.

I glance to Chris, Coombs, and el-Masri. I'd be lying if I said my dick wasn't stiff.

"Who," I ask, "is Bravo's target?"

Salter gives me a look that says he's sure we've sussed this out long ago. "Qazi Ahmed Razaq, our old friend 'Razz.' "

Petrocelli hands us our orders packets, which we skim as Pete briefs us. Qazi Ahmed Razaq is the son of Habibullah Mohammed Razaq, the legendary Tajik warlord and current president and head of state of Tajikistan.

He—Razz—is the young Takfiri with whom el-Masri was imprisoned in Egypt in the early teens, whose life el-Masri saved by killing the guard Ephur. It is Razz who went on, seven years later, to become a warlord and drug trafficker on a scale even greater than his father. It is Razz who, many believe, was the funding source behind the 11/11 dirty-bomb attack on the port of Long Beach. And it is Razz, on that account, whom our TacOps team was pursuing in the mountains of northern Yemen when we were ambushed and Salter performed his "crawling man" heroics.

Today, more than another decade gone, Razz is the mullah/mass murderer/messiah of the IMT, the Islamic Movement of Tajikistan, the country's most militant insurgent faction—and the most passionate and dangerous enemy of his own father, who, in Razz's eyes, has sold out his people and his faith by becoming a stooge of the Russians.

Petrocelli affixes satellite and UAV surveillance photos to the whiteboard on the bulkhead, along with topo maps marked with mission-specific GPS grids and site nomenclature. Dupes, he says, are in our orders packets. Ground zero of the satellite imagery is a fortified compound—a torture house, Pete tells us—on the outskirts of Dushanbe, the Tajik capital.

"Sometime within the past six days," Pete says, "the target has been captured and taken into custody by agents of the Sekorstat, the Tajik secret police. Reliable intel—and I use that word advisedly—has Razz being held at this site. The situation looks grim. Our young friend is days, if not hours, away from public decapitation, if not worse, at the hands of his old man, unless Team Bravo can haul his miserable, U.S.-hating, smack-dealing ass outa there."

Bravo will have as assets, Pete tells us, significant host-country assistance. A team will meet us, guide us in, get us out.

Coombs will be our political representative; he'll handle whatever negotiations and undertakings of surety (meaning cash) are necessary to secure an alliance between Salter and Razz. El-Masri will be our interpreter and personal link. I'll run the tactical show and handle coordination with Tim Hayward and Team Alpha.

Petrocelli conveys this to us in under five minutes, while Salter looks on, saying nothing. The briefing takes place not in the aircraft's conference area (which is packed with suits and uniforms burning up the broadband), but in the galley immediately aft of the flight deck. Salter stands by the exit hatch, with a red fire ax on the bulkhead behind him and the rest of us jammed in anywhere we can. Jack Stettenpohl attends as well, along with our old battalion S-2 from East Africa, Cam Holland, both with dark circles under their eyes from too many nights without sleep. Salter himself, Pete has told me, has been going nonstop longer than anyone, but he looks flush with energy and resolve.

Now he steps forward.

"Gentlemen, events have propelled Bravo's—and Alpha's— mission to a level of supreme urgency. If you feel that I'm asking more than you're ready to give, speak up now."

Salter lays out the situation with the Saudis. Force Insertion's funding has been pulled, along with 99 percent of its political cover and 100 percent of its logistics and resupply.

Coombs asks how this affects Team Bravo's mission. Hasn't the Saudis' betrayal cut us off at the knees?

"Fuck 'em," Salter says. He is cold sober. "The world is witnessing a scenario it hasn't seen in four hundred years. A mercenary army has invaded a sovereign state and not only taken it over but convinced its indigenous constituents to support and embrace it."

"But can we carry on, sir, without the backing of our employers?"

"I don't know and I don't care. We're the power on the ground, not them."

The hair on my neck stands up.

Salter's voice has altered. I've never heard this tone before. It's electrifying.

The briefing finishes. Faces turn toward the exit.

"Wait a minute, Gent. Stick around."

Aides and principals take off. Salter dismisses Chris and Coombs. He leads me, Hayward, and el-Masri down the ladder to the aircraft's second deck, to a waist-high hatch along the inner curve of the air-frame. "Let's get some air," he says.

Salter wriggles ahead; we follow.

We emerge outside, onto the wing.

El-Masri is shaking his head and grinning. He's never stood on the wing of an airplane. Neither have I. I didn't even know you could go here. "Sorry," Salter says, indicating the AVFUEL stencils beneath our feet, "the smoking lamp is not lit."

We sit cross-legged in a half circle where the fuselage slopes up from the wing. A part of my brain is still spinning from what Echevarria confided. That part wants to quiz Salter for the full story. What's really going on, what's the big picture, what do you know, sir, that you're not telling the rest of us? But no one can ask that. The whole concept of a chain of command is that the boss gives the orders and the troops carry them out without question.

Then, too, there's awe. Though it's Salter's gift to make you feel like he's your pal and best buddy, closer to you than your own father, you can never forget who he is. Standing next to Salter is like standing beside Patton or Rommel or MacArthur. He's as near as your own flesh and as remote as Hannibal or Caesar.

"Gent, you and I have never spoken, have we, about Rob's death . . . and what you and Tim and el-Masri did to get my son's body back?"

"We haven't, sir."

Salter tries to continue. He can't. He turns his face away. I feel his hand reach out and touch mine. Every hair on my body stands up.

"I would have drained my blood for you, sir. We all would've — and we will now."

Salter still can't speak. He curses and blows snot from his nose. He straightens and turns back.

"You are my sons," he says.

He coughs and spits and swears again. He peers out into the night.

"What I say now," Salter begins, "is among us four only. When I'm finished, each of you is free to back out, with no hard feelings and your full fee paid."

I don't need to glance to the others; I know they're thinking the same thing I am. Nothing can make us pull out. This is what we live for.

"I want to install Razz, the son, in place of his old man as head of state of Tajikistan. Your job, Tim, is to eliminate the father. Gent, you and el-Masri will grab the son. Your two teams will be operating hundreds of miles apart, depending on changing circumstances, but you both have to strike at precisely the same hour, so that one team's move doesn't compromise the other's. It ain't gonna be easy. Gent, I want Razz alive. You'll have to babysit him. He's a handful." Salter tells us not to worry; the fix is in. "He'll go for this deal like a shark for a ham sandwich."

I glance to Tim and el-Masri. I love it that Salter can so casually declare, I want to install so-and-so as head of state of such and such a sovereign nation—and not only mean it but fully intend to carry it off, for reasons that he isn't about to confide in me, Hayward, or el-Masri—and about which none of us gives a damn anyway. Salter knows this. It's why he picked us.

"I know you're wondering," Salter says, "what I want from Razz and whether or not he can be trusted. The answer is I don't want anything and I don't care what he does. Just get him installed. One more thing: I may have to withhold information from each of you. Orders may change. Be ready for it. You yourselves may have to misdirect your men. Prepare them for that too.

"If the operation goes south, you'll have to make your escape on your own. I won't be able to help. In fact, I'll disavow all knowledge of your existence. I'm sorry but I can't tell you more. And I can't give you any glorious reason for hanging your asses so far over."

Salter meets our eyes, each in turn.

"You understand," he says, "that I wouldn't send any of you on a mission that I would hesitate to undertake myself."

We understand.

I understand.

"Two questions," I say.

First, why Tajikistan?

"Remember that briefcase," says Salter, "that you delivered to Maggie Cole in Scotland? It contained a geoengineering report about a newly discovered field at a place called Kooh-e-Khushruhi — 'Beautiful Mountain' — in eastern Tajikistan. That field is as big as Ghawar. A second Saudi Arabia. The most massive find in seventy-five years."

In other words, Salter says, out with Razz's father (who, if he's allowed to live, will no doubt sell the oil to the Russians), and in with Razz who, we hope, will make a deal with us.

I'm impressed.

"This is world changing," says Salter.

He asks for my second question.

I tell Salter that, since Scotland, I've had the feeling that I've been followed — and that the sensation has doubled and tripled since Cairo and PSAB.

"Russians," he says. "Gazprom probably, or Lukoil or the government, which amounts to the same thing."

From his expression, Salter has clearly anticipated this element; it is integral, apparently, to his design. "The Russians know you're working for me and they know you don't know anything yet. That's why you're still alive."

El-Masri nods appreciatively. "May I ask, sir? How many moves ahead do you plan?"

"As many as I can when men's lives are at stake. And it's never enough."

14

THE MERCENARY CODE

THE LAST THING TEAM Bravo does out of Hantush is sign contracts and make out our wills.

I've been through this drill with half a dozen outfits. The process is always the same: a rote speech delivered by some shaved-skull ex-colonel in an airless and sweltering (or freezing) Winnebago; then a short, lamely produced video hyping the (totally bogus) traditions of the company. There's an oath you swear and an appeal to your pride and self-respect. You promise you'll be loyal to your employer and won't bolt for Neptune the first time a bullet whizzes past your ear.

This time it's different. The contract with Salter has no talk and no video. It's one page. Each man signs individually. Then there's a group contract, which you all sign together, like the Declaration of Independence. It's meant to be emotional and it is.

We part from Team Alpha, then load up and board.

The two War Hawks take us on our first leg, south to Shatt-al-Arab (the town is still stinking from incinerated cement and human flesh). There we transfer to longer-range craft for the main haul — across the gulf and over portions of southern Iran to a hidden landing ground in the Panjshir valley in Afghanistan, northeast of Kabul. The first plane is a Russian An-24, which we had preloaded forty-eight hours earlier at PSAB. This will carry all the team gear, plus Coombs, Q, and Chutes with the UAE commandos and five Tajik mercenaries who've been added at the last minute by Pete Petrocelli. The second is an ancient PBY Catalina, which will carry me, el-Masri, Junk, and Chris Candelaria. The split-up into two elements is to ensure that the mission can carry on in the event of a mishap to one component.

A PBY is what they used to call a flying boat. Ours is a bona fide antique, complete with a brass WWII service plaque—rebuilt God knows how many times over the years and leased now to Force Insertion from one of its Bulgarian subcontractors, Teddy Ostrofsky's TulipCo, but owned and operated by an Alabaman who calls himself C.C. Ryder and copiloted by a corpulent cracker who C.C. claims is his son but who is obviously the same age he is, if not older. The purpose of using a seaplane is to defeat Iranian radar by flying so close to the surface of the gulf, says C.C., "that a boy can hang his dick out the hatch and drag the knob in salt water."

It's night and he's wearing Iraq-era NODs, notorious for their blunting of all depth perception. After the third unplanned skip off the surface at 140 knots, el-Masri unbuckles and crabwalks forward to the cockpit, where he attempts to incentivize C.C. to increase his altitude. When the pilot tells him to return to his seat because his fat ass is upsetting the trim of the ship, el-Masri bumps his offer to outright purchase of the aircraft. "How much are those Bulgarians paying you for this piece of shit?"

C.C. shoots him a baleful eye. "If you don't stem from the U.S. of A., partner . . . fuck off."

The plane's two engines are set close together on the wings, which themselves are mounted above the crown of the fuselage, so that the aircraft can make a water landing without the props churning into the sea. This setup provides exceptional visibility (PBYs had been search-and-reconnaissance planes during the war in the Pacific). You look down and see everything. This scares the snot out of el-Masri, who can discern only too clearly the whitecaps skimming a few feet below our boat-shaped prow, into which the dry-landing wheels are retracted and rattling around with an unreassuring clamor.

To check in with Petrocelli via satphone, I have to crawl forward past the pilots to what had been the observation bubble. This is a single-seat perch, where a hood ornament would be, so cramped that you have to breathe through your nose to keep your breath from fogging the plexiglass.

Sure enough, Pete has bad news. Our target, Razz, is no longer in the torture house in Dushanbe, where intel had said he was. His Islamists have tried to break him out. His father's secret police have fought these attackers off and spirited Razz away, Pete says, just before the whole hideout blew up.

"Where is Razz now?" I ask.

"No one knows."

I ask Pete about Salter and the Saudis. Any sign of reconciliation?

"I forgot," he says. "You haven't heard."

"What?"

"The boss just told the whole world to go fuck itself."

Salter had assembled his warriors, we will learn later, on the parade square before the Ministry of Justice in central Basra. This was four hours after we left him at Hantush airstrip. Those present on the square represented less than a twentieth of the deployed mercenary forces (the rest being occupied fighting or preparing to fight), but the cameras and video feeds of Fox/BBC, Trump/CNN, FARS, al-Arabiya, and al-Jazeera carried the pictures live to the full contingent—and to every street corner and public square around the world.

Men who were there said Salter showed no anger. He was cool. Nothing about him had altered.

He addressed the troops, standing on the hood of an I-SAM missile truck, amid a half-brigade-sized amphitheater composed of MRAPs, AA-11s, and Iraq-era Marine War Pigs. Apaches and Black Hawks streaked overhead. The show looked like a video game. It was a gun geek's wet dream.

In the center stood Salter, with his M9 pistol in its shoulder harness and his skull shaved high and tight.

Salter told his mercenary troops that their employers had gotten cold feet and had ordered the operation discontinued. Pressure from the United States and the European powers, from Russia and China and India and Iran, from the UN and world opinion, not to mention panic in the global oil and stock markets, had induced the venture's backers to agree to a cease-fire in place.

We troops on the ground, Salter said, have received orders to halt all offensive operations. We will advance to no farther phase lines and seize no additional objectives. United Nations peacekeepers will arrive within ten days. At that time, we are to surrender our posts and our weapons and deliver ourselves into the custody of such wardens and keepers as the world community shall appoint over us.

At these words, the first groan ascended. Salter held up his hands; the square quieted. Salter spoke into a hand mike. Huge rock-concert speakers had been erected behind him.

"Who would be a warrior for hire? What kind of man would hazard his precious life for something as coarse and easily acquired as money? Only a fool or a madman. That's what I am — and that's what you are too, brothers, or you wouldn't be here with me. But there is wisdom in our lunacy and cunning within our folly. For war, we have learned, is the crucible within which all that is base and unworthy is purged from our impure and polluted hearts. The god of strife sees to that. I worship him. He is my teacher.

"What principles has this divinity taught me? To hold true to my brothers, to subordinate my self to the greater whole, to donate freely the last drop of my blood — and to ask nothing in return.

"We are warriors. Our trade stands a handbreadth from that of the murderer and the assassin. Perhaps in another lifetime, you and I have committed grave crimes. This life now may be our purgatory. How do I absolve myself of those transgressions, which I cannot even remember? By sacrificing my ego, my greed, my fear, my hesitation, and my selfishness on the altar of strife.

"How do I perform this rite? By striding into harm's way for no cause, no dream, no crusade, but only for the striding itself and for the comrades at my side. Brothers — and when I call you my brothers, I speak the most profound truth, though I have never met most of you and may never see you again — I will die for you this instant. My life is yours, not because of anything I can gain from you, because I have that already, but as an expression of, and fulfillment of, the bond we share.

"Every warrior society has lived by this code. Drain your blood. Make yourself nothing. Stand at the shoulder of a tribesmen whose language you cannot speak, in a country you cannot locate on a map, and let him know without a word that you will give your life for him and his family, his clan, his tribe. What do you ask in return? Nothing. An unmarked grave on a hill with no name, in a cause you cannot understand and that no man will remember. That's what I offer, gentlemen. And as I look in your eyes, I see that you accept."

No cheers came yet. Instead the mass of men seemed to press, like a wave, more closely around Salter.

"We have been given guarantees by the world community," Salter declared, "that none of us will be prosecuted for actions taken outside of, or contrary to, the international conventions of war."

At this the men, who were already hot, tired, and pissed off, broke into a roaring jeer. Salter held his arms aloft, calling for quiet.

"Those are the instructions from our employers. I don't know about you, brothers, but I have four words for them:

" 'Take it to hell.' "

The first great cheer ascended. Salter again called for silence. It took what seemed like a full minute for the troops to stop whooping and whistling. Salter told them that he had pulled out of an operation like this once before; he would cut his own throat before he would do it again. Monumental ovations greeted this.

"Where am I gonna go if I back out now? Where are *you* gonna go?"

He told the troops that their employers had broken faith with them.

"Brothers-in-arms have been killed and maimed and blinded, acting upon the assurances of those who engaged us for hire. These brothers' blood is our surety. We've held up our end. Now all bets are off. We here are free to elect a new and independent course."

Riotous citations saluted this. The men cheered and pounded the flats of their weapons against their armor; they beat their rifle butts and the soles of their boots on the ground.

"Don't worry about money," Salter cried. "I'll get you your pay and I'll get you your bonuses. Our share of the oil in this ground will make every one of us richer than he ever dreamed. But that's not why I'm here and it's not what this is about. This is about us. It's about who we serve — ourselves or others? It's about whether we stand or kneel!"

Salter called for a vote. He would not compel anyone, he said. If you fault me, fire me. Strip me of command. But if you elect me as your leader, then follow me with all your heart.

"Do you trust me, brothers? Will you follow where I lead?"

Salter called upon the people of Shiastan to stand with him. Why shouldn't they? The rest of the world hated them as much as it despised him and his warriors. He appealed to the civilian drivers and contractors, and to the logistics teams who had come ashore with the expedition, whose role was to supply the troops for the next ninety days. Join us! Stand with us!

Then came the peroration that would be played over and over on cell and video around the planet:

> The world wants to know who we are. I'll tell them. As this force stands here now, it comprises the fifth-richest nation on earth and the ninth-largest mobilized army. You and I, brothers, represent the best-trained and most experienced military professionals in the history of the human race. We've got twenty-seven thousand on the ground here in southern Iraq and another nineteen thousand at Prince Sultan Air Base with all their fuel, ammunition, and transport. The Americans, the Chinese, and the Russians command us to stand down. The Saudis and the Iranians have ordered us to back off. Europe calls us criminals. They demand that we lay down our arms and go home. Go home to what? I've bowed beneath that yoke before; I'll die before I do it again. Are you with me, brothers? We stand in this hour upon the threshold of history. Do you trust me? Will you go forward at my side? Then stand by for orders. This campaign isn't over. It has not yet begun.

Aboard our PBY, my half of Team Bravo knows none of these specifics. We get only what Petrocelli can compress into a twenty-second sound bite — the troops have backed Salter. We've all jumped off the cliff. I relay this to Coombs, Q, Chutes, and the others aboard our sister plane.

All hands still in?

Fuck, yes.

Twenty minutes later an encrypted reroute comes in. We are to proceed to the old U.S. base at Pasni in Baluchistan, now in the hands of friendly elements of Pakistan's ISI, from which other air transport will convey us to Dalbandin, fifty miles south of the Afghan border, and from there across the Registan desert, up the Helmand valley and past Kabul. Our aircraft will have landing clearances at Bagram (our designation code is IC3, "humanitarian assistance"), but when we reach the Shomali Plains, we will drop off the scope and make for the original secret strip in the Panjshir. We'll overnight there at the Afghan HQ of RNI, the private intelligence agency that serves as Force Insertion's CIA. Two of Teddy Ostrofsky's Soviet-era Mi-24 Hind helicopters will take us north in the morning. By then hopefully some genius will have developed a lead on Razz's whereabouts.

This alteration in timetable is no joke, as the execution of our assignment must be coordinated with Tim Hayward and Team Alpha, as well as several other operations of whose specifics our team is not yet "need to know," but of whose schedule imperatives we, according to our instructions, will be apprised at the appropriate moment.

To further complicate matters, a coup is apparently in progress in Tajikistan. Chutes is our comms specialist; his plasma repeater can pick up regional radio and TV in real time even if the broadcast isn't satellite relayed. The system translates and closed captions too.

The army of Tajikistan numbers only thirty thousand; what holds the country together are an equal number of Russian "volunteers." According to our intel, these poor bastards are luckless conscripts, yanked off the streets and assigned to what, even to Russians, must feel like the asshole of the universe. Chutes reports that IMT rebel television on the far side of the mountains is reporting that one armored regiment has mutinied and seized a critical pumping station along the TUC, the Tajik-Uzbek-Cerna gas pipeline. Whether this is true or not (Tajik state TV makes no mention of it) or what its import may be for us, I have no idea. I remember only the wisdom of my old enlisted mentor, Master Sergeant Vaughn Telamon of Arcadia, Mississippi, regarding behind-the-lines insertions:

Change is never good.

But the pea keeps rolling. Both halves of the team reunite on schedule in the Panjshir. Morning of day three we fly out of Ahmed Shah Massoud's old base, bound north over the Pamirs into Dushanbe and Tajikistan.

BOOK SIX

TAJIKISTAN

15

JINGLY-JANGLY

DOWN WE COME INTO the disused Russian airfield at Kurkan, which is nothing but a flat pitch beside the Varzob River that looks like it was paved sometime in the 1950s and hasn't seen a patch of asphalt since.

The field was once a bustling Soviet base — Coombs has briefed us from his own time in service here — but is now used only by opium and armaments smugglers, most of whom are Russian military personnel using army aircraft. We ourselves have flown in, as I said, on two hired Soviet-era troop helicopters (which have had to make a pair of unscheduled stops, at Faizabad and Khoja Bahauddin, to replace clogged fuel filters), having braved the Amjuran pass in the predawn darkness to avoid getting stovepiped by the mujahideen rocketeers who camp at 12,500 feet in the narrow gorges waiting for a shot.

Dushanbe is the capital of Tajikistan. Coombs had been stationed here in 2024 with the SAS. Flying in, while the rest of us eyeball the terrain from a tactical point of view, our Brit launches into a rant on aesthetics.

"Look at this bleedin' arsehole, will you? Have you ever seen such hideous architecture?" We're banking in low, past a massive crenellated mosque sited amid an urban wasteland dominated by a desolate main drag upon whose flanks squat soulless apartment blocks, cube monoliths, and vast barren plazas. "This is Soviet totalitarian architecture, Stalinist Modern. God, what a horror!"

Coombs says he'd rather be in Afghanistan, which at least possesses aesthetic integrity, if only of impoverishment. "Look down there. That's not third world, it's fourth!" Our ex-SAS captain declares that he despises all isms, "ideologies that are based on some lunatic intellectual concept like the perfectibility of man or the efficiency of free markets. Give me a bleedin' break. This is what it comes to. Look at this place!"

I love a guy who knows how to bitch. Any moron can gripe about chow or rotations, but someone who can get exercised over architecture is my kind of dude.

Another of Coombs's tirades takes off on the abuse of the word *insurgents*. "What bloody 'insurgents'? It's their flippin' country! If you and I defend home and hearth, do we call ourselves insurgents? 'Stand still, insurgent! Hurry up, insurgent!' I'm glad I never got promoted past captain. The higher one rises, the more deranged become his faculties of discrimination!"

Kurkan airfield is vacant. We're supposed to be met by Russian contractors, who will provide us with ground transport and deliver the latest intel regarding Razz's highjacked location. But the tarmac is deserted; dust devils scour the weedy flat.

The Hinds whoomp-whoomp away as we deploy on the double, packing our 120-pound gear bags. Suddenly three Kamaz trucks appear out of the blowing grit, a thousand yards east, trundling toward us in echelon with their topside-mounted PKM machine guns and gunners muffled to the eyeballs in the whipping gale. It's September but it feels like midwinter.

We're caught in the open. Chris, Coombs, Chutes, Mac, Tony, Junk, and I spread out at as wide an interval as we can, prone and ready to fight. The Kamazes brake about three hundred yards out. A form pops from a topside hatch, waving both arms.

It's our Commies. They're late.

The most recent hot wire from Pete Petrocelli has informed us that we'll be met by a Russian contractor named Suvorov, a civilian. Instead we get a Tajik colonel who introduces himself as Amaz. He knows my name and asks if I speak French.

"The bayou kind."

El-Masri has come forward, ready to translate Tajik. Col. Amaz wants to communicate with me directly. He and I stand by the trucks in a freezing blow. My team has formed an HDP, a Hasty Defensive Position, facing inboard and out. I ask Col. Amaz where Suvorov is.

"*Il fallait eliminer Suvorov,*" he says.

"You killed him?"

"I command now."

This is my third crisis. The first two are ongoing: how to coordinate with Tim Hayward and Team Alpha, which can't make its move until they know we've completed ours, and with Petrocelli, who's juggling other in-country elements that I don't know about. The second is the coup, which these Tajiks may or may not know about or even be a party to. The clock is ticking and I'm the guy who has to watch it.

"All right," I say. "What now?"

Amaz's trucks take us off the tarmac to a double-wide trailer parked at the southern extremity of a mile-long junkyard of cannibalized Antonovs and Ilyushins. Inside, on a table, spreads an array of brown and white powders; red, yellow, and black capsules; bottles of vodka and trays of cigarettes of dubious origin. Amaz's men ring the vehicle, packing S74Us, the snubbed-up AKs with grenade launchers under the barrels. The men are dark, stocky Tajiks, clearly a different race than the lean Pashtuns of the south or the black-eyed, black-haired Mongoloid Hazaras of the north.

"*Pourquoi avez-vous assassine Suvorov?*" Why did you kill Suvorov?

"He wanted the money all for himself," says Amaz in French.

The colonel tells us to help ourselves to the alcohol and drugs. "*Pour votre equipe.*" For your men. His boss, who had been Suvorov's superior, expects us in an hour for a banquet. There will be plenty of blond Russian females with big chests and big asses who will do anything I or my men want.

Then he, Amaz, will take us to Razz.

I'm translating this for el-Masri, and louder for Chris and Coombs and our three Emirate operators who are just outside the door, trying to look nonchalant with their fingers on their trigger guards and their eyes on the horizon.

"How far to Razz?" I ask Col. Amaz.

"*Pas loin.*" Not far.

"Take us now."

"*Non. Mon chef.*" His boss. And he shrugs as if the decision is out of his hands.

My mentor Telamon has an axiom for occasions like this:

When in doubt with tribes or criminals, break out the cash.

I do.

I call for Coombs, who enters immediately. Amaz's share (what would have been Suvorov's) is a million bucks, which Chutes, Q, Junk, and Tony are packing in hundreds, eleven pounds apiece. From Coombs's North Face ruck that holds a reserve quarter mill I remove $25K, also in wrapped hundreds. "*Pour votre chef.*"

I set this wad on the table alongside the powders and pills.

Col. Amaz is too well mannered to take it himself. Instead he nods to one of his men, who with a practiced motion scoops up the parcel and stuffs it into his field jacket. It's a safe bet that the colonel's *chef* will not learn of, let alone acquire, a dime of this.

From the North Face ruck, I count out another fifty grand. I do not set this on the table. Instead I deliver it for safekeeping to Coombs, who stands at my shoulder in the posture of a second in command or bagman.

"Which of your men," I ask Col. Amaz, "will guide me, right now, to where Razz has been taken?"

"Comment?" Say again?

"Right now," I repeat. *"Tout de suite."*

It works. Within minutes Col. Amaz has split his motorcade, ditching the lesser players (who will, for certain, also be cut out of the revenue stream) and cramming Team Bravo into their slots.

We head east for the Pamirs.

Jingly-jangly is SAS slang for running a mission in hajji-flage, meaning dressing up like the natives. That, we learn later, is also the MO for Team Alpha. Alpha is eleven men, all former Turkish and United Arab Emirates Special Forces, commanded by Tim Hayward. Salter has promised each operator a quarter of a million bucks (and Hayward and his team leaders a million apiece) if they pull this off. Tajikistan, as we are beginning to grasp, is not really a country. It's a criminal narco-fiefdom locked in a death struggle with an Islamo-narco-fiefdom, which will soon become, with the integration of the new "Beautiful Mountain" oil field, a criminal Islamo-petro-fiefdom.

Razz's father—el-Masri tells us as our convoy speeds east—had been at one time an idealistic young revolutionary, an Islamist back when Islamism was unheard of. The old man had fought the Soviets, then the warlords and, after them, us. To buy guns and pay his militiamen, he needed money. The only way was drugs. Razz's father's men acquired and transported the raw poppy out of Afghanistan into Tajikistan, then shipped it via the Caucasus to Turkey, where it was processed into heroin and transported to Europe and the United States. Apparently the elder Razaq had become a little too close to his product.

El-Masri continues: "The old man never touched the shit himself, but he got addicted to the power. We heard about him originally in Egypt because he was a Salafist and a Takfiri like we were, a warrior of God. At least half the dope that funneled through Suez came from Tajikistan via the elder Razaq. The heroin trade was regarded as God's work because the poppy was destroying the infidel. Tajikistan became independent in 1991. The Soviet Union broke into pieces. The killing was worse than in Chechnya but nobody gave a shit because the Western press didn't cover it. The Spetsnaz was in there big-time, along with mercs from China, Uzbekistan, Vietnam, Mongolia. When the smoke cleared, Razz's dad was the last man standing. Only he was no longer God's holy warrior. He was a narco lord, who ran the country like hell is run by Satan.

"The Russians love that shit. They want countries on their borders to be as weak and as fucked up as possible, so they can pull the strings. I knew a woman named Irina, the wife of Razaq's finance minister, who used to run whores, and maybe still does, out of Syria, Egypt, and the north — Russians, Poles, even Swedes and English. Koverchenko and the others made it flow. The whole country ran on skag and overseas pussy. They had no courts. If you ran a red light, the cops killed you. If you published a pamphlet or a newspaper, they chopped your head off.

"The old man had a palace built for himself that looked like the imperial residence at Persepolis. He began calling himself Kyros, after Cyrus the Great of Persia, who, he claimed, his ancestors had killed in 550 B.C. Which actually was true. Not that anybody gave a shit. But Razaq/Kyros had this huge fucking palace filled with long-legged Russian poon and that was it, until young Razz the son came along."

Hayward and Team Alpha, el-Masri figures, are on their way right now to that very palace to knock off Razz's father, while we, Team Bravo, liberate the son.

"How much longer?" I shout in French to Col. Amaz.

"Bientot." Soon.

We are speeding into the mountains in a column of two GMC Kodiaks (with Amaz in the passenger seat of the lead truck and me, Coombs, and el-Masri in back) and the rest of our outfits in the Kamaz trucks and two Russian BMP-4s, tracked amphibious personnel carriers that can do forty miles per hour on paved roads while cornering like Cadillacs. El-Masri continues the story while Amaz, who supposedly speaks no English, plays a handheld video game up front.

The Egyptian recounts his days with Razz in prison, their release together, then the pursuit of Razz through the mountains of northern Yemen.

"For five years after prison I hear nothing from this bitch. I figure he's ashamed because of what happened; he wants to put it behind him — and he certainly doesn't want his new smack partners to learn anything they can use against him. I've got my own problems. I'm out of the secret service, trying to get a visa back to the States. I haven't thought of Razz in years. Then one morning an overnight package comes from DHL, from Lebanon. What the fuck? I open the box. Inside is a gold coin in a glacene bag with the profile of Alexander the Great on one side and the goddess Victory on the other, with a certificate of authenticity from the Central Asia Numismatic Society. A gift from Razz. The coin is from Scythia, 320 B.C. It's worth seventeen hundred bucks. Razz himself is in Beirut, he says in a note. He wants me to fly over. He has a job for me.

I can't of course. I'm on an entry list for the U.S.; if I leave Cairo, I'm fucked. I write him back and explain. I hear nothing. Now I'm curious. What is this sonofabitch up to — and why does he want me?

"You know the story, Gent, I told you in Cairo, but I'll tell you now, Coombs. Razz has fallen afoul of his old man. Since prison he has gotten even more militant; he reads Sayyid Qutb and Ibn Taymiyah; he's become a hard-core Takfiri like we were with the Brothers, which means he believes he can decide who's a good Muslim and who isn't and then kill whoever isn't — which he has decided, now, is his old man. He breaks off all dealings with his father. Now they're competing for the heroin routes. The roles have reversed! The kid has become the zealot that his old man used to be. He's playing mullah in the mountains, trying to take down his father, and he's got followers all over the country. This goes on for years.

"To make a long story short, three weeks ago I'm watching Trump/CNN in my factory in Damietta and suddenly there he is — freakin' Razz, in the Pamir mountains with a jihadi beard, a *shalwar kameez*, and packing an AK! So I put him on RSS. Two nights later . . . he's busted! The old man has put ten mill on his kid's head, dead or alive, and his secret police have snatched him, no doubt intending to disembowel the ungrateful pup on Tajik national TV. Two days later I get a call from the son of my old boss, Col. Salem (the son is now a captain in the Egyptian Islamic Police), telling me to expect a visitor from the States. That's you, Gent. I thought Salter might have sent you to whack me, to shut up everything I knew about Razz. But when you said you had a job for me, I knew we were going after the bitch. Which brings all of this up to the moment."

El-Masri indicates Col. Amaz and his driver in the front seat.

"These fuckers we're riding with work for the old man. That's why they killed Suvorov. But they're selling their boss out for that ruck full of greenbacks." He turns from me to Coombs. "After they waste us of course."

"How?" asks Coombs.

"If it was me," says el-Masri, "I'd set up a fake checkpoint. Our trucks stop, the guards walk up . . . *b-b-b-brip,* we're statistics. Or they could take us alive and saw us off at the neck on the six o'clock news alongside Razz."

I ask el-Masri what he thinks we should do. Up front, Col. Amaz is still thumbing his PlayStation. His translator is riding in back where he can't hear us. "We can wax these assholes now," says el-Masri, "but then how will we find Razz? Plus that squad radio on the colonel's shoulder is hot miked. If we make a move, those BMPs behind will light us up like the Fourth of July."

Coombs observes that these Kodiaks have 800 cc batteries. He's thinking of slotting the lot, as the SAS would say, then wiring the colonel's testicles till he comes up with a road map to Razz.

At this moment, my own satlink chirps. It wants an encrypt code. Around my neck is a thumbnail-sized randomizer; I read the code on its LCD display and enter it into the phone terminal. I press the headset tight to my ear. From the receiver comes Petrocelli's voice.

Pete spits out a change in orders.

"Understood," I say. "Copy all."

Coombs and el-Masri turn toward me.

"That was Pete. The mission's blown. Someone has put the old man wise to the plan. He's moving now to cap young Razz. If we can't get to him in an hour, our orders are to get out."

Silence. Our host keeps playing his video game. I lean forward to the front seat and speak in French: "What do you think of all this, Col. Amaz?"

He answers in English. "I think it is rude for your friends to speak with one another in a foreign language, in front of one whom they believe cannot understand it."

16

TEAM BRAVO

COOMBS PRESSES THE MUZZLE of his 9 mm against Col. Amaz's neck.

Our vehicles are careening up an unpaved mountain road above the Varzob River—night, no lights. Blinding dust from the Kodiak in front coats our windshield so thick that the beating wipers only smear it into an even more impenetrable paste.

Amaz has made a deal with us. He wants all the money. He admits that he had planned to kill us. But now he likes us. In return for both rucks of cash, he will deliver Team Bravo to Razz's jail, get us in safely, and get us out of the country when it's over.

"But I want the money *before*."

The colonel is communicating now over his squad Motorola, in some Tajik dialect, guiding the Kodiak ahead of us. The Kamazes and BMPs have long since been left in the dust.

"Time?" Coombs quizzes me, meaning how long since we started on our allotted one hour.

"Ninety-five minutes."

No need to confer. We're all in till the finish. We'll break Razz free or make our widows rich trying.

Suddenly the lead Kodiak slews off the track and brakes. Amaz's driver follows. We screech to a stop in a tornado of grit. The mountain rises on the left; a precipice plunges to the right. "We walk from here," says Amaz.

Coombs drags the colonel out. Amaz's posse covers us with AKs and one Russian PKM. "Where are they?" I demand.

"Where are what?"

I press the cutting point of my K-bar knife beneath his jaw.

Chutes hurries over with the GPR, the ground-penetrating radar. "Three artillery shells," he says, "buried right beneath us. One-five-fives, daisy chained."

I tell Chutes to scan both sides of the track.

"You will find two more across the road," says Amaz. "They will not be detonated while I live."

I order Amaz to bring all his men down from the hill. Six appear, bundled in *pettus* and winter cloaks—plus his interpreter and the three in the lead Kodiak.

"Tell them to man this point as an ambush. Hit anything that comes up behind us." I grab Amaz myself. "You and your guide come with us on foot. When we've got Razz, we'll bring you back here with the cash. And remember: no Razz, no money."

I know Amaz is planning on cutting his confederates out. He's got a backdoor somewhere up ahead; either that or he's in with whoever is holding Razz. But he's smart. "How do I know you won't kill me and never come back?"

"I'll leave two of my men here. If I'm not back with you safe and sound, your buddies can do their worst."

Ten minutes later we're humping up a goat trail so steep we have to claw our way by hand and so narrow we have to walk it like a tightrope. The night is ink. I have left Chutes and Q with the Kodiaks. We have stripped down for a cross-country hump, jettisoning body armor and half the contents of our gear bags, though the load for each of us still makes nearly seventy pounds. If we have to assault a fortified compound, we'll need all that and more. Every man voluntarily packs the max in rounds, grenades, and water—plus boots and heavy woolen shalwar kameez, K-bar knife, squad radios, PVS 24 unit radio with headphones, two GPSes, batteries for all, NODs, ropes, grapnels, explosive kits, hooligan tool, med packs, smoke grenades, flash-bangs, two PDMs (Pursuit Deterrent Mines), M67 frag grenades, chemlites, extra headset for radio, M9 pistols with ammo, M4-40s with M240 grenade launcher underslung (four grenades in bandoleer), EO TECH sight, PEQ-4 laser sight, and ten 20-round magazines. I'm carrying a sawed-off Winchester 101 twelve-gauge. Chris Candelaria packs an SPR sniper rifle with suppressor for killing dogs.

"Set the GPS for behind that rise," I say, indicating a hide three hundred yards downhill from this site. Chutes and Q will net up and camouflage the Kodiaks there. "That's our rally point."

Chutes and Quinones are bitterly disappointed not to be in the assault team, but they make no complaint. They help with the load-out.

Amaz estimates the distance at one mile to the compound where Razz is being held. The trek will take at least two hours. I form up the men at the high side of the road.

"Everyone hydrate. Eat. Get something into your belly. Piss and shit now."

I note the time.

El-Masri and Amaz jostle at the trailhead. They hate each other already.

"Go on," says the colonel, indicating the rising slope.

El-Masri bows like a courtier.

"After you."

———

The compound where Razz is being held is an abandoned Russian radar installation, sited in a barren, stadium-sized bowl beneath peaks whose summits are already dusted with snow. It has taken us three hours and ten minutes to get within sight of the objective, climbing straight up and straight down across three five-hundred-foot gorges. We are all so cold by the time we reach the overlook that we can't make our fingers close around our weapons, and so exhausted that our body heat has dialed down to a flicker. We have left our winter gear behind to save weight. That's the bad news. The good news is the sentries guarding the compound are just as cold and miserable as we are. Two at the central chicane have bundled themselves inside sleeping bags on the seats of a UAZ jeep with the motor running and the heater going. Two of the three guard towers are unmanned.

Amaz has not stopped bitching the whole way. At each crest he has sworn on his children's souls that the post is just over the next ridge and demanded his money and the keys to one Kodiak. At each crest: nothing. We haul him upslope and belay him down. Three times Coombs and I have had to stop el-Masri from chucking him off the mountain.

"Where are you leading us, you lying dickwad?"

The Egyptian has stripped Amaz of his pistol and two concealed blades.

"What do you think this sheepfucker will do with Chutes and Q if we let him get back to the trucks—not to mention us, before or after?"

Amaz has guts though. He keeps demanding his money and keeps vowing that the compound is just over the next hill.

Now there it is. I send Chris and one of the UAE men ahead to take out the snoozing sentries. The rest of the team enters the compound from the upslope side, bolt-cutting a fence and a six-foot band of concertina wire, then dashing through the shadows of the two dozen corrugated tin buildings that make up the ancient post. Junk sprints to the gate and lets Chris and the UAE men in.

Col. Amaz points out the building where Razz is being held. "He's lying," says el-Masri.

I take Chris and one UAE man, who calls himself Mike, to recce the site from inside the wire. We pass through one section of the compound and discover a second area, on a flat downslope from an abandoned radar dome. Mike taps his ear, meaning "What's that sound?"

Music.

Five corrugated tin buildings squat in a cluster. We creep closer. Loud Rooskie rock is blasting from Building Five. I swear I smell hashish. I call Amaz up.

"That's the one," he says.

"What about the earlier one?"

"Things look different in the dark."

I call up the team and divide it into two assault elements and a security element. I'll go in first, through the rear. We crunch closer. I'm stacked with Coombs, Junk, and el-Masri, who holds Col. Amaz on a leash, flush against a generator shack twenty frozen feet from the building. Mac, Tony, and the Emirates guys dash into position, sealing forward egress. Techno-trash blares from inside. Junk pads up beside me with the hooligan tool. I'm so cold that the muscles of my jaw have entered rigor mortis. I can't speak.

I motion: ready. Junk sets the hooligan's claw against the jamb. He braces to spring the lock. Suddenly the door opens from inside.

A man in a Russian fur hat stands there.

I pile into him like a linebacker, jamming the muzzle of my Winchester beneath his jaw and body-slamming him to the deck. Coombs, Junk, and el-Masri burst in behind me. I hear women screaming. A table overturns. Guards have been playing poker.

There's no firefight. In ten seconds Chris, Coombs, and Junk have stripped every man of his weapon and spread-eagled them facedown on the floor. I throw my guy into the pile.

A stream of profanity pours from one captive beneath the table. Chris kicks the man in the head.

"That's him!" shouts el-Masri.

Razz.

Coombs and Chris drag him out. Junk is flex-cuffing the others. The guards are shouting something in Russian that either means "Fuck you!" or "Don't shoot!" Probably both.

Razz unloads a broadside of abuse at Chris and Coombs. He tries to thrust himself between them and the security men, who are all civilians in European garb. He trips and crashes.

"They're with me!"

Now we see the women. Four blondes and a brunette, all impossibly gorgeous. "Russian hookers," says Coombs, who is already jabbering with them in Russian. I can't believe how good-looking they are. They're in furs and silks. One wears a Cossack cap; another sports a top hat.

Razz is on his feet now. He has figured out I'm the boss and is cursing me furiously in Tajik or some other alien tongue. I cross straight to him and punch him in the face. He drops like a sack of shit. Techno-rock continues to blare. Coombs is interrogating the Russians. Who else is outside? I send Junk with the Emirates guys to form a hasty perimeter. I want to be out of here in seconds, not minutes.

El-Masri hauls Razz to his feet. I have been curious to see how the Takfiri youth will act toward the Egyptian secret policeman who saved his life in prison. Razz gives him zero props. Instead he demands money—the million bucks that he knows we've got for Amaz, plus the five million Coombs is authorized to deliver on top of that. El-Masri cuffs him hard. The Egyptian has reverted to his secret-police role. He seizes Razz by the hair. "What are you on, you fucking shitworm?" He backhands Razz across the mouth.

"I will eat your heart," says Razz.

"Answer me!"

Now they're both bawling in Dari. I hear el-Masri call Razz a bitch. Razz spits in his face. I grab him. "We're outa here — now!"

Razz won't go.

"Friends!" he shouts. "We are friends!"

Razz hauls two of the prostitutes forward.

"These are for you," he says. He swears he has brought these beauties here specially, just for us. "Take a look. You ain't seen nothing like this never." He tears the top off one six-foot blonde, revealing the most spectacular pair of headlamps any of us has ever seen. "And these jugs is real!" says Razz, grabbing my hand and giving me a test squeeze. "Not plastic like your bitches in Hollywood."

He shows off the other babes' legs and asses.

"I am not going nowhere," Razz declares, "till every one of you has fucked every one of these. You think I'm kidding? You! Team leader!" He grabs my arm. "Go first. Show us how Americans fuck!"

Col. Amaz creeps forward toward the women. His eyes are the size of pie plates.

"What are you afraid of — HIV?" Razz confronts our team. "These girls go to university! Here is snatch that can quote Dostoyevsky!" He accuses us of having no balls. "Are you queer? What is wrong with you? Prove you are not pussies like the Russians say you are!"

I order Chris to flex-cuff Razz. We go now!

"If you Americans got no sack," Razz says, "let this Tajik show you." He claps Col. Amaz on the back. "His dick is standing tall. He knows world-class poon when he sees it!"

Razz turns to Coombs, as if to clap his back too. Instead his hand slaps the Brit's shoulder holster, jerks hard, and pulls free. Razz's right arm straightens, into Amaz's face. I see muzzle flash and hear the walloping bang of a Czech Nagy 9 mm.

Amaz's body hits the deck before I can even turn.

The girls shriek in terror. The room rings from the gunshot. El-Masri seizes Razz; I wrench the pistol from his grasp. Everyone but Razz is too stunned to speak.

"Now," he says. "Give me my money."

It's almost dawn as our Kodiaks weave at high speed along Rudaki Prospect, the only civilized sector in the capital, Dushanbe. Crowds flood from side streets. Masses are streaming in aboard buses, minivans, farm tractors. Q drives; Razz navigates, up front.

We have given him Amaz's million; the rucksack lies on the floorboard beneath his feet.

The plan has changed half a dozen times since our party started down from the mountains. First, emerging from the compound, Team Bravo comes face-to-face with at least a hundred Islamist militiamen, Razz's mountain guard, streaming down from the hillsides, where apparently they have been under cover for days. At Razz's order they empty the prison building, marching the prostitutes and the security men into the dark. God help all of them. The militiamen drag Amaz's body outside the gate and leave it for the wolves.

Us? We are aces in the insurgents' eyes. We have come for their prince and will soon install him on the national throne. When I ask Razz about Amaz's men waiting below at the roadblock, he mimes a pistol shot, execution style.

"They have left this earth an hour ago. Your men are safe."

Razz tells me his father has been executed too. Team Alpha has taken care of that.

"I rule now," Razz says.

This new reality is confirmed by hot wire from Pete Petrocelli, which comes as our Kodiaks speed into Dushanbe. Pete tells me that militant *lashkars* — tribal armies — are converging on the capital. I tell him I can see them; they're on the road with us — Pajeros and Hi-Luxes and BMPs.

Pete tells us to pull up GlobeNet on our handhelds. An armored regiment of the 201st Motorized Rifle Division (which had been Russian but is now Tajik) has revolted, says al-Alam and al-Jazeera, seizing a key distribution junction on the TUC pipeline. The commander is calling on his brother officers to take their units out in Islamic revolt. Razz is their Osama bin Laden. They have oil and power; the world belongs to them.

I'm watching this on Chutes's laptop. "Are you sure these are our guys?"

Pete laughs. "I'm bringing in Trump/CNN right now to interview 'em." He asks me have I got the kid, meaning Razz.

"In the seat in front of me."

"Tell him the TV station's blown. He's gotta do the palace."

Petrocelli and I trade ninety seconds of coded instructions, by the end of which I have a new timeline and GPS coordinates for extraction and a new mission.

Pete clicks off. I turn to Coombs, Q, Chris, and el-Masri.

"Remember Mussolini on the balcony?"

They don't get it.

"According to Pete, there's a hundred thousand crazed Tajiks massing right now in front of the presidential palace." I indicate Razz in the passenger seat. "Our boy's gonna address 'em."

Eight in the morning and the palace has been looted to bare bones. The hundred thousand mad Tajiks have turned into three hundred thousand. At least five hundred pack the royal edifice; a body-guard of bandits clamors around Razz, ecstatically swearing fealty. El-Masri is jabbering with them in Tajik. The outlaws pound Team Bravo's backs and thrust bottles of anise liquor into our fists. They will erect statues of us. We have brought them their prophet.

Razz climbs out of his Adidas tracksuit, which he has decided is not presidential enough. One thug donates his pettu and shal-war kameez; another chips in boots and a Doctor Zhivago wolfskin hat. Someone hands Razz an AK. Razz tugs me aside. Grimly: "You know what you must do?"

"Do your thing first."

We squander the next hour, struggling to satisfy the aesthetic caprices of the camera crews from Trump/CNN, SkyNet, and Fox/BBC. They don't like Razz's beard. They don't like the balconies. The sun isn't right on the first one, sound is lousy for the second, there's no angle for the cameras on the third.

Petrocelli is back on the wire to me, demanding that we get on-air ASAP. The time difference to London and the States is criti-cal. "This has to go live, Gent."

"What am I, Pete, a TV producer?"

"Gent, get the dude on the air!"

I tell him I'm a warrior, not Captain Kangaroo. I turn to Razz, who has been slugging Stoli Cristal from the bottle for the past forty minutes. "You're on, Mr. President."

Razz spits a mouthful onto the floor. "You don't set the timeta-ble, asshole," he tells me. "I do."

"Please," I say. "Pretty please."

The virus of acquiring real power has only infected Razz for the past four hours; already he has become Tito, Saddam Hussein, and OBL. His royal guard of mountain mujahideen has been augmented by an armed-to-the-teeth posse of city gangsters, tribal man-killers, and narco hoodlums.

I turn to Chutes, who's got the INMARSAT radio. "How close is the bird?"

"Here in twenty."

I tell Chutes to have the chopper that will extract us set down directly behind the palace, on the paved plaza. And keep its rotors cranking.

A TV producer waves Razz forward, onto the balcony. The heir steps up to a battery of mikes. An ovation ascends.

"He's the fucking pope," says Q.

El-Masri and I move back out of the cameras' sight line. The office and its balcony belong to the Ministry of Agriculture. Pillagers have looted everything, down to the curtains, even the poles.

Razz begins speaking. El-Masri translates. Razz is talking about oil. The new find at Beautiful Mountain will be "a second Saudi Arabia." Its wealth will restore Tajikistan to its ancient glory.

A bark of approval rises, then a low rolling cheer. Razz cranks up the emotion. He's good. Like Hitler, his rhythm is mesmerizing.

"The motherland possesses wealth," Razz declares, "on a scale beyond imagining. But we will not let it be stolen this time. Not by my father, may his soul find peace despite his crimes and greed, who would make deals with the Russians and steal for himself whatever was left over . . . not by the Russians themselves, who would make us their slaves if we let them . . . nor by the Chinese, whose lust for the property of others knows no limits and whose armies will be massing on our borders in a matter of days if not hours."

Ecstatic applause ascends. I eye the Western cameramen. They're zeroed on Razz like a school of piranha. History. They are recording it. They are making it.

Razz ratchets the rhetoric higher. Tajikistan's riches, he swears, will not be plundered by native criminals either. He himself will stand guard over it, night and day, unsleeping, to ensure that each Tajik warrior, each family, each clan, each tribe gets its fair share.

"Neither, brothers, will the insatiable Americans thieve our bounty. I have manipulated the friendship of General James Salter and his mercenary armies to the purposes of our God, our nation, our freedom, and our glory. He will make us rich, but we will not bow to him. We thank you for your assistance, friends" — he gestures to me and Team Bravo — "and now begone!"

At this erupts the mightiest cheer yet. Razz's muj and narco-underworld posse brandish their AKs and S7s at us, whooping and jigging.

Three hundred thousand Tajiks surge beneath the balcony. Razz calls down the blessings of heaven upon them and their countrymen. He dedicates himself, body and soul, to their service. The crowd goes orgiastic. With a flourish, Razz vacates the podium, sweeps back inside, pushes through the ecstatic embrace of his worshippers, and marches straight up to me.

"Now," he says with blood in his eye, "finish it."

I turn to Chris and Chutes, indicating el-Masri. They seize him. The Egyptian goggles in bewilderment. I level my shotgun at his solar plexus.

Razz is waving his bodyguards back.

El-Masri understands. "You motherfuckers," he says.

Chris and Chutes react, as thunderstruck as he is.

"Orders," I say.

"Salter," says el-Masri.

Razz leads us down the stairs, into an office off a rear hall. He bolts the door, leaving his posse packing the corridor. "Do it now," he commands me.

El-Masri shakes free of Chris and Chutes, with an expression that says, *You don't need to hold me, I can face death on my own.* Coombs, Q, and Junk cover him reluctantly with their weapons. They know nothing either. It's all me. I'm the only one who has received the orders.

"Prison," says el-Masri to Razz. "That's why."

"I rule Central Asia now. No one may know the things you know of me."

"You were a bitch then and you're a bitch now."

Razz backhands el-Masri across the mouth.

The Egyptian wallops him back.

Chris and Chutes seize el-Masri again. I raise the shotgun.

The Egyptian meets my eyes. "Once I called you sentimental, Gent. But I'm the guilty one. I believed you were my brother."

I release the safety.

"Do him now!" shouts Razz, wiping blood.

I raise the muzzle and pull the trigger.

Point-blank the blast has no range to disperse. The pellets hit Razz's chest in a tight group. Lungs, heart, and dorsal spine explode out of his back. His body blows rearward and crashes to the floor like a wad of dirty laundry. El-Masri and the others gape in befuddlement.

"Change of orders," I say.

El-Masri's knees are wobbling. He grabs my shoulder. "You scared the shit out of me, bro."

Sixty seconds later Team Bravo is piling into the waiting War Hawk. The mass of Tajiks take half that time to grasp what has happened. That's our head start.

In twenty minutes our chopper has set down at Kurkan, the abandoned strip where we originally landed. Ninety seconds more and we're wheels-up aboard an L-100 piloted by Dimitri and Dimitri, climbing over the cotton country west of Dushanbe, bound for Karshi-Khanabad Air Base in Tashkent, on our first leg back to Basra.

I can't raise Petrocelli on satellite or AKOP. Someone's jamming all transmissions. It takes an hour, till we're clear of Tajik airspace, before I get through to Pete's stateside counterpart, Tim Mattoon. Mattoon has monitored Razz's speech and the hysteria in the aftermath of his assassination live on FARS, Trump/CNN, and Interfax.

"Well done," he says.

I'm more than a little sickened by the act I've committed — and I still don't understand its purpose.

Col. Mattoon tells me to key the encryption tab on my handheld. I do. Onscreen appears a live feed from ITV-Moskva.

"Those are T-79 tanks," Mattoon says, "rolling south from Mother Russia through Kyrgyzstan and across the Tajik frontier. Three Chinese armored divisions will be crossing from their own border within twenty-four hours. The Russians and Chinese will be fighting over Tajik oil for the next twenty years."

Now I'm completely confused. "That's why we took out Razz and his old man?"

"You mean you haven't seen SkyNet?"

I tell Mattoon that we've been a little preoccupied, trying to save our own asses.

He keys in a patch for me. My screen flickers. Into focus comes a live feed of Salter leading a column of I-SAMs — state-of-the-art mobile antiaircraft batteries — along a desert highway with a massive petroleum-processing complex in the background.

"While your team was in Tajikistan," Col. Mattoon says, "Salter struck at the Eastern Province of Saudi Arabia."

"What?"

"He just took the Saudi oil fields. We've got Ghawar, Shaybah, and Khurais. Force Insertion is sitting on fifty-seven billion barrels. Fifty years' worth of crude."

BOOK SEVEN

POTOMAC

17

PLAYERS

I LAND AT DULLES International Airport at 10:37 P.M., 13 September 2032. A.D. is waiting, standing next to a limo driver with a handwritten sign:

GENT

My wife had flown back from Basra two days earlier; she and I have been communicating by handheld throughout all three of my flights home. She won't tell me what has pulled her off such a hot story. It can only be one thing—an even hotter story.

For thirty-six hours the news has been wall-to-wall Salter and the Saudi oil fields. The coup is so brilliant (and so bloodless) that the U.S. press doesn't know whether to react with outrage or exultation. The presidential campaign has been body slammed; the blow is a blind-side hit to the oil, credit, and stock markets, the banks, and the economy. At one stroke, Salter and Force Insertion have turned the world on its head, and no one knows when or if it will ever be right side up again. Our mercs have wired half the globe's oil, ready to blow it to kingdom come if any force attempts to wrest it from them. I confess I didn't see this coming either. All Salter has done is misdirect the world's attention for a few days to Iraq, Iran, and Tajikistan, then turn loose his seventeen thousand troops at PSAB. The columns waltzed to Ghawar, Shaybah, and Khurais and took them in a day without firing a shot.

I descend the escalator at Dulles to discover A.D., beaming. A big kiss and we're off for the limo.

"Come on," she says. "We're going to Maggie Cole's."

The flight from Amman to Heathrow has been aboard an Air Martiale business 767. Ninety percent of the passengers are Force Insertion legionnaires and tech and psyops guys out of Prince Sultan. As for me, I've had no time to shower or change since Karshi-Khanabad, Basra, and PSAB, the three prior legs. When I board at Queen Alia, it's in the same hajji-flage I've been stinking in since Dushanbe. Jack Stettenpohl is on the flight too. I grab him for thirty seconds, before he squirts away to meet with a gaggle of mil/industrial types in the rear of the aircraft.

My question: Why am I here?

Why did Salter pull me away from my team and put me on these flights home?

Jack answers as we stride aft. The plane has no conventional seating; it's divided into conference areas and sleeping compartments along one bulkhead, like a European train. "There's only one issue right now," says Jack, "and that's keeping Salter safe. We need ten days and the deal's done."

"What deal?"

"Gent, you might not realize it, but you're about to become a player."

"Me? Why?"

"Because Salter trusts you."

There's an inner circle, Jack is saying, of under a hundred. Himself and a number of other congressmen, senators, and Pentagon people, media, lobbyists, the brain trust. "And Maggie and her connections, of course."

I, if I want to, am about to see things I never knew existed.

"What," I ask, "are we trying to do?"

"Change the world."

Stettenpohl hurries off, promising to catch up with me later. I make my way to the sit-down bar. Along the bulkheads are three thousand-channel 3-Ds — one tuned to Trump/CNN, one to Fox/BBC, and one to English-language al-Jazeera. No one is paying attention; they all have their iSats and Skyscreens tuned to mil/nets, FARS, and raw feeds from combat comms.

Two American and one Chinese aircraft carrier group have taken station in the Gulf. Between the missile cruisers and other screening vessels, not to mention the nuclear subs, there's so much naval hardware, a TV analyst says, that there's not enough blue water to hold it.

I run into Cam Holland at the bar — Salter's longtime protégé and my old battalion intelligence officer from East Africa. Holland is drinking vodka tonics with a former Special Ops colonel named Broussard, from Lafayette, Louisiana. It's Broussard who honchoed infil and exfil for Alpha and Bravo over Tajikistan. I thank him for getting us out in one piece. He's an ol' coon-ass cracker; in two minutes he and I have become blood homies.

The obvious question, now, is will all this carrier air go after Salter.

"Not the Chinks," says Broussard. "That'll be World War III."

Our own guys?

"The navy'll fly five hundred sorties but they won't drop a single munition. Salter's troops may be mercs but they're still American boys. What U.S. politician has the nuts to say, 'Take 'em out?' "

The Iranians and Syrians won't make a move, I know, even though they've got plenty of armor and more than enough incentive. The Eastern mind is so tribal, so inured to systems of patronage and blood influence, that it can't conceive that a venture of this scale could be mounted without the full knowledge and approval of the United States at the highest level. The major powers will believe the same. Even Salter's inflammatory speech, broadcast live to the world, will be viewed as brilliant theater, a sham that the global players are too shrewd to be taken in by. The only credible threat, I say, is the Russians.

"Not anymore," says Holland, shoving a Black Label in front of me. "You and your guys took care of that with your little stunt in Tajikistan."

Sure enough, FARS and ITV-Moskva are broadcasting cellphone video of the presidential palace in Dushanbe, being leveled by Russian rockets and M-79 tanks. Columns of Russian armor are rolling over the Kyrgyzstan border in the north, while two Chinese armies are invading from the east. "Nature abhors a vacuum," says Holland. "Particularly when that vacuum is smack on top of the second-biggest oil find in the world."

That was Alpha and Bravo's mission, Holland says. To create chaos. He clinks my glass. "To you and Tim Hayward!"

World opinion, Broussard says, will pile onto Moscow and Beijing for this aggression, eliminating whatever thin sliver of moral high ground might remain, from which the Russians or the Chinese could have expressed outrage at any action of Salter's — that is, seizing the Saudi oil fields — and, more important, ending all possibility of either power launching a *second* intervention, this time against Salter.

Stettenpohl comes back and joins our group just as Trump/ CNN London begins speculating on this precise scenario. Reliable reports, the network declares, have Salter's forces wiring the complexes at Ghawar, Shaybah, and Khurais with high explosives. If the mercs blow up the pumping stations and processing facilities, it will take a decade to rebuild them. By then, says the news, ocean trade will be by sail and land transport will be horse and wagon.

Which way will Salter jump? Trump/CNN reports him negotiating right now with India, Japan, the EU, and South Korea — and communicating by back channels with Russia and China. ITV-Moskva runs a clip of Koverchenko, the Russian premier, landing in Riyadh. BP is there already, along with ExxonMobil, Sinopec, PetroChina, Royal Dutch Shell, Lukoil, and CNOOC, with ConocoPhillips and Petrobras jetting in. Salter is dining, a report says, with the same Saudi princes who had left him in the lurch four days earlier. It goes without saying that all existing oil contracts are null and void.

How, exactly, has Salter taken the oil fields? Jack and Cam Holland confirm what Broussard and I have guessed. The Saudi army is more a family affair than a true national defense force; regiments are loyal to their commanders only, and these give fidelity to whichever faction of the royal family their network of influence dictates. Only the Royal Saudi Air Force, a few elite Special Ops and counterterrorism units, and the corps of royal bodyguards are true professional formations. The main of these have vigorously opposed the cabal of young princes who staged the initial coup — meaning these units are, if not exactly on Salter's side, then at least realistic enough not to stand in his way.

What Salter has done is simply to hold back more troops in Saudi Arabia than he dispatched to southern Iraq.

In other words, the base at PSAB was a Trojan horse.

The Gulf region right now, Jack tells us, is major-league madness.

Southern Iraq has broken away from the central Baghdad government, as will the Kurdish north momentarily, triggering who-knows-what response from the Turks. There are Russian tanks in the streets of Dushanbe and Chinese armored columns steaming west from the Tajikistan-Peoples Republic border. The whole world is howling in outrage, and no one has the slightest clue what to do.

Japan, South Korea, India, Brazil, and the European Union are dispatching brokers and diplomats to Riyadh, eager to kiss ass for the next big contracts. But there's nothing left in Riyadh. Salter holds the fields and he's taking orders from no one. No one knows whom he's negotiating with or what tricks he's got up his sleeve. His weaknesses are logistics, keeping his men fed and supplied and making sure that no force gets the jump on him. "He's holding jacks over nines," says Stettenpohl. "And that may just be good enough to take the whole pot."

"What I still don't understand," I tell Jack, "is why I'm here and not back in the fight."

"This *is* the fight, Gent. And you're here to be a player. You're here to make plays."

In the movies, limos always have a bar in back, stocked with liquor and ice. Now, speeding out of Dulles with A.D., this one's got warm Fiji water and G-7 Gatorade. "Can I smoke?" I ask the driver.

"Sorry, sir."

"Gent, will you knock it off and listen to me?"

A.D. is wearing tight leather pants and a pair of $3,000 come-fuck-me heels that I bought her at Cesare Pacciotti on Fifth Avenue with my first bonus from Iran-Iraq II. Her blouse is black silk, one of those see-through numbers that can pass as business-casual only if it's night and you've got a chest like she does.

"Gent, stop staring at my tits."

"I missed you, baby . . ."

A.D. switches off the news, which has been reporting poll figures for the upcoming presidential election. The incumbent President Murchison and the challenger, Senator Dodd, are splitting 40 percent of the vote. Salter, whose name isn't even on the ballot, stands at nearly 50 percent — trouncing them both combined.

I reach for the fly front of A.D.'s leathers. It's not the most sophisticated move, I know, but my estranged bride has been known to let her guard down, on occasion, in the backseats of vehicles driven by others.

She swats my hand and slams her thighs shut tight enough to crush a walnut. "This is serious, Gent! Will you listen to me?"

A.D. tells me Maggie Cole wants her to write an article. About Salter.

"Not 'wants,' " A.D. says. " 'Commands.' "

The article will be what they call a "lead piece." Ten thousand words. It'll have the cover of *Apple imPress* next week. Mrs. Cole will see to that. In addition to first-generation exposure ("1gen," as they say in the biz) from the virtual mag and its online and Holo-Net hooks, tweets, and links, the piece will generate massive "wrap-around" on the mil and pol blogs, Politico, SinoNet, rChive, not to mention on-camera time on all the beltway talk shows. A.D. personally will be part of the story, Maggie Cole has made clear by way of incentivizing her, "because that Lord Jim hit piece you wrote was the one that originally took Salter down."

"In other words," A.D. has asked Mrs. Cole, "I'm recanting."

"You're reporting with your customary fearlessness and objectivity."

We speed east on 267. I'm grilling A.D. about the poll figures. Can Salter run? Is it too late to get his name on the ballot? Does he even want to run?

"Whether he runs or not doesn't matter. Salter's holding every card. The only questions are how long can he hold them and what deal can he drive."

"I thought you hated this shit, A.D. I thought Salter was Caligula."

"He's Caesar, or wants to be." Her expression becomes sober. "Maybe that's what this country needs."

A.D. admits that Maggie Cole scares her. Players are coming out of the woodwork; established powers are jockeying for position like warlords in Kabul. The world is shifting on its axis, A.D. says, and no one knows who'll be on top when it finally settles.

"I feel like, if I tell Maggie no, I'll be sleeping with the fishes."

My bride lights a Pall Mall. When the driver says she can't smoke in the car, A.D. tells him she'll put the cigarette out on his face if he gives her any more shit. I can see the dude's glance flick to me in the rearview.

"She's got 'em like this, Jack."

He laughs and keeps driving.

A.D. briefs me about the event at Maggie's place this evening—who'll be there, how I'll recognize them, what is expected of me. A.D.'s skin flushes when she gets hot with ambition. I can smell the Chanel No. 22 steaming between her breasts.

"What are my chances," I ask, "of getting laid?"

"By me? Zero. I'm going home to start on the article."

The piece on Salter, she says, will take five days. She already has her assistant cranking out research—and two freelancers on the way to her office as we speak.

"What's the hook?" I ask.

"Alcibiades."

I get it. The unwilling exile. The misunderstood patriot.

"Your idea or Mrs. Cole's?"

A.D. pulls a single sheet of buff-colored stationery from her laptop bag. On it, in a woman's handwriting that is not A.D.'s, is a subject-head outline, start to finish.

"I didn't think cut to measure was your style."

A.D. cracks the window and flicks her cig into the night. "It is now."

The limo drops me at Maggie Cole's town house in Alexandria. The driver will take A.D. to a separate soiree at *Apple imPress,* then return to Mrs. Cole's and wait for me.

I ask A.D. if she herself has come over to Salter's side.

"Let's say I'm riding the story wherever it takes me."

This bothers me.

I step out; the limo creeps forward. I rap the driver's glass to make him stop. A.D. rolls down her window.

"One last question, babe. Where does the Constitution stand in all this revolution?"

"The Constitution," my wife says, "is a living document."

18

A GOVERNMENT IN WAITING

I STAY UP TILL FOUR, AKOPing friends still with Salter in the kingdom—Chris and Chutes, Tony, Q, Mac, Junk, and Pete Petrocelli—asking them what they've heard about this stuff. Grunts and operators never know shit, and care even less. I wind up phoning Ariel Caplan, waking her at dawn in her Manhattan condo. She doesn't seem to mind.

"Have you heard," she asks me, "of the Emergency Powers Act?"

I have not.

"I shouldn't be blabbing over a satline that's almost certainly being pinged by both sides, but the merest cupcaking would bring this out anyway, so what the hell?"

The Emergency Powers Act of 2024, Ariel tells me, was passed by Congress and enacted into law in the aftermath of the nuclear attack on Long Beach.

"Under the Act," says Ariel, "Congress, in circumstances of immediate national peril, may vest extraordinary—some would say dictatorial—powers in the president as commander in chief. The Act gives the chief executive power, under his own initiative, to declare martial law; impose military conscription; employ wiretaps and electronic surveillance without the supervision of the courts; arrest and detain individuals without trial; nationalize the banks and all air, sea, rail and truck transport, as well the oil, coal, steel, and auto industries; order forced internment and deportation of individuals and groups; suspend habeas corpus and freedom of the press and a lot more. That's nasty enough, wouldn't you say?

"Well, now, today, before several committees in the House and Senate are measures that would amend this Act, so that the aforementioned commander in chief need not be the president. He or she may be a military person. The precedent being cited is the run-up to the Six-Day War in 1967, when the Israeli democracy, believing the state's existence to be in jeopardy in the face of imminent invasion by the armies of Egypt and Syria backed by the Soviet Union, created a 'unity government'—which basically meant that Prime Minister Levi Eshkol stepped aside while Moshe Dayan was brought in as defense minister and took over.

"Clearly this current American measure is being brought by partisans of your friend General Salter and is designed for one purpose only—to bring him home in a position that places him beyond the law and, by the way, reverses 245 years of constitutional checks and balances."

Ariel tells me that private poll numbers, which she has accessed through her own independent databases, indicate that somewhere between 66 percent and 73 percent of the electorate would support such an amendment if it would result in bringing Salter home with sufficient powers to deal with the current crisis.

"This is not nothing, Gent. This is tyranny on its face. It's Roman. And I'll tell you something else."

I can hear Ariel dragging on a cigarette. The tinkle of cubes in a glass comes over as well.

"I have it from an unimpeachable source," Ariel says, "that the

Republican presidential candidate, Senator Dodd, has privately intimated that he will cede this power. If elected, he'll voluntarily surrender C in C to Salter. Why? To get elected in the first place! If he's saying this, you can bet that President Murchison will make the same deal. Remember what Osama bin Laden said once about people wanting to follow a strong horse? That's your friend Salter. He's the horse *and* the rider."

I sleep all day, tossing with fever dreams, then go to work that evening.

Can what Ariel said be true? And if it is, does it mean what she says it does?

"Evening" in Beltway-speak means business. Evening is when things get done. The meetings and conferences that take place during working hours, I am learning fast, are only for exercise. It's not till after hours that deals are actually struck.

Nor does anything happen in the District at the hour it's announced. By the time a decision hits the press or the blogs, it's been a done deal for days. And the decision maker is never the one to tell you. You find out from some nobody three and four levels down.

That's what I am. I have been sent here as a nobody to do business with other nobodies.

It's the nobodies, I come to understand, who get things done. Change happens at the nobody level. The nobodies craft the memos and prepare the policy papers. It is the nobodies who stuff a page of notes into a senator's hand, which he then reads cold for the cameras as if he had penned every syllable himself.

Why has Salter sent me to Washington? To serve as a back-channel conduit between him and the third- and fourth-tier representatives of power who want or need to talk to him but either can't risk the consequences of overt contact or who wish to sound out a situation unofficially or even — this is the tricky part — to conduct, or initiate, actual negotiations. Does Salter trust me to do this? Hell no. I report to Maggie Cole, who then confers with whomever she must confer with. After that, I get my instructions.

What sort of Deep Throat shit am I doing? Here's one. TataLux, the giant Indian CNG car company, is threatened by the proposed Takhar Valley–Karachi pipeline that, if completed, would be able to deliver vast quantities of liquefied natural gas by sea to Indonesia, the Philippines, Japan, and Korea (their second-most-profitable market) and, more critical, to China, their number one. The primary selling point of these compressed natural gas vehicles, which cost peanuts and get over a hundred miles per gallon while polluting at near zero, is that when you purchase the car you also sign a contract to buy three years' worth of CNG from TataLux. If the new pipeline delivers the same juice for half the price, TataLux is hosed.

The company wants to come to an understanding with Salter. If he will torpedo the pipeline (which he can do with a single phone call to any of fifty players in Central Asia who are now dependent upon his good graces), TataLux will put a hundred mill in his pocket, give him a seat on the board, and cut him in on the action. TataLux can't communicate this directly to Salter because (a) he's not a businessman; he has no apparatus of commercial representation by which he can be approached with deniability; (b) the situation is so fluid (and Salter's hold on power so precarious and impossible to evaluate) that there are no precedents to establish price or compensation for influence; and (c) if they get caught, the company loses credibility big-time as a reputable force in the industry. So they have to work in the shadows. They have to operate through nobodies. Nobodies provide deniability.

I sleep at Maggie Cole's town house in Alexandria. Each morning at six thirty I teleconference with Mrs. Cole, who works out of her horse property in Middleburg. The connection is encrypted by Force Insertion's domestic security firm, Rhinehart Norton International. As I make coffee, a day sheet containing my appointments scrolls out of the printer. Maggie or her staff update this via my handheld every thirty minutes.

I am not allowed to phone A.D., or anyone else not on Maggie's secure list. I have a "correspondent" named Deeana (no last name) who travels with me to every meeting, to act as a witness both to what I promise (which is always nothing) and what is pledged by others (which is often something) and to record officially all exchanges for Salter and his network; a Lebanese-American driver/bodyguard named Tomas who speaks Arabic, Farsi, and Dari; and a stylist named Gerri who cuts my hair, orders my meals, and both buys and lays out for me my shirts, shoes, and jackets. When I ask her to articulate her job description, she says, "I'm here to accessorize you." She is also here to fuck me, thank you Maggie, to keep me out of trouble, running around town, but for some reason I never take her up on it, though she is very cute and very willing. I'm being faithful to A.D.

While I'm doing this, my own self-imposed priority is to get el-Masri and his family back to the States. Salter can't pull strings yet; there's still too much fear and uncertainty within the bureaucracy, not to mention he's got ten thousand items higher up on his to-do list. No one knows if the general will be escorted home in triumph or tried for treason. I'm trying to work in the cracks. Every time business puts me in the way of someone connected to Immigration, I pump him for the inside track. Simultaneously I'm working with Maggie and her people, rolling bones, and calling in favors. It's incredible how difficult it is. El-Masri knows nothing of what I'm doing; I don't want him to get his hopes up.

Here's a typical day, reconstituted from memory and notes on matchbooks and cocktail coasters, because Maggie's minders shred each twenty-four hours' schedule as soon as it scrolls by.

7:30 Breakfast w/Xiang X of PetroChina (at McDonald's in Bethesda, continue discussion in walkaround)
9:00 To Spy Museum for drivearound w/Cong. Z (R-FL), House Approp. Comm.
10:30 Meet immigration lawyer Nate L at Equinox on K Street
12:00 Lunch and conf call w/Turkmen-Uzbek consortium/ South Yolotan-Osman to Caspian Basin pipeline
2:30 Helo to AWC, Army War College, Carlisle, PA; Georgian (Tbilisi) "individual of interest" is supposed to contact me but doesn't show

At the same time that I myself am meeting with agents and representatives of corporate, political, or governmental interests, other operatives working for Salter are doing the same thing. How many are there? I'm guessing several hundred, though, from my worm's-eye view, there is no group planning and no sharing of intelligence. Each of us is a law unto himself. I report to Maggie and others above me, but have no official contact with peers on my level. The only people I know are the reps of interests who conspire with me.

Who are these guys? I meet them in tapas bars, at ball games, and in locker rooms at health clubs. We take a steam. We ride around in taxis or on the metro, always someplace loud to defeat audio surveillance or self-bugging. I confess I'm impressed by these players. They are not goons or boiler-roomers; they are hip young hotshots—Americans, Brits, Japanese, South Africans, Brazilians, Dutch, Russians, Arabs, and Indians. They all went to Harvard or Sloan/MIT and they all get picked up, when the pitching is over, by five-foot-ten Stanford-grad blondes driving Daimler biodiesels or fuel-cell Fiats. "Have we got a deal?" they ask.

"I'll get back to you."

I record everything in after-action reports and shoot it up the line. But the real work happens past midnight in Maggie Cole's home gym, which has had the Stairmasters and Cliff Climbers removed and replaced by two big war-room tables, wall maps, and carrels for multilingual tech jockeys who are tapping out encrypted dispatches to Hong Kong, Seoul, Riyadh, and fifty other capitals of finance, while Maggie and her staff of whiz kids wheel and deal with an ever-mutating cavalcade of shape-shifters — corporate, tech, military, financial, governmental, and nongovernmental actors. The latter category includes such unsavory entries as warlords and tribal chieftains, exiled businessmen and royalty, scholars and clerics, rebel and faction leaders (demarked in communiqués as GIWs, governments-in-waiting), gangsters, narcotraffickers, even the odd celebrity and media titan.

All are supplicants seeking Salter's favor.

Salter himself remains in Arabia. Neither Mrs. Cole nor any member of the kitchen cabinet dares serve as his official channel of communication. That role is performed by the lobbying firm of Gershater/Kahn/Valentino, who represent in addition to Salter not only the Kingdom of Saudi Arabia but four of the top eleven energy giants, including Russian Lukoil and Chinese Sinopec. GKV's law firm is Lowther Schapiro & Bloom, on whose board sit four former senators and two ex-Speakers of the House, as well as Maxwell "Marty" Bloom, secretary of state under Jack Cole and secretary of defense under the incumbent Murchison. Bloom was the Jedi knight who restored the Supreme Court's credibility after the electoral scandal of 2016 and whose half-hour speech in prime time as a private citizen, paid for out of his own pocket, single-handedly quelled the panic on Wall Street during the crash of 2019. Arrayed around Bloom is an unofficial but fully functioning network of current and former cabinet members, senators, congressmen, and long-ball hitters in the corporate, legal, financial, and military universes.

In other words, Salter possesses his own government-in-waiting.

Where were all these sonsofbitches, I ask Maggie, when Salter needed them?

"Doesn't matter," she says. "They're here now."

A few nights later I witness firsthand a sample of this GIW.

Adm. Harley Spence is chairman of the Joint Chiefs. He drives to Maggie's farm by back roads at one in the morning and meets with her in the kitchen with all the shades drawn. I'm sitting beside Maggie on a banquette that runs along one wall of the breakfast nook while Adm. Spence, who is suffering with back spasms and can't sit in a chair, perches across on a low-rise stool, leaning forward with his elbows on the tabletop like an old man desperately trying to take a crap.

I remember Spence from East Africa. He was the three-star commander of the carrier battle group sent to back up Salter's Task Force 68. Spence was the one who presided over Salter's dismissal and termination of command; it was aboard the admiral's G-5 that Salter flew home to face his congressional tarring and feathering.

Meeting the admiral now in person, I must say I like the guy. He's in civilian clothes, accompanied by his son, a midshipman at Annapolis. Spence opens his HoloTab and fans through a sequence of video news sites— *Wiki Washington Post, NYGT,* MurdochNet and Trump/CNN, along with *Politico,* ITV HuffPost, and *The Situation Room* —which he displays for Maggie to see. The featured sections are solid with stories about Salter in Saudi Arabia and the imminent collapse of the global financial, security, and energy structures. The collective U.S. psyche, the admiral declares, can't take much more of this chaos. Something's gotta give.

"What I know you understand, Mrs. Cole," says Adm. Spence, "is that Washington is in bed with the Saudi royal family on every level. Petrocash pays the salaries of half the think tanks and three-quarters of the lobbying firms. Wives are on the payroll; every DoD guy above GS-15 has his snout in the trough, including me the second I retire. But it's way more than that. It's the economy. It's society. It's Western Civ! What falls next, Maggie? Manufacturing is overseas, housing has tanked, finance is history. The country's been hanging by a thread since '08, based on Chinese paper, cheap Saudi oil, and smoke and mirrors. Now Salter's in Iraq and the kingdom, with his fist around America's lifeline.

"What does the U.S. military do? Drop JDAMs on American boys? Do we let Iran push the button? Then what? Anarchy? Global collapse? World War III?

"Do we wait till Salter sells us out to Gazprom and Sinopec? What happens when the Russians or Chinese take our oil? Will some crazed actor nuke the fields? Or just blow Ghawar and Shayba with a few truck bombs? And Salter knows all this. The sonofabitch is brilliant. He's run rings around Europe and the Iranians and Iraqis; he's totally screwed the Saudis; and now he's got us by the short hairs too. I'll step down if I have to. If Salter wants me to fall on my sword, I'll do it."

Mrs. Cole asks the next question. "For whom are you speaking, Harley?"

"I can't answer that."

Maggie assures Adm. Spence that Salter bears no personal grudges. He is not that kind of man. She asks Spence if she can count on him. "A moment will come soon," Maggie says, "when all the chips will have to be put on the table."

The admiral expels a weary breath.

"I'm speaking for the president of course. But I'm also looking out for the chiefs and for the military as a whole. Jim has put us in a helluva spot and he knows it. What does he want? Money? Redemption? He can't sit on those fields forever."

"Why not?"

The admiral glances to his son, then back to Mrs. Cole.

"Godammit, Maggie, I surrender! I know Salter's got more cards up his sleeve and I know he's smart enough and jacked up enough to play 'em."

I glance to Maggie Cole as she watches the admiral squirm. I can't help but flash on the code name that her Secret Service detail gave her when she was first lady: Livia, after the Roman empress in *I, Claudius,* who poisoned every pretender to the throne including, in the end, her own husband, Augustus.

"I have a question for you, Admiral," says Mrs. Cole. "What do *you* want?"

"Me?" Clearly the chairman thinks of himself as just another handcuffed bureaucrat.

"How do you want to come out of this? And what are you willing to do to make it happen?"

Before Spence can answer, Maggie turns to the midshipman, the chairman's son. "You're a football player, aren't you, Edward? A defensive back, I hear, and a good one." She observes that the young man has been silent all evening. "Tell me, what is your impression of the events of the past two weeks?"

The midshipman blushes and glances to his elder.

"Don't defer to your father, Edward. You're in my house now. Tell me, please. What is your impression of General Salter?"

The young man sits up. You can see he has brains and guts. "I can only speak for myself, Mrs. Cole. But I think it's about time we had an American commander who wasn't afraid to kick the world in the ass."

This answer seems to please the former first lady. "Even," she asks, "if he's not doing it under the American flag?"

"I don't care what flag he's doing it under. He's one of us and he's through taking shit."

Later, when father and son are taking their leave, the chairman speaks aside to Mrs. Cole. This is in the foyer, as he's pulling on his overcoat.

"Dammit, Maggie, what the hell does Jim want?"

Mrs. Cole hands the admiral his muffler and gloves. "That's easy, Harley. He wants to come home."

19

THE NEAR ENEMY

19 SEPTEMBER 2032. I'M meeting a rep from Petrobras, the Brazilian oil company, at a fund-raiser at a restaurant in Georgetown called Melisse. The event is upstairs, in a private room; our group is chatting before dinner at the service bar, when I feel an iron fist seize my shoulder from behind. "Gent, is that your sorry ass?" I turn to discover a stranger of about forty—six foot, 190, clean shaven, business suit.

"It's Hayward, bro!"

The Team Alpha leader.

"Sonofabitch!" Hayward and I clasp hands and clap each other's backs. "Sorry, man, I didn't recognize you without the beard."

"Yeah, they made me shave the fucker. You too, I see."

We laugh and make our way to a quiet corner, exchanging stories of how each of us has wound up in this candy-ass capital and what's up with various friends still fighting the real fight back in the sand. I ask Hayward how long he's been here.

"Since right after," he says. "They flew me back in the same stinking rags I was wearing in Tajikistan."

"And you've been here in D.C. the whole time?"

"D.C. and other places."

I eyeball my fellow warrior. His sandy hair is cropped in a straight-up buzz cut. His Popeye forearms bulge beneath the sleeves of his suit jacket, which are so short his full shirt cuffs are showing. Hayward's blue, Oklahoma-panhandle eyes scan the room like an assassin's.

"How do you like doing all this deal making?" I ask, indicating the guests, who are networked around the chamber in twos and threes, churning out predinner business.

Hayward gives me a look. "Yeah," he says, "I'm doing some really cool deals." And he draws a thumb across his throat.

I catch his arm and pull him closer. I can't imagine Hayward, even in a suit and tie, making social chitchat with Beltway politicos. The dude is a man-killer; it sticks out all over him.

I want to know what he means by "really cool deals." But from the head of the room comes the peal of a butter knife against a crystal goblet. A blond staffer materializes at Hayward's shoulder, tugging him back toward their table. I flash him the call-me sign and add emphasis to make it urgent. He grins and shoots a lascivious eyeroll in the direction of the blonde.

The conversation over dinner is of nothing but the Emergency Powers Act. When coffee arrives, the host rises and introduces a series of prominent guests — a senator, a lobbyist, and former secretary of state Echevarria (whom I hadn't noticed till then) — who stand and briefly address the room. Each speaks passionately of his fears for liberty, for the very survival of the republic if this amendment passes and Salter is brought home under its unconstitutional provisions. As the dessert plates are being carried away, I catch Hayward shooting me a second look. I want to get him alone, but, just as I stand, I see him receive an incoming text. In seconds he's on his feet and out the rear exit.

Outside, guests pile up at the valet stand, retrieving their cars. I wait for Echevarria. I want to ask him about his "Catalog of the Elect." Is it for real, as he declared that night at Hantush? And did he succeed in getting his name on it?

But I can't find him. Has he left by another exit? My own car is just being brought curbside when a voice booms from the restaurant doorway.

"Colonel! Are you avoiding me?"

The secretary works through the crush. I'm surprised at the affection I feel, seeing him again. But when he comes up, his expression is stern. With him is a fiftyish gentleman whom he introduces as William Agocopian, deputy director of intelligence for the FBI. Their wives wait with a couple of other matrons.

"I saw you inside, chatting it up with your friend, Colonel Hayward," the secretary says. He glances to the FBI guy. "I'd like to have recorded that conversation."

I tell him Hayward and I were talking about beards.

"I didn't think," Echevarria says, "that Salter would play so rough so fast."

I ask him what he means by that.

"Please, Colonel. You and I are friends. We both understand how the game is played."

I tell him I'm serious.

"They're calling it a 'unity government,'" says Echevarria. "A felicitous turn of phrase, don't you think? I didn't make the cut. But apparently you did, Colonel, along with your brother-in-arms Hayward."

I repeat that I don't know what he's talking about.

The FBI deputy snorts. "Cut the crap, partner. We know what business your pal is in — and we know what you've done too."

"And what exactly is that, partner?"

"We know about the Pakistani village that disappeared into a river, and we know about Mbana's Brown Bombers who disappeared altogether."

I feel the blood surging in my temples. "If you're accusing me of something, motherfucker, spit it out."

Echevarria slides his bulk between me and the deputy. Two security men glide in. I dish out a dose of profanity to this son of J. Edgar Hoover. But already I'm getting the sick feeling that he's right and I'm wrong.

The secretary's car comes. Echevarria apologizes for the unpleasantness as he and his party move off. At the curb, he turns back.

"If you really don't know, Colonel, ask your wife. Or better yet, speak to Maggie Cole."

I'm driving home, trying to reach A.D. when my earbud pings. The numeral "1" appears in the text window on my handheld:

Need you Dubai soonest. S.

20

THE NEAR ENEMY, PART TWO

A.D. IS WITH ARIEL Caplan at a bar in Alexandria. When I find the two of them in a back booth, they're arguing.

"We'll call the guy," Ariel is saying. "We'll get him on the phone right now."

I sit. "What's going on?"

"Tell him," says Ariel.

"It's bullshit," says my wife.

I order a Johnnie Black and tell the girls I'm off for Dubai in the morning. Ariel wants me to report everything that happens. Then she tells me the news.

Two men have turned up dead in the past week, and a third is missing. Lavalle Courtemanche. Do I remember the name? The blogger, who outed Rob Salter for the Brown Bombers massacre. The cops dragged his body out of a ditch seven days ago — and not one mainstream outlet is covering it.

The second corpse, Ariel says, belongs to DeMartin White of CyberLeaks, who published the Marine Corps report that confirmed Rob's complicity. White dropped dead of a heart attack seventy-two hours ago—at forty-one, a marathoner in the prime of health.

"Ariel," A.D. says, "thinks they've been murdered."

"The Third Amigo is Jake Fallon, the congressman from Montana who put Courtemanche's and White's material in front of every camera in the country. He's supposedly hiking now in the Bob Marshall Wilderness. Except the place has been shut down for two weeks."

"And you think he's been murdered too?"

"Someone's sending a message. To let Salter's enemies know he's playing for keeps."

I ask Ariel where the first two men died.

"Here. Courtemanche in D.C., White in Anacostia."

Ariel hears something in my voice.

"What do you know, Gent?"

"Nothing."

I can't believe Salter's behind this. I won't.

"You know who did it," says Ariel. "Who? Some mercenary? Someone who knows how to kill people—"

A.D. laughs. "They *all* know how to kill people." She dismisses the whole narrative as coincidence.

"Two bodies?" says Ariel. "Both linked to the biggest story in the last fifty years? And a third missing?"

"People die, Ariel. It happens."

"What kind of horseshit answer is that, A.D.? You're a journalist. Don't tell me why it's *not* a story; tell me why it is!"

Ariel insists we go back to her apartment. It's two in the morning. A.D. refuses. She's got work to do—for her meeting tomorrow at *Apple imPress*.

"What work?" Ariel asks.

A.D. confesses that she has contracted to do a second cover story, this one on the "adaptability" of the Constitution.

"Adaptability?" Ariel scoffs. "What, have you gone over to the fucking dark side?"

"Look," says A.D. "I'm working."

Ariel tells me what apparently she and A.D. have been arguing about. There's a young reporter for a McClatchy Webpaper who's been working the Blogger and Leaker story. He's the only one. He's in Sacramento. He works for the *Bee*.

"I've been tracking his pieces," says A.D. "They're all speculation."

We're outside the bar now. It's raining. Ariel says she's going to dial the reporter right now. She puts her phone on speaker.

While the ring sounds, Ariel gives A.D. a hard look. "A second cover story? Your little pussy's getting wet, isn't it?"

"Fuck you."

"She smells a Pulitzer."

The phone picks up. "Tumulty."

"Andrew Tumulty?"

"Who is this?"

"Sorry to disturb you so late, Mr. Tumulty. This is Ariel Caplan of Agence France-Presse. I'm phoning from Washington with A.D. Economides of *Apple imPress*. Do you have a moment to answer a question or two?"

The reporter sounds like he just woke up. "What time is it?"

Ariel tells Tumulty (a total fabrication) that she's just had a report that the body of Montana congressman Jake Fallon has been found at the base of a cliff in the Bob Marshall Wilderness.

"That's not true," says the reporter.

"You mean he's alive? I have the story from a reliable — "

"It's not true."

"Then he's dead? From a different cause?"

The reporter says he knows nothing. He has dropped the story. He says he's going to hang up.

Ariel won't let him. She threatens to write her own story, naming Mr. Tumulty as a source and suggesting that he knows who murdered Congressman Fallon. "What aren't you telling me, Andrew? Is Fallon dead by some other cause?"

The reporter says he has to get off the phone.

"Why? Is it bugged? Are we being recorded?"

Why, Ariel asks the young newsman, has he pursued this story on his own if he doesn't believe there's something to it?

"I changed my mind."

"Who got to you, Andrew? Did your editors order you off? Who got to them?"

"Nobody talked to me and nobody got to my editors. I dropped the story because it was going nowhere."

"Horseshit. Show some balls! Tell me something."

"What's your problem, bitch? You want the story yourself? Take it!"

Rain beats down. A.D. is tugging at Ariel, to get her to hang up. I crane closer to the speaker. The reporter's voice pipes, high pitched:

"Stop calling me, you got it? Quit bothering me!"

The phone clicks dead.

Ariel turns to A.D. "Still think this is nothing?"

"I'm going home."

A.D. stalks toward her car. I chase her. Her phone rings. Ariel tramps behind me. "Gent," she says. "You have to tell me what you know."

A.D. answers her phone, still striding. She pulls up, pressing the phone to one ear and covering the other with two fingers. "What? Say that again."

Ariel and I come up beside her. We're all drenched.

"Are you sure?" A.D. says into the phone. "There's no mistake?"

She clicks the phone off.

"That was my office," says A.D. "Calling with real news."

Ariel and I wait.

"Salter and Maggie Cole are getting married."

21

TOP OF THE WORLD

THE LION SUITE IS THE premium crib at the Burj Khalifa in Dubai—summit floor, twenty-eight hundred feet up, tallest building in the world. The suite comes with three pairs of Zeiss binos to watch the peregrine falcons soaring a thousand feet below.

Salter has installed himself in this aerie, but I don't get to see the digs till a day after I arrive. In-flight newscasts are bumper to bumper with stories of the upcoming Salter-Cole nuptials. Two handlers, a man and a woman, pick me up at Dubai International; they zip me through Customs in about forty seconds. Chris Candelaria is waiting with Chutes and Junk Olsen. They look like kids at Christmas. "Welcome to the rocket ship," says Chris.

"Where's el-Masri?"

"In Mosul, making deals with the *peshmerga*."

"What about Hayward?"

No one knows. I've tried him twenty times, by phone, Skype, and AKOP. I've even phoned Agocopian, the FBI guy. Hayward has gone invisible.

Chris tells me the political scuttlebutt. A hot wire has just arrived from Salter's law firm in D.C: the decisive votes are in hand. "The Emergency Powers Act. The amendment's gonna pass."

Dubai is the Miami Beach of the Arab world. Right now it belongs to Salter. CSPs, concentric security perimeters, ring the Burj at three thousand yards. Passing the Karama Center I note four I-SAMs, mobile surface-to-air missile launchers, and count a dozen more as we approach the tower itself. Antimissile drones swarm above the summit like hornets. I hear the thwack-thwack of Apache rotors, juking along the urban canyons, and the whine of F-35s high above. Every corner seems to sprout a colony of security contractors, mostly Arabs, packing AK-47s with Russian PKM machine guns behind sandbagged emplacements. Primary checkpoints are blocked by MRAPs and other armored vehicles, parked sideways, with troopers on .50 cals topside.

Entering the Burj's defensible space, our Suburban, which is bristling with security IDs and clearance freqs, is shunted through three additional checkpoints. First,

TURN OFF ECM

where we are inspected to be sure the vehicle's electronic countermeasures — a humming pod that takes up the entire rear luggage compartment — have been disabled, as well as searched by thermal scan and bomb-sniffing dogs; then

CLEAR WEAPONS HERE

where we dismount, eject all rounds from chambers, remove all magazines, then hand over our weapons entirely; and finally

STOP FOR BIOMETRIC ID

where we are individually retina scanned and argon IDed, and at last patted down by hand.

"And this is for friends!" says Junk.

Inside, our foursome is met by other new faces, who greet us politely but professionally and escort us to a belowground level of the lobby. From there we ride a freight elevator to the third subbasement, where another phalanx of security men processes us again, including a second patdown.

Stairs and two passageways take us even deeper into the skyscraper's bowels, to a blast-proof bunker that, inside, looks like a convention suite at the Holiday Inn in Topeka. Steel folding chairs are arrayed in a U around two military-style tables. A buffet spreads along two walls: coffee in industrial urns, stale turkey and roast-beef wraps, wilted Caesar salad served with plastic forks, and bowls of M&Ms for dessert.

Salter enters, preceded by Petrocelli and Cam Holland and his old combat team leader, Gunnery Sgt. Dainty, with Col. Klugh, the security chief, and four other gunslingers that I don't recognize. They're all in cammies, dirty, coming straight from the desert, Salter as always with his M9 in a shoulder holster. Next in the door is Jack Stettenpohl. He looks as trim as ever, in a gray business suit and modified Semper Fi haircut. Three Lowther Schapiro & Bloom lawyers accompany him, whose names I can't recall but whose faces I've seen a dozen times at capital evenings in the past couple of weeks. With them are a half-dozen young Saudis in tribal robes. The senior, Chris tells me (the prince can't be older than thirty), has been the kingdom's ambassador to China but will now fill that post to the United States. Present via satellite, displayed on a battery of flatscreens and holos, are two dozen Euro, Asian, and North and South American power players. Finally, on a video screen set up just east of the M&Ms bowl, shimmers Maggie Cole, in jeans and Western-cut shirt, via satellite from her farm in Virginia.

Champagne toasts are drunk out of paper cups, saluting the wedding. Cigars are broken out. Petrocelli lifts his Dixie cup, addressing Salter.

"Do you realize, sir, that as we stand here at this hour, you're not only the happiest man on earth but also the most powerful!"

The confab's subject is how to get Salter home. He's trepidatious; he trusts no one in the U.S. government. A homebound plane can be shot down at the push of a button, he says, and he believes his enemies are more than capable of such an act. He feels no more confident about his personal security, even after safely arriving home. "I'm not stepping down onto the tarmac at Andrews or Dulles to find myself being zip-stripped and arrested."

On cue, a "breaking news" story appears on Trump/CNN: demonstrations are being held in twenty-one cities, calling for Salter to be brought up on charges of treason. A motion before Congress calling for the revocation of Salter's citizenship has not been rescinded, nor has its companion proposal stripping citizenship from all Force Insertion operators and their subcontractors.

While Salter's brain trust debates, I find a quiet corner and try to get through to el-Masri. Channels bounce me from one link to another; it takes twenty minutes to determine that the Egyptian is in the field and unreachable. I leave word that I'm in Dubai and will try to get north to see him before I fly home.

When I return to the group around Salter, they've got Marty Bloom, the lawyer, and a couple of his associates on video teleconference from D.C. Apparently the vote tally for the passage of the Emergency Powers Act amendment is shakier than the firm had believed. Bloom names a specific congresswoman from Indiana, who is being negotiated with as we speak.

"Her vote is everything," says one of the partners on-screen, adding that he's confident that the lady's requirements can be met. "One last hurdle, Jim, and you fly home with F-35s on each wing."

Marty Bloom addresses Salter, cautioning against premature self-congratulation. "When the amendment passes, the gloves really come off. Your enemies will hit you with everything they've got."

"I don't blame 'em," says Salter. "I would too. In their eyes, my return equates to tyranny."

I hear myself speak up. "Then why do it?"

Every pair of eyes swivels in my direction. Salter smiles.

"Because if Force Insertion sits tight in Arabia, Gent, we're dead meat in ninety days. The troops starve. The U.S. gets a president it despises. We lose the oil. In four years there's nothing left of the United States but a damp spot by the side of the road."

I ask Salter why he can't simply link with the new president, whoever he is, and put Force Insertion under U.S. command.

"Because I won't," he says.

Cheers fill the room. I'm caught by surprise.

"I've done that before, Gent. I'll never do it again."

Approbation swells from every man in the suite. As this emotion crests, one of Salter's aides cues up a video that has apparently just appeared on Trump/CNN. The scene is a Pentagon press room. The Chairman of the Joint Chiefs, Harley Spence, reads a statement. He is flanked by his colleagues in full dress before a wall of Stars & Stripes.

It is not the role of the Joint Chiefs to establish policy, but to enforce policy once it has been decided upon and, when requested by our civilian superiors, to contribute to the debate preceding its adoption. Still, in extraordinary circumstances such as those faced by the United States at this hour, the Chiefs would be derelict in their duty, should we fail to go on record in a matter in which we, collectively and as individuals, are professionally and personally involved. We favor the lifting of all charges against General James R. Salter, USMC (R), and we urge Congress to enact his formal repatriation as expeditiously as possible.

More cheers from the room. I'm thinking, can Spence and the chiefs be making such an extraordinary statement on their own? Surely they have conferred with both the president and his challenger. Is this a ploy by the chiefs to position themselves for a future dominated by Salter or is it a signal by them and the next president that the city gates have been opened, the besieger is free to enter?

> Jim Salter is not only the finest fighting general of his generation but a leader whose gifts and talents the nation, at this hour, cannot afford to deprive itself of. Bring him home!

Later, I pull Chris, Chutes, and Junk aside. What do they think of this shit?

"Whatever the man wants," says Junk.

"It ain't by the book," Chutes says. "But what other choice is there?"

Jack Stettenpohl comes up. He tells us excitedly that it looks like the Emergency Powers Act will pass — and that some sort of unity government will be formed, with Salter at its head.

"What's a unity government?" asks Chutes.

I want to hear this myself.

"A wartime apparatus," says Jack. "Like Lincoln had, or Churchill, or the Israelis during their wars of survival."

"Meaning what? No Bill of Rights? No vote?"

"Meaning the people who count will be in power. Meaning the country can finally get something done."

"Jack," I say. "This is bullshit."

He stares at me as if he's never seen me before. "Gent, don't scare me like this."

"What the fuck, bro. Do you hear what you're saying?"

Jack glances to Chris, Chutes, and Junk, as if to confirm that they're with him and I'm crazy.

"What do you think has been going on, Gent? Whose side did you think you've been fighting on? Since East Africa we've all seen how fucked this country is — and we all agree there's only one man who can unfuck it."

I try to reach A.D., then Ariel when I can't find her, but all channels are coming up goose eggs.

Around midnight, a text comes in from el-Masri. I shuttle to the comms room and get him on a secure line. He bitches for twenty minutes about getting screwed on pay and bonuses and thanks me (he has sources, he says) for my efforts on his family's behalf. Unprompted, he gives his dish on Salter and the Emergency Powers Act.

"Let me tell you something, my friend. When a man has lived under a police state like I have and, worse, been part of the apparatus himself, he appreciates the hell out of a Constitution. New Jersey is heaven. Get me back there, dude! I pray to wake up again in that shithole, where at least a man can say what he thinks without some motherfucker in a uniform kicking down his door in the middle of the night."

Hanging up, I try for another two hours to wangle a ride home for my Egyptian brother. Still no luck. I don't get off till two in the morning. My handheld has a message from Salter — find him and report. He wants me in on the current discussion.

Salter has settled now in the Lion Suite on the summit floor. He's working on a room-service Cobb salad when I enter. A Steelers game is on TV. Petrocelli and Holland perch in separate corners, pecking away on secure text lines. Half a dozen security men man the room, including Dainty and Col. Klugh, with a dozen more covering this floor and the one below. I note two ATAs, Airborne Threat Assessors, coordinating the various satellite defenses, AWACS planes, choppers, and fighters screening the sky for the surrounding 240 miles. Against one wall stands a pair of dry-erase boards full of notes and a wad of PowerPoints and printed leavebehinds. Four official-looking suits exit as I come in.

"Know who those guys are?" Salter asks. He passes me a room service menu and points me toward the bar to make myself a drink. "That was the A.G. of the State of California. He's here to offer me forty thousand early-release inmates."

Sacramento, Salter says, is prepared to issue special pardons, turning these prisoners over to Force Insertion as volunteers (all drug-free and in the prime of health) to be trained and employed as legionnaires. And of course to ingratiate itself with what it believes will be the new power in Washington.

"We'll have an Aryan Brotherhood brigade, and one from the Mexican Mafia. What do you think, Gent?" Salter is laughing, but he's serious too. "Forty thousand is more than the United States had in Afghanistan for nine years — and that's just from one state."

Dainty mutes the tube as a commercial comes on. "Everybody loves a winner."

Maggie Cole's face appears on the VTC screen, as well as a number of laptops around the room. It's lunchtime in Virginia; Mrs. Cole sits at the banquette nook in her farm kitchen, wearing a flannel shirt and sipping from a mug of coffee.

She listens for a few minutes as the group discusses the predicament of Salter's Force Insertion troops in-country — in Arabia, southern Iraq, Iran, and Central Asia. Salter, through his representatives in Washington, has made it known that full amnesty must be granted to all personnel serving under his command and, further, that they and their formations, in their current configurations, must be integrated without prejudice into the armed forces of the United States. He wants American citizenship for all Third Country Nationals who desire it — and, most important, the legitimization and inclusion of the full force under conventions consistent with the troops' present station — meaning salaries and bonuses commensurate with those paid by Force Insertion, as well as medical, education, and death and dismemberment benefits for field operators and their families — and for the force as a whole to remain under command of its current officers, in an autonomous position outside of DoD chain of command and commanded by Salter for life.

"Are we talking to Salter," one columnist has demanded upon hearing this, "or Caesar?"

Salter's response: "How about gas at forty bucks a gallon?"

The officers in the suite are deliberating Salter's options. They're talking power in military, economic, and geopolitical terms.

Now Maggie Cole weighs in.

"You're searching for the solution in the wrong arena. Forgive me, gentlemen, but at this hour, General Salter possesses the most unstoppable power of all — the force of political momentum. The American people love him, and they're going to love him more tomorrow and more the day after that.

"Jim," she says, speaking directly into camera, "you're riding a once-in-a-century wave, like the ones that swept Churchill and FDR into office. You can ride it to whatever height you wish, but ride it you must. This is the force of historical necessity that you've always embraced in theory. Now it's real. The moment is irresistible, but it's perishable, too. It must be seized *now*."

The Steelers game is still playing. Nobody's watching. Maggie wraps it up with a minute more of specific technical suggestions, then signs off. Salter shuts down all screens. The suite gets very quiet.

"Gentlemen, I've always prided myself on thinking three and four jumps ahead. That's my game; it's what I'm good at. But I never saw this coming."

Everyone in the room has turned toward him.

"Maggie's right. The American people will call me home in any capacity I choose. They'll make up a new office if I want it. And here's the tricky part: I can't say no."

I glance to Jack Stettenpohl and to Chris and Chutes and Petrocelli and Holland. The men in this room have been with Salter for years. They are his circle. They have come of age serving under his command and have had their worldview shaped, willingly and indelibly, by his intellect.

"You've heard me talk many times," Salter says, "about 'the intersection of Necessity and Free Will.' I believe in such moments. I've studied them my whole life and prepared myself not only to recognize them, but to be ready to act upon them. The moment compels me to seize it. If I don't, someone or something worse will step in."

He pauses and turns to the company.

"But if I perform the bidding of Necessity, I violate the code of the republic to which you and I, all of us, have sworn allegiance. I cross a line, beyond which there can be no return. Do I lose you, brothers? Tell me now. Will you cross that line at my side?"

A rush of concurrence follows from every man in the room. Salter scans the faces. Pledges of fidelity issue from every officer. They stand with him. They will never abandon him.

"If we fail, gentlemen," says Salter, "every one of you crashes with me."

"Fuck that," says Mattoon.

Laughter all around. Obscenities issue from every quarter. Salter is not the type to weep, but I see emotion, profound and authentic, in his eyes.

"Thank you, gentlemen. Thank you, my friends."

22

EMERGENCY POWERS

I'M BACK IN D.C. Still no Hayward. I have grilled Dainty and Col. Klugh in Dubai. Both claim Tim is on assignment in Indonesia. I tell them I don't believe them. Klugh grabs his crotch. "Believe this, fuckhead."

One other thing has happened regarding Hayward.

After the confab at the Burj Khalifa, I catch a C-130 up to Mosul to see el-Masri. Chris Candelaria is on-site too, working the same pipeline deal he had been negotiating when my team and I originally ran into him south of Nazirabad. After a drunken day and an even more drunken night, Chris piles me and el-Masri aboard the Iraq-era Humvee that is his personal car/office/sleeping hooch and drives us south along the Tigris.

He has something he wants to show us.

While el-Masri and I carve out seating space amid a small landfill of tech journals, ammo, MRE boxes, and cases of bottled water, Chris confesses to me that our original meeting south of Nazirabad was not an accident. He was sent there, he says, with orders to link up with me.

"What?" For some reason, this unnerves me. "Who sent you?"

"Salter."

"Salter? What for?"

"To protect you."

I don't get it.

"I should've told you before," Chris says. "But my instructions were to keep my mouth shut."

This is seriously pissing me off. Was all that stuff with the tuxedo and the financial team bogus too?

"That was straight," Chris swears. "Salter just wanted a few extra guns to look out for you."

We've turned east now, past a sign for Qaraqosh and Al-Hamdaniyah. Terrain is treeless semidesert. An irrigated greenbelt runs along a tributary of the Tigris. "Where the hell are we going?" asks el-Masri.

"Trust me," says Chris.

I ask him what he knows about Tim Hayward.

"Nothing."

He's lying. Godammit. I feel the veins in my neck start to swell.

"Chris, what the fuck is going on?"

"Bro, you gotta learn to stop asking questions."

"Why?"

"Because you might get answers."

Chris tells me I don't understand how important I am to Salter. "Gent, you don't realize the exalted place you occupy in his heart. Salter loves you, man."

"What are you talking about?"

"To him you're the pure warrior—the man who fights for the fight alone. In a way, I think you've replaced his son. Or maybe he sees you as who he himself used to be before—"

"Before what?"

"Before he had to become what everybody becomes when they rise beyond a certain level. Politics. He doesn't want you contaminated with that shit."

"Then why did he send me to D.C.?"

"He sent you as a warrior, Gent. He knew he could trust you. He knew you loved him as much as — "

A flyblown turnout appears on the left. Chris pulls in. The lot is untended and unpaved. Rolling grassland rises inland toward a range of foothills. There's a sixty-foot obelisk and a crumbling monument that looks like it came out of a 1954 Cecil B. DeMille movie.

"What is this place?"

"Gaugamela."

Chris tells me and el-Masri that this site is where Alexander the Great defeated Darius of Persia in 331 B.C.

"This is what you brought us here for?"

"This is a cosmic place, dude! Gaugamela was — "

"I don't give a fuck about some ancient battle, Chris. I want to know what's going on now. Hayward's back in D.C., waxing people. I want to know who gave the order!"

Chris brakes at the crest of a rise and kills the engine. He turns toward me.

"Gent, I don't know Hayward and I don't wanna know him. But I do know that anything can be bought. You and me are contractors. So are ten thousand guys stateside."

"What does that mean?"

"It means this is high-stakes chess, baby. Salter's moving multiple pieces around multiple boards — "

"I get it."

" — and you and I are players."

"We're pawns."

El-Masri leans in from the back, sets his hand on my shoulder. "My friend, this is why you must always ask for double. Because guys like you and me . . . we will always get fucked in the end."

I turn to Chris. I see in his eyes that he's told me all he knows.

"All right," I say. "Show us the fucking battlefield."

Now, in D.C., the capital is nearing its breaking point. Only four days have passed since I flew out, with Salter's repatriation looking like a gimme. Suddenly, resistance has doubled and redoubled, not only inside the Beltway but from scores of power centers around the country.

ITV HuffPost calls the general's return "de facto despotism," "a crypto-coup," and "the end of the republic as we know it." Its editors vow to shutter the office and take their outrage to the streets. On the same day, no fewer than eleven political action groups made up of lawmakers, business leaders, and concerned citizens take out above-the-fold banners on the *NYGT, WSJ/CBS,* the *WikiWashington Post, Politix,* and *FaceTime*—all declaring the proposed amendment to the Emergency Powers Act unconstitutional. Salter's poll numbers have plunged fourteen points.

A powerful, organized resistance has arisen, led by a significant minority of senators, oddly enough from both sides of the aisle; a triad of ex-presidents; and numerous representatives of the retired military and the diplomatic corps, the most prominent and outspoken of whom is former secretary Echevarria. A number of legal challenges are being mounted, the press reports, not only to the proposed amendment but to the Emergency Powers Act itself.

On the second Monday after Labor Day, the House of Representatives votes on, but fails to pass a motion stripping Salter of American citizenship. On Tuesday an unnamed Justice Department source is quoted in the *WSJ* stating that the attorney general is in fact drawing up an indictment for treason. The story is retracted online two hours later, but not before the blogs and pol/boards short out on tens of thousands of rabid posts, pro and con.

Chaos in the Gulf is driving the country nuts. Will the U.S. lose its oil? A story on MurdochNet has Salter meeting in Abu Dhabi with Vitaly Salaquin of Gazprom, aiming to sell "our" Saudi oil to Russia. Fox/BBC broadcasts file video of Salter with premier Koverchenko during the Ingushettia crisis of '27 when he, Salter, had hired out a Force Insertion armature to protect the pipeline and other Russian interests.

What is the truth? No one knows. Salter has sealed the kingdom to the press and all outsiders. In place of news, rumors abound. Trump/CNN publishes a schematic purporting to depict the high-explosive wiring rigged by Salter's mercs across the entire Saudi pumping/pipelining/processing infrastructure. This act, which may or may not be fiction, prompts a photo-op denunciation by a phalanx of congressmen, mostly from Texas and Louisiana, who declare Salter no better than a terrorist. Nuke the bastard! Send in the Marines! Two carrier battle groups continue to cruise the Gulf. Hellfire-packing Predators circle over Salter's head. Nuclear-missile subs remain on-station; B-1s, B-2s, and B-52s from Diego Garcia do racetrack runs 24/7.

A thousand inflammatory fables ricochet around the blogosphere, from which they are tweeted and retweeted, rChived, Holo-Tubed, magnified, inflated, and bloviated, before metastasizing onto the mainstream airwaves. Salter, the myths declare, has concluded a pact with Revolutionary Guard Iran; he now has nuclear weapons. He is in bed with China, India, Brazil. One story tells of a deal with Japan. Tokyo, flush with Salter's promise of limitless oil, is preparing demands for the annexation of the Hawaiian Islands; the Japanese want Pearl Harbor. Salter, other sources proclaim, has orchestrated a giveback to the Saudis. He has converted to Islam, taken a Saudi bride, and been adopted into the royal family.

A.D's article comes out — the lead piece of a double issue of *Apple imPress*. The story is unapologetically pro-Salter, portraying him as a misunderstood patriot, a champion of vision and virtue who has been stabbed in the back by envious, craven, and careerist colleagues. A.D. makes the rounds of talk shows. Could this article bring her third Pulitzer nom? She blogs and pens op-eds. This one, posted on zenpundit.com, goes instantly viral. It is titled "Coalition of the Bewildering."

> The nation hasn't seen a figure as populist or as polarizing as Salter since Andrew Jackson. "Strange bedfellows" doesn't begin to sum up his partisans. Where he is loved, he is worshipped, and where he is suspected, he is abhorred. Start on the left. At the same time that Gen. Salter is feared and loathed as a warmonger and Lone Horseman of the Apocalypse, he is admired by equally rabid elements of the pink who see him as perhaps the last serious military/political intellectual, a writer and thinker on a par with John F. Kennedy and, to some, Lincoln (not to mention National Book Award–winning author of *In the Shadow of Appomattox*), and the sort of thinking man's ass kicker who possesses sufficient street cred to make accommodations abroad without squandering what little armed-force capital the republic still retains.
>
> On the right, Salter's enemies include throngs of conservative Christians and "values voters" whose alarm is monumental at his indifference to (not to say boredom with) the social issues that are near and dear to them. Wall Street hates him. Big Oil is terrified. He is vilified by true-believer patriots for whom he is and always will be a renegade and turncoat, if not an outright traitor. For them, the 2021 photo of Salter with Premier Evgeny Koverchenko never fails to

elicit blood-boiling rage. And yet, last weekend, when Agence France-Presse journalist Ariel Caplan and I attended a stock car race in western Pennsylvania, we counted hundreds of SALTER NOW stickers (and several tattoos) on the fenders of biker babes and Rolling Rock–guzzling truckers.

Gas prices have hit fourteen bucks a gallon. Desperation mounts. The United States teeters on the brink of collective hysteria.

Then comes September 27, 2032.

Crown Prince Faisal bin Abdul Aziz, speaking for his father, King Nayif bin Abdul Aziz, Guardian of the Two Holy Mosques and Sovereign of the Kingdom and the House of Saud, appears on forty-seven international nets simultaneously to announce that the Ministry of Petroleum and Mineral Resources has finalized a contract with ExxonMobil and ConocoPhillips for 66.6 percent of Saudi crude for the next forty years. It will all go to the United States. The other 33 percent will be reserved for the people of Saudi Arabia.

Salter is not on the platform for the announcement. No officer of Force Insertion is available for comment. But every prime minister and head of state, every president and premier, crown prince, magnate, mogul, CEO, every Peterbilt-driving cracker waiting to fill up his saddle tanks . . . they all know whose hand is on the wheel.

Salter has made peace between the princes and their elders — and between both royal factions and the commons. He has taken nothing for himself and nothing for his legionnaires beyond their promised pay and bonuses.

Two days later the *Financial Times* announces a 50/50 split of the natural gas field at Takhar in Afghanistan between Royal Dutch Shell and Russian Lukoil, also for forty years — and a matching deal for thirty-three years for the Umm Qasr, Majnoon, and Rumayla fields in Iraq with BP, Russian Gazprom, and Inpex from Japan. According to the *Wall Street Journal,* Salter has also taken under his protection the LNG fields in Qatar and occupied with thirty-five hundred mercenaries and forty I-SAM, surface-to-air missile trucks the Ras Laffan gas plant, from whose offshore terminal, R-LOT, the Qatari prime minister, Sheikh Ali Hassan bin Jamad bin Salem, signs contracts with Unocal, US Shell, and Pacific Richfield for a hundred billion cubic meters per year.

In other words, thanks to Salter, U.S. markets for the next two generations have locked up nearly 40 percent of the crude oil and gas from seven of the largest and most productive fields on the planet and, because the deals are tied to Russia, the EU, India, and Japan, they are stable and, theoretically at least, proof against incursion, overthrow, and insurrection. The Dow takes off on a rocket ride. Overnight, Uncle Sam's national manhood soars from broke dick to world-class stud.

I'm driving home from a Wizards game (a meeting on Kurdish oil), on the phone to Jack Stettenpohl, when the Saudi announcement breaks. What does this mean for the Emergency Powers Act amendment?

"It'll take a couple of weeks," says Jack. "Opponents need time to shape-shift and cover their asses."

"But this thing is happening?"

"Slam dunk, bro. Salter is about to be anointed emperor."

I sign off, about to speed-dial Ariel. She phones first.

"Log on to page 22," she says, "in tomorrow's *Post.*"

"What is it?"

"Fallon. The Third Amigo. Dead in his condo at Rehoboth Beach."

23

MAGGIE'S FARM

IT'S ELEVEN THIRTY BUT Maggie's awake. She leads me into her kitchen. We sit. I tell her what Ariel has told me.

"And you think," Maggie says, "that I know something about this."

"If you'll forgive me, Mrs. Cole, not much happens inside the Beltway or out that you don't know something about."

The former first lady pours Johnnie Blues. Her Secret Service detail hovers but, at a sign from her, the nearest two agents withdraw.

"Gilbert," Maggie says. "Are you still my nephew?"

"Are you still my aunt?"

Mrs. Cole declares that she's aware of my encounter with Colonel Hayward and of the suspicions I harbor concerning him. "What I want to know is what you intend to do about it."

I repeat the events as Ariel has reconstructed them. "The Cyber-Leaks chief dies of a heart attack. A marathon runner, in the pink. Courtemanche, the blogger, crashes his Lexus on a dry road, alone, with no other vehicles in sight. Now Congressman Fallon suffers a stroke — at age fifty-six — and kicks."

"With respect, Gilbert, you haven't told me what you intend to do."

"With respect, Mrs. Cole, you haven't told me a damn thing."

The former first lady studies me for a long moment. Clearly she is making up her mind whether to spare me or send me to the guillotine.

"Will you believe me, Gilbert, if I'm completely candid with you?"

Maggie swears she has no firsthand knowledge of any action taken against these three men who were responsible for ruining Rob Salter's career and ending his life. "But I understand," she says, "how the game is played. This country is fighting for its survival. Sometimes messages have to be sent."

She glances into the adjacent dining room, making sure that the Secret Service men are out of earshot.

"The world changed for Jim Salter," Maggie says, "the day Rob was killed. Jim worships this country. But he came to understand, then, that he had lost it, or rather that it had become a different country—one he didn't know, one he no longer recognized.

"We started then. He and I and others. Believe me, there was no want of patriots who shared our desperation, our fear for the nation, and our refusal to stand by and permit it to perish."

Maggie tells me to take a drink. I do.

"This is not the first occasion in history when a nation has banished her noblest son, only to call him home in her hour of need. The days of the United States pretending to be a republic are over, Gilbert. History has moved past that place, and you, as much as any man, have been a part of it."

The first lady's eyes fix upon mine.

"You blew an entire village into a river. I applaud that. It was justice. When unspeakable crimes were committed in East Africa, you struck at the villains, though you knew the act could cost you everything. I salute all you've done, in the service of General Salter and on your own. But you are no innocent. You're in this game up to your eyeballs, my friend, and you have been all your life."

My blood turns to ice.

"I've put people in the ground, Mrs. Cole, plenty of them. But never Americans — and never in the cause of trashing the Constitution."

"The Constitution is a piece of paper. Men wrote it and men can rewrite it. It was made to be amended!

"Then amend it by law, not by murder!"

"It *is* being amended, Gilbert. Read the news! Ask your precious friend, Miss Caplan!"

A rustle from the dining room; the Secret Service agent appears in the doorway. "Are you all right, Mrs. Cole?"

"I'm fine, Richard. Thank you."

Maggie recovers herself.

The agent withdraws.

Maggie turns back to me. She tells me she wants me at her wedding. She wants me up front — with the family.

"Jim's flying back. He and I decided tonight, just a few hours ago. It'll be the first time he's set foot on U.S. soil since Rob was killed."

The wedding, Maggie says, will be held in the chapel at Annapolis. She and Salter had reserved the National Cathedral but have changed their minds. Modesty is more seemly. And it is critical, they both agree, that the ceremony be held on ground sacred to the military, particularly the U.S. Navy and the Marine Corps, which are and always will be Gen. Salter's home.

"Jim loves you, Gilbert," Maggie says. "You have no idea how deeply."

She lifts her Scotch and throws it down at one belt. Then, looking over my shoulder into the night:

"This country is fucked. Who else is there but Salter? No one."

24

A DISH BEST
SERVED COLD

THE PHONE RINGS AS I'm driving home. It's Jack Stettenpohl. The dash clock says one thirty. "Gent, I love you, man. Don't do anything stupid."

"Did Mrs. Cole just phone you?"

"Biscuits and gravy tomorrow. I'm buying."

Jack makes me promise to meet him for breakfast at the Hay-Adams.

"Gent—"

"What?"

"Don't do anything stupid."

I turn onto Jeff Davis Highway, heading home to Crystal City. A black SUV turns behind me.

I try to reach A.D., but her phone's on work-block. I call Ariel. "Put a pin in me. Come now." I sync the GPS in my phone to hers, so she can follow me.

"Where are you?"

"In trouble."

I turn off Jeff Davis. The SUV turns after me. Crystal City is high-rises built in the 1980s; you turn onto a frontage road that leads to underground garages serving corridors of aging residential towers.

Ahead, a Chevy Suburban angles in from an alley. In three seconds they've pinned me. I've got a .45 under the seat but it's too late.

"Gentilhomme."

It's Agocopian, the FBI man. He presses an ID against my driver's-side window and points to the locked door.

"Open it."

Secretary Echevarria's house is an 1850s historical landmark near Lee's Hill in Georgetown. It's past two when Agocopian and two other agents, one a woman, shove me up a flight of Civil War–era stairs and down a long, unlighted hallway.

Into the secretary's bedroom.

He's sitting up in bed, with papers and documents strewn around.

"Here he is," says the FBI guy, pushing me forward.

Echevarria doesn't look up. The room is flooded with video lights. A cameraman runs a disk-cam on a tripod. The secretary is speaking into the camera — something about Salter and the Baku-Ceyhan pipeline. A boom mike extends above him, held by a soundman.

The FBI female tries to clip a microphone to my shirt. I tear it off. "What the hell is going on?"

Echevarria continues speaking into camera. I stare at him. He has lost fifty pounds. He looks like death.

The deputy, Agocopian, approaches me, with a Fed-issue 9 mm pointed at my chest. "Put on the mike."

"Fuck you."

The female wallops me with a steel baton behind the right knee.

I won't go down. I refuse to give them the satisfaction. "Stop it!" cries the secretary.

The female has come around in front of me; she is itching to shatter my shin. She's strong as a man.

"That's enough!" shouts Echevarria, stopping the agents with his voice. He has finished dictating to the camera. He turns to me. For the first time I notice medical monitors and IV drips.

"Colonel," he says, in a voice that sounds like his insides have been hollowed out, "you want to know why I've brought you here."

A nurse helps the secretary sit up.

"You're here to testify," the secretary says. "And, by God, you will or you'll never leave here alive."

Echevarria wrenches himself free of the nurse. He tells me the video crew has recorded his "last testament" — everything he knows about Salter and how Salter has generaled his way to tyranny: whom he's eliminated, whom he's co-opted; whom he's cut deals with. I see the cameraman unload the finished disk and set it on top of a case. The secretary swings his legs over the side of the bed as if they were made of concrete.

"You did this to me, didn't you? You or another of Salter's murderers."

He struggles to stand. I start forward, instinctively, to help him.

"Get away from me!"

The nurse helps Echevarria stand. I'm telling him I've done nothing; I don't know what he's talking about.

"Colonel, you're either the world's most accomplished liar — or the dumbest bastard I've ever met."

The secretary stands and tears off his hospital gown, exposing his chest. His skin from neck to belly is livid with lesions and ulcers.

"What did you use? Some untraceable isotope? How did you get it into me —"

The secretary's chest looks like hamburger. The nurse and the male FBI agent catch him before he falls. They settle him onto the edge of the bed. I'm repeating that I know nothing; I'm stunned to see what I'm seeing. The old man greets this with contempt.

"I know," he says, "that I'm just a fat old fuck to you. But I flew F-15s in Desert Storm, goddamn you, and I don't deserve to check out like this."

Agocopian and the female agent cover me with weapons drawn. "Now talk, Colonel." The soundman swings the boom over my head. "Tell what you know and what you did."

There's a principle they teach you in SERE School, for escape and evasion. It says *Escape right away.*

I spin toward Agocopian and hit him with the heel of my right hand as hard as I can under the cartilage of his nose. This is no martial arts move; it's just a street shot. The agent drops like a bag of dirt. I tear the 9 mm out of his hand and dive laterally onto the floor. Two sharp bangs explode behind my back. I roll and twist, turning to fire back at the female agent.

At that instant, the main doors burst open. Into the room charge four armed men in booties, hairnets, and latex gloves. Two silenced shots drill the female and male agents. Right behind the four men comes Tim Hayward. Hayward sees me on the floor with the 9 mm. His expression is almost comical with shock and puzzlement. Agocopian, the nurse, and the camera crew have thrown their hands in the air. In seconds the operators have flung the whole bunch facedown and flex-cuffed them. Two more, carrying body bags, race into the room.

"Gent! What the fuck are you doing here?"

"What does it look like?"

I'm thinking as fast as I can. Half my brain is scrambling for some bullshit story to keep Hayward from doing to me what he just did to the female and male agents; the other half is desperately afraid for

Ariel outside. Has Hayward's team spotted her? Have they killed her already?

"You mean Klugh sent you here —"

"The fuckers snatched me." I point to the camera, the lights, and the sound boom.

Adrenaline and surprise are keeping Hayward, for the moment, from seeing through me. "Help me then," he says.

Two of his men have crossed to Echevarria. The secretary is blistering them with profanity. "I know you, Hayward, you're a hero," the secretary cries. "Why are you doing this?"

The old man shouts to Hayward and me that we should be killing Salter, not him. The operator beside the secretary opens a medical bag. Hayward nods. The medic spikes a syrette into Echevarria's thigh, right through the hospital gown. The secretary convulses and spits blood.

Two men haul Echevarria to his feet. "There," says Hayward, indicating a spot at the edge of the carpet, halfway between the bed and an adjacent bathroom. "So it looks like he was trying to get to the toilet."

Hayward's men start body-bagging the corpses. The rounds they have used are low-speed "pop-and-stops," which shred inside the victim's rib cage and leave no exit wounds, no blood, no mess. The team gets the others to their feet and starts herding them out. Two men sanitize the site and start policing up the documents and the camera gear.

"Chief," the medic says to Hayward. "the fucker's still breathing."

"Get him up again."

While they lift Echevarria, I get to the camera case and snatch the disk. I jam it into my shorts.

Hayward supports the secretary upright over the hardwood floor, then drops him with a skull-cracking crash. Echevarria's eyelids flutter; his chest convulses. A final fall of fluid spills from his lungs.

"There he goes," says an operator.

The medic kneels, setting two fingers alongside the old man's carotid. He nods to Hayward. Hayward checks his watch. "Sixty-five seconds."

We're outside, in the service alley behind the house. Operators are shoving the flex-cuffed captives into two vans. The vans peel away. An operator in booties sprays the pavement with methyl chloride. I glance over Hayward's shoulder toward the street. Ariel stands in the shadows. Hayward comes up beside me.

"This is some fucked-up shit, ain't it, Gent? If my guys had been five seconds later, we'd be zipping you in a B-bag too!" A black sedan pulls up to collect him. "You should have had backup. A team should have been covering you." Hayward is already speed-dialing. "Somebody's ass is gonna pay."

He asks again if I'm okay.

"I am now, Tim."

Hayward raps me on the shoulder. "Get outa Dodge, dude. We've had enough fuckups for one night."

25

A PATRIOT

SIX MINUTES HAVE PASSED. Ariel's dash clock reads 2:32. I'm keeping to the speed limit on Pennsylvania Avenue approaching Washington Circle when I see a dark sedan coming up fast in the rearview. I've told Ariel everything. She's downloading the camera disk into her tablet, ready to send it to her editors in Paris.

Here comes Hayward behind me. It has not taken him long to see through my bullshit. I punch the gas and speed into the circle. The sedan accelerates right behind. I turn south, hard and squealing, onto Twenty-third Street.

"Ariel," I say as calmly as I can. "Take the wheel."

She sees me cock the 9 mm.

"Gent, what the —"

We roar down Twenty-third Street toward the Lincoln Memorial. The sedan kicks on its brights; blinding dazzle fills our cockpit. I grab Ariel's left hand and plant it on the steering wheel just as the sedan rams its prow against our rear bumper and shoves with all its power. Our car lurches wildly. Ariel is flung backward into the seat;

the wheel spins. Ahead I see sidewalk and concrete construction barricades. I grab the wheel and jam it back into Ariel's hand.

"Drive!"

I'm half-out the driver's window, facing rearward. I can see Hayward's buzz-cut in the sedan's passenger seat.

"Help!" Ariel is screaming. "Help, anyone!"

She jams the accelerator through the floorboard. We're bombing down Navy Hill, past the State Department. I get off two shots that ricochet harmlessly off Hayward's windshield. The sedan locks onto us again. It's got vertical push-bars on its front bumper, like state patrol cars. It shoves. Our car fishtails right; its front wheels hit the curb. I'm slung into the cabin post; my head smashes into the outboard mirror.

We're under elms. Ariel is screaming. Our tires are on grass. Over Ariel's shoulder I see a wall of timber and then we hit.

Both airbags inflate with a bang, but I hear Ariel's skull hit the windshield anyway. She has unbuckled her passenger-side seat belt to take the wheel; the crash over the curb has flung her between both bags. The horn blares; the alarm screams. I'm tumbling end over end on the grass. Hayward's sedan slaloms past on the pavement, braking furiously.

I'm on my feet, scrambling toward Ariel's door. Ariel's body lies broken between the two limp airbags, face-down in the floorwell with her bare legs splayed grotesquely and her neck snapped like a doll's.

Here comes Hayward and the other man. I roll under the car.

"Watch his weapon!" "Take him from both sides!"

My only advantage is I know they won't shoot; their game is to make this look like a car accident.

I'm scanning for legs when I hear liquid being sluiced. Gas. I roll madly out from under. A baseball bat swishes half an inch above my skull. I roll onto my back and pull the trigger. The slug catches

Hayward directly beneath the solar plexus; his mass blows backward and up as if he had been kicked by a mule. Hayward still hasn't hit the ground before I'm on my knees scanning for the second man.

He's running. I try to sight but he's too far away. I don't even fire. The man dives into the sedan; the car screams away.

A bus stops; I lurch aboard, bloody and reeking of cordite and gasoline. The driver doesn't make a peep.

I'm speed-dialing A.D. when the bus passes the Lincoln Memorial. The illuminated columns look grand in the night, enshrining the Great Emancipator. Goddamit, I love this fucking country.

I get my wife's voice mail.

"Pick up, baby! Ariel's dead. Pick up!"

She does. I tell her to meet me at a spot by the river. I tell her in code. "Lose whoever tails you. And be ready to run."

At the river, I give A.D. the disk.

"Here's your Pulitzer, baby."

"Where are you going?"

"To Salter."

26

THE BLESSING
OF THE GODS

NEXT EVENING, THE AMENDMENT to the Emergency Powers Act passes. I get the news over the phone from Jack Stettenpohl. I'm in Fort Erie, Ontario. "I did something stupid, Jack. And I'm gonna do something more."

Jack knows everything of course.

"Gent, where the hell are you?"

It has taken me two stolen cars and one ferry to get north of the border.

"I want to talk to Salter."

"Impossible."

It takes sixty seconds to tell Jack my side. Now, I say, tell me yours — and tell me the truth.

I hear my old friend take a breath. "Gent," he says, "there's nothing on the news about your friend Ariel or about Hayward. And there won't be. Ever." He promises me that nothing will happen to A.D.

"Where is she?"

"Safe. She called me."

My old friend tells me I have to come in. It's not too late.

I tell him I've got something to do first.

"Jack, I want you to take care of two things for me."

First, I tell him, retrieve Ariel's body. I know he can do it. Get in touch with her family in France. See that her remains get home in a manner that's worthy of her.

Jack promises. "What's the second?"

"Get me in to Salter."

"Can't be done."

You're a man-killer, Jack says. Even empty-handed, you're too dangerous. Klugh and Dainty won't let you without fifty feet of the man.

"I'll come unarmed. I'll show up naked. Klugh can stick both his fists up my ass."

"Gent, tell me where you are."

"I'll phone you."

I'm in Halifax when Salter and Maggie get married. The Annapolis Chapel ceremony is carried live on all four networks plus twelve cable news channels, as well as every gossip, celebrity, and polito-tainment site on the Web. It's the biggest public matrimonial, says Trump/ CNN, since Elizabeth and Prince Philip in 1956.

I'm waiting, moment by moment, for the video I gave A.D. to break in. When it doesn't appear, I start worrying for her. Did someone get to her? The only secure way to reach her is by cupcake, accessing our shared database.

I text:

R U OK?

Yes, R U?

Did U file the story?

Why?

My phone rings. It's A.D. in the clear.

She starts explaining that to run the story will accomplish nothing. The American people want Salter. Nothing anyone can do or say . . .

"Don't shit me, darling. I know, with you, it's not lack of guts or ambition."

A.D. goes silent.

"Gent," she says. "It's over."

Now it's my turn to draw up.

"You're with them," I say.

"Give it up, baby. It's over."

I ask my wife if she means the republic or us.

"Both."

I watch Salter and Maggie's wedding on my handheld in the freezing Canadian rain, hunkered under a camouflage hunter's poncho in a sniper's hide I've scraped out of a wooded mound overlooking the motel I've checked into but have not set foot inside except to wire the door and windows of my room with motion and thermal sensors (both bought, no problem, at a hardware store three towns to the south) and a baby video monitor (from Target half a mile down the highway).

Whoever's after me will catch up in a matter of hours and will be real-timing me from a satellite minutes after that. I'm under cover, armed with a used Remington 750 deer rifle, bought at a local gun fair (a $900 weapon for a hundred and a quarter cash) and registered via the counterfeit Canadian passport that Force

Insertion provided me to get into Egypt when I first recruited el-Masri. I've zeroed the scope on the beach, targeting clamshells at 150 yards.

The sun is shining at Annapolis when Salter and Maggie exit the chapel, pelted by blizzards of rice and photographed by a galaxy of video and cell cameras, paparazzi, helicopters, and waterborne telephoto lenses.

Salter has returned to the States, says the news, for a flying seventy-two hours, primarily to take Mrs. Cole as his bride, but also to coordinate in person with the prez and the Pentagon his triumphal repatriation twenty-one days hence — and to reassure those who have bet their futures on him that he is for real and all is well. Short as this trip may be, it still produces ecstatic mob scenes everywhere Salter goes. The change of site for the wedding — from the National Cathedral, as originally planned, to the less pretentious and more military-respectful chapel at the Naval Academy — has elevated even higher the couple's, and Salter's, stature. I'm watching Anderson Cooper from my shooter's nest when the newsman comments on the symbolism of the union.

> By wedding Margaret Cole, widow of the president who sacked him over the 2022 nuclear facedown with China, General Salter receives, if not the formal pardon of his countrymen, then at least the implicit benediction of those who had condemned him before. Marrying the former first lady puts Salter on a par with the president in the firmament of stature and celebrity.

I try to shut off the wedding but the damn thing is everywhere, including the ads and pop-ups bracketing every phone and search app. Fox/BBC's Martin Bashir remarks on the political brilliance of the Naval Academy venue.

The Annapolis symbolism represents the conventional military embracing its prodigal son, himself a Naval Academy grad — and his reengagement with the establishment in return. This takes the curse off Salter's mercenary past and present. Then there's the long-lost love angle. Gossip-show and femme-journo outlets are playing over and over the legend (which is perhaps even true) that Maggie Cole spurned Salter when he proposed to her as a young midshipman because he had chosen glam-deprived Marine infantry as his specialty rather than the dress-white naval service that more aptly suited Maggie's pretensions as a young Bryn Mawr society filly. Now forty years later, says the symbolism, the mature Margaret has seen the light. She recognizes that she — and by extension the nation — needs a champion on horseback, a man with *cojones,* a jarhead general.

The marriage is more than that. It's the benediction of the gods. By granting him her hand, Margaret Rucker Cole — America's Lady Liberty — forgives Salter's excesses (and even revels in them) and takes him to her bosom. Even the honeymoon becomes a statement: Salter and Maggie don't take one. Instead Salter returns straight to work — to Kazakhstan and Central Asia, to the Caspian Basin and then to Kurdistan, seeking to conclude even more oil and gas deals, in concert with Russia and China, so as to further secure the nation's energy future. The act demonstrates that Salter is husband and savior now not only to his bride, but to the nation.

27

TRUST NO ONE

NO KILLER TEAM SHOWS up at my Halifax motel. Instead a van scans the site, passing without stopping. Its electronics pick up my motion and thermal sensors. At least that's my surmise, monitoring traffic minute by minute from my sniper's nest. My phone vibrates midafternoon. It's Jack. Conrad the pilot will pick me up in a G-5 at the Supermarine hangar at Stanfield International and take me to Mosul nonstop. Jack gives me his word that I'll be safe.

Will I?

My voice mail has two recent messages from A.D. Both urge me to come home. It's a creepy feeling, hearing the woman you love try to set you up for elimination. Who can I trust? Not Chris. He's a good man but he's picked his horse. Jack, for sure, has priorities that don't include my longevity. My old teammates — Chutes, Q, Junk, Mac, Tony — love me still, I know. But the world has turned upside down and they have to turn with it. Who's left?

El-Masri.

That's why I've insisted on Mosul.

What do I expect there?

Klugh will kill me, or Dainty or someone in Salter's praetorian guard. I don't care. All I want is to get my minute.

My minute to speak in my own voice for the first time in my life.

28

AL SALIM

EL-MASRI MEETS ME IN Mosul, on the Tigris in northern Iraq. The Egyptian has quit Salter. He is living out of a truck. His brothers, Jake and Harry, are with him.

El-Masri says he'll protect me. He'll get me away to the tribal areas. He won't let me go in to see Salter.

"They'll slice and dice you before you're in the door, bro."

I tell him I don't care. I'll make Salter face me, one way or another. We're in el-Masri's 5-ton, an AfPak-era relic that he's got rigged with a camp stove, sleeping mats, and a .50 caliber on an X-mount under the highback tarp. Behind the cab el-Masri has an nCryptor masking station, which makes the vehicle invisible to satellites. He has two Dragonfly surveillance drones, the kind you launch by hand like paper airplanes—and the Chinese-built InCom repeaters to monitor and control them. With his brothers, he takes me off road through the desert to Al Salim airstrip in the desert southeast of the city—Salter's HQ in the north—which had been a single un-hardened runway but is now a fortified air-and-ground complex be-hind a twenty-foot berm topped with razor wire and studded with gun towers. El-Masri's truck pulls up in a wadi five miles out; the brothers, Jake and Harry, camouflage the vehicle with nets and brush. El-Masri puts up a Dragonfly. We hunker around the InCom screen, watching the green glow of the real-time readout.

"See this gate? Salter will enter there, in a convoy coming from the airfield. Then they'll call you. Klugh will instruct you, or maybe Petrocelli, to enter by this eastern gate. See the chicane?"

Resolution from the fly is so good, I can make out the clearing barrels where friendlies returning to base eject the rounds from their weapons' chambers before proceeding past security.

"They'll kill you right here," says el-Masri, indicating a site along-side a row of Porta-johns. He mimes a shot to the head, execution style.

He joysticks the Dragonfly out of its loop, heading home.

"You got to remember, Gent, that you're a dangerous man. They can't take no chances. Even unarmed, you scare the shit out of them."

Jake and Harry plant "eyeballs"—robot cameras the size of a dime—at six sites atop the ridge overlooking Al Salim. "Salter's plane will come in cloaked, but we'll know he's here from the activity at the security posts."

We drive west to a cave complex carved from the walls of another wadi. There's good water from an ancient Roman cistern. Smugglers, camel- and truckborne, use the site regularly, says el-Masri, so our vehicle will not stand out to even the most sophisticated drone or satellite surveillance.

El-Masri has something important he wants to say to me. He pours gin in tin cups and we sit across from each other, cross-legged on a carpet on the sand.

"Forget this thing, Gent. What can Salter possibly say to you—even if you could get in to see him—that would make any difference? He's got the world by the nutsack. You ain't gonna change that. And he ain't gonna back off."

The Egyptian wants me to come away with him. Now. Tonight.

"To the tribal areas. I got peeps there; no one will fuck with us. After that, Cairo. I still got money. These people who want you now, they will forget. We can live like humans."

But I can't.

El-Masri shakes his head. "What went wrong with you, my friend? You used to be hard. The hardest I ever knew. But you have changed. You have committed the one sin that God himself cannot forgive. You have come to care."

29

THE PROFESSION

I DRIVE IN TO Al Salim, big as life.

Jack Stettenpohl has cleared me; I have pass-through papers from Col. Klugh.

If the guards have orders to waste me, they haven't gotten the memo. I cruise. Within ten minutes, I've been escorted to a holding area adjacent to Salter's HQ—a sandbagged, revetment-flanked hangar—and five minutes after that, ex-gunnery sergeant Dainty appears, with three black-suited security contractors, to take me back to the man himself.

I have been disarmed and strip-searched twice. My mouth has been scoured. A girl has been sent to trim my fingernails. "I'm surprised," I tell Dainty, "you guys don't wheel me in in a straitjacket like Hannibal Lecter."

"Klugh thought of that, but we didn't have the leather mask."

The headquarters complex is constituted of two big Drash J-Shelter tents, air-conditioned and butted together at right angles to form an L. The rear wing houses the JTCC, the Joint Tactical Control Center—or so I'm told; they won't let me back there. The forward limb of the L holds individual offices and conference rooms, comm stations, and a fifty-seat briefing theater.

I enter from the rear, with Dainty on my right, another contractor on my left, and two behind me. Salter stands up front at one corner of the stage (which is plywood and so freshly built you can smell the lumber), finishing a press interview with a handful of journalists. Col. Klugh stands above him on the platform. Jack Stettenpohl is there, looking red-eyed as if he has flown in minutes earlier, as are Cam Holland and Tim Mattoon.

Dainty stops me at the entry and points me to a theater seat. I take it. I count four exits, including the rear one by which I have just entered. Each is manned by a three-man security detail. I recognize faces from the Marine Corps and from Force Insertion — contractors now, armed with their own idiosyncratic weapons choices, H&K 416s and 420s, Israeli KM submachine guns, U.S. M6A carbines. Another team of six protects the stage rear.

Several of the journalists are familiar as well. Senior is the Englishman John Milnes. He's nipping some kind of sauce from an airline minibottle and asks permission to put a question that he calls "a stinker."

Salter agrees to answer.

"The world knows, sir, that a primary tenet of your political philosophy is that concept that you characterize as 'the intersection of Necessity and Free Will.' By 'Necessity,' one assumes you mean 'force of history' or perhaps 'momentum of events.' Clearly something very like that has propelled you to this hour. Yet you retain, as your philosophy asserts, free will. It lies within your power, then, to preside over the extinction of the American republic or to refrain from this overthrow — to step back, as it were, from the threshold of what would appear to be incipient tyranny. Will you, sir? Will you accept the crown that your countrymen seem so keen to place upon your brow? For history has shown that few men, however honorable their intentions, have been granted such powers as you will soon possess and failed to succumb to their charms. It was Pericles, I believe, who said, 'Tyranny is a fine perch, but there is no way down from it.' "

Salter laughs good-naturedly. The query, he observes, is indeed a stinker. He will answer it, he says, though perhaps not from an angle that the distinguished journalist will approve of.

"I am a mercenary soldier, Mr. Milnes, and the warrior-for-hire lives by a code. That code looks upon the world without illusion. It regards all motives, including its own ambition, as equally expedient and self-serving. The code can be cruel or it can be kind. It can save and it can slaughter. It can slaughter in order to save. This is the era in which we reside, Mr. Milnes, whether we like it or not. History has brought us here.

"Any time," Salter continues, "that you have the rise of mercenaries or the evolution of a code like that of the Samurai, society has entered a twilight era, a time past the zenith of its arc. Before then, no one needed a code; the thrust of history was so irresistible and so self-evident. Raise a flag and you raise an army. It was that easy and that satisfying.

"But when a nation's sun has passed the meridian, particularly when it encounters enemies whose own despair is so great and whose application of violence so extreme that, to contest such forces, that nation must lower itself to a level of barbarism incompatible with standards of civilized conduct, then despondency enters the hearts of the people. In response arise noble but dark codes like that of the mercenary and the samurai. I'm not saying there's not great wisdom in such philosophies of willing self-effacement, of nonattachment to outcomes, of voluntary sacrifice of the self to some abstract standard of excellence or skill. That's the ground that spawns legends. But it's ground that's already been fought over and lost."

Has Salter changed? Or was he always like this? As I watch him,

I realize that his power, monumental as it was even a week ago, has doubled and redoubled in the interval. He is the only man in the world who can resolve disputes between Russia and China, make peace between India and Pakistan, Iran and Iraq, Israel and the Palestinians. Plans are in motion, I know from the morning's news, to triple the size of American mercenary forces, 90 percent of whose funding will derive from corporations and overseas entities, energy producers, mineral and resource extractors for whom military and political security has been the final impediment to their own empire building. Volunteers for Force Insertion and its subcontractors are lining up by the thousands, not only in the United States but in every developed and developing country from India and Brazil to Turkey, Japan, Russia, China, even Kenya, Somalia, Eritrea, Uganda. The U.S. (or at least that element represented by Salter and Force Insertion) seems at last, after decades of near eclipse, to have found its role in the twenty-first century — as private military guarantor of a Pax International and custodian and distributor of the world's oil and energy.

"The mercenary code," Salter continues, "is the standard of a fallen soldiery and of heroes in a time past heroism. Mercenaries serve empires and they serve houses of crime. Soldiers for hire enlist under banners of conquest or of self-preservation. The former means stealing something that has never been stolen before, the latter protecting the employer's right to keep stealing it. What is either except a felony?

"The United States is an empire, Mr. Milnes. But the American people lack the imperial temperament. We're not legionnaires, we're mechanics; De Tocqueville nailed that in 1835. In the end the American Dream boils down to what? 'I'm getting mine and the hell with you.'

"What happens now? I don't delude myself that I've generaled my way to this moment. History has tossed it into my lap. The country wants a 'strong man.' Horseshit. The rocket ride is over. The very ascension of someone like me—a mercenary general plucked from the provinces—is history's sign that the nation has lost its way and is struggling desperately, merely to hang on.

"But what, I ask, is the alternative? If the presidential election is held without authority passed to me by the Emergency Powers Act, the United States will break down into revolution. The nation can't go on as it is, and everyone knows it. If not me, who? If not me, what?"

Salter turns toward the rear of the auditorium, toward me.

"Do you see that officer sitting there? This man has traveled twelve thousand miles to assassinate me. I have brought him here and I have let him in. Do I fear him? Watch and see."

Salter turns back to the journalists around the stage. Four are filming with minicams.

"The American people, Mr. Milnes, are no longer put off by the idea of mercenaries; they *like* mercenaries. They've had enough of sacrificing their sons and daughters in the name of some illusory world order; they want someone else's sons and daughters to bear the burden. The American people are willing to pay for this privilege, in cash and in the circumscription of their own liberty. Do I approve? No. I hate it. But this is what the times demand—and what the people insist upon. They want their problems to go away. They want me to make them go away.

"So, yes, I will go home. And yes, I will accept whatever crown, of paper or gold, that my country wishes to press upon me. Not because I believe such a coronation will make any difference in the long run. It won't. But maybe in the short term, it's better that my hand be on the wheel (since I at least understand how fucked the situation is and possibly how to unfuck it), rather than some other self-aggrandizing sonofabitch whose motives might not be as well intentioned or whose consciousness so painfully evolved."

Col. Klugh shifts behind Salter. The teams at the exits straighten and come alert. Dainty raps my seat.

"Come up here, Gent," Salter calls. "Come here, my friend."

The reporters turn.

Dainty lets me advance.

Salter stands, not on the stage but at ground level in front of it. I stride up. No one stops me from coming close.

"Say what you came here to say," Salter says.

I'm unarmed. Across Salter's chest, as always, stretches the holster rig with the M9 Beretta. He withdraws the weapon, cocks the slide, and holds it out to me.

"It's loaded," he says. "The rounds are live."

Security teams step closer. Fingers move beside triggers.

I take the pistol.

I have rehearsed nothing. My secret self will act. He has become me at last, and I him.

"These other sonsofbitches," I address Salter, "won't say anything to your face because they're afraid of you and because they don't love you enough. But I'll say it. Not for myself or for the country, but for you. I've followed you my whole life. I believed in you. But what you're doing is wrong. It's wrong, Jim. I've never called you Jim, but I'm calling you by your name now."

I feel Klugh's P220 zero on my skull. "Let me paste him, *Jefe*," he says. Salter raises a hand to hold him back.

Reporters watch. Minicams record. I'm aware that I look like a madman, that every word I speak makes me seem crazier and makes Salter appear more courageous and self-assured.

I indicate Klugh. "Is this who you're with now? Have you chosen men like him, instead of me? What kind of country will they stand for — one that worships you and nothing greater, the way I did for so long? I want to hear it from your lips: that you understand what you're doing and you're still gonna do it."

A terrible sorrow fills Salter's eyes. "I wish I didn't understand, Gent."

He tells me the time for choice is over. History has carried us past it.

"It's never past," I say. "I'm choosing and so are you."

I still love Salter. In my eyes he's still a great man, the only one I've ever known. But that doesn't stop my right hand from elevating the M9 — or my index finger from tightening around the trigger.

"Go ahead," Salter says. "You'll be saving the republic. And me too."

Reporters are scampering clear. I hear chairs overturning and laptops clattering onto the floor. The security ring tightens around me.

"Sir!" says Klugh. "Give the word!"

I feel no fear in Salter. His raised hand keeps the teams back.

"What are you waiting for, Gent?"

In my mind I feel the recoil of the M9 and smell the blast of its powder. I see the round punching a hole between Salter's eyes — and the bright spray blowing out the back of his skull. I see him dropping to the deck, like dead men do, as fast as a marionette when its strings are cut.

But I can't pull the trigger.

I lower the weapon.

"Now," I say, "I'm guilty with you."

I drop the pistol. It clatters onto the floor. Klugh and Dainty seize me. I feel my wrists being yanked behind my back. A kick sweeps my feet from under me.

The deck rushes up and smacks me in the face.

30

A BROTHER

I'M FACEDOWN IN A truckbed with my wrists zip-stripped behind me. It's dark. The floor is sandbagged, a precaution against roadside bombs. Dainty and another operator pin my ankles. Klugh's knee, with his full weight behind it, digs between my kidneys; the muzzle of his 9 mm presses against the base of my skull. At least four other contractors complete the execution team.

I feel the truck—and hear two others in front and behind—zig through a series of chicanes.

"Finish it here, Klugh. Save yourself the gas."

"Shut up!" He wallops me with the shank of the pistol, then mashes my face into the sandbagged floor.

I twist forward. Against the bulkhead behind the cab squats the mass of the ECM—Electronic Countermeasures—transmitter, the anti-IED jamming device. The 7-ton slows for the final checkpoint. I feel the trucks rattle over the scanner grid. I'm thinking one thing: all the ECM in the world can't protect against a buried pressure plate—and that kind of trigger can be as primitive as two hacksaw blades wired to a battery and tucked under an inch of sand.

As I'm thinking this, the bomb goes off.

The truck elevates, stern first, tilts forward onto its nose, and rotates 270 degrees before crashing to earth, upside down and on fire. I have been flung out over the tailgate. I smell the bomb and blood and the contents of somebody's guts opened by the explosion. Machine-gun fire and RPG rounds are tearing into the vehicles fore and aft. I'm on the ground, facedown, swimming. Someone turns me over. A voice shouts into my ear, "You okay? Gent!"

El-Masri.

He and another man lift me. I see tires, a floorboard. Explosions are going off so close I feel the impact in my eyeballs and my kidneys.

I'm in the backseat of something. Hands probe my guts and limbs. "Relax, bro!" the Egyptian yells in my ear. "You've still got your balls!"

We're moving fast. A tribal warrior is packing a wound on my left shoulder.

"Can you fight, Gent?"

I'm back in my body.

"Fuck yes."

I'm trying to turn to see if there are vehicles behind us, but my neck won't crank past my shoulder. El-Masri is slipping the pistol grip of an M4–40 into my fist and jamming a couple of thirty-round magazines into my belt. "Hang on to your ass!" he shouts as a fireball of orange flame erupts fifty feet behind and twenty-five feet to starboard. I feel only the shock wave. El-Masri's vehicle — an Iraq-era Humvee — yaws left, dumps onto its side, and skids to a stop.

The tribal warrior and I clamber out of the passenger-side window, which has become the roof. El-Masri follows. Floodlights are racing toward us. We dive into a ditch just as a Javelin antitank missile reams the wrecked Hummer right up the wazoo. The blast blows all three of us over a berm and tumbling down a thirty-foot slope. When I try to stand, I fall flat on my face. A shard of steel the size of a spatula is embedded in my heel. I jerk it out; it's sizzling like a skillet.

Somehow we're in another vehicle, pounding across country. El-Masri's brother Jake drives. The truck's roof has been torn off by something, probably another missile blast; there's no driver's door, no flank at all on my right side. Ahead of us speed two hajjis on motorbikes, leading the escape.

Explosions detonate in front, behind, and to the sides.

"Goddam drones!" shouts el-Masri.

We're back on a road. The Tigris dazzles on the right. A warrior in a turban mans the .50 above me; another in a pettu rides forward in the right-hand seat. El-Masri points east. "The tribal areas."

We've got no chance. Klugh's drones will have us locked down by thermal, infrared, motion, and XGPS. Apaches will be overhead in minutes. Even the chase vehicles can smoke us from beyond the horizon.

Somehow I've still got my M4–40. I have no concept of time and distance.

"How far have we come from Al Salim?"

"Farther than we deserve."

El-Masri points ahead.

A sixty-foot obelisk looms out of the dark.

"What the fuck's that?"

"The battlefield."

"What?"

The bikes slew off the pavement; our truck follows, zigging wildly. Drone strikes explode right and left.

The ancient battlefield.

Gaugamela.

Where Chris took us a few weeks ago.

Bikes and trucks buck east on farmer's tracks into the cultivation. I look back just as another javelin blows the hell out of the obelisk. Stone blocks rain down like meteorites. The chase trucks race, right behind us.

Then we see the Apaches. Four attack helicopters in line abreast, east, a quarter mile ahead under the moon.

I can see rocket flash as the Wildfire missiles erupt from their pods and streak straight at us. The bikes scatter. Our truck swerves hard left, behind a berm and down into a dry watercourse. The missiles scream overhead; a wall of stone and fire erupts behind us.

Our truck is doing sixty between boulders the size of Cadillacs. "There!" shouts el-Masri, pointing to a rise of ground with a rubbled stone wall on its crest.

A place to make a stand.

The truck ascends from the wadi just as a second broadside of Wildfires explodes in front and to our right. I feel the right front wheel buckle. The axle shears. The tribesman on the .50 snaps his spine as the truck whiplashes with the impact. The Apaches blast overhead, strafing us with their cannons. The whole front half of our truck disintegrates. Jake's chest shreds; the warrior in the commander's seat is torn in half.

El-Masri and I scramble on foot toward the rise and the wall. Here come the chase trucks. The Egyptian clambers on all fours, ahead of me, up the slope. I see the wall above him. Ancient. Rubbled. Three worn stone columns.

It's the wall from my memory.

I fall.

"Gent!" El-Masri comes back; he lifts me. I can see the Tigris to the west, foothills to the east.

This is it.

" . . . I thought it was the sea," I say.

"What?" El-Masri hauls me to the crest. We both plunge to cover behind the wall.

"I thought it was the sea. But it's the river."

He looks at me without comprehension.

Machine-gun fire rips the slope. Two chase trucks attack from the south; two more maneuver to take us from the north.

"We've had it, bro," says El-Masri.

He and I have wedged ourselves into fissures in the floor of ancient stones. All I want is one clear shot. I read el-Masri's eyes; he wants one too. We hear drones above us. Survival time is seconds now.

El-Masri's eyes lock onto mine.

We'll die in the open.

We rise together. A chase truck is rushing up the slope. I kneel and fire the 40 mm. El-Masri has one shoulder-fired rocket. He stands. The truck is roaring straight at him. El-Masri puts the rocket right between the headlights. The truck's front end rises, shredding like a can of peas. But the mass of the vehicle keeps coming of its final, fatal momentum. It rolls right over the Egyptian, burying him under its wheels and frame.

I race to him. More headlights mount the rise. Rotor wash blasts down.

El-Masri lies under gravel and shingle, with no part of him visible aboveground except his left hand clutching the launcher of the rocket.

The chase trucks brake at the crest. Men leap down; a dozen muzzles zero on the center of my chest. Search lamps blind me. I hear the static of radio transmissions.

Salter's voice.

Pete Petrocelli dashes forward in the lights. I see Jack Stettenpohl.

A final chase truck mounts the rise and brakes. Rotor blast from the Apaches turns the hill into a hurricane. Someone on the truck waves the choppers back. They withdraw; the gale abates.

Salter stands in the turret of the final chase truck. Search lamps from the trucks and helicopters light him from the side and behind.

I see his eyes move from the rise to the rubble wall to the three worn, eroded columns.

He orders his men to hold their fire.

I'm kneeling beside the broken remains of el-Masri. Salter's truck edges forward until the general stands, in the vehicle's turret, directly above me.

"Whom do you bury, soldier?"

I answer, "My brother."

Security men look on, baffled, waiting for the order to blow me to hell.

Instead Salter bares his head. He straightens into a posture of respect for the fallen el-Masri.

"Take this man's weapon. Leave him as he is. Let him bury his brother."

Two contractors scramble forward. They disarm me. I glance to Petrocelli and to Jack Stettenpohl. Both look on in mystification.

Salter meets my eyes one last time. Then he reaches forward and, with his knuckles, raps his vehicle's armored roofline directly above the driver's station.

The truck shifts into gear. Its front wheels turn. The vehicle peels away and descends the slope.

One by one, the others follow. The column moves off toward the road and the river. The Apaches bank eastward and ascend. Even the drones withdraw, the tinny whine of their propellers receding.

Darkness swallows the site.

From the foothills I hear the two tribesmen's motorbikes, coming back to collect me.

I feel neither grief, nor anger, nor fear. Only waves of love rising from the earth at my feet.

EPILOGUE

COL. ACHMED CROSSES THE courtyard toward the mud-brick hooch I share with el-Masri's brother Harry. It's January, but the temp in the sun sits at thirty Celsius — eighty-five Fahrenheit. "Here comes your news," says Harry. He was one of the motorcyclists at the ancient battlefield. It was he who rescued me and got me here.

Nine weeks have passed. I'm well enough now to walk, according to Dr. Rajeef. But the physician advises me not to push myself. "Healing takes time," he says.

Indeed it does.

Col. Achmed brings the *New York Google Times,* the English-language version downloaded from the satellite, which his militiamen have run off on the printer in the office in the main house. He does this every day. I don't know why. I get the news online three hours earlier.

"Your President Murchison has died." Achmed tosses the paper onto the bed. "Guess who has taken his place."

Harry's room and mine compose a small but comfortable apartment. We've got every modern convenience, from our host's stores of loot — a brand-new 12BTU A/C, a Lucas espresso machine, two LG 3-D flatscreens, and high-def Internet 24/7. We even have women — Dutch and Polish prostitutes who come out once a week from Husseinabad.

Col. Achmed and I have become friends. He practices his English on me, and I struggle with my Farsi and Arabic. He has a sense of humor. Dr. Rajeef is a good man too.

They and their tribesmen love to mock me about my stateside celebrity. Video of my verbal confrontation with Salter has set the all-time Web record for hits. "Why didn't you shoot the bastard? Now we are all fucked!"

Once, when I was a kid, some gangbangers tried to screw with my sister, Jane. She was fourteen, I was nine; we were on our way to the market. I took the bullies on. They kicked the crap out of me of course, busted my face up good and proper. Later, Robbie, the boss in our town, came by our house in his black Lincoln. "Let me look at you." He turned my face this way and that in the light. "So," he said, "you are a fighter." And he gave me fifty bucks.

Not long after that, I had my first vision of the ancient battlefield. I never told anyone. Not my sister, not anybody. I had the vision again a few years later, and again when I was seventeen. That was what made me join the Marine Corps.

I have experienced my life, from within, much as Robbie expressed it from without. "So . . . you are a fighter." That's how it came to me. Before that day with my sister, I had never thought of myself in that fashion. After that, I could not conceive of myself any other way. It was like I was discovering, as I grew, not who I might become, but who I already was.

My secret self was me already.

When I met Salter for the first time, in Mosul in 2016, I associated him with the commander in my vision. I thought, *This is the man I was born to follow. He will lead me and my brothers to our collective destiny.* Salter was indispensable to my conception of myself. I could not function without him.

The love that arose in my vision from my brother's grave, I took to mean his approval of this vision. Go with this commander, I thought it said. You belong to him.

I was wrong. That love said instead, "Be true to me, brother. Be true to us, and true to yourself."

I killed my brother by leading him to war. I'm responsible for his death, because he looked up to me and to the certainty I projected. He followed me, as younger brothers will, wishing to be like me and to earn my love and respect.

But my brother was wiser than I, in his ancient incarnation and again as el-Masri.

His love, both times, was forgiveness. He forgave me for being the engine of his extinction. Next time, his love said, we'll get it right.

Will we?

I cannot blame Salter for exploiting my love and loyalty, as he has done and is doing with so many others. I made up my story. I told it to myself and I believed it. The myth was my creation. I am responsible for every act I performed or failed to perform in its service.

I cannot hate Salter either. He has acted by his lights, in full awareness of the peril to himself and to the peoples and nations over whom he will rule. Will he be able to navigate those waters? No one ever has.

I am his enemy now. His reach could finish me with ease, even here in the rugged land of Persia. But he won't come after me. He spared my life, not out of love, as I wish he had—but out of cunning, so that I would be cast in the public imagination as the mad and futile emblem of opposition to his ascension.

I'm okay. I'll be walking soon. Harry is well already.

We'll make our way to Cairo, as el-Masri said, traveling via the tribal lands, where you need no papers and where friends hand you on to other friends. We'll be safe in that city of millions, and from there we can go anywhere.

I no longer have my brother. But I have my brother's brother, and he has me.

As for Salter, he and I are quits. What he has been to me, he is no longer. I see him plain, and I see myself.

He did not spare my life out of love. But I spared his.

SPECIAL THANKS

Many friends have helped me try to get this right. For geography, finance, politics, language, and lots more, my gratitude to Fred Lowther, to Christy Henspetter and Nadine Uzan, to Gisela Eckhardt, Sallie Shuping Russell, Justin and Lissa Pressfield, and to Monty Freeman.

To Dave Danelo for demolishing an earlier version of this story (which deserved demolition)—and to Nancy Roberts for laboring mightily to help build it back. To Shawn Coyne, for understanding this tale better than I did and for elevating it to a level higher than I had envisioned or hoped. To Callie Oettinger, for being a rock for me amid turbulent waters.

And to Major Jim Gant, U.S. Army Special Forces, for friendship and wisdom beyond the call of duty.

ABOUT THE AUTHOR

Steven Pressfield is the author of the fictional works *The Legend of Bagger Vance, Gates of Fire, The Afghan Campaign,* and *Killing Rommel,* and the nonfiction book *The War of Art.* He lives in Los Angeles.

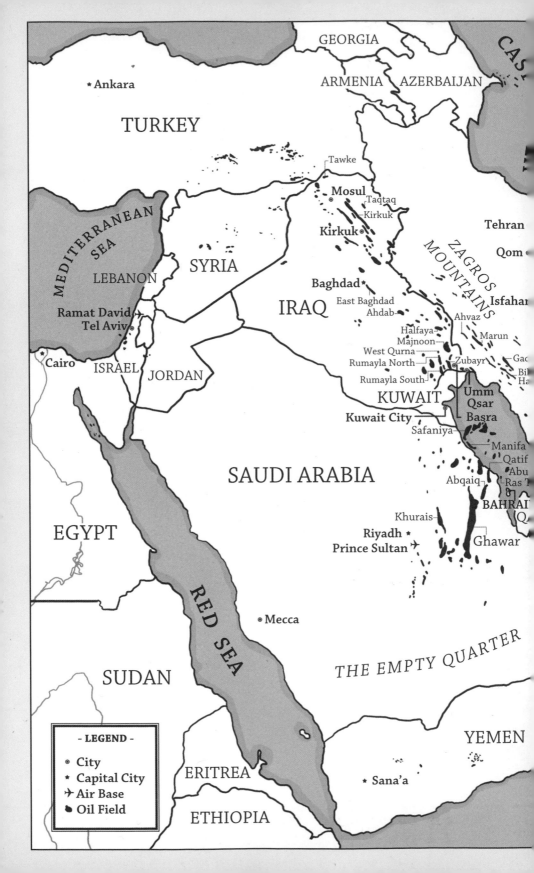